THE ONLY GIRL . . .

She was the handmaiden, and they
were the high priests of the great
gambling Mecca in the desert. Her
job was to lead the lambs to the
altar, to keep them happy at the
tables where her partners slaught-
ered the suckers for sacrifice.

*This masterful dissection of the backstage
life of a gambling casino on the famous Vegas
Strip will show you why John D. MacDonald
has been acclaimed as one of the most com-
pelling storytellers in America today.*

the only
girl in
the game

JOHN D. MacDONALD

FAWCETT GOLD MEDAL • NEW YORK

THE ONLY GIRL IN THE GAME

Published by Fawcett Gold Medal Books,
a unit of CBS Publications, the
Consumer Publishing Division of CBS Inc.

ISBN: 0-449-14032-6

Printed in the United States of America

19   18   17   16   15   14   13   12   11

IT WAS THE MIDDLE OF APRIL, AND THE MORNING SUN LAID its white weight across all the architectural confections along the Las Vegas Strip, and shone with bright impartiality upon the grubbiness of the town itself, upon the twenty-four-hour-a-day marriage chapels, the sour little rooming houses and anonymous motels.

In the big hotels . . . Sahara, Desert Inn, Tropicana, Riviera, New Frontier, Sands . . . the guests slept in too darkened rooms, in the chilly whisper of air conditioning.

At the Cameroon, the front desk phoned at the customary nine o'clock, bringing Hugh Darren, the assistant manager, up out of a submarine nightmare where he had been fleeing through endless coral caverns from a Thing which wore the red compulsive face of Jerry Buckler.

He put the phone back on the cradle and swung long legs out of his bachelor bed and sat there for a time, making the transition from the fading terror of the dream to a bright Wednesday, to the shifting intricacies, the partial projects of this day. He was nearing the end of his twenty-ninth year, and he sensed that thirty was a label of a significance he could not yet comprehend. He was a big lean limber man who gave the impression of leisure and indolence and low-pressure amiability. He moved with that elusive look of style and special favor that some athletes achieve. His hair was a crisp short brown, with ginger highlights; and his eyebrows were a lighter shade, unusually bristling and heavy over gray-blue eyes set aslant in the bony, slightly freckled, asymmetric face. It was an ugly-attractive face which had adjusted itself to a habitual expression of mild irony. He could not have imagined for himself any kind of life work which would not have required a constant involvement with people. He had the detectable composure of a man who knows he is very, very good at his work, and the humility to appreciate the luck that led him into it.

Hugh Darren rubbed a coppery stubble with his knuckles, stretched until the flat muscles of his shoulders popped, remembered the last of the dream before it was all gone and mumbled aloud, "Son of a bitch nearly caught me that time."

He walked to the window and yanked the cord to open the slats and let the desert sunshine into the room. It was a second-floor room in the rear of the building, in the old original wing. New construction had made these rooms unsuitable for paying guests, and they had been assigned for staff use. They used to look out across the brown floor of the desert toward the eroded mountains. Now they looked out at a blank wall of the new convention hall, and down into the rerouted service alley. He squinted at the too-blue sky and had a glimpse of a commercial jet swinging into its landing pattern before it disappeared behind the cornice of the convention hall. He looked down into the service alley and, with a professional eye, checked the neatness of the long rank of garbage cans outside the rear doors of the main kitchen.

After he took his shower, and before he shaved, he phoned down for breakfast. It was wheeled in just as he finished shaving. He looked out at Herman, the bald maestro of the Cameroon Coffee Shop, and said, "Currying favor again, I see."

"Good morning, Mr. D.," Herman said with broad gold-flecked grin. "We got the good sausage again. So I serve myself. So you remember Herman with pleasure, is it not so?"

Hugh walked out of the bathroom in his robe, drying his face. "And you bring it up yourself when you want to be the first with the news. And it is always bad news. So where is the pleasure in that, my friend?"

"No special news, Mr. D."

"But there happens to be one interesting little thing?"

Herman inspected his place setting carefully and stepped back and shrugged. "Just a small thing. Mr. Buckler came back earlier than anyone expected. At three this morning, I think. Mr. Downey, the new man on the night desk, displeased him, and so he was fired."

Hugh Darren lowered his head, closed his eyes and told himself to count very slowly to ten.

"Herman, I don't know how I'd ever get along without you. Get Bunny Rice up here on the double."

Hugh Darren had barely begun his breakfast when Bunny Rice arrived. Bunny, when summoned, always arrived looking as though he had run all the way. When Hugh Darren came to the Cameroon the previous August to rescue what was possibly the poorest hotel operation on the Strip, he had given the most careful consideration to the selection of

6

people to help him. Bunny Rice had then been working the front desk on shifts that changed from week to week.

He was a spindly man whose greatest flaw was his tendency to come apart when faced with a crisis. But he knew his job and knew the town and the special problems of the area. He had energy, imagination, and a capacity for loyalty. And Hugh had judged him honest. And so Hugh had made him a special assistant in charge of hotel operations from midnight to eight A.M. In a normal hotel operation this would have been a job that held no challenge. But Vegas runs twenty-four hours a day.

Bunny Rice, at his own volition, came on duty at eleven, and did not leave until Hugh was in his own office. Bunny Rice was pallid, with bulging blue eyes, thinning mousy hair, jug-handle ears, a long severe upper lip, and a mouth which tended to tremble when he was upset, as though he were fighting back tears. He nonetheless seemed to enjoy his new scope, new responsibility and increased pay. He lived with his wife and three children in a new housing development on the far side of town.

"Sit down, Bunny. Relax. What's this about Buckler firing Downey?"

"There wasn't a darn thing I could do about it, Hugh."

"Why didn't you wake me up?"

"Because there wasn't anything you could do either."

"Jerry was loaded?"

"He was ugly drunk, Hugh. You know how he gets. If he'd gone right to bed there wouldn't have been any problem. But he stopped at the desk to see if he had any mail. Downey may have seen him at a distance, but I don't think he ever talked to him. Downey thought Mr. Buckler was a drunk trying to check in. I guess Mr. Buckler wasn't talking very clearly. In the confusion, he got abusive, and Downey tried to get help from the casino guards to have him put out. So he fired Downey. Downey left right away. I filled in at the desk."

"Let me do some thinking. No, don't go yet. Stick around a little while."

Hugh Darren finished his breakfast. He poured a fresh cup of coffee. "I guess it's time, Bunny. I guess that's the final straw. He goes or I go."

Bunny licked his lips. "It . . . makes me nervous, Hugh. I don't like to think of how it'll be here if you're the one who goes."

"I won't like it either. I've never made this kind of money before. And only a damn fool could say this kind of money doesn't mean anything. And the job I want to do around here is only half done. But I just can't keep taking the responsibility without having the authority."

"Who will you go to with this . . . ultimatum, Hugh?"

Darren shrugged. "The man who can say yes or no. Al Marta. Who else?"

Bunny Rice looked as though he wanted to wring his hands and sob. "I think you ought to . . . to talk to Max Hanes about it first, Hugh. Really I do."

"Max runs the casino operation. What's that got to do with this?"

"Just talk to him, Hugh. Please. Tell him what's on your mind."

"Max and I aren't what you'd call buddies, you know."

"He's a very smart man. And . . . excuse me for saying this . . . he knows a lot about how things work around here . . . things you might not know about, Hugh."

Hugh Darren felt the quick anger tauten his body. "Bunny, I told them when I came here, and I'm telling you again, I have no interest in knowing anything about any clandestine arrangements. I'm no conspirator. I don't give a damn about the casino and the money room, or any foxy tricks those boys practise. They had a sick horse here, and so they had enough sense to go out and hire a good vet. They hired a pro, Bunny. They hired me away from one of the biggest operations in the Bahamas. They said I'd have a free hand. I don't have a free hand. All I want to do is run this hotel operation."

"Just talk it over with Max, Hugh. Will you do that first instead of going up and hitting Al Marta with it cold?"

Darren studied his night manager's anxious, loyal face. Byron B. Rice, condemned from the very beginnings of pinkness and trembling to be known as Bunny, robbed by that inevitable name of both passion and authority, never to be called Mr. Rice even by the bus boys.

Darren sighed. "All right, Bunny. I'll do it your way."

Hugh Darren's office was at the end of a short corridor which opened off the lobby near the registration desk. The door to that corridor was marked "Private." In the smaller offices opening off the corridor were the nerve centers of the hotel operation—bookkeeping, accounting, billing, purchasing, credit, payroll. Since taking over the game, if not the name, Hugh Darren had made clear and specific a functional division of all his complex activities.

In simplest terms, he was concerned with every aspect of food, drink and shelter—their acquisition, preparation, serving of and collection for. And he was responsible for maintenance of the whole plant, inside and out. And so he had pinned—in a triumph of the obvious—the specific responsibilities onto specific people: hiring sullen temperamental gifted George Ladori away from the Casa Vegas and loading him with all the functions concerned with food served everywhere in the hotel; promoting humorless reliable John Trabe to supervise all liquor operations; leaving bitter old Walter Welch in charge of all inside and outside maintenance, and giving him a freer hand than he had had before, because he was good.

That left Darren with nothing to do but run the hotel, handle lease of concessions, supervise all non-casino personnel, solicit trade, control Ladori, Trabe, Welch and the front desk, clean up after Jerry Buckler's mistakes . . . nothing he couldn't handle in a ninety-hour week . . . based always on what is known as the First Rule of All Hotels, "If something hasn't gone wrong, it will."

He walked into his office a few minutes after ten. This morning time in the office, an hour or so for the analysis of operating reports and the signing of this and that, and quick conferrings with key personnel, was the nearest thing to established routine that he was able to manage—though sometimes he arrived there after sleep, other times before he had had a chance to go to bed.

He pushed the office door open and wished the lettering on it could miraculously cease to irritate him. Jerome L. Buckler, Manager. Hugh J. Darren, Assistant Manager. In the practical mythology of the hotel trade, the average assistant manager has approximately the same status as the elevator starter, and usually works for less money.

But he could not fault the decor of the office. The wall-to-wall rug matched the Williamsburg blue of the draperies. The walls and the formica desk and table tops were oyster white, matching the white leather of the furniture. It was hushed, soundproofed, air conditioned. There was an intercom, tape dictation equipment, a noiseless electric typewriter at the secretarial desk in the corner. There were two custom executive desks. The larger of the two, seldom used, belonged to Jerry Buckler.

Hugh Darren went directly to his desk and began to check

the daily operation summaries placed in perfect alignment in the center of his large dark blue blotter by Miss Jane Sanderson.

She came back into the office thirty seconds after he had begun to read the summaries. "Good morning, or is it?" she said. She was a slat-thin woman, very tall, with legitimately white hair in a cropped tousled cut which should have been too young for her and wasn't. In spite of her indoor employment she managed to maintain a hickory tan. After too many disheartening weeks trying to make a secretary of various slothful dumplings, he had found Jane through a blind ad placed in the Los Angeles papers.

"It is another one of those same mornings, Miss Jane."

"That's what I was afraid of."

"Try to set up an appointment for me with Max Hanes, whenever he's up and about. Neutral ground, I guess. So make it the Little Room. Then see if you can get Downey on the phone."

"I think he's still in that motel. His wife found something they like, but they couldn't move in right away, and I guess maybe that was a good thing."

He went through the summaries, jotting down brief notes in his pocket notebook to use during his daily inspection trip, and then began to study the checkout-checkin list. The name of each guest had coded information beside it, indicating how many times, if any, he or she had previously been in the house, the type of accomodations, his occupation —if available, credit arrangements, any special services requested, the total amount of the bill on checkout. A note from the desk indicated that 603 had been reported by the housekeeper to have been stripped before checkout. A salesman from Denver, who should know better. Hugh made a note for Jane to send the usual letter. If the man ignored it, he would suddenly find himself unable to make reservations in fine hotels in many places.

"Mr. Downey on the line," Jane said.

Hugh Darren picked up the phone and said, "Tommy, there was an elective course you should have taken, all about how to cope with a drunken boss man."

Tom Downey's tone was chilly. "I had the four-year hotel administration course, Mr. D., and I had a year and a half at the L.A. Ambassador, and maybe the only thing I've learned is I don't have to take abusive crap from anybody."

"You're just as sore as I figured you'd be, Tommy."

"I get mad once a year, Hugh. And I stay mad."

"I brought you in here, Tommy. And I've got good reasons for not letting you go like this."

"I was fired, remember? I'm long gone. Sorry."

"Suppose we had a big change here? Suppose all of a sudden it's all mine?"

In the long silence he heard Downey sigh before he said, "In that case I'd come running back and you know it. Not loyalty, Hugh. But I guess there is some of that. Self-interest. I can learn so damn much from the way you operate. But right now you're dreaming. Buckler is Al Marta's buddy."

"All I'm asking is for you to sit tight while I give it the big try. Then either you can come back, or we'll both be looking for work. Okay?"

"On that basis, sure, Hugh. And . . . good luck."

After Hugh had set up an appointment with Max Hanes for two that afternoon in the Little Room, he made his rounds, conferring with his lieutenants. He went with his maintenance chief, old Walter Welch, to the men's shop in the arcade off the lobby. The concessionaire wanted to take out a wall at his own expense. Walter said removal wouldn't affect structural strength, so Darren gave his conditional approval based on a final approval by the hotel architect. He went back to his office and called his food chief, George Ladori, in for a forty-minute fight over the price changes on the dummy of a new menu overdue at the printer's, and he won those points he had expected to win, while giving Ladori the feeling, so necessary to that man, that he had achieved victory.

Next came John Trabe, Hugh's liquor chief, with a satisfactory accounting for the discrepancy in the last liquor inventory, and the worried information that one of his best bartenders had been reliably reported as having been seen at the Showboat, gambling heavily. Hugh told John Trabe to perform his own discreet investigation and take the action he thought best. Trabe had obviously hoped to duck that responsibility, and so he accepted the orders grudgingly.

After signing the letters Jane had typed up, Hugh once again prowled the big hotel. He went up to the sun deck and looked at the new sun lounges which had recently been delivered. He checked on the progress of redecoration of two suites on the fourth floor. He cautioned Red Elver, the head lifeguard, that two of his boys were hustling the guests too strenuously for tips.

By the time he had returned to his office and dictated

11

more replies to current correspondence, he barely had time for lunch before meeting Max Hanes. He angled across the main casino floor to the Little Room. In all the big hotel casinos of Las Vegas, it is always a few minutes after midnight. The sun never touches these places. The lighting is clever and directional—so that the playing surfaces are bright enough, and all the rest is shadowy—a half light that fosters indiscretion. They are big rooms, all darks and greens, sub-sea places. He saw the guests clotted close around one of the crap tables, their faces sick in the reflected light, the smoke rising, the stick man chanting, a casino waitress taking drink orders.

The Little Room is a shadowy place of leather, dark wood, white linen, small lamps that give a flattering orange glow. At the raised dais in the far corner there is always someone at the piano. It never stops.

Max Hanes was alone in a big leather booth on the far side of the room. He was a man of medium height with an astonishing breadth of shoulder, a hairless, shining head, a face that sagged into saffron foldings yet had a simian alertness. People frequently thought him an Oriental. The rumor went that from time to time during his life people had tried to nickname him Chink. And he had hospitalized each of them with his hands. He was thought to be a Latvian, and it was known he had been a wrestler long before the days of gilded bobby pins. The people who worked for him gave him that special, undiluted respect that can only be achieved through pure terror.

As Hugh sat opposite him, Max Hanes said, "I was listening to the slots. A man spends his life by the sea, he can tell you the size waves coming in without looking. I can tell the casino take for the afternoon to within a thousand bucks. The slots give you the picture of how the tables are going."

"That's interesting, Max."

"Everything in this place is based on the slots, Darren. And that includes me and you, and all your fancy plans. Don't ever forget that."

"It's a lousy way to start this little conference, Max. When I first came here you told me you're more important than I am in this picture. No casino—no hotel. Okay. So you keep telling me. Should I put it in writing?"

"Maybe you should. You keep forgetting."

"You won't let me forget it, Max. I can depend on you."

"Ten years ago it was easier around here. Not in this

12

place, because this place wasn't built then. But the liquor was on the house, and a good meal was a dollar, and a room was three, and we didn't have these problems. We didn't need guys like you. Hotel managers!"

Hugh Darren leaned forward. "And when I came here eight months ago, Max, you were supposed to be running the casino and Jerry was supposed to be running the hotel. But both of you were messing in each other's back yards, and the place was such a mess they had to bring somebody in to straighten it out. Now stop telling me how good it used to be and tell me something I want to know. Is your life a lot simpler and easier than it used to be?"

"I don't know. I guess so. If you tell me it is."

"You know it is, Max. You want all the hotel operations run in such a way that you get maximum play in the casino. That's what I'm giving you. And when you have any beef, you know where to come. People who have had bad food, short measure on their drinks and dirty rooms don't come back and play your tables. So I'm building a new reputation for this place."

"It's slow play out there this week. How come?"

"You know how come. You booked a dog into the Safari Room, and when that show moves out and the Swede opens in her show, you're going to get more play. So it's your own fault, isn't it? You book every bit of entertainment in here, and it comes out of the casino take, and I have nothing to do with it."

"Too much comes out of the casino take lately."

"Max, when you request me to give away food, drinks and lodging to special people who gamble heavy, I *have* to charge it to the casino. Otherwise, how can I keep logical books on my own operation? And the thirty per cent of all overhead wasn't set up by me. You know that."

"What you're trying to do, Darren, you're trying to operate the hotel part with a profit," Max Hanes said accusingly.

"That's what I was *ordered* to do, damn it! And I should be almost over into the black by the end of this year."

"It isn't right. The hotel should run at a loss. It's a service to bring the big play around, to sweeten the casino take."

"Don't argue with me, Max. Argue with the management of every hotel on the Strip. That's what they're all aiming for. It's the trend."

"It's a bad trend."

A waitress came over to the booth. Hugh ordered a pot of coffee. Max Hanes asked for another sherry. The wine glass looked incongruous in his hairy, thick-fingered paw, as out of character as the ancient yellow of his long ivory cigarette holder and his salmon-pink sports jacket. He always reminded Hugh of some cynical old chimpanzee who goes through his act for the sake of the bananas.

Hugh grinned at him. "No matter how much it bugs you, Max, we *are* working together, and it *is* becoming a better place to eat, sleep, drink and . . . lose your money."

"Every operation is getting so goddam legitimate lately," Max said. "So I got to put up with changes. What do you want now? I should move out some slots so you got room for tea-dancing?"

"You know damn well you're stealing half my lobby next month."

"One third."

"Max, I want your advice. I want Jerry Buckler out of my hair. He's a problem drunk. I spend too much time patching up his mistakes. I want him out of the picture as far as running the hotel end is concerned."

Max Hanes leaned back and the sallow lids hid most of his quick black eyes. "*You* want him out of the way. You're a pretty ambitious kid."

"Max, is he a drunk?"

"Yes. It didn't used to be so bad. The last couple of years, yes. And it gets worse, so old friends got to care for him."

"Is he incompetent?"

"Would you be here if he wasn't? At fancy pay and with a free hand?"

"It should be a free hand, but it isn't."

"You must be getting smart, talking about this to me, Darren."

"How do you mean?"

"Suppose you took it right to Al. Al checks with me. I say I don't see any reason to change anything so Al Marta says to you to take it the way it is or get out, and we get another smart boy who *will* take it."

"But why?"

"Don't you have the picture yet? One of those big New York hotels, a manager starts to fall apart, they fire him. It's a cold business. Here you got to figure on sentiment."

"I can't feel very sentimental about Jerry Buckler, Max."

"A lot of people can, kid. Al Marta, for one. You take Jerry, he operated a place on the Florida Keys way back. Way, way back, when the stuff was coming in from Cuba in thousand-case lots. It was, like you could say, a gathering

14

place. Lots of deals were made there. Later on Jerry was in on the Miami thing when it was going good, managing one of Fats McCabe's places out near Miami Shores. Then he managed one of the places in Havana. From there to Reno, and from Reno to here, and it was Al Marta brought him in here. It goes way back, Darren, to old times and old places. Al let him run this until he damn near ran it into the ground before Al went out and brought you in to clean up."

"I'm not saying throw him out into the street."

"You just want to keep him from having any say at all in the running of the hotel end. That would hurt him, wouldn't it?"

"Probably."

"I don't think Al would want to hurt him, and I don't think I would want to hurt him."

"Because he knows too much?"

Max Hanes gave him a pitying look and shook his head sadly. "Honest to God, how do you get the time to watch that crime crap on TV? That's the only place you could get an idea like that. First, you never let a drunk know anything he might hurt you with. Second, if he ever tried to use old stuff to pressure you, he'd get himself a shallow hole out on the lone praireee. Third, you take care of your own all the way down the line because there comes a time when maybe you need it yourself. This isn't the Hilton Hotel Corporation, kid." He made a gesture with an ape arm that included all Las Vegas. "A lot of this town is just a bunch of old buddies taking care of each other."

"The Cameroon Corporation is paying me too much salary to have me wasting my time patching up things after Jerry goes staggering through, Max. So is there any way he can be kicked upstairs—so his pride won't be hurt?"

"You might not like that as well as you think you would."

"What do you mean?"

"You might not have the whole picture."

There had been a sudden shift in the direction of the conversation. During his eight months at the Cameroon it had happened to Hugh before, and it annoyed him each time. It was like being a school kid again and, while standing and talking to several kids, suddenly realizing from a veiled comment that they all belonged to some secret society. You had not been invited to join, and you knew you would not be.

"Max, I don't want the whole picture, or whatever it is you're talking about. I want to run a hotel."

15

"You listen close, Darren. Learn a little. I'm on the casino end. Jerry is on the hotel end. I can come to you with the routine stuff. But suppose something special comes up, something where the hotel and the casino have to work close? Jerry talks my language. Together we do what has to be done."

"Why is this special thing, whatever the hell you're hinting at, something I can't do?"

"You could do it. But these special things, you never learned them in college. Maybe you wouldn't want to do them."

"Why not?"

"Two reasons. First, being the kind of kid you are, maybe your conscience gets in the way. Second, if you go along with what we want, Al Marta and me, maybe that gives us a handle, so some time if you want to leave and we don't want you to, we've got some good arguments to use for you staying."

"Blackmail, Max?"

"Back to the TV again," Hanes said in a disgusted way.

"If I got some clue from you as to what you're talking about, maybe I could make more sense."

Max Hanes closed his small eyes for nearly ten seconds, and sat with his heavy lips pursed. He opened his eyes. "I'll make you up one. All the tables are straight. We don't dare operate any other way. So we set the rules to give us the biggest percentage we can. There can still be streaks of luck. Mr. Smith comes from Oklahoma and stays in the house. He wins a little, loses a little, and then he has a long hot streak and cashes out sixty-two thousand bucks. That's a bruise we don't want to take. He's lined up for a flight out of here, to take all that bread back to Oklahoma. So Jerry and I get together. There's plenty of ways the hotel side can help out. Maybe you can think of some. We want to get him back onto a table so the percentages will catch up with him. If we think of the right things, and we usually do, Al okays a little bonus, maybe five per cent. It comes right out of the money room, kid. Right off the top before any accounting takes place, so it's nice loose money."

"Bonus? Off the top? You're going too fast, Max."

"You got to have it like a grade-school reader, maybe? I see the cat. Okay. You've got no way to prove I told you this. On every table there is a slot. Every mark who buys chips, his cash money goes down the slot into the lock box fastened under the table. I got boys who make the rounds.

They unlock the money boxes from the underside of the tables and put empty ones in place. They take the boxes to the money room. In the money room it is sorted and counted and bundled, and it goes into the vault. We keep a three-hundred-thousand cash float on hand. If the float is running low, the table take builds it up to where it should be. If the float is fat enough, we make cash deposits in the bank. You've seen the armored car come for the pickups."

"That's clear enough, but . . . ."

"In the money room we keep records. Right? For the books. For the owners. For the tax guys. Everybody keeps books. But when I talk about a bonus off the top, I'm talking about money that never gets on the books at all, kid. Take that Mr. Smith from Oklahoma. He's cashed out sixty-two thousand. He figures to grab it and run. But he gets sucked into trying for more, so he puts it all back. So Al says to the people who helped Smith put it back, cut yourself three grand, boys. So the next time the table boxes are emptied, I just take out three thousand in cash, right off the top. I can do that because there is no such thing as any kind of outsider getting into any money room in Vegas. No tax cop has ever seen the inside of a Vegas money room. That's the way it works."

"But if Al can . . . approve that kind of a bonus, doesn't it mean the owners are being screwed out of that money, Max?"

Hanes stared at him with sad impatience. "Just when I begin to think you're maybe bright, you. . . . Listen, kid. Al is an owner. There are two kinds of owners. There are the 'inside' owners and the 'outside' owners. We don't ever let the casino show up too fat, for tax reasons. So there is money coming off the top all the time. It gets spread to Al and the other inside owners, and all the outside owners get is their share of what shows on the books after taxes. But they can't prove anything and they aren't what you call anxious to sue."

"But. . . ."

"Al has to play it straight with everything that comes off the top. The most stupid thing he could do would be try to pick off more than his share. And he has the okay from the other inside owners to spread around some of the money off the top in the way of bonuses to guys like me and Jerry when we've done something special to fatten the take, like suckering that Mr. Smith into some more heavy play. It's a fat green world, kid. It's a money machine. You should

17

ought to come in for a piece of it here and there, not hurting anybody."

"I . . . don't think so."

"In a barn where they got cows, what are those things hold the cow's head?"

"Huh? Head stalls, I think."

"So we got the barn and we got the cows, but no head stalls, and no lock on the barn door. So, a cow with a lot of milk, you got to use psychology to make it stand still, and like every minute of it. Psychology around here, kid, means women and liquor and the red carpet, and sometimes little tricks Jerry Buckler and I cook up."

"Tell me one."

"Once we had a fat Greek fairy in the shipping business, got into us heavy and was about to leave. Jerry come up with the idea of a fake morals charge, so we hired the right kid and put him in a bellhop uniform and gave him a pass key. We brought in fake detectives and even an imitation lawyer, and we hung him up for four days and scared him green and then cleared him, with big apologies. He was so damn glad to be in the clear, he settled down nice with Jerry and nibbled on free champagne and Jerry steered him down to the casino and we plucked him clean. And so for that kind of cooperation, Al tells me to go ahead and give Jerry a slice off the top—the kind of bread you don't report. Can you see me coming to you on a deal like that?"

Hugh Darren thought it over. "No."

"So face it, kid. Drunk that he is, we need Jerry more than we need you."

Hugh finished the dregs of his coffee and banged the cup down. "Damn it, I hate to leave here before the job is running the way I want it to."

"So why leave?"

"I told you. He's too often in my hair, Max."

"In some ways you're stupid, kid, but I think I can help some. I think I can keep him from laying it on you so much. I'll talk to Al. Al will talk to Jerry. He'll make it sound as if the beef came from me. Then here's what you do for me. When I'm about to work on one of those . . . special problems . . . with Jerry, I'll let you know. Then he'll have the right to mess a little with the hotel end. Pay no attention to whatever he does. And I'll let you know again when the problem is over. Any other time he gets in your way, let me know."

"It isn't . . . exactly what I hoped for."

Max stood up and edged out of the booth. "But the way things are, it's all you get. Right? So you take it and smile, because it's more than I thought I'd give you, Darren."

After Max had walked away on his tough bowed legs, Hugh Darren sat alone for ten minutes. I should get out of here, he thought. I knew that in any setup like this there'd be a stench here and there, and I thought I could stay clear of all that, but somehow it seems to get closer all the time. And maybe I get a little more indifferent to it all the time. And perhaps one day I'll find out I'm right in the middle of it, and then it will be too late to get out.

The strange, almost superstitious, feeling of foreboding had been growing stronger these past two months. He had the sensation that he was moving toward some inexplicable disaster. And so, sitting there alone in the booth, he shook off apprehension by retreating into his dream. Four years ago he had found the island. A sixty-acre tropical island, part of the Berry Islands group, an island that stood by itself ten miles from Fraziers Hog Cay. Last year he had finished paying for it, had made the final payment to Her Majesty's Government, and Peppercorn Cay was his. It had a small natural boat basin fronting on deep water.

When he had saved thirty thousand dollars of his own, he would begin to build the small, perfect resort hotel he had visualized. Thirty thousand was a dangerous minimum. He knew the people in Nassau who would back him with an additional ninety thousand.

So he would and could endure this place, and consort with people like Max Hanes, Al Marta, Gidge Allen, Harry Charm, Bobby Waldo, Beaver Brownell, Jerry Buckler and the rest of the hoodlums, just for the sake of the wonderful way his bank balance was increasing. Food and lodging were free. He could bank almost his entire salary, and the amount that remained after taxes was still impressive and comforting. Eight months were gone. Three full years would do it, and maybe an extra year could be endured if he wanted a better margin of safety.

He had nothing to fear from these people. They could touch him in no basic way. He had a hotel to run, and run it he would. So that one day, sooner than he had ever dared hope, he would have his own to run in the good ways that would suit him.

He signed his outgoing mail at a little after three, returned two phone calls, and then went to his room, changed to swim trunks, went down the rear stairs and through the service alley and the big gate at the end of it, and across the perfect and velvety lawn toward the pool and the main patio, lengthening his stride with a pleasurable anticipation as he looked among the sunbathers for Betty Dawson.

● ● ● two

BETTY DAWSON SAW HUGH DARREN APPROACHING THE POOL area, turning his head from side to side as he looked for her. Though she had been expecting him, and had expected him nearly every day since this pleasant routine had been established, something reached in and gave her heart a sly rude pinch in that moment of recognition. And, as always, it gave her a feeling of mixed tenderness and exasperation which, vocalized, would have come out, "*Now* they tell me!"

It was a damnable thing, she thought, that They waited so long before exposing me to this kind of a guy. They threw all the clowns at me. They paraded their battalions of bums, and They said, "Sorry, this is all we got in the store." So I made the best of it, and the road was full of rocks all the way. So after They bounce me until my heart is all over calluses, *then* They wheel Darren in and say, "We just didn't happen to have this sort of thing in stock when you first started to trade with us, Betty."

Today she had asked one of the pool boys to put the aluminum-and-plastic chaise over on the grass away from the pool apron, near but not shaded by a contrived clump of narrow trees, with a table nearby for drink, book, sun oil and cigarettes. She wore today the blue bandanna bikini, knowing well that it was the most demanding costume any woman could wear, and taking considerable justifiable pride in being able to wear one at twenty-seven. She knew she could take no credit for her basic structure—wide shoulders (almost too wide, almost boyish), high round breasts placed well apart, short waist, long legs, a straight and reliable framework of bone—but she felt damn well smug about keeping things the way they should be, devoting all the tiresome hours to keeping the waist limber and narrow, the belly tight and flat, the long thighs unpuckered.

You had to earn the right to wear a bikini from age seventeen on, and no matter how confident you felt in it, you could not afford to forget you must never never walk away from your beloved while wearing one. This angle of vision turned even a Bardot into a slapstick comic. And so a certain amount of tactical maneuvering was required.

She was a tall brunette with unusually dark blue eyes, and a loveliness of face that was reminiscent of Liz Taylor, but without the flavor of self-satisfaction. It was a stronger face, and because strength breeds resistance, life had marked it here and there in small ways, bracketing the corners of the mouth, drawing little half-moon lines over glossy, quizzical brows.

When Hugh Darren paused she raised her arm, and he spotted her and came over, smiling. She moved her legs and he sat on the foot of the chaise and said, "You look like an import—brought here by a rich guest."

"Ho! A week-end companion. A chippy, hey?"

"Rich guest with good taste."

She huffed on her fingernails, looked at him with disdain, and pretended to buff them on her bare midriff. "I'm on duty out here, sir. Part of my employment contract, decorating the pool area."

He looked at her meaningfully. "Any smaller suit than that one, Betty, and you'll be running competition to those bare broads in the Safari Room. You'll be taking business away from our headline talent—two shows nightly."

"That mess is taking business away from itself. Max must have had holes in his head when he booked that crew into the big room. It's so bad it's giving free material to every comedian in town. And what do you mean, a smaller suit than this? There's no such thing."

"Don't go away," he said. He dropped his towel and went to the pool and dived in. She kept her head turned and watched him do his fast laps and the racing turns, watched the long arms reaching, the muscles of the shoulders sliding and meshing under his red-brown tan. She could sense the complete way he was expending himself. He came back to her, winded and gasping, and spread his towel beside her chaise and stretched out there.

When his breathing had quieted down, she lit a cigarette and reached down and placed it in the corner of his mouth.

"How went the battle last night, mother?" he asked her.

"My four exciting performances? The midnight and the two o'clock were square, so damn square I had to back away from my own stuff and do them ballads, which I do poorly and which I despise doing. The four o'clock was empty. Two drunkey couples, not together. But the five-thirty aye em was a warming thing. Old fans rolled in, a party of fourteen, by gosh, with requests for this and that, and the excitement even brought some spooks in off the casino floor, jangling their silver dollars. So I had to nightcap my old buddies, and I didn't get into the sack until seven, or out of it until two-thirty. Tonight I'm off, but tomorrow night if you could hang around for the midnight, I've got a new one I want you to catch. I'll lead off with it right after the standard opening, so you won't lose too much time."

"What's it about?"

"I won't tell you much because I don't want to spoil it. It is a lament-type thing, about a young girl who has grown up in the sports-car era, and who had adjusted well to love in Jaguars, M.G.'s, Triumphs, Mercedes and so on, but now she is in love with a guy who loves classic cars and he drives an ancient sixteen-cylinder Cad, and she just doesn't know what the hell to do with all that space."

"It sounds choice."

"I'm saving it for a time you can catch it, Hugh."

He sat up and grinned at her, and she couldn't let him guess the weird way it made her heart thump to see that crooked wonderful grin. "I am so damn glad," he said, "that the entertainment around here is entirely a casino operation and Max Hanes handles it with Al Marta's help and advice, and nobody asks me anything about it."

"So you don't have to face up to the sad job of firing me?"

"Hell, I'd give you a single in the Safari Room."

"And *that* would be a gasser, lad."

"I mean I like it because I can be with you with no stress and strain, Betty. I know you're under no obligation to be pleasant to me. Maybe you've never thought of it, but the job I've got is lonely. If I set up any teacher's pets, it starts cliques and jealousies."

"Some of those waitresses would make dandy pets."

"Yes indeedy."

"You don't have to smack your chops like that. Jerry Buckler doesn't have your scruples, Mr. D."

"And I wouldn't hire Jerry to throw water if I was on fire. He bitches me every chance he gets."

"Don't buck him too hard, Hugh."

"Why do you say that?"

"I'd like to keep you around for a while, that's all. I'm a fixture here, dear. Two and a half years. Good ole Betty Dawson and her little songs of love and stuff. There's no

22

room in any of these palaces along the Strip for . . . some kind of perfectionism, or idealism, or whatever you want to call it."

"I just want to do my job and ignore all the rest of it."

As he was not looking at her just then, she could look at him with most of her heart in her eyes and say, "I hope that's the way it will work for you, Hugh. I really hope that's the way it will be, until you can leave with all the bread you need for Pepperbox Island."

"Peppercorn Cay. I'll take you with me when I leave, Dawson."

"Sure enough?"

"And you'll be the only entertainment in my joint. Dawson of the Islands, they'll call you. Of course, I'll have to clean up some of your blue material."

"My God, not that! I've got no voice and I can't play much piano, so what would I have left? Oh oh! Here comes a flaw in your coffee break, Mister Manager."

Jane Sanderson was walking toward them. She stopped at the foot of the chaise and said, "It's nice to get out here once a day and find out how the rich people live. How are you, Betty?"

"Broiled. I endure this discomfort for the sake of my vast following. They appreciate a spurious look of health."

"Oh, sure! Mr. Darren, this wire came for you."

He began to smile as he started to read it.

LOYALTY DEMANDS WE FOLLOW OUR FAVORITE BONI-FACE EVEN TO DEGRADING PLACES. CAN YOU SUITE US FOR A WEEK, STARTING FRIDAY? WE'RE ARRIVING ANYWAY, SO BE READY WITH ACCOMMODATIONS OR APOLOGIES. VICKY AND TEMP.

"They'll be through redecorating 803 Thursday, won't they?"

"That's the schedule, Mr. D."

"Have the desk set it up for Mr. and Mrs. Temple Shannard of Nassau. Fruit, flowers, free drinks on arrival."

"Will they be billed at all?"

"Yes. And thanks, Jane."

As Jane Sanderson walked away, Hugh handed the wire to Betty, saying, "Wonderful types. Real people, for a change."

"They sound nice."

"Temp owns a piece of the place I managed in the

23

Bahamas. He helped me fight my battles, backed me up when I needed it. He's loaded. He inherited a little and made the rest out of the tourist business in the Islands. Vicky is English. Temp came originally from New Hampshire. He's one of the guys who has promised to back me when I'm ready to go. You'll like them and they'll like you, Betty."

"How old are they?"

"I'd say Temp is fifty, but he doesn't look it. Vicky is close to thirty, I think. His first wife died. His kids are grown. He's been married to Vicky for seven or eight years. They've wanted kids, but they haven't been able to have any. They've got one of those . . . good relationships, Betty. They don't have to go around patting and cooing for you to sense it. It's just there, all the time."

"Whenever I run into that bit, I get wistful. Wigwag that high-heeled dolly over there so we can drink some free liquor, buddy." As the waitress started toward them, Betty sat up and snapped her white bathing cap in place and said, "Tell her another rum collins for me, please." She was pleased she had timed it perfectly, so that while she was walking away from him he was too busy with the waitress to turn and see the rear view of the bikini.

She felt unaccountably depressed as she slid down into the dance of the blue water and began her slow and lazy trips up and down the pool. When the reason for the depression occurred to her, the realization created a sour, guilty amusement. She wanted him all to herself, to be his only friend, the only person he could talk to unguardedly. Now old friends were coming to restake old claims and talk to him of times and places she had never known, shouldering her out of the way for a little time.

Be careful, girl, she told herself. When it gets this strong and this important to you, it means that you'll have to work twice as hard to keep it from showing, to keep him from guessing. With a man like Hugh, should he ever learn how deeply it goes with you, how it has become love, then he would respond to that love out of a sense of responsibility to you, if nothing more. And you don't want that. It's too late for that. And it has been too late for over two years.

It is just simple logic. You cannot give yourself away totally to any man, no matter how great your need, if you no longer belong to yourself. And you do not belong to yourself, girl. You are leased out, in perpetuity. You belong to Them, and They are very relaxed and casual about their ownership until it is time to use your special services. Then if you try to refuse, They know exactly how to explain the fact of ownership to you, and there is nothing to do but take your orders. You no longer belong to yourself.

Max Hanes gives the orders and, when it is over, you have the bonus—which he did not have to give you—and another smutch that won't scrub off, and more material for bad dreams.

It is your problem, and nothing to be wished on Hugh, bless him.

As she swam there, feeling the long good stretch of her muscles, all her years were with her, clotted darkly in her throat, gagging her. And, as was her habit at such times, she cursed that girl she hardly knew, that Betty Dawson of nine years ago, that Stanford sophomore, that only daughter of Dr. Randolph Dawson, that girl of irritable restlessness, who felt cloistered and frustrated, and believed with all her heart she had great talent. Dazzled by the show biz dream, she was a perfect setup for the first cruel selfish bastard who came along and saw the dream and was willing to take it in trade.

Jackie Luster was the one who happened along. He had grinned at her out of the sleazy covers of two score fan magazines. He was glamor and importance and Her Big Chance. Naturally, the despair and heartbreak of her father meant nothing. The world had turned into a dream. When her father started to take legal action to get her away from Jackie, they went away together. They left the state. She was eighteen. She learned later that Jackie was at a low point in his career. He needed something fresh and young to set him off, so he bought material and worked up a double, and he trained her in heartless ways until she was the image he wanted. It was too late then to turn back.

They auditioned in Chicago and got a spot in a sleazy club in Cicero, and they were on their way. Somehow it was never the time or the place to get married. He had a vile temper, and he knew how to use his small hard fists so they hurt, and nothing hurt too much if you used a few drinks for a pillow. But, bruised or hungover or heartbroken, you always had to stand up in front of the baby spot and do it the way you were taught to do it—in Cicero, Chicago, Bayonne, Miami Beach, Biloxi, Mexico City.

Dreams die in strange ways. The show biz dream persisted longer than it should have, while she lived in shabby places with Jackie Luster and served him in the ways he demanded. But on a strangely disorganized houseparty

25

given by people who owned a club they were working, Jackie found it either politic, or a gesture of protest against her humble possessiveness, to load her up drunk enough so he could turn her over to one of the owners, in whose bed she awakened, at whose bedside she vomited. And though it was only peripheral, it killed what was left of the dream. It buried the wide-eyed sophomore. From then on, of course, there was much less chance of turning back, no chance at all to be Doctor Dawson's pretty daughter ever again. And she continued to fulfill Jackie's requirements, in an icy acceptance of a bargain made for better reasons.

Three years ago they were booked into Vegas, into the Glad Room at the Mozambique, and Jackie was beginning to get it all back, that perfect edge of timing, and a more judicious selection of material. As the room began to jump for him, he began to cut her material, shortening the musical bits, fattening his end of the monologue. After six socko months he had pushed her far enough out of it, close enough to the edge so he made that one last effort and dropped her.

"Who needs you?" he said. It seemed an apt summary of the whole thing.

But when you know you can't go back, you have to make do with the little bit you have. She made a connection with a local agent-manager, a shy confused guy who had no idea how to sell talent, but knew how to build up the talent he was trying to peddle. So he added three factors—four if you add the looks and the figure and the sexy wardrobe: the true and husky voice of limited range, the piano playing—which was at best an accompaniment with chords, a la the late Dwight Fiske—and her knack of writing wry little lyrics and the music to go with them . . . a talent Jackie had scorned. Jackie had beaten timing into her. The little agent made her work with a mirror, made her concentrate on the mobility of her face until she had fifty clown faces to match the husky naughty lyrics. And then he showed her around, but she was nervous and could not put it over.

Max Hanes saw something in the package. And he knew she was broke and desperate and beautiful in her own special way, and he knew most of the things that can be done to desperate people, and he talked to her and learned what would work best with her.

That's how they install the button. That's how they wire you for chimes.

See what you did to me, schoolgirl? See where you put me? Many thanks, little sophomore. Many, many thanks.

26

She clambered up out of the pool seal-sleek and spectacular. As she walked smiling back toward Hugh Darren, she yanked her bathing cap off and fluffed her midnight hair, and then, on impulse, clowned for him, making a big wet Marilyn Monroe mouth, with the chin up and eyes hooded, and giving her hips all the roll and swing she could manage.

"They could pass laws about you, even in Vegas," he said.

"It was all for you, dear."

"The bystanders suffer, though. One of my younger lifeguards just walked into the ladder on the slide."

She winked at him, toweled her face and shoulders dry, and clambered lithely back into the sun chaise with a sigh of contentment. "Just a bawdy impulse, I guess. Didn't mean to destroy poolside morale. Just thought, mmmm, there's ol' Hugh and I'll walk him a girl-type walk."

She lay back, her face turned toward him. He sat on the towel beside the chaise, his gray-blue eyes level with, and less than a foot from, her dark blue eyes. And with that magic that was but a month old for them, they were suddenly enclosed in their own area of special and personal privacy.

"It was girl-type," he said. "I will give you that. Yes."

"Some days your eyes look green, even." And she did something with her lips that so specifically invited his kiss that she saw his inadvertent leaning toward her.

"Oh, fine," he said, scolding her in a mocking way. "We establish this poolside routine and some other routines of meeting here and there, and now you are giving me the walk, and trapping me into the kiss. So why don't we just have the information tattooed across our foreheads so nobody will be in any doubt at all?"

"You have made me see it all, Mr. Darren. I have been unfair to you. I have been undermining your authority. I am causing your employees to whisper about you behind your back. The only decent thing I can do is to . . . sever our clandestine relationship right here and now."

"Hey!" he said. "Hey, now!"

"You've made me see the error of my ways at last." She did that thing with her mouth again.

"Stop that, dammit!"

She produced a tragic sigh. "Here it is Wednesday, the only night I have off in the whole week, and I was all set to be sly and sneaky and sort of skulk around so as not to completely destroy your reputation by having anybody see one of the entertainers sneak into your room. But now it is all over.

27

Indeed. Forsooth. Verily. I shall spend the evening reading something uplifting."

He stared skyward for strength, wiped his hand slowly across his face, then glowered at her and said, "Why, O why do you give me hell on Wednesdays?"

She giggled. "No girl wants to make things *too* easy."

"Skulking is splendid exercise, Miss Dawson."

"But should you really be so smug about all this, Hugh?"

"Smug?" His expression changed. "I'll be serious for once, without you changing the subject. Now shut up and listen. Not smug, Betty. Eternally, quietly, humbly grateful. And not quite able to believe my own luck. I didn't know there was such a thing as this kind of a relationship between a man and a woman. I thought there always had to be love or it was just a sort of cheap opportunism. But there's a special, wonderful honesty about this. You are a hell of a nice guy, Betty. We became good friends before . . . we added the physical part. And now this whole thing of . . . giving and receiving pleasure seems to be such a logical extension of friendship and affection that it seems a damn shame more people can't find it the way we have, without tension and friction."

"That's right. You're unbearably smug. I'm just another fool woman. You are using me, you cad."

"Sure am," he said, grinning. "Couldn't possibly stop now. Don't you ever want to say anything in a serious vein?"

"You, my managerial friend, are serious enough for both of us. Let's not pick at things and analyze them and make a lot of goopy comparisons, Hugh. That bird over there in that bush will never need psychiatry. He just busts his throat singing, and takes things as they come."

"And so should we?"

"Don't you think so?"

"Of course I do, Betty. Like this is Wednesday night, so let's take it."

"Trapped," she said. "Outmaneuvered again. Ah, sir, you are too clever for stupid broad in entertainment field, no? Broad condemned to career of skulking to save reputation. But may humble girl ask favor from mighty manager?"

"Anything your shriveled little heart desires, cutie."

"Honestly, I am exhausted, Hugh. So, with your permission, I'll sneak into your room about seven or maybe a little later, and please see if you can keep yourself busy long enough so I can have a long nap. May I say, solemnly, that it is one of those little favors you won't regret?"

He looked at her eyes and her lips. "Damn this secrecy kick. I'd like to brag about you. Take ads in the paper. Buy air time."

"Let's just keep it to ourselves, hmmmm?"

He stood up. "I've got a five o'clock date with some gift-shop people who don't like our standard lease."

"Give 'em hell, Mr. D. Tell them what for."

"You have a happy nap."

She winked at him. He turned and walked away from her. When he reached the service-alley gate he looked back and waved from the distance. She lifted one long leg in sardonic salute. When he was gone she said, moving her lips, making no sound, "I love you, I love you, I love you with all my heart, Hugh Darren."

And that is the message I cannot give you, ever. And it is that love, you dull darling, which keeps it all from being cheap. I wrap everything in my love, all for you, and it is all right if you call it friendship, because I'm going to take all of it I can get, drink deep and fast of it, because I know it is going to end and I just don't know how soon.

A man hairy as a bison, and almost as large, moved in on her, bringing his chair and planting it next to the chaise, facing her. "I certainly admire your work, Miss Dawson. I caught your midnight show last night."

She saw, with weary amusement, that his eyes were tracking back and forth from her ankles to her throat as though he watched a midget tennis match. "Ummm," she said.

In a soporific drone he began to tell her all about himself. She thought about her nap in Hugh's bed and she thought about Hugh with great precision of erotic detail, and thus comforted, baked by a slanting sun, she slid off into a cat nap right in the middle of the bison's explanation of how it had practically stolen the tract of land on which it had erected its third shopping center.

. . . three

As BETTY DAWSON WAS DRIFTING INTO HER CAT NAP DOWN by the pool, Al Marta, in his penthouse apartment atop the east wing of the Cameroon, was awakening from his afternoon siesta. The master bedroom was of sufficient luxury to remind Al Marta, each time he returned from dreams of ancient violence, that he was safe and well and rich. The decor affirmed his heavy ownership—even though it was partially a front—of the Cameroon. It spoke of his freedom from the indignity of any kind of arrest for many years. It was safe harbor, rich, protected, loaded with all the niceties of the standard hoodlum dream. With Max Hanes down there operating the casino, and the Darren kid running the hotel, and with good talent running the other aspects of his local operations, the days were made of silk and broads, bourbon and laughs, and there were a thousand important people who loved him and called him Al.

He checked and learned he had napped alone, knuckled his eyes, dug at the coarse gray thatch on his chest and got up, yawning so vastly that he tottered. He pulled on a pair of rumpled linen slacks, smoothed his thinning hair back with the palms of his hands, fired up a cigar and walked barefoot out into the main living room of the apartment to see who was around. There had to be someone around. He had arranged his life so there would be. He had to have people near him. He needed them close, where he could touch them, look at them, laugh with them.

The music was turned low. Gidge Allen and Bobby Waldo were playing gin. Beaver Brownell was slumped on a low couch, soft-talking, with practiced insistence, a young blonde broad from the chorus line of the current show in the Safari Room. She sat, glass in hand, her expression rapt and blank, while the Beaver emphasized the highlights of his muted lecture by touching, lightly and often, the golden convexity of her right thigh just below the hem of her shorts.

Jerry Buckler was asleep on one of the other couches, blowing small bubbles in the corner of his mouth.

Al went over to the control panel and boosted the volume of the music. He wandered over and watched Gidge throw the seven of hearts. Bobby Waldo hesitated over his next discard, then threw the seven of diamonds. Gidge snatched it up to fit right in the middle of a diamond run, and Bobby Waldo mumbled, "Advertising son of a bitch."

"Stay alert, son," Gidge said smugly.

Al made himself a light highball and said to the group at large, "Where's the action? Who's ahead?"

"The home team," Beaver told him.

"What's the score? Don't tell me. Nothing to nothing, the way it looks around here. You people are dragging it. Where the hell is Artie?"

"He ought to be along any minute," Gidge said. Gidge Allen had been with Alfred Addams Marta for over twenty years, serving in various capacities, all of them relatively confidential. Allen had the voice rasp and knowing eye of the carny pitch man. He had a shock of gray Will Rogers hair, a strong youthful body, and a saddle-brown face so deeply seamed and lined it was like some strange new kind of corduroy, contrasting in a startling way with glassy white dentures and eyes the color of mercury.

"Make it a three-way game," Al said. "We'll play Captains, okay?"

"Okay, soon as I finish out this blitz," Gidge said. "I got a pigeon here and I need the money."

Bobby Waldo snorted with exasperation. "Gimme some cards one time," he demanded. He was young, huge, bulging, sun-raw, with an eighth of an inch of carroty bristle on his square skull, invisible eyebrows and lashes, extravagant fading tattoos on his fleshy freckled arms.

Al Marta felt annoyed with all of them. He was a stocky, powerful man with a sallow, fleshy face. He was almost exactly half bald, with no hair growing forward of an imaginary line drawn from ear to ear across the top of his skull. He had a thick growth of long black eyelashes, a small snub nose, a broad sensuous mouth, liquid brown eyes.

He owned, in the patois of Vegas, thirty points in the Cameroon. Thirty per cent of the corporate stock. Though it had been some sixteen years since he had suffered the indignity of an arrest, he had what is called a heavy record. Twenty-six arrests, three convictions. He drew probation on two of them, and had served one year out of three on the third. The criminal record should have kept him from owning anything in Nevada, but he had gotten in well before the so-called cleanup of 1955, and by then it was too late to move him. Nominally he was the largest shareholder in the Cameroon, but no one could say exactly how much of that was actually his own. And on the total list of shareholders, no one could say who was fronting for someone else and who was not. The quiet word in town and in Los Angeles and New York was that the Cameroon was Al Marta's place, and thus a syndicate operation.

He knew a thousand people in the entertainment world by their first names, and most of them were such fools as to be flattered by this hoodlum attention. He smiled readily, laughed loudly and easily, listened with flattering attention, and told jokes with an almost professional timing. He lived

31

well, dressed well, entertained well. No, there was nothing at all sinister about Al Marta. He remembered birthdays and sent expensive presents, and if you were in any kind of a jam he was always glad to help out.

Al Marta used the Cameroon as a base of operation. In downtown Las Vegas, in a new office building, was X-Sell Associates, the nerve center for a random collection of corporations dealing in real estate, transportation, communications, wholesale supply houses. In one sense, Al Marta owned X-Sell. In a truer sense, and in one that would never be unraveled because of the obfuscating skills of the attorneys and accountants employed, Al Marta was a regional manager, taking his orders from a Los Angeles district headquarters which in turn was directed, through a Chicago setup, by the national council on syndicate policy, operating on the eastern seaboard.

A portion of every dollar, legal and illegal, declared and undeclared, eventually ended up in the war chest of the national council, where it was expended with such thought and care that people like Al Marta had been able to go for sixteen years without an arrest. Some percentage of each dollar was sidetracked for each station along the way. Nobody could say how much Al kept. But it was enough for a new Lincoln each year, a twenty-thousand-dollar wardrobe, lavish presents, luxurious entertaining, the maintenance of a special staff of "assistants" not covered by either the casino payroll or the hotel payroll, and the procurement of and proper entertainment of those young women who pleased him.

"No action today," Al grumbled.

He stared with habitual wonderment at the operational technique of Wilbur "Beaver" Brownell. Beaver was a gaunted, spindly, fragile-looking man somewhere in his forties. His cheeks were so hollowed he had a death's head look. The protruding angle of his large yellow teeth had supplied his nickname. His hair was dyed a curiously unreal shade of brown, like the color of cheap shoes. He had a reedy, monotonous voice, a sparrow-chested stance, and some mysterious source for the type of clothing that was called sharp during the thirties. He wore too many large yellowish diamonds, and he doused himself liberally with cologne, and yet this ridiculous man was never known to have less than three women on the string at the same time. Nor were they dogs in any sense of the word. And their inexplicable love for Beaver kept them in a state of torment.

32

The intensity of Beaver's focus on the new blonde gave Al an idea. He went over and stepped into the conversation and took the blonde by the hand.

"I got to borrow this broad a couple minutes, Beaver."

"Hey, Al. Hey now!" Beaver said, alarmed. The girl giggled.

"I got to get my back scrubbed, Beaver. This here is a good strong-looking blonde and she can do a good job, can't you, honey?"

The girl giggled again and Beaver said, "What the hell, Al?"

Al looked directly at him and said, "I'd hate to think you were being selfish about this, Beaver."

"Huh? Oh, hell no, Al. I mean, we were just talking. Go ahead, Al."

With a sudden muscular tug, Al hauled the girl up onto her feet. She glared down at Beaver. "The big hero!" she snarled. "The big shot!"

"Just be a good kid and do a little favor for a pal," Beaver wheedled.

Al led her into the bedroom by the hand and closed the door. She yanked her hand away. "Lissen, I'm not scrubbing your back or anything else."

"What's your name, darling?"

"Gretchen Lane."

"How old are you, sweetheart?"

"I'm . . . twenty-one."

"Stand right there a minute, sweetheart." He went to the bureau and took a fifty-dollar bill from the top drawer. He went to the bathroom and came back with a bath brush. "Put your hand out, dear." He put the bill on her hand and the brush on top of it. "One goes with the other, dear. Take your choice. It's a good pay scale, don't you think? I'll leave you right here. If you don't like the offer after you think it over, leave both items and take off. Fair enough? But don't leave one and take the other, because then you might be in a hurry, and you might fall and break one of those pretty legs, sweetheart."

She gave him a skeptical look. "Just for scrubbing your back, Mr. Marta?"

"That's all, sweetheart."

He went into the bathroom and, as he started his shower, he left the glass door of the shower stall open. When he felt the first tentative touch on his back he smiled to himself. She did an efficient and vigorous job. When he sensed she was about to stop he half turned, pretended to slip, grasped her arm, and pulled her under the roaring water. She leaped out, gasping and cursing, her hair pasted flat, her blouse and shorts drenched.

He apologized profusely and with great sincerity, and gave her a big fresh towel for her hair, and went to the extra closet and selected a hostess coat in pale blue satin that he knew would fit her.

"You'll have to accept this as a gift, sweetheart."

"It's beautiful!"

"You shut yourself in there and get organized, darling. Throw your wet stuff out and I'll have maid service take care of it."

He dressed quickly, then picked up the wet blouse and shorts from the floor outside the bathroom. He balled them up, walked into the next room, closing the door behind him, and hurled them against Beaver's chest. They hit with a damp substantial sound and fell into his lap. Beaver stared stupidly down at them, and picked them up, holding them gingerly.

"Where's Gretch?" he asked.

"That little broad is resting, Beaver. She got real tired."

"What the hell, Al?"

"She thought you'd like those things as a keepsake. Sleep with them under your pillow, buddy. Sorry they got wet, but we got so eager we were in the shower before either of us remembered she should have taken them off. So I helped her get 'em off."

"But she's a *nice* girl," Beaver said in such a heartbroken way that Gidge gave a high hard yelp of laughter.

"Oh, and I nearly forgot," Al said sternly. "Get the hell out of here. That's one thing she asked me to do, like a favor. She doesn't want to see you when she comes out."

"Me? Get out?"

"Need Bobby's help?"

"Hell no," Beaver mumbled. "I'm leaving."

Al had just started to explain what he'd done when the girl came out. "My hair is pretty messy but I guess it. . . . Where'd Beaver go?"

Al had to fight to keep a straight face when he took hold of her hands. "Sweetheart, we had a pretty ugly scene here. I'm glad you missed it."

"Whaddaya mean?" she asked blankly.

"Beaver said we'd both lie, but he said that no matter what we said, he knew a lot more than back scrubbing went on."

34

"Why that dirty. . . ."

"So I ordered him out of here, sweetheart. As he was leaving, he left a message for you."

"Yeah?"

"He said to tell you he'd be looking you up soon, and tell you he wants his back scrubbed, and he said you'll know what he means."

The girl turned chalky white and then a violent spastic red. She unleashed a howling stream of vituperation, semicoherent, so loud that it jarred Jerry Buckler up out of his deep sleep. Her general opinion was that one Beaver Brownell could work on his project thirty hours a day for ten years without ever getting close enough to give her a phone call that would cost less than a dollar toll. As she still spouted, Al eased her out to the private elevator that serviced his suite and, at the last moment, tucked her damp raiment into her hand.

When he walked back in, grinning, Jerry said, "What the hell was that?"

Al went over to Gidge and slapped a hundred-dollar bill down on the table. "I say he doesn't score, not on ole Gretch."

"Odds?" Gidge asked.

"Two to one?"

"Done," Al said. "Come up with your fifty. You got confidence, friend."

"That Beaver," Gidge said, "he hardly ever gives up."

"There's one thing for sure," Bobby Waldo said. "If Gidge wins it won't be hard to check. Beaver's women follow him around, howling like stomped dogs."

"Ready for three-handed?" Gidge asked.

"You guys play. I don't feel like it right now," Al said. He walked slowly over to the window and looked down at the half-full parking lot, spangled with pastel cars. He saw a young couple get out of a convertible and run, hand in hand, toward the front entrance, laughing at some joke.

Suddenly he knew the laughter of Gidge and Bobby Waldo had been forced. It hadn't been a good gag. It had been too complicated and clumsy. A stupid young broad, half stoned, and the old Beaver. Gidge had covered the bet because he knew Al wanted it covered. What had happened to all the good gags and the good laughing times? There wasn't any action any more. The world has flattened out. The score is nothing to nothing every day lately.

He heard the steady glug-glug of a bottle and turned sharply and saw Jerry Buckler, his hotel manager in name only, at the bar making himself a half-pint highball of bonded bourbon. He moved quickly and quietly over and put his hand on top of the glass just as Jerry tried to pick it up.

Jerry looked at him with an uncertain smile, waiting for the punch line. The liquor route, Al realized, had been shrinking the man lately. The belly still bulged and the red face was puffed, but the jacket sagged on him, and the neck was stringy, the shirt collar too big and slightly soiled.

"You're leaning on my little drink, suh," Jerry said in a forced way.

"I'd hate to see you mix a big one, for chrissake. Let it sit right there. Come on in the bedroom, Jerry."

Al closed the door as they went in, and he let Jerry fidget as the silence grew. "Something on your mind, Al?"

"How was New Orleans?"

"It was fine, fine. Everybody was fine."

"What the hell would you remember about it?"

Jerry shrugged. "It did get a little drunk over there, Al."

"It gets a little drunk everywhere, doesn't it? For you?"

"Hell, Al, I can take it or leave it alone. But why should I leave it alone?"

"You look like a drunk, Jerry. You got the shakes. You got a dirty shirt and dirty hands. You smell dirty. You *are* a drunk, Jerry."

"God *damn* it, Al!"

"I love you, baby, but you bore me lately. You really do. I don't like to see a man let something get on top of him. He isn't a man any more then."

"What's on your mind, Al?"

"I know. Get it over with. That big drink is sitting out there getting lonesome."

Jerry smiled, and Al could sense what the smile cost him. "It's such a waste of good booze, boss."

"Max and I had a little talk about you today, Jerry. You're making Max and me unhappy."

"How? What am I doing wrong?"

"You aren't being an executive, Jerry. We bought you a good boy down there, that Darren. We bought you the best we could get. That was so you could let him handle all the details for you, baby. But you keep messing around, bitching up the routine for him."

"I've known you a hell of a long time, Al. I was running big places before that punk learned to feed himself. Are you all of a sudden going to listen to Darren instead of me? He's got no beef. I just straighten him out once in a while."

"Who said I listened to Darren? Who said he isn't happy as clams?"

"Then what's wrong anyway?"

"Max likes the new deal around here, Jerry. He likes the way things are running now much better than he liked the way they used to be. Max has strong ideas, Jerry. He's got the idea you've turned into a foulup. He thinks you suck on the bottle until you don't know what the hell you're doing. So here is the way it's going to be. You stay the hell out of running the hotel. The time you come into the picture is when Max has a special problem. And when he has a problem, you handle it cold sober, baby. No other way. And when the problem is solved, you get off the pot and you keep hands off Darren's job until the next time you get your orders from me or Max."

Jerry stared at him with fury and indignation. "I manage this hotel, Al. And when I happen to feel like straightening that punk out, I'll. . . ."

Al reached him in two strides and, smiling, he pinched the loose flesh of Buckler's cheek and gave the man's head a painful little shake. "Baby, baby, what're you trying to prove?"

"I just. . . ."

"You got a home here, baby. You're a drunk, but we all love you just fine. And so I'd hate to have you get hairy with me, Jerry. I'd hate to have to tell Harry and Bobby to take you out on the desert and break you up a little. They wouldn't like doing it, and I wouldn't like telling them to do it, believe me. But it would be better than letting Max handle it with a couple of those casino guards of his. They aren't pro the way Harry and Bobby are. So just give me a little smile, Jerry, and tell me you're going to cooperate a thousand per cent."

The smile, when it came, was ghastly. "Sure, Al. Sure. I can see it your way." He made a noise like a laugh. "I shouldn't get into any detail work now that I've trained Hugh Darren to handle it. It'll be . . . better this way, Al."

"Now go nibble that big drink, baby," Al said. As Jerry ducked his head and scuttled by, Al gave him a gentle, re-assuring pat on the shoulder.

At the door Jerry turned, frowning, and said, "Do I get to keep my desk and my name on the door? And, you know, tell people I'm manager?"

"You *are* the manager, Jerry! You want your name bigger? You want it in gold? You want a fancier desk, just say so."

"No. Everything . . . the way it is . . . it's fine, Al. It's just fine."

When they walked back out Al found that Artie Gill had arrived, bringing two burr-headed beatnik broads and a defensive linebacker from the Rams. By seven o'clock there were twenty people in the big room One of the three "owners" of the Cameroon had even appeared quite unexpectedly. At the time the hotel was being built, the public relations specialists decided the place would have more glamor if the general public was led to believe, through column plants and other devices, that three of their idols held substantial interests in the Cameroon. The three they carefully selected were each given a half point in the enterprise.

The first was a middle-aged, corseted, western-hero faggot, with a lisp hidden somewhere in his drawl, and a permanent expression of noble, enduring humility. The second was an often-married, stupid, lazy, arrogant, photogenic blonde whose sole shred of acting ability consisted of being able to take a very deep breath on cue. She had not worn well, but continual head-to-toe cosmetic surgery plus top cameramen and lighting specialists had maintained her in the role of pneumatic goddess to the pimpled set long past her time. The third owner, the one who showed up unexpectedly, was a famous jazz musician who hadn't blown a note in years. Too many kinds of addiction and too many kinds of abuse had worn him down to a stunned half-world where an eighty-word vocabulary was sufficient for his needs, and he was carefully led around and displayed by nervous retainers who made a nice thing indeed off his old record royalties.

At one noisy point in the evening, before they split up, Al Marta drew Max Hanes aside and told him Jerry Buckler had bought the new deal with no fuss at all. Max looked gratified and said he'd let Darren know.

"Let's bump that kid one more hundred a month, Maxie."

"Isn't he making out pretty good now?"

"There's two things to think about. First, he handled this thing pretty good. Second—" Al tapped Max on the chest and winked at him—"the more a man makes, the more he's got to lose. Right?"

"You always make sense, Al."

"I think ahead. And because I'm thinking ahead, I'm telling you this. Don't ride the kid. Suck him along. Do him favors here and there. I mean don't change all of a sudden, because that looks phoney, but sort of come around gradual, so he'll feel . . . you know, like obligated. Just in case you need a little favor, and need it fast, and Jerry is hiding in a bottle someplace."

"Okay, Al."

"Maxie, you got a lousy taste in garments, you know that? A color and a cut like on that jacket, it's for a college boy."

"In my heart, Al, I'm young forever. You know, all we can take off the top this week is maybe twenty grand? And even that doesn't depress me. Want to know why?"

"Tell me why, Max baby."

"Because, Al baby, Homer G. Gallowell checks in here on Saturday, fresh and ready from Fort Worth. And we put a 200G bruise on Homer last time."

"So he can stay here, but why will he give us the play? Maybe he'll figure this place is cold for him and take his bread up or down the line."

"I know the way his mind works just like he had a window in his head, Al. He believes in the law of averages. So we'll get the play because, according to his law, we've got his money. I'll even bet he'll hit the same table and bet the same way."

"How does he bet?"

"There isn't any good way, Al, as you damn well know, but he goes for it the wrong way, doubling up on the losses. For a mark like Homer I'll happily set a new house limit, just like last time. A nice brand-new big fat house limit that'll make him very very happy. Then we lay back and watch the dice whip him again. Nothing in the world ever whipped him before, and he can't take it."

"He gets all the red carpet we got, Maxie."

"Why waste your breath? I'll check it out with Darren. If he wants a cruiser on Lake Mead, I'll lay that on him too. If he wants a pair of twin Jap blondes, I'll giftwrap 'em for good old Homer G. Gallowell."

"How big a party?"

"Just Homer, like before. He's maybe got the faint suspicion he's being a damn fool, so he's taking care nobody else he knows well gets to watch him."

"What's he worth?" Al asked.

"If it's less than fifty million, I'll eat his biggest ranch with a tin spoon."

Al clapped him on his solid shoulder. "So let's take it all."

"We'll take all we can get of it, boss."

At ten o'clock, while Hugh Darren was checking the front desk, Max Hanes said he'd like a minute in private, so Hugh took him back to the office and turned on one hooded desk lamp.

Max walked over and sat at Jerry's desk in the far shadowy corner, sighing as he sat down. "Jerry is out of your hair, kid. I thought you'd like to know."

"It's a good thing to know, Max. It makes everything a hell of a lot easier for me. Thanks."

"We can talk things over together once in a while, and it should all run smooth. Right?"

"No reason why not," Hugh said guardedly.

"You get a hundred a month bump as of May first, Darren."

"Why?"

"Don't you think you're worth it to the joint?"

"I know damn well I'm worth it."

"Then that could be the reason you're getting it, couldn't it?"

"For a minute there, Max, I had the idea you were recruiting me for extra duty."

Max Hanes chuckled in the darkness. "A clean-cut American boy like you, Darren? Hell, you'd write an indignant letter to the governor. We're a bunch of thieves, like you learned all about on the TV. Dirty gangsters. Mafia, maybe."

"I didn't say that, Max."

He heard the chair squeak as Max stood up. He came over into the cone of light. "Bill the casino account for everything on Homer G. Gallowell of Fort Worth."

"I saw his name on the reservation list and I checked him back and saw that he got the best, on the house, before, so I set it up that way. But I planned to check with you, of course."

"When you're set on the suite you'll give him, tell my assistant, Ben Brown, the number. I'll have him put a one-dollar slot up there, and a hundred silver dollars to play around with." He strolled toward the door, an ape-like figure in a yellow raw silk sports jacket. "See you around, Mister Manager."

"Max . . . this is just idle curiosity, but when you put a one-dollar slot in a room like that, is it the same payoff you have on the floor?"

"I like the way your mind works, kid. The state doesn't like for us to rig the slots too lean. But they don't care at all if we make one real fat. It gives a man a lot of confidence, pulling that handle, listening to the payoff crash into the scoop. It makes him happy. That's why we're here. This is a happy little city, full of fun and games."

"I know. That's why, on some of the checkouts, I have to charge the freight to the casino account, because somehow the happy people haven't got one dime left. They're so happy they can't stop smiling."

"You've got to learn that a mark is going to give it away to somebody, kid. There's no way to stop a real mark. So when he's ready, you just try to be first in line."

By the time Bunny Rice, the night manager, reported in at eleven, everything was so well under control that it required only a ten-minute briefing to catch him up on the problems in process of solution.

Hugh had tried to make himself stop thinking of Betty Dawson, but by the time he walked down the corridor toward his room he had a good vibrant alive feeling, as though his skin fitted particularly well, as though he could do front flips all the way down the empty corridor. There was a prickling of the skin on the backs of his hands and the nape of his neck. Her burlesque bikinied strut came into his mind and it seemed to him that he was unable to take a deep breath.

He fitted his key into the lock and opened the door as quietly as he could, and made himself close it again with the same stealth and shoot the night bolt before he let himself look at her. She lay tousled in his bed in a sweetness of sleep. She had thrown a towel over the bedside lamp, and there was a soft orange-pink glow against her sleeping face. She was on her side, facing him, both hands under the crumpled pillow, with a crow wing of her dark tumbled hair curling down her cheek and around to her throat.

There was a note for him under the light, a sheet with large printing on it, one corner under the lamp base. SLIPPING BEAUTY it read, AWAKEN WITH TENDER KISS. A crude arrow pointed toward her. Her slacks, cardigan, big purse and wisps of underwear were arranged in severe order on a straight chair beyond the foot of the bed. She wore a nightgown, pale blue-and-white net and lace, as evanescent as a mirage, a tenderness against the brown of her throat and shoulders. Her lips were slightly apart, and the thickety lashes were closed over the secrets of her eyes.

Moving without sound, he undressed in the sweet silence of the room, he paused once when he caused a harpsichord jangle of hangers, but she was not awakened. He went to her then with eagerness, but paused and sat slowly, with the patience of a thief, on the edge of the bed, so he could watch her for a little while and enjoy the gentle guilt of one who watches the face of a sleeping friend or lover. By forestalling his own hunger he sharpened his desire.

It was, he thought with a proper humility, a rare kind of luck, and a seldom thing. Back in August when he had begun work, he had been tense about the size and complexity of the operation and the almost total lack of proper administrative controls. There had been no one to break him in on the job. Buckler was a compulsive fool, obviously jealous of the assistant who had been forced upon him. And Hugh could define the limits of his authority only by testing them.

The employee situation was difficult. The good ones were glad to see the change, and the thieves were frightened. He had no one to confide in, no one whose judgments he could trust. And so his first project was to familiarize himself with every aspect of the operation, from linen inventory, to printing receipts for guests, to rejuvenation of wilted lettuce, to window-washing schedules, to shot-glass dimensions, to the uniforms of maids, to furniture repair and replacement. He worked a fifteen and sixteen hour day, roaming, watching, scribbling notes, assessing personnel. He knew they were all watching him, wondering when he would suddenly stop being an observer and start chopping off heads.

It was during the nights of his roving that he became aware of Betty Dawson. She worked the Afrique Bar just off the main casino floor to the right as you came into the casino from the lobby. She was working the midnight to six, doing her four shows in alternation with other entertainers. He found that she could provide the closest thing to relaxation and forgetfulness for him, and he fell into the habit, when he was around during the small morning hours,, to go in and sit at the curve of the bar nearest the small stage and listen to her. She had a limited range. She talked her way through a lot of her songs. But her face was very alive and, at times, wonderfully comic, and she had the refreshing trait of seeming to be sourly amused by her own antics. The lyrics of her songs were quick and tart—and blue without being tasteless.

He began to have a preference for some of her songs and to await them with pleasure. He liked ALICE WAS AS BLUE AS HER GOWN, and THEY'RE STILL RECRUITING GIRLS FOR THE NAVY and THE GIRL OF THE WEEK CLUB. She seemed to enjoy truly horrible puns, and he wondered who wrote her material, and he was more pleased than he should have been when he learned she wrote it herself.

By a quiet question here and there, never betraying more

than the most casual interest, he learned that she was the nearest thing to an entertainment fixture the Cameroon had. She had been there almost two years, and her room was but three doors from his. Knowing that Max Hanes handled the entertainment, with approval, when necessary, he made the obvious assumption that there was a special relationship between Betty and Max, between that curiously sinister ape-like old man with his playboy wardrobe and this handsome woman who, behind the practised facade of an entertainer, had the ineradicable perceptions and instincts of a gentle-woman.

With that nagging question still unanswered, he had begun to move, doing the things that needed doing, installing checks and controls, weeding out and strengthening the staff. In this process he had learned he could trust Bunny Rice. One dawn while they were discussing individuals, Hugh casually mentioned Betty Dawson as being Max Hanes' girl.

Bunny looked pained. "No, it isn't that way, Mr. D. I've never known of Max to take that kind of interest in any girl, or any boy either, in case I'm giving you the wrong idea. Max is maybe in love with the money room."

"I guess I got that idea because Miss Dawson has been here so long."

Bunny had shrugged. "She's not a big draw, but she's got a following. She's on the tab for room and food, so what Max pays her makes hardly any dent in his budget. She doesn't make any kind of trouble, and she knows how to handle a drunk."

"Shouldn't she get better hours after being here so long?"

"Betty likes that shift, Mr. D. She really does. She has a point. She can sleep late, get up in time to catch some sun, have herself a nice evening before she has to go on. Other entertainers, you keep them on that shift too long, they start to bitch about it. Not Betty."

"So she's found her home away from home."

"I guess she'll stay quite a while."

"Bunny, you gave that little remark a strange sort of emphasis."

"There's some kind of an edge working for her."

"I'm getting goddam tired of the little hints about wheels within wheels around this place. What kind of an edge? What kind of an angle?"

"Don't get sore. I didn't mean anything by it. And it isn't just this place. It's the whole town. You hear things, that's all. I don't know anything specific about Betty Dawson. But

43

I've gotten the impression that . . . there's some other kind of tie-up with Hanes and Al Marta, something that makes it unlikely they'll fire her or that she'll quit. I think she comes from a good family. I guess you can tell that. She's a doctor's daughter, they say, and she went to college, and for quite a while she had an act with Jackie Luster, and nobody ever got mixed up with him without coming out on the short end. He can pack any room in town and name his own price, but nobody in show business who knows him well can stand being in the same room with him except when working."

And so Hugh Darren had added all the bits of information together, but it was not until nearly the end of his second month on the job that he got to know her. They had nodded and smiled and said the appropriate greetings whenever they met in the corridor or on the staircase or in the elevator.

He came out of his room at dawn one morning in October just as she was walking slowly toward her room.

"It's time I thanked you, Mr. Darren."

"For?"

"Nice little things going on. Nice, and appreciated. Better food, better service, and the whole gaudy joint is cleaner and smarter, inside and out. And all your little service people are . . . I don't know how to say it . . . getting a better attitude about working. They act less like they're doing you an enormous favor to fill your water glass or hand you your mail."

"I didn't know whether it was beginning to show, Miss Dawson. I've been too close to it to really see it."

"Oh, it's showing. And it's wonderful. Living here was beginning to seem a hell of a lot like camping out, or like one of those collection points for refugees from disasters. You're a pro, Mr. Darren." She smiled at him. "And do you know what I like best?"

"What's that?"

"The way you kinda drift around, no sweat, no strain. Just ambling around in a slow smiley way."

"I keep pretending I'm not getting an ulcer."

She yawned. " 'Scuse please. I guess I hate fidgety, nervous little managers who trot to and fro, bobbing and wringing their hands. It wears me out watching them. You apparently get no rest at all, but you're still restful."

"And thanks for that too, Miss Dawson."

"If it wouldn't be showing too much familiarity with the hired help around here, you could make me more comfortable by calling me Betty."

"And Hugh, if you please."

"Hugh when we meet in the corridor. Mr. Darren in front of the troops, sir."

"I like your work, Betty."

"I know you do."

"How?"

"You laugh at exactly the right places. And you keep coming back for more. So it hasn't been any secret. So thanks, Hugh. And this is just about all the mutual admiration I can take at the moment. Seventy-one seconds from now I either fall into bed, or flat on the floor. It's a delicate problem of timing. And a good morning to you, and a good night to me."

From then on it was very easy to talk to her, so easy and so pleasant that he found himself making little adjustments in his schedule so that it would happen more often. He learned the likely time to find her out by the pool, or in the coffee shop, or having dinner in the Little Room. His was a lonely job and a hard job, and she was the only person he could talk to in an unguarded way. He learned that she was observant, and he found it to his advantage to check some of his conclusions about members of his staff with her. In one way it surprised him that she should know so much about the personal problems, the domestic situations of bartenders, bellhops, waitresses; she seemed to have little time to learn such things. But on the other hand she was a warm and sympathetic person, and her interest in other people was not forced, and so they talked about themselves to her. He found himself doing the same thing.

By Christmas their friendship was close and comfortable, and very probably it would have leveled off at that point had she not decided he was looking a little too drawn and weary. She did not work on Wednesday nights. She talked him into taking a Thursday off, and she was most mysterious about the whole project. They left the hotel early in the morning on the seventh day of January, in her stodgy, elderly Morris Minor which she called Morris in a way that turned the designation into a personal name. There was a giant picnic basket resting on the back seat. She drove thirty miles out of town, and then three more miles over a track so primitive the small car moaned and sighed at each hump and dip. They were in the burned and ancient land on a morning clear and bright, dazzlingly new.

In country where for reasons unknown even the shacks of the desert rats are fashioned of boards brought from far away, the place where she stopped, at the end of the road, was of the red-and-brown native stone. It was a small place, which blended against the lift of a small, angular hill.

She had a key for the crude, heavy door, and she was very much at home in the place. There was wood stacked for a big fireplace. There was a deep well gasoline pump with manual controls and a big pressure tank, a gauge to be watched carefully. There were propane tanks for a small stove and a gas refrigerator. There were gasoline lanterns.

Most of the interior was one big room—living room and bunk room, with the kitchen at one end, and a small bath. She enlisted his aid in getting the utilities operating. When all chores were done she looked at him with a pride in this feat, in this special place, and said, "See? Like for hermits."

She stood, smiling at him, wearing pale tailored whip-cords, a bulky white cardigan, and soft desert boots, her black hair ponytailed with a thick white length of yarn. Mirrored sunglasses made her eyes unreadable.

"It's exactly ten thousand years from the Cameroon," he said.

"And so it is exactly what we need, Mr. Darren dear. And first comes the picnic-type breakfast, and you build a fire to take the chill off this place, and then comes a walk to places I know, and then back here for drinks, and then lunch out on the picnic table in the sun, and a nap for the weary ones, and more drinks and the final eating, and some more fireplace-type atmosphere, and then back through the night to the tired old workaday smell of money. I'm going to schedule the hell out of your day, truly."

She did. They were in the middle of fifty thousand years of silence, and it was a restoring thing. They moved the luncheon table to a sunny place out of the chill wind. They ate like wolves, and later they talked and they napped, Betty on the fireplace couch, he atop a gray blanket in one of the wide deep bunks.

It wasn't until after dinner, sitting on the Indian rug in front of the fireplace flames, that he said, "Okay, so you won't volunteer any information until I ask. Or, if it's a secret, I'm out of order. But is this your place?"

"In a funny kind of way, I guess it is, Hugh." Her voice was soft and thoughtful, and she was looking at the flames and mesquite coals, half frowning, hugging her legs, chin on her whipcord knees.

"Mabel Huss actually owns it," she said. "She's a fat, sloppy, ignorant woman, Hugh. Ignorant in book ways. She

46

runs a motel in Vegas, a little old junky place on one of the old streets, all crowded in between a furniture store and a big shiny operation with a name that haunts me because the neon used to flash in my window. Super-Drug, Super-Drug, Super-Drug, it said, all the night through. It was a cheap place, the cheapest I could find, and I was way down, Hugh. There are little pockets of despair in Vegas for people who are way down, Hugh. Down as far as they can get. The thing is, in Vegas or anywhere, you aren't put down by the cruel world all by itself. You have to get in there and help the bastards bring you low. That's something hard to learn. It's so easy to blame everything and everybody else.

"I can skip the stinking details, except to say Mable was carrying me on credit for no good reason in the world, and there was one way I could get out of the whole dreary deal, but it was a way that made me feel a little sick to my heart to think about. But I was scared, and even though it wasn't long ago, I was inconceivably younger than I am right now. I had that special kind of stupid pride which made me feel I couldn't get on the collect phone and yell help to my father in San Francisco. So I decided to be real hardcase about it, and I told myself it was that kind of a world, and I walked right through the door the bastards were holding open for me. And it was worse than I had thought, Hugh. Don't ever romanticize evil.

"I solved my problems in what they call one fell swoop, buddy, and I caught the brass ring, and it was so damn bad, every implication of it, I knew I had to die. I had lost myself. And though I didn't have to, though I could have started going first class right away, I went crawling back to Mabel's Comfort Motel, knowing that all the trouble I'd thought I was in before was nothing at all. I spent twenty hours in a stupor of self-disgust, and then that fat woman, without saying much of anything, loaded me and some cartons of food in her old car and drove me out here and left me. It was a special kind of wisdom, Hugh. This is the kind of aloneness you need when you have to mend yourself, when you have to form some kind of adjustment to the sort of person you have suddenly become through making a bad error.

"She left me here for five days, and when she came out and got me, I'd put myself back together. Her husband built this place. They had good times here. He died. She's never wanted to sell it or rent it, and she hadn't wanted to spend time here herself. But she knew what it would do for me.

47

She knows I still need to come here from time to time, to put myself together, so I have her permission to come here any time. I stop at her place once in a while and tell her how I'm making out. This is the first time I ever brought anybody here."

"I feel honored, Betty."

She turned her head to smile at him. "Ah, you should be! If you're real good, maybe I'll bring you back sometime."

"A day like this can be like taking a whole week off."

"I know."

She had her head turned, looking at him in a quiet way, and it was in those long moments their relationship changed to something else that perhaps neither of them particularly wanted. He had had a perfectly normal physical awareness of her as a handsome and desirable woman, but this awareness had the objective and rather abstract quality of admiration he would have given any woman equivalently endowed. But in those moments it became a personal, emotional awareness, a strong and specific desire for her, underlining their isolation and building new tensions between them which became all too tangible.

He had long since learned that his habit of sexual continence was no indication of basic coldness or meager drives. He drew upon this unused energy and channeled it into his work, driving himself harder with this extra fuel. Many men in his situation of bachelorhood and wide opportunity would, he well knew, have indulged themselves in all the meaningless available ways, but he suspected that such men had some well-concealed doubts about their own adequacy, so that they needed chronic proof of their own desirability and potency. He had no feeling of self-righteousness about his policy of continence. At times events had conspired to make a minor conquest too easy and too attractive to be ignored. But he sensed in himself an idealism which made such casual episodes unsatisfying. It was that same streak of idealism which had blocked the marriage he had almost made when he was twenty-five, and had left him with rather more skepticism than was healthy.

They looked into each other's eyes by firelight for those long moments, and then a coyote made a quavering, gibbering cry of despair in the starry night. She shivered and then rose lithely to her feet and said, "Time we policed the area and took off, Hugh."

The relationship had moved into another dimension, as yet unexpressed, and it created awkwardness between them

48

in small ways. He felt it on the way back in the little car. And he felt it during the days that followed. It left small and curious gaps in their conversation, as though they had begun to speak to each other on a new wordless level.

They went to the little house in that desert again in January, and on only one Thursday in February—because that was a very busy time for him—and they managed it again on the tenth day of March, which was, if her phrase was correct, the day of their reckoning. They had taken every sane effort to make their excursions inconspicuous. They sensed there was some staff gossip about them, a thing unavoidable in the encapsulated social complex of any large resort hotel, but they knew it was intelligent to provide the gossipers with as little factual information as possible.

On that tenth of March, a rare blowy blustery day, all the tensions were stronger and more obvious to each of them. They had known each other for seven months. And it did not come about through the accidental touch, through any half-accidental blundering. He had replenished the woodpile, and it was midafternoon. He had fattened the fire and was standing, one hand braced on the stone mantel, watching the wood catch. He was aware, suddenly, that she was very still, and he looked toward the kitchen end of the room and saw her standing, looking at him, her dark blue eyes wide. She wore a soft white leather jacket, dark flannel slacks, a yellow silk scarf around her throat.

She squared her shoulders and marched directly to him. He turned to face her and she put her hands on his shoulders and looked up into his face, her head tilted, her expression odd.

"Should we say, like the man on the train from Minsk to Pinsk, enough of this luff-making?" she asked.

"I don't want anything you don't want, Betty. I want anything you want."

"I am, and remain, in the best sense of the words, very truly yours, your friend, Betty Dawson."

He had placed his hands gently on the nimble, narrow waist. "Very sincerely yours. Hugh Darren. His mark."

"Let me draw a picture first, darling. I like you much. So I give me to this liking of you, and so let's just have it for joy. We'll indulge ourselves with a pleasure thing, Hugh. Without angles or tensions. We take what's here, with gladness and respect, and we stay proud of what we are, and nobody has to own or dominate anybody, ever, because we're grown up and we don't need that."

49

"Can it be done that way, Betty? Is it possible?"

"I don't know. But if it isn't, I think we can come as close as anybody. And if it starts to turn into anything else, into the kind of thing neither of us are looking for, then we knock it right in its pretty head and bury it under stones."

"Agreed, sure, but isn't that kind of a thing much more advantageous for the man?"

"The man? The woman? We start, buddy, by not type-casting ourselves. We're Hugh and Betty, and there isn't any rule says we can't make up our own rules. And this room is warm now, and this is a mouth to be kissed, and these little round things are an interesting invention called buttons, which will yield to a clever man. And there are a zipper and snaps and things which should cause no terrible problems, and that thing over there is a rustic bunk. And my darn knees feel as if they could bend either way, and my heart would give Gene Krupa a feeling of awe, and if you wanted any coy, shy little thing, brother, you came to the wrong store, and I have the feeling we've waited just about long enough."

It began then, in crescendo, and it kept right on from that explicit starting point, becoming better for them in the same ratio that they were apt students of each other, each so much more intent on the giving than on the taking of their pleasure that it became different from anything they had ever experienced.

He sat at her side as she slept so soundly in his bed, thinking of this little-more-than-a-month of their love-making. They conspired, in shameless ingenuity, but with no overtones of coarseness, to find every opportunity to be together. If it could be hours, they took them gladly, and if there were only minutes, they could make do with minutes. It was, he knew, obsessional and compulsive with them, but with none of the dark overtones he had always thought went with intensively physical affairs. There were sly laughter, and rude ridiculous jokes, and only the very slightest easily ignored suspicion of guilt. Nor did this sweet excess drain his vitality or hamper his work. It gave him, instead, a vibrant, bounding feeling of fitness and capacity. The work was easier for him. And, whenever he could watch her act, he knew that it was doing the same for her.

It would, he thought, be a nice thing if she was always here, if I had her for always. Wherever I might go. Watch it, boy! It isn't what she wants. She said so. We defined the limits of this thing, and if you try to own her she will suddenly be long gone, and it will become a damned drab world around here.

He stood and lifted the corner of the covers, and slid in beside her, leaving the small light on, finding her sleeping lips with his. As he felt her lips wake up and her drowsy arms move to encircle him, he made the little adjusting moves that brought her long against him. He relaxed against the fragrant, sleep-warm, silken length of Betty Dawson, with her little murmur of contentment that went with the kiss, and her little languorous flexings to the slow stimuli of his hands, and the quickening pace of her breath as her arms grew more strong. . . .

She had nuzzled into his throat and she could tell from the slow rise and fall of his chest that he was now asleep. His heart, so very fast not long ago, was now a slow, heavy, comforting sound to her.

"Darling, darling, darling," she said in the smallest whisper, and felt the tears welling, sliding out of her eyes.

It was always best, every time. And it was a good thing that had to end badly because there was no other way it could end, so you wept for that. She had thought, this time, that she would see that it was all for him, with the greatest perfection she could manage, thinking only of him, being for him the sweet enveloping vessel for this strong and tender voyage, creating for her man a completion unlike any other which had gone before. And just when she thought she had managed it, deadening, with an effort of will, the eager claims of her own body, and, seeking to please him with false testimony to a final objective timed to match his own, the faking turned without warning to a tumultuous, roaring, blinding reality that was an unbearably long time in spending itself. When it finally released its harsh hold upon her, she floated back to shore on a midnight tide, buttery, boneless, helpless, and obscurely indignant with herself for having been so vulnerable that she had been unable to do as she had planned.

"My darling, my beloved," she whispered against his throat, and she let the tears come slowly and endlessly. When one would touch her lips she would find it with the tip of her tongue, tasting the salt of it.

Daddy used to say to save them in a bottle, and he would get me one of those little medicine bottles and I would hold it so tears would roll into it, but they would always stop then.

51

Don't ever love me, Hugh. Just let me love you. I'm ready for hurt. I'm braced for it. You are worth too much ever to fall in love with what I have become. Sleep deep, my darling. Dream of me, but not too much, please. Just a little unimportant dream or two. The same kind of dream I want you to have a long time from now, far from here, in that pink hotel on Peppercorn Cay. You'll be married then, and she won't have to know about the little unimportant dreams that come to you sometimes, in the Bahama night. Dream of a girl you once knew. God give me the continuing strength, my darling, never to damn you and hate you because you came along too late—because by the time you came along this was all that was left for us to have.

The tears followed her down into sleep.

... four

TEMP AND VICKY SHANNARD OF NASSAU, NEW PROVIDENCE, Bahamas, arrived at the Hotel Cameroon by taxi from the airport on Friday, the fifteenth of April, at four o'clock in the afternoon. Checkins were heavy at the time they arrived. There were bellhops loading luggage onto the rubber-wheeled service carts, and people pressing close to the long desk for their turn to sign registration cards, and a confusion of goings and comings and people being paged and people demanding service and attention.

Vicky Shannard stood quietly by their luggage, well out of the confusion, over by a low dividing wall which was also a planter luxuriant with some sort of evil broad-leafed growth. The small lobby was about five feet higher than the casino floor, and as she waited for Temp to take care of things she looked out across the ballroom length of the shadowy casino, bordered by gaudy thickets of slot machines to the right and left. There was a curious continual clattering metallic roar which she identified as the combined sounds of all the slot machines in play. Forty feet away, she saw an old woman engaged in a strange ritual. The woman was oddly dressed—in a bright red sweater, a powder-blue skirt far too short for her, a conical coolie hat in venomous green. She teetered on reedy old legs as she fed the dime slot machine, using both hands to give the handle a savage yank, then turned her back to the machine each time in a tension of waiting for the payoff. She kept her dimes in a paper cup.

How odd, Vicky thought. What a strange thing for an old lady to be doing! And could she be staying here? And why should there be something alarming about her? Perhaps all ritualistic frenzy is alarming. But I think I shall like this place not at all.

Vicky Shannard was in her thirtieth year, a cuddly dumpling, a pwetty wittle pigeon, a blonde, pink and white, cushiony little cupcake, with a brain as lean, functional, indestructible and survival-oriented as a pneumatic hammer.

She stood there, five foot one, solemn as a child dressed for a party, with a hat of maximum frivolity atilt on an expensive contrived tangle of Greek curls, in her little tailored beige suit from Bay Street, and her little seal cape from Montreal, and her little lizard pumps from Rome, holding her purse from Paris. She had a round pretty-pretty face, unmarked by turmoil, a suggestion of a double chin, chinablue eyes that protruded slightly and always had a bland, please-like-me, innocent appeal. Tailored suits were never quite right for her, though she adored them. Her breasts, impossible to minimize, did odd things to jackets and lapels and the placement of buttons. And her little rump thrust heartily at the skirts in a way that dismayed her tailors.

Few people have ever been able to make a journey as long as the one made by Victoria Purcell, child of the slums of York in the north of England, fatherless daughter of a parttime whore, cuddled by an illogically numerous succession of "uncles". By the time she was thirteen she had experienced more of the filthy underside of life than most women ever hear about, much less endure. She had experienced rape, a term in a house of correction, malnutrition, savage beatings. She had seen murder done.

But to her this had all been but a series of tiresome annoyances, little irritating obstacles to clamber over on her inevitable way to a future of gold and grace. She could not particularize that future. She just knew it was there, and if she kept moving she would be moving toward it. At fifteen she was Vicki Vale, doing an Alice-in-Wonderland strip in a London cellar. She would come out with blonde hair combed long, wearing childish frills and bows and pastel satins, first to sing obscenities in her thin tinkling little voice, and then to dance her way slowly to nudity. Between her acts she sold cigarettes and hustled drinks.

At seventeen she was Vicky Morgan in a Tangiers club, singing seldom, as befitted the mistress of the owner, a fat and gentle man, half Turk, half Egyptian, who used her also for profitable courier duty for the Tangiers gold combine. At twenty she was Vicki Lambeth, working in a club at Atlantida Beach, thirty-five miles up the South American coast from Montevideo. She was working that summer season after being stranded when the man who took her there died in his sleep in the Nogaro Hotel, in one of their finest suites. At the end of that season she left Uruguay on the ocean-going yacht of a wealthy Brazilian. It was the beginning of her three years in the international set, learning the special attractions of the Riviera, Acapulco, California, Havana, the Bahamas, moving with whim and season, learning to be so agreeable that she could move from one relationship to another without causing the tensions of jealousy or anger.

A little over six years ago she had been a guest on a yacht out of Galveston tied up at Bimini for the Tuna Tournament. She had been, in a sense, an unofficial hostess for the large party of guests aboard. But a handsome woman who was a special friend of the owner had flown out from New Orleans. Vicky was deposed and the situation became slightly awkward. She was trying to decide whether or not to send some carefully worded cables which would result in the expected invitations, when Temple Shannard came into her life. She was twenty-four and he was forty-four. He knew one of the guests, and came aboard. He had sailed over from Nassau alone in his Abaco-built ketch, a tidy dancing vessel. She learned about him quickly, with the ease of long practice.

An unfortunate accident had made him a widower two years ago. He had two teen-age children in college in the States. He was an American who had moved to the Islands right after the war, with a very few thousand dollars to invest, and with a fine optimism tempered by shrewdness. He had done very well. According to the standards of the alley that ran by the house where she was born, he was a rich man. The owner of the Texas yacht could have bought him forty times over without critically impairing his economic position. But Vicky had become aware of the relativity of values as you move through time and space.

Temple was a lonely man, and she liked his manner, and liked his appearance. He was brown and weathered, with strong blunt features that came alive with his frequent smile. He was not tall; he had a broad hard body which he moved with a youthful lightness and economy. He was that special sort of man who needs someone to cherish and protect, and is not emotionally fulfilled unless he has such a love-object at hand.

Soon they could walk hand in hand along the narrow roads in the Bimini night. She knew this situation was one she had been waiting for, and it had been a long time of waiting. She did like him, and found it pleasant to be with him, and she felt no guilt at all over the necessity to fake the attitudes of the opening scenes of love. She had her own sense of equity, and knew she would not strike any bargain wherein he would be cheated of what he needed. She had known for some time that it was only her youngness and carefully achieved freshness and manufactured enthusiasms that had kept her welcome green at the estates and ranches and villas and on the yachts of the big restless rich, and it could all end with a dismaying quickness. Being a professional guest is the most precarious of all careers. It was time to leave the game with a profit.

Temp Shannard was a little too awed by her, and so she found it necessary to force his hand. This was readily accomplished by forcing a quarrel with her New Orleans replacement, so that she was no longer welcome on the yacht. Then she was ready, with the appropriate air of helplessness, a plausible story, and her ten pieces of expensive luggage, for Temp to help her.

Inevitably he sailed her back to Nassau, back to the big waterfront house which had been too empty for him, with terrace and tropical gardens and small staff of servants. Her papers were in a frightful mess, but he had friends at Government House who straightened them out quickly, so that she and Temple could be married three days after they arrived. It was a big festive wedding, and everyone seemed marvelously friendly, and just as skeptical of her as she had expected them to be.

They took a month-of-May honeymoon touring the Out Islands in the *Party Girl*. She learned about rigging and handling lines and reading the water and spotting the buoys and markers, at the same time that she came to realize she had at last reached the place she had been expecting with bland confidence all along.

She knew the limitations of her position. She could never achieve complete acceptance in the top social echelons of New Providence. Even were she from titled stock, marriage to an American immigrant would have nullified that goal.

Temp, in his marriage contract, in the unwritten words

between the spoken lines, assured her the pleasant stature of a nice home, servants, a circle of reasonably amusing friends, charge accounts at good shops, visits to interesting places, and the warm security of feeling adored. Should these factors change, the bargain would be, by her standards, voided.

She would, if he kept his side of it, live up to her own bargain in all respects, and she felt it was rather a good one for Temple Shannard also. He had acquired a young wife in remarkably good health, sound of wind and tooth and limb. He had acquired, along with her, the history she had invented for herself. It was plausible, interesting, and impossible to check, and she had lived with that invented dossier long enough so that it was highly unlikely she would contradict herself. She had felt compelled by honesty to tell him before they were married that she could not have children, but the fact was not important to him.

She knew that she would give him complete faithfulness and loyalty. She would give him all the help in his work she could. She would see he ate properly, got ample exercise and did not drink too much. She would care for him in sickness, and she would, at all times, suppress her own moods in deference to his. She would learn what pleased him most in a sexual partner, and she would become exactly what he desired, never denying him. She knew she would be expensive to maintain, but she would not require more of him than he was able to provide.

She well knew the world was full of wives who supplied considerably less.

Had Vicky been endowed with more imagination, more sensitivity, her past would have marked her too deeply to be concealed by any playacting. But she was a realist of unusually stubborn fiber. In the back hallway of her memory was a rather nauseous tangle of black deeds and twisted acts and horrid requirements. She had been badly used by an indifferent world. At the time of her marriage she went into that back hallway with housewifely bustle, dustpan, broom and cleaning powder, and piled it all into a crate which she dragged out to the roadside for the trash men to truck away. She dusted her hands and went confidently into marriage.

And thus Temp Shannard, insulated forever from truths that would have buckled his knees, acquired a young, pretty, warmly eager bride, unsoiled by the fingerprints of strangers. She had a remarkably even disposition. She was fastidious as any kitten, wholesome as a milkmaid, trying always to look and act to suit his pleasure. She had lost all the accent of her origin, and she had absorbed the manners and the outlook of the better environments she had known. Throughout that May of honeymoon, his bride renewed him, and it was the youth he thought was gone forever who sat at the tiller and grinned at his girl. And it was that same youth who, during the moonlit nights, at anchor in tropic harbors, would fall asleep in the small cabin, in the sweet bridal arms, his graying head cradled between her truly marvelous breasts.

They had had six good years and she was thirty, and now, standing in the lobby of the Cameroon, she could feel the queasy shifting of fear, as though it were a small scaly animal who slept poorly in a pocket close to her heart. Before marriage she had never felt this kind of fear. There had been times of anxious planning and a careful weighing of alternatives, but she had known all the time that everything would come out right for her. In the last six months she had lost this confidence. It was a feeling she did not like. And it was the first thing in six years of marriage to affect the way she had kept her half of the bargain. It was not a case of scenes and quarrels. It was, instead, a subtle alteration in the entire spectrum of their marriage. It was as though she had spent each day painting a bright and joyful and affectionate picture, and suddenly the pictures had become a little bit drab. The colors were not as pure and distinct. The oils she was using were fading, and there was no way to buy fresh supplies.

Lately it had begun to seem to her that she and Temp were people who said memorized lines to each other in an empty theater.

A bellhop wheeled a cart over for their luggage, followed closely by Temp in his pale blue hopsacking jacket, white shirt, the inevitable gray silk bow tie. He walked in the eager lunging way characteristic of him, a grin for her cracking the hard brown face and accentuating the sailor's wrinkles around his eyes. His cropped hair was more white than gray of late, and there was a nervous tic near his left eye that occurred in times of stress, annoying him exceedingly.

"We're set, honey," he said. "Come on. What's that number again, son?"

"Eight oh three, sir. Would you follow me, please?"

"Wherever is Hugh, dearest?" she asked him.

"They're looking for him to tell him we're here, Vick. He's well past the point of working behind a registration desk."

"Of course."

Touching her arm lightly in the protective way she liked, he took her into the elevator—a fit brown urbane man with all the brisk confidence of the born promoter, escorting his expensive little confection of a wife who wore, here and there, the discreet, faceted gleamings that betokened his pride, his success and his devotion.

As they walked into the suite, Vicky was acutely observant. She had always been responsive to her immediate surroundings. She saw the size and luxury of it, the panoramic windows that looked out along the wide bright ribbon of the Strip to the brown silence of the low mountains beyond. It all had a freshness that meant recent redecoration. There were floor vases of fresh flowers, a huge bowl of fresh fruit and candies, and an ice bucket containing a bottle, next to a tray with three shining wine glasses. A penciled sign propped against the neck of the bottle read "Do Not Touch". She looked into a bath suitable for a sultan, touched the nubby material of the sand-colored draperies and said, "You know, this is rather nice, isn't it?"

Temp tipped the boy and, when the door was closed, went to her and put a light kiss on the immature tip of her nose and said, "The red carpet, mouse. With bugles and drums."

"This is utterly vast, you know. Did we really need a suite, dearest?"

"What is this economy kick you're on, Vick?" He grinned at her. "After this many years of you, it comes as a shock, somehow."

"I definitely wouldn't want anything cheap and tiny, Temp, but this seems like so very much more than we need. That's all I meant."

"Leave things up to me, please." He was still smiling, but there was a trace of harshness in his tone. "The accommodations fit a business purpose."

"Of course, dearest," she said. "I'll settle us in, shall I?"

"You do that."

Though they had traveled overweight, she found more drawer and closet space than they could possibly use. She put everything away with neatness and method and, after she had arranged her cosmetic array on the dressing table, she laid out what they would wear after they had bathed. She glanced through the doorway into the sitting room of the suite from time to time, looking at Temp as he sat reading the newspaper they had given him at the desk. The bedside radio, adjusted by the bellhop, changed from music to soap opera, and so she changed it to another place, to Latin music,

58

all gourds and chantings and marimbas, turning it just loud enough to carry into the other room, but not so loud that she failed to hear the quick knock at the door.

Hugh found himself smiling with the anticipation of pleasure as he strode down the corridor to the suite he had assigned the Shannards. Temp, as a part owner of the hotel at Governor's Harbor at Eleuthera, had come to his rescue at a very crucial point in the career of Hugh Darren. He had not only resolved the immediate difficulties, but he had set it up so that Hugh had a much freer hand to pursue his own policies in the future. Friendship had developed from this contact. Temp and Vicky had never made any attempt to patronize Hugh. He had gone sailing with them, gotten slightly drunk with them, and had stayed in their Nassau home.

Temp opened the door of the suite, and went into vast, loud, energetic greetings. Vicky came smiling, hurrying from the bedroom, with a quick embrace to be given, and a cheek to be kissed. They all tried to talk at once, all stopped at the same moment and did the same thing again, and had to laugh at themselves.

Vicky told Hugh he was looking wonderfully fit and happy. Temp told him he was looking too damn fatuously successful. He told them they were both looking wonderful, and he hoped he made it sound convincing. Neither of them looked the way he remembered. He could sense tension and see the traces of it in their faces. Their cheer seemed forced and, what was more distressing to him, he sensed the cool, withering breath of estrangement.

"What the hell is this 'Do Not Touch' routine?" Temp asked.

"He wouldn't say a word about the lovely flowers, of course," Vicky said. "He would only complain about the wine. He's a greedy, impossible type."

"Do not touch until I get here," Hugh said. "And I am here." He took the bottle out and showed them the label. "Champagne, of course."

"What a gloriously low habit!" Vicky cried. "Champagne at this time of the day."

"It's a very low town, doll," Hugh said, twisting the wire off and working at the cork. It clicked off the ceiling and into a low chair by the windows.

They touched glasses. "Old friends, old times and old places," Temp said. And they drank and smiled and moved over to the grouping of low blonde chairs, and Temp told

Hugh the news of the Bahamas since he had been gone—from the Jack Paar invasion at Christmastime, to all the vast new resort projects and the continuing incredible increases in the cost of land in the developments on New Providence. When the champagne was gone, Vicky stood and said, "Aircraft erode me horribly, chums. I look a dreary old bag for days, so it's me for a steaming tub and a champagne nap. Will one of you gentlemen please knock me up when it's time to get festive?"

"Love those limey expressions," Temp said fondly. "We'll *awaken* you."

She looked with mock disdain at their grinning faces. "You both have dreadfully dirty minds, dears." She winked at them and went into the bedroom, closing the door behind her.

"Marvelous girl," Temp said.

"Best of the breed."

"Can you chat for a while, or should you be running around managing things, Hugh?"

"This place is in practically full operation twenty-four hours a day. I live right on the premises. They know where I am, Temp, and somebody will yell if there's a jam they can't handle, so I'm working right now. But I can't talk with an empty glass. Bourbon?"

"Ingenious idea."

Hugh phoned down for a bottle and setups and went back to his chair.

"Hell of a big operation you've got here," Temp said.

"Service staff of four hundred and sixteen, as of right now, not counting casino personnel, or the entertainers, of course. And it was such a loose operation, Temp, it's taken me this long to begin to feel I'm getting on top of it. It's been a brute of a job, but they're paying me damn well—so well, in fact, that I may be around to see you for that construction loan a lot sooner than I thought."

"That's fine, Hugh. That's great!" Temp said, but it was strangely forced. Hugh felt a small new worry, one he had not anticipated.

"What's the matter, Temp?"

"Nothing. Nothing at all. Just that it's a damn good thing you're not looking for that money right now."

The waiter knocked. Hugh let him in. Temp Shannard made a very uncharacteristic half-hearted attempt to get the service check. In past days it had been almost impossible to pay for anything when Temp was in the party. This was an additional clue that made Hugh increasingly uneasy.

As he was fixing the highballs he said, "I could be knocking on your door in about two years, Temp, the way it's going. You'll have it then, won't you?"

"Of course, dear boy! Of *course*."

"You remember the way we laid it all out that night with Alec Whitney. I put up Peppercorn Cay free and clear, plus thirty thousand. You and Alec each come in with sixty thousand, forty of which will be a loan, and twenty will be for fifteen per cent of the limited partnership." He handed Temple his drink.

"Don't look so worried about it, Hugh. I'll be flying like a big bird again by the time you come for the money."

"What's happened, Temp? Are you in trouble?"

Shannard gave him a smile of confidence, but there was an uncertainty, a shifting, half-apologetic expression around his eyes that spoiled the effect. "Nothing I can't work my way out of, Hugh."

"What went wrong?"

Temple Shannard leaned back, holding his glass in both hands, frowning at it. "Quite a few things went wrong. The law of averages should have protected me from such lousy timing. Damn it, I was a tiger in the backfield, playing offense and defense. I could diagnose all the plays and pick off those passes, and I could call the right sequences and make those first downs, one right after the other. But it has been like I'd lost a half step somewhere. They're red dogging me now and smearing me in the backfield, and on defense they're passing just over my head. If I was part paranoid I'd begin to think it was a conspiracy, that the whole damn world was out to get me."

"It's serious, then."

"It didn't seem so in the beginning. Maybe I was too damn confident. I've moved fast, Hugh, because I've been willing to extend myself so far it would give a nervous man a chronic spastic colon. I've operated out of pure faith in the Bahama boom, and God knows, except for that strike a few years back, it hasn't even faltered. So when a few things soured, I didn't get too upset. A bad title mixup smeared one deal. On another an insurance company found a way to eel out of their responsibilities on a technicality, and it fell back on me."

He upended his drink, got up and made himself a heavier one, and began to pace as he talked. "Things like that, Hugh. Damnable, unforeseeable things, as though I had to have a run of bad luck to make up for all the good. If I'd been playing it close to the vest all along, I could have rolled with it, but it all started to hit me just when I'd stretched myself as far as I dared. And you know how fast bad news travels. So the people who would have been delighted to give me extensions have all tightened down on me."

"What can you do?"

Temp gave him a fighting grin. "I had to find a way to lick the bastards. If I let them force me to liquidate right now, not only would I be dealing myself out of potential millions to be made in new projects, but I'd end up in such a lousy net-cash position I wouldn't have a big enough lever to pry my way back into the big-time deals down there. I'd have to start again with the little stuff, and I just haven't got the patience for that. I can't get money down there because now they have the idea they can lay back and pick off my good holdings for less. So I made up a brand-new package, Hugh.

"I've got a prospectus that would knock your damn eye out. I sold the pieces of the hotels because I could get a fair price there. I've put the house and the insurance and every other damn thing in hock, and I paid off just a bare minimum of the people who are leaning on me, and I'm stalling hell out of the rest of them, and I've got a hundred thousand bucks cash I moved to the Morgan Guarantee Trust so nobody could get too wise down there and put any kind of attachment on it. I know this much, Temp. You can't sell a big deal unless you can show that you're willing to go into it in a respectable way yourself. Otherwise you're a dubious promoter. I've consolidated my personal holdings in raw land, all the stuff on Andros, Eleuthera, Abaco, Spanish Wells and San Salvador. I have maps, descriptions, mortgage deeds, and exhaustive reports on the future of the islands based on the past growth record. I've got all the papers on Island Associates, Limited, set up and ready to go."

"Who's in with you?"

Shannard ignored the question. "The way it will work, I will put my equities in the land and my hundred grand into the pot in return for thirty thousand shares worth four pounds a share . . . call it ten dollars a share. I take in seven hundred thousand dollars for the remaining seventy thousand shares. That money pays off the balance on all the land, leaving over three hundred thousand to begin the development of the Eleuthera piece first. That property adjoins the Arvida piece, and I've got an engineering and development study that's a gem. It can't miss, Hugh. I know those islands. It just can't miss. Fix you a fresh one?"

"I'll ride on this, thanks."

Temp brought a fresh drink back to his chair and sat down a bit heavily. "That's the picture. With that much backing I can then pledge my Island Associates shares for the line of credit to handle the stuff I've been dodging, and then I can save those deals where I'm in with other people. It's a hell of a lot of scrambling, but I'll come out the far end smelling like a rose, believe me. In the meantime I've been living it wide and handsome. I've been the most confident-looking man in town. You have to keep it up, Hugh, even when it hurts."

"Like asking for a suite?"

"You're getting the message."

"Not all the message, Temp. Who do you have to impress here, for God's sake?"

"I don't know yet."

"What do you mean by that?"

"I tried to peddle the deal in New York, Hugh. That's why I went there. I had good contacts. I was dickering with two groups. They both liked the sound of it. I had my chance to grab one or the other, but it looked like a golden chance to improve my end of the thing by playing one against the other. And one day they both turned ice cold. I couldn't imagine why until one of them was kind enough to tell me to look up a gossip column in a paper of the previous day. I can quote the stinking thing by heart, Hugh. 'Temple Shannard, golden-tongued promoter who operates in the Bahamas, and whose dreams lately have been turning to nightmares, is in the city with his luscious wife trying to scare up those heavy funds which may or may not keep his tottering tourist empire solvent.' That did it, old boy. That did it to me good. I couldn't trace the tipster who did me the dirty, and I can't sue even if it is actionable, which I doubt. That's the way my luck has been running."

"What do you do now?"

He smiled at Hugh in a somewhat apologetic way. "I take a suite in Las Vegas and throw myself on the mercy of my good friend, Hugh Darren."

"If I understand what you mean, I don't think I like it, Temp."

"The money is here, Hugh. It's a resort business. Men who run deals like this know how to analyze deals like mine. And according to my . . . ah . . . researches, there is a lot of homeless, unidentified cash in this area looking for a legitimate home away from home."

"I guess I better have that next drink, Temp."

"Let me make it, boy. I know what you're thinking and . . . what you're remembering."

"A long talk in your house one night, Temp."

"I knew you'd remember that. I was very noble and idealistic, wasn't I?"

"I wouldn't have called it that."

Shannard turned and said in oratorical tones, "We men who love the Islands have an unwritten agreement to keep important holdings out of the hands of the hoodlums and sharpshooters, and the front men they use. We have been largely successful in this, and we will continue to keep the Islands clean." He brought Hugh his drink and said in a soft and empty voice, "I wasn't being squeezed then, pal. I could afford high principles. Now it gets down to survival. I need the money. And I can't let them bring me crashing down because of something I once thought I believed. But I will try to set it up in such a way that I'll have a long-term contract to operate the venture."

"They would have seventy per cent to your thirty, so how long would that last?"

"Just so long as I run it the way they want it run."

"Exactly."

"Hugh, I love you like you were my kid brother." There was a thickening of his voice that surprised Darren. Shannard used to be more immune to the effects of a few drinks. "I love you dearly, but I could get a little goddam tired of your attitude of righteousness and disapproval."

"I do disapprove, Temp. Hell, those islands are my future. Castro ran the syndicate operation out of Cuba—for all the wrong reasons—but he ran the boys out, and it would be a nice new place to light, and I don't want to spend my future in a spread-out version of Batista's Havana."

"No sir! You're too decent a fellow for that to happen to. But still you'll come to this town and work, and you're not too proud to take their money. That's a double standard, isn't it? This town is a big milking machine, milking the innocent, and you're right in here, doing your part."

"You better get something straight, Temp. I don't want to get sore at you. I operate this hotel. Food, rooms, drinks. I have nothing to do with the casino operation. The hotel problems are the same as you'd find in New York, Miami or Montreal. I'm worth what I'm paid. It was a good offer and I took it. So kindly don't confuse what I'm doing with what you're thinking of doing."

"Aren't you a little naive?"

"I don't think so."

"Hugh, you remind me of an old old joke about the innocent virgin who took a job in a whorehouse, doing mending and light housework. A friend tried to talk her out of it by saying to her that even though it was honest labor she was doing, she would be affected by the dreadful environment. She insisted that she would be untouched by what might be going on around her. Several months later the friend met her on the street and asked her how her job was going. She said it was going very well, and the friend had been wrong in thinking it would change her in any way. So the friend asked her if that was still the limit of her duties, the dusting and scrubbing and mending. The maiden said, 'Yes, that's really all I do.' She paused and blushed prettily. 'But sometimes, like on Saturday night, when there's a big rush of business, I just come in and help out a little.' "

"That's hilarious," Hugh said stiffly.

They stared at each other. Shannard said gently, "I'm nearly fifty-one years old, Hugh. And I haven't got the guts to start from scratch. You're a little bit younger than Vicky. Somehow I don't think we should be fighting."

"I don't think so either."

"I'll see what I can do to develop my own contacts, Hugh."

"There's no need of that. I'll set up an appointment with Al Marta."

"Is he . . . well-connected?"

"Temp, they don't publish a list of officers and directors, and they aren't listed on the exchange, so you can't get hold of a balance sheet. He lives here. He owns thirty per cent of the place. He has a whole slew of other business operations here and over into Arizona. And I have the idea he is one of the men in the area you could talk to who could check the deal out with . . . the top brass you have in mind. Okay?"

"So let's be grateful we don't have to talk about the damn thing any more tonight."

"I've got some rounds to make and errands to do." Hugh looked at his watch. "Suppose I meet you two at about eight o'clock in the Little Room for dinner, and after that we can catch the acts in the Afrique Bar."

"Sounds like fun," Temp said.

As Hugh walked back toward the elevators he experienced a feeling of depression that surprised him with its bleakness. Temple and Vicki had always seemed so invulnerable, so securely stationed in their gay and profitable world, accustomed to a kind of success that required short periods of very hard work by Temp which freed them for long times of the fun they had together. This revelation of crisis made Hugh feel more vulnerable, less confident of his own plans and purposes.

When Hugh met the Shannards at eight o'clock in the Little Room, he told them he had asked Betty Dawson to join them for dinner, explaining that she was an entertainer working at the Cameroon. He had hoped to state this in a way that would give them no particular clue, but he saw a quick interest in Vicky's eyes.

"Please don't tell me there is a woman who has gotten past your guard, my pet," Vicky said.

"She's a nice gal and a good friend," Hugh said, slightly annoyed.

"Drink to all nice gals," Temp said thickly. They both looked at him with concealed apprehension, trying to guess whether he would spoil the evening. He was not really bad, but he was as drunk as Hugh had ever seen him.

"Hugh has no drink yet, and mine is gone, darling, so let's make a loving cup out of that lovely toast, shall we?" Vicky said, and reached for Temp's double bourbon on the rocks.

He surrendered it with suspicion and reluctance. She drank and handed it to Hugh. When Temp got his glass back he glowered at the amount remaining and tossed it off and said, "Surrounded by spongers, by God."

When Hugh ordered the next round he gave the waiter an inconspicuous signal. From then on Temp would be given drinks that would look hearty, but would be as innocuous as a light wine. His bourbon would come out of one of the special bottles filled with liquor which had been simmered until little alcohol remained. And his previous drinking would keep him from detecting the subterfuge. It was a much more civilized device than refusing to serve the unruly drunk. And considerably more gracious than the chloral hydrate which would end all drinking for the evening.

It was a local solution to a special problem. A man who became too drunk could not gamble. A man refused service would go elsewhere. A man knocked out could not gamble. But a man could, with doctored drinks, be sustained at the outer limits of his own precarious control until he had made his appropriate donation to the house percentages. Temple Shannard was not at the point where a waiter or bartender would have made that decision, but the availability of the device gave Hugh a chance to make the evening more pleasant.

Betty Dawson found herself unduly tense about meeting Hugh's friends. She took time and care in the selection of what to wear, and with her makeup. After her final inspection of herself in her full-length mirror, wearing the strapless sheath top in dull coral, and the long full skirt in a fine stripe of black and coral, she decided she looked as well as she could look. The top seemed to exaggerate slightly a sweep of bosom she believed unduly bountiful, but it also emphasized the shoulders, which she hoped were wide enough to sustain that hammocked abundance.

"You'll have to do, babe," she told herself. "And what the hell am I trying to prove anyway?"

As she went to the table, and throughout the introductions and the first few minutes of small talk, she was so involved with reinforcing the impression she had planned to make that she had no time for observation. But with all the facets of her entrance accomplished, she was able to be aware of Hugh's friends, and she felt a sense of disappointment as she overtly studied them. They did not match his glowing descriptions. The blonde had an empty prettiness, but there was a look of frigid calculation in her eyes, and a slight cast of piggishness to her nose and mouth. The man was just drunk enough so it was difficult to say what he was like.

And, for a meeting of old friends, the attitude at the table was all wrong. There was a strain which shouldn't be there, and she had the wisdom to know she was not responsible for it. She detected, in Hugh, a faint flavor of apology. These things, she knew, could happen. Perhaps this pair was marvelous over in the Bahamas, but inadequate here. And sometimes people outgrow each other in as little as the eight months since he had last seen them. She knew from the tentative glances Hugh gave her across the round table that the apology was for them rather than for her. Had it been for her, she could not have forgiven him.

Vicky, on her left, chose a time when the men had started to talk of Bahama politics to say, "What sort of bit do you do, Betty?"

"Horrible people say it's a magic act. Without a voice, I sing. And accompany myself with a no-talent piano, Vicky."

"But you're so marvelous to look at. That must be a help. I do hope we'll be able to see you tonight."

"You can, if you don't collapse early. I start at midnight."

"Hugh has been telling us you've been here for years."

And that, Betty thought, is a sharp switchblade you carry around, little blonde. "If I can hold out for ten, they'll give me a gold watch and a testimonial banquet."

"I should think your agent would want you to have bookings in other places."

Betty looked at her with amusement. "I didn't know you'd ever been with it, pal. That's an inside comment, isn't it?"

"It was all a very long time ago."

"What did you do?"

Vicky gave a little lift of her snug, padded shoulders. "A spot of singing and dancing. I wasn't very good, actually. My voice is too small."

"What sort of places, Vicky?"

The blonde's little smile was very bland. "Oh, you wouldn't know any of them, darling. I never worked in this country." She sipped her drink. "As a matter of fact, I gave it all up when I was twenty, over three years before I met Temp. My guardian was always raising such a horrid fuss about it, you know. He didn't think it a suitable thing for me to do. And I guess it wasn't, really."

"Performers are socially unacceptable, of course."

"But I didn't mean it that way, darling! Don't be cross with me. It's really very different in this country, you know. People have so much more chance to do what they want to do. Without criticism. It must give you such a wonderful sense of freedom."

"Oh, it does!" Betty said. "I'm a free spirit, all right. Self-expression. Admiration. Free meals."

At that moment one of the desk clerks approached the table. Hugh apologized and stood up quickly. They talked in low tones and Hugh said he would be back in a few minutes, to go right ahead. Their dinner was being served. With Hugh gone, Temp found it necessary to explain to Betty how you went about getting a ketch built at Abaco, ignoring Vicky's attempts to divert him to a more suitable pattern of conversation. In spite of her absolute indifference to how you went about getting a boat built, Betty found herself liking the man. He was deeply troubled by something. He was trying to sustain a flavor of holiday in his own way.

When Hugh came back he seemed upset. "What was it?" Betty asked.

"Some damn foolishness in the parking lot. The problem was to find the quietest way to handle it. A married man from San Diego is in town with his girl friend. Somebody tipped the wife off. She's been laying for them. She tried to run them down in the parking lot when they were walking out to his car. She missed him, broke the girlfriend's leg, and clobbered the hell out of three parked cars."

"How veddy violent!" Vicky said.

"The police in this town are good. They have to be," Hugh said. His mouth twisted in a sardonic way. "Nothing must upset the fun times of the merrymakers, or bring any realistic note to fantasyland. My people are trained to put the lid on as quickly as possible. And so I had to coordinate how three very chastened people should be handled. Attempted murder by motor vehicle isn't an attractive story. So a lady lost control of her car. That's all."

"Do you have this sort of thing often, actually?" Vicky asked.

Hugh looked at her patiently. "Vicky, dear, when you give people the maximum opportunity to make damn fools of themselves, sexually, financially and alcoholically, in an environment that makes movie sets look like low-cost housing, all sorts of things happen often. We get one fat spectrum of trouble out here along the Strip, and down in town they get all the other kinds. Down in town they have fun with the floaters, the winos, the junkies, the bums and tramps and sharpshooters who drift in looking for enchantment. The thing that spices the whole pudding is the divorce-mill operation. The severed ones have a kind of emotional trauma that makes them reckless."

With a sidelong glance at Betty, Vicky said, "You must be getting a *very* extensive education here, you poor boy!"

Betty turned directly toward Vicky Shannard. "At least, darling, he's learning to identify a phony at forty paces, and that's something that will benefit him all his life."

"But I think Hugh always had good instincts about people," Vicky protested.

"In that case, we should both be proud to be his female friends, darling," Betty said, and enjoyed the sudden pinkness of Vicky's dainty little ears.

After dinner the four of them sat at a good table in the Afrique Bar, and at a little after eleven Betty excused herself to go change for her night's work.

"What do you think of her?" Hugh asked, and then cursed himself for his illuminating display of eagerness.

"All in all," Vicky said judiciously, "I think she's quite

nice, Hugh. It must be very . . . satisfying to you to have a close friendship with her. But I rather suspect she is considerably more attractive in . . . this particular context than she would be, say, in the Islands. She seems so . . . suitable to this sort of a place."

"*Murrroooww*," Temp said.

"Do be quiet, ducks," Vicky told him firmly. "Hugh asked us, and I felt an obligation to give him my opinion, my veddy honest opinion. If I suspected for one moment that he had more than a . . . casual interest in this . . . entertainment person, I would certainly be much less kind in my remarks."

"How do you mean?" Hugh demanded.

She smiled at him and reached to touch his cheek. "You're so wonderfully loyal to your friends, my dear. It's very earnest and becoming. But shall we drop it, please? She is really, as I said, quite nice. But it would take a very long search to find any girl nice enough for you. Remember how I used to try?"

"She's still trying," Temp said. "She's still giving you the hard sell in Nassau."

When Betty did her first forty-minute session, Hugh was conscious of a subtle lack of control and conviction. She lacked her usual ability to silence her audience completely, so that at times it was difficult to hear her. Her timing seemed slightly off.

After she rejoined the table he eventually excused himself and said goodnight to them. He had been up for twenty hours, and they had not been easy hours, and no week end was ever without constant demands on his energies and attention.

He clambered slowly up and out of sleep at six-thirty, squinting through the glare of his bedside light until he could make out Betty's smiling face. She sat close to him on the edge of his bed in her skin-tight gold lamé costume, wearing her professional makeup. She bent over and kissed him.

"This is a brutal invasion of privacy, my dearest," she whispered. "But I was lonely. I didn't get to say word one to you all evening."

He found her hand, turned it and kissed the palm. "I'll give you a special medal for each invasion, lady."

"Now I *know* you're awake! Darling, I am sorry I was so lousy on the first set. I think that female got to me. I shouldn't have let her, but she did."

70

"I couldn't understand why she was using the needle."

"Can't you? That one is an acquisitive bitch. She has to keep a firm hold on everything in sight. I got back into the swing when I went on again. But I didn't rejoin them. I didn't have a chance. I had to stop at the bar a moment on my way back to the table to do the greeting-old-fans bit, and when I looked over I could tell they were having one of those grim quarrels, so I prolonged the stay at the bar. She marched out and Temp came over and said a very gracious goodnight. You know, I like him, Hugh. But what the hell is eating him?"

He raised himself up on his elbow. "It isn't the way I thought it would be. How about grabbing my cigarettes off the bureau over there?"

"I don't want to keep you up. You're very tired."

"I want to talk about it, Betty."

She brought the cigarettes and ash tray, lit his cigarette for him, snapped the lighter shut with more force than necessary and said, "Me, I have this lousy honesty about my opinions, Hugh. They can be your dearest friends in all the world, but I think she is a dumpy, vicious little pig."

"She's made Temp a good wife, Betty."

"And lived damn well while doing it, I presume."

"Sure. But I never felt close to her, particularly. I'm fond of Temp."

"I can understand that."

"And they aren't at all the way they used to be." As Betty listened, he explained the whole thing to her. He finished the story, stubbed out his cigarette and lay back on the pillow. "So he came here for my help."

"And you'll set it up with Al Marta?"

"There isn't much else I can do."

"If any deal is made, Hugh, it won't be as nice for Temp as he wants it to be."

"He's at a point where he hasn't got a hell of a lot of choice. Time is running out for him. He can't go to reputable money. They'd take a year to case a deal this size. He has to have the fast money, and so he has to deal with the kind of people who have it."

"Don't get caught in the middle, Hugh."

"How could I?"

"I don't know, but be careful." She looked down at him with her warmth and with a look of wry curiosity. "I suppose she found a chance to badmouth me?"

"Sort of."

71

"What was the general drift of it?"

"Oh, how you wouldn't stack up so well anywhere else but here."

"If I could be guaranteed an all-female jury, I'd strangle that little monster. They'd never convict me. How do *you* think I'd stack up elsewhere, friend?"

"Wherever they put you, old buddy, you're well-stacked."

She stood up. "And on that note of reassurance, I shall take to my lonely bed and cry my eyes out, I betcha."

He lunged and caught her wrist and pulled back, bringing her down upon him. "There are better kinds of reassurance, girl."

"No, Hugh. Really! I didn't come in here to. . . ."

He stilled her struggles with a kiss, and when it ended she looked owlishly down at him, their noses an inch apart. "I've got no character," she whispered.

"When somebody tries to cast a shadow over our beautiful friendship," he said, "I figure it gives us a sort of obligation to reaffirm it just as soon as humanly possible, don't you?"

"Your thesis is unarguable, sir."

She went into his bathroom and sponged away the theatrical makeup, came out and, in the rosy-gray light of dawn that leaked through the almost-closed slats of the blinds, rid herself of the golden gown and two wisps of nylon and her diaphanous hosiery and her tall golden sandals. Then, standing there, she undid the blackness of her hair until it fell about her shoulders, and came to him, bringing to him in special pride the deft abundance of her love.

• • • five

GIDGE ALLEN TOLD HUGH OVER THE PHONE ON SATURDAY morning that eleven o'clock would be a pretty good time to talk to Al. When Hugh took the small private elevator up to the penthouse at the stated time, he found a dozen people milling around the big living room, most of them working on Whisky Sours and Bloody Mary's. Morning television was on full blast, ignored by everyone. A slight Negro with a mustache sat at a small electric organ, seeking out lugubrious chords. Two men argued heatedly over a racing sheet. A redhead was proving to a mildly interested group how long she could stand on her head. Hugh nodded to those he knew as he worked his way over to the windows where Al Marta stood talking to a dumpy swarthy little man in a cheap suit of electric blue, a dirty striped shirt, and shoulders thick with dandruff.

As soon as Al noticed Hugh's approach, Hugh heard him say, "All you're doing is wasting my time, Mario. I can't give you no answer. Go away and get it set up and come back with it all laid out and maybe we can talk about it."

As the man trudged sadly away, Al gave Hugh a wide white grin of welcome and said, "You don't come up here enough, Hugh. You should come around any time. We always got some kind of action going. We always got laughs. You work too hard down there, you know that? Take it easy sometimes. Everybody's going nuts about the wonderful job you're doing. We got Jerry off your back, right?"

"I appreciate that."

"And another bump in pay. You heard about that?"

"Max told me, Mr. Marta."

"Mr. Marta was my father. He's dead a long time, God rest his soul. If you don't call me Al you get me sore, Hugh. Let's go where we can hear ourselves think." He took Hugh through the bedroom and into the small study beyond. The walls were almost solid with framed photographs of celebrities, fervently inscribed to Al Marta.

Al settled himself in a deep chair, put one foot up against the edge of the pink desk and said, "Sit right there, Hugh. You know, boy, the way we got it set up now, we got the strongest team on the Strip. You and Max. The way you two are working together, everybody is nuts about the operation we've got. Thank God I got the sense to stay out of it. All I do is represent the owners, being one myself. And thanks to you, I'm living better here every day. I wanted to get that across to you, Hugh, how much everybody thinks of you. Now what is it you got on your mind?"

"It's an investment opportunity, Mr.—I mean Al. I don't know if you or any of your associates would be interested in it. There's an old friend of mine in the house right now. He asked me to . . . vouch for him."

"Sometimes I'm interested in putting money in something good. How much is involved?"

"Seven hundred thousand. And it would have to be cash."

With no change of expression, Al said, "Until you said that, kid, I was ready to reach for the brush. You better give it to me slow and careful."

Hugh explained what he knew of the deal. He outlined Shannard's background. Suspecting that careful checking would be done, Hugh did not make the mistake of minimizing Shannard's current difficulties.

"Temp has maps and all the facts and figures, and he can talk to you at your convenience, Al."

"This is prime land, you say. And you've worked out there."

"You can't find Island land that desirable now, in tracts that size."

"Suppose it went through, kid. Maybe you got your heart set on a finder's fee? Or do you get your end from Shannard?"

"I get nothing at all. I wouldn't want anything."

"You don't like money?"

"It isn't that."

"Then what is it?"

"I'm just doing a favor for an old friend. That's all."

Al studied him with quiet amusement. "Sure, kid. We understand each other. Tomorrow your pal gets the chance to make his pitch. Some time tomorrow afternoon. I know some guys who'd like to listen to it. They got to have time to get here. I'll let you know when to set it up. You want to sit in?"

"Not particularly."

"Tell your buddy the wheels are starting to turn. Okay? Now why don't you go out and have some fun and drinks with the kids while I make a couple calls?"

"Some other time, Al. I've got to get back to work."

"You're way ahead of the game already, so why don't you relax a little?"

When he got back downstairs he called Temp's suite, but there was no answer. He put a note in a sealed envelope and left it in Temp's box at the desk. He had a very late lunch after a long and bitter conference with a food wholesaler who had been trying to squeeze George Ladori for special kickbacks. He was able to take a break at four o'clock and make a quick change to swim trunks and go out to the pool.

When he located Betty he walked over to her and said, "Why don't you pick the same place every day?"

"I love having you hunt for me, darling. It keeps you off balance. I finished breakfast not ten minutes ago. I am truly a slob."

"A lovely slob, with little telltale shadows under her eyes."

"You don't exactly look as if you were bristling with energy yourself, friend."

"Hell, something woke me up at dawn, and it was quite a

little while before I could get back to sleep. You know how it is."

"No I don't, really. How was it?"

"Keep that up, and we could get thrown off the premises for bad behavior."

"Braggard!"

He noticed the towel spread on the grass by her chair. "You found a friend?" he asked, with an edge of annoyance in his voice.

"Your friends are my friends. It's Temp. He's swimming at the moment. Vicky has gone shopping. He's much nicer sober. But, then, aren't we all? Did you talk to Al?"

"It's all set up for tomorrow afternoon."

Temp joined them, grinning, thumping the side of his head to get the water out of his ear. "You showed up too soon, Hugh. I was just about to start the sweet talk."

"She's listened to experts. She doesn't need beat-up types from Nassau."

"*I'll* decide what I need, gentlemen."

"Get the note?" Hugh asked.

"Yes, and thanks. Today I've got my confidence back."

Hugh looked at him. Nothing bad would happen to this brown man who sat in the expensive poolside sunshine, droplets of water shining against the brown of his shoulders. Temple Shannard would not be defeated.

Homer G. Gallowell of Fort Worth, Texas, arrived in Las Vegas in his own Piper Apache at four o'clock on Saturday afternoon, piloted by a prematurely bald young man called Scotty. Homer had dozed most of the way. Scotty felt more at ease when the old man was asleep. It seemed a little better, somehow, than having him sitting there beside you not saying a word, just sitting and staring straight ahead, never looking down or to the side.

In his four years of employment by the Gallowell Company, this was only the second time he had ever piloted the old man himself, and the first time he had ever been alone with him in so small a ship. Parker, the chief pilot, had given Scotty his instructions.

"You fly by the book, boy. You run that check list like you had an inspector with you. And in your landing patterns, you make those turns loud and clear. You pretend like you're wheeling seventy people commercial, and you'll have no trouble. Don't you say à word to him you don't have to say. And for God's sake, don't try to help him in or out of the airplane. When he says something to you, you give him the shortest damn answer you can come up with, and give it fast. When he gives orders, you listen so good you hear everything."

"You make him sound rough, Joe."

"Man, I mean he *is* rough. He's got twice as many million dollars as you have years on you, and he didn't get 'em by being a nice guy, that's for sure. He's an old lizard, baking hisself in the sun, dreaming about foxy tricks, and he doesn't miss a thing goes on around him. He's tough and spry as an old lizard too."

"Why's he want to go to Vegas?"

"How do I know? Maybe he owns it. He could have owned the whole place for years and nobody would ever know about it. He pays smart men four times what he pays us just to keep his name *out* of the papers, Scotty. You just bear down on the flying, and let *him* think about why he has to go to Vegas."

As they came over the mountains Scotty was thinking how little the old man looked like the traditional image of the rich Texan. He was spare, fairly tall, and he had the look of one who had been powerful in his youth, but the years had shrunken the slabs of muscle to hard gristle and string. He wore a rusty black suit and a vest with a gold watchchain looped across it, and steel-rimmed glasses that rested in a slightly crooked way on the sharp old beak of a nose. He wore high black shoes, bulbous at the toes, a cheap bright necktie soiled in the area of the knot from many tyings, and a black ranch hat, old and worn and dusty. He had the hard, lean, grooved, wind-bitten face of a man who has spent the front half of his life sleeping on the ground. His hands, thickened by the toil of years ago, rested on his thighs, scarred, red-knuckled, looking too big for the rest of him.

See him in a bus station, Scotty thought, and you'd figure him for an old ranch hand on his day off. You'd never guess about all that damn oil and more land than he's ever had a chance to ride across, and the other stuff they say he owns—newspapers, radio and television stations, chemical companies down on the Gulf, oil-well-supply outfits. You could never guess it from the way the old son of a bitch looks.

They say he married once and she took sick a year later and lived twelve years in pain before she died, and that was the end of it for him. They say if you cross him, he'll wait until he's got you set up just the way he wants you, and then he'll grind you down into rubble. Power is what he lives off, they say. He eats it and drinks it and rolls in it. Most times he travels with all those serfs around him, bowing down, yessiring, doing the paper work for his big deals. They say he used to have a U.S. Senator he tamed and treated like a dog. But sometimes, like now, he moves alone.

Scotty made his tower contact, waited his turn, brought the plane around and set it down, and taxied to where they told him.

The old man dropped down lightly and Scotty handed his old square-cornered suitcase down to him.

"You get the aryplane checked over good and gassed to go and put in a place that suits you, Scott. I'm going to be at the Cameroon. You locate you a place and phone the name of it and phone number to the Cameroon for them to put in my box so I can get you when I need you. You stick close by that number up to five in the evenin' every day, and from then on do like you please because we wouldn't be leavin' later. Don't get yourself too drunk to fly the aryplane, and beyond that I don't give me a damn what you do." He took a long black old bill case out of the inside pocket of his jacket and gave Scott a hundred-dollar bill. "You'll charge gas to the company, and you'll get expenses back from the company, and this here hondred dollars is to amuse yourself with on account of you kept your gawddamn mouth shut and flew good and steady."

By the time Scotty could open his mouth to thank him, the old man was fifteen feet away, lugging the heavy bag without apparent effort, heading toward the cab rank at the terminal.

As Homer Gallowell rode toward the Cameroon in the cab, he felt a cold and savage excitement in his belly, strong enough to outweigh his own dry amusement at himself. It had been too many years since he had felt this way. He was walking right back into the polished machine that had taken one fifth of a million dollars away from him the last time he was here. He had come to Vegas the previous time because it had been selected as neutral ground, and there had been some dickering to do. He had not been interested in the gambling. He had found himself with unexpected time on his hands, and he became interested in the mechanics of the crap table as he watched, with contempt, the sweaty fools being parted from their money. In time he thought he saw a way the odds could be beaten, and so he had tried it and suffered a humiliating defeat. The damage to his cold pride had hurt much worse than the loss of the money.

And now he had come back, prepared for a laboratory experiment in the methods that had made him an enormously powerful man. And what was sweeter to him was the knowledge that he was bucking somebody else's system. It had been too many years since he'd had a chance to do that. Men challenged him from time to time, but he knew all the uses of power in the areas where he was challenged. They had to play his game, and their defeat was so inevitable it often bored him. Long long ago he had whipped other men at their own games, and the memories of those times were still sweet. This was a rather childish opportunity to try it again.

The men at the Cameroon would be delighted to see such a valuable sheep come back for a second shearing, he knew. And they had no reason to suspect it would not go exactly as it had gone the previous time. Possibly they thought him senile. And, he thought, possibly I am. And this return visit is a sign of it.

But there were some things they could not know. They could not know that he had installed a crap table at the old ranch south of Dallas, and he had spent a few hundred hours estimating odds and methods of play before calling in one of the bright young mathematicians from the Gulfport outfit. Once the young man got it through his head he was to take this seriously or get fired, he settled down. He compiled figures, took them back and checked them against the electronic calculator at Gulfport, then came back to the ranch.

The problem was to find the most plausible way to win three hundred thousand dollars with the smallest chance of loss. All systems of doubling up except one were eliminated, and that one would only work if Homer Gallowell could achieve a very generous hike in the limit on any one bet. After intensive study, that system was also eliminated. The critical factor seemed to be the provable assumption that the more bets placed, the better the house percentage against the bettor. Patient and bewildered ranch hands, who wondered if the old man had begun to lose his mind, threw dice for hours. The opinions of professional gamblers were secretly sought. And the final plan was an apt combination of the sterility of higher mathematics and the superstitions of the accomplished gambler.

It had as good a chance of working as Gallowell had hoped for. It depended on his exercise of a rigid discipline. He knew he would not deviate from the program in any way. Yet, in spite of all the planning and all the caution, the casino might take his money just as easily as before. It was that chance which kept him in a state of cold anticipation as the cab pulled up under the marquee of the Cameroon. He had grown weary of sure things in the last decade.

He was treated with a bored indifference right up until the moment he signed the registration card, and then the red carpet was unrolled with awkward haste. Yes sir, Mr. Gallowell, sir, your suite is all ready, sir, this way, sir.

The spacious beauty of the suite amused him. Had he been paying for accommodations, he would have picked the smallest, cheapest room in the house. This was not so much frugality as it was an indifference to his surroundings. He needed a roof, a bed, a toilet, a tub, a sink, a chair and a window. Anything else was superfluous.

The stacked silver dollars amused him too. The note of welcome was signed by Max Hanes. He remembered him. Looks like an old ape, that feller. Guess I was one of his favorite people last year. So he fattens me up for another crack at me.

Gallowell fed three silver dollars into the slot machine standing next to the bedroom door and got ten back. That was the end of his interest. The gain was not worth the effort of pulling the handle and the boredom of watching the colored wheels go around.

He unpacked with an old man's fussy neatness, washed up and went down to the casino, the side pocket of his jacket sagging under the load of silver dollars he had taken off the bureau. He went directly to the crap table where he had dropped the two hundred thousand and began to play without any feeling of interest, wagering one dollar at a time, losing a little more often than he won. He was waiting for Max Hanes, and he knew it would not be a long wait.

"Welcome back, Mr. Gallowell," Max said.

He turned and shook hands with the squat bald man. "How you, Hanes?"

"Fine, sir. Just fine. Going to try us again?"

"Haven't decided. I guess maybe I'll just stick to dollar bets this time. Then you fellers can't get to me so bad."

"Think your luck would run as bad as it did last time?"

"It might. It just might. I guess I couldn't get much interested unless it was arranged a mite different, Hanes."

"How do you mean?"

"Got a place where we can talk it over?"

Max Hanes took Gallowell back to his office, a rather small and shadowy room with a bright light that shone directly down on the dark top of his desk.

"Can I get you a drink, Mr. Gallowell?"

"Bourbon and branch water'd cut the dust some." He waited until Hanes had hung up after ordering the drinks and then said, "On second thought, I'd do better sticking to one-dollar bets. I learned long ago you can't get rich playing the other feller's game."

"Some do, Mr. Gallowell. Some do."

"But do they stay rich? I got myself in that habit, sort of."

"Here's our drinks, sir."

"Good fast service you get here, Hanes."

"You talked about a different kind of arrangement."

"Last time I was here . . . this is fine bourbon . . . I could maybe have made out better but I kept a-running head-on into that limit you set on me."

"We made it sixteen thousand on any single bet, didn't we?"

"You remember pretty good. I must be the kind of customer you like to remember."

"Always glad to welcome you back, sir. What kind of a limit were you thinking about?"

"I didn't have any special idea in mind. I think maybe. . . twenty-five thousand. How does that sound?"

"High."

Homer put his empty glass down. "Then thanks for the drink, and I better get back to my dollar bets. . . ."

"But not too high, Mr. Gallowell."

"Then you'll give me a twenty-five-thousand-dollar limit on a single bet?"

"And one bet of that size on the table at one time."

"Now that sounds neighborly of you. Another thing, the last time I was here, that damn big crowd gathered round and watched me make a dang fool of myself, and if they could have found out who I was, it would have been all over the papers. So I want to bet inconspicuous like. I want you should fix me up with some chips worth twenty-five thousand apiece. You could maybe use hundred-dollar ones and put a little bitty piece of tape acrosst them, with your signature. Could you do that?"

"Yes, but. . . ."

"Now I got right here a check for two hundred thousand, which is the same as I lost last time. I want you to fix me up with eight of those special chips, and you better fix up another fifteen or twenty more of them in case I have to buy more or I should start winning some. Put them at that same table where I lost last time, tell those boys working that table all about it."

"But. . . ."

"I don't want to be conspicuous, Hanes. If you want any more of my money, you do it just like I want it done. I guess there's places in this town that will do it my way if I ask polite."

"Don't you want to make . . . any smaller bets?"

"I sure do. Dollar bets, like I was doing when you come along. And every once in a while, when I happen to feel like it, I'll throw one of those special chips into the game."

"It's unusual, Mr. Gallowell, but . . . we can do it."

"I'll go get my supper now, and I guess you can have it all set up the way I want it when I get back."

"It'll be just the way you want it, Mr. Gallowell."

"I'll just hold onto this check until you get my special chips fixed up." Homer Gallowell walked out of Max Hanes' office, concealing his feeling of triumph. Had he been unable to set it up exactly as he wanted it, he would have given up the idea and gone back home. His experiments had proved that any other approach would very probably result in a loss. Hanes, believing he was going to use a doubling system, had approved the big limit, knowing that any doubling system would collapse when any long run brought it up against the house limit. Even if he started with a one-dollar bet, doubling each time, betting against the shooter, sixteen consecutive losses would bring him to the point of a twenty-five thousand-dollar bet and, winning that one, he would make a one-dollar profit.

Sixteen straight passes was an event of utmost rarity. But it could happen. Following such a system, he did not have enough years left to get his previous losses back, even if he never ran into such a string of passes. His previous fiasco had been the result of using a bastardized doubling system on eights and sixes, betting one thousand, then two, four, eight and, because of the limit they had imposed on him, sixteen thousand. He had done reasonably well at first, had been, in fact, thirty-five thousand ahead after three hours of play, waiting for each shooter to roll the point he had to make before making his bets on eight and six.

But the dice at that table suddenly turned exceedingly cold for all shooters. Time after time they would make points and seven out. He was pushed up to sixteen apiece on both six and eight. As he kept covering for five straight rolls, the shooters would roll a point and then seven out. He dropped a hundred and fifty thousand during those five rolls, as people crowded thick around him and the table men kept the play slow so as to give him time to get the bets down. He came back a little bit, and then limited himself to the big eight, and ran into the same sort of run again, and that was the end of two hundred thousand.

Max Hanes, he realized, had missed the one essential factor in the personality of Homer Gallowell. He always prepared himself for any venture. His methods were never the result of hunch, superstition or blind stubbornness. His was that optimum flexibility which permits quick adjustments to new problems, based on the acquisition of facts by hired experts. He looked rigid, inflexible, opinionated and stubborn. Yet this was the practised deception of the poker player. In his lifetime he had found the inflexible men easiest to devour.

He knew that what he accomplished or failed to accomplish at the crap table was a matter of great moment to Max Hanes, and he felt an easy contempt for the man. A great military leader, between campaigns, can amuse and refresh himself by playing a game of war on a board, using counters, and despite his desire to win he can feel comfortably superior to his professional opponent who has spent his life at the game rather than the reality.

It was a little after seven o'clock when Homer Gallowell picked up his eight special chips from Max Hanes. He found room at the rail of the crap table, and he was immediately aware of the special attention he was given by the three men operating the table. The other players didn't notice this. Homer began to play, using silver dollars, betting with no particular plan or pattern. Max Hanes and two of his floor men hovered in the background for a time. Homer's tough old plainsman face was expressionless. He waited and he watched and he counted, with the tireless patience of a lizard awaiting the random beetle, inconspicuous against sun-brown rock.

At twenty minutes after eight the special circumstances he had been awaiting occurred. There was a new shift working the table, but he knew they were completely aware of him. A woman at the far end made eight straight passes. She lost the dice. The next shooter was a man at her left, half drunk, noisy, aggressive, ready to be belligerent. Homer slipped two fingers into his vest pocket and took out one of his certified chips. The man rolled a nine, a three, a ten, a three, a nine. The noisy man let his come bet ride.

Homer reached over and put his special chip on the Do-Not Come line.

"Hold the dice!" the stick man said sharply.

"What the hell for?" the shooter demanded.

"Your bet is down, sir?" the stick man asked Homer.

"It's just about exactly where I want it," Homer said.

"That old man need help placing his lousy bet?" the shooter said. "Dad, you should know better than to bet into me. When do you guys break down and let me roll myself a seven?"

"Roll, sir," the stick man said.

The shooter rolled another nine, and then eleven, trey, ten, six, seven. The bank man went to the bottom of one of the stacks in front of him, took out a special chip and placed it neatly on Homer's. He picked them up and put them in his vest pocket.

"You put the hex on me, Dad," the noisy one said. "You ride with me next time. Hey, are you hearing me, Dad?"

Homer Gallowell slowly lifted his head, unhooded the odd yellow-gray reptilian eyes and gave the man the same long look that had quelled men of considerably more stature than the drunk. "Keep it shut, son," he said gently.

"No offense," the man said in an entirely different voice.

Between that moment and midnight, Homer had three more chances to follow the same procedure, to put his bet down against the second roll of the shooter who followed anyone making at least eight passes. He lost once. He won twice. He left the table fifty thousand dollars ahead.

The method he had used violated the mathematical theory of the young mathematician in one respect. "But, Mr. Gallowell," he had pleaded, looking close to tears, "Dice have no *memory*! If, with honest dice, a man rolled forty sevens in a row, on the forty-first roll his mathematical chance of making a seven is exactly the same as it was on the first roll."

"Son, you've been a big help. We know the optimum size of the bets I got to make. We know I'm putting them on the best percentage bet on the table. I got this table you made up for me, telling me I can only bet nineteen or twenty times before it starts to run too sour against me. I got that part from you. I got the other part from the professional gamblers I had my people contact. Every damn one of them says that after a long hot roll, the next shooter is lucky to make one pass, and sometimes he makes two and he hardly ever makes three. Understand, son, this is what *generally* happens. Sometimes dice will stay hot all the way around the table, shooter after shooter. But those professionals, they see the shape of something you can't measure with your little tubes and transistors, and I think, for a patient man it's maybe enough to give me that little extra edge I need. Now if I was a *gambling* man it wouldn't work, because I'd get all fired up over winning and I'd try to win so damned much I'd just naturally give it all the hell back to them. But I'm no gambling man. I just like to plan things out and see how they work. And if this don't work, son, then I've settled once and for all there's no way under God's sun a man can beat those tables."

Mr. Homer Gallowell of Texas walked from the table to the Afrique Bar, took a corner table and ordered a ham sandwich and some bourbon and water. He was near the door where the entertainers entered the bar. When she came through the door he stood up with grave courtesy and said, "Evenin', Miz Dawson."

"Well, hi, Mr. Gallowell!" she said with evident pleasure. "I heard you were back."

"Can you set for a spell?"

"I have to go on right now, but I'll be glad to after my act, if you're still here. I know you don't approve of my line of work."

"I guess I can stand waiting for you, if I don't listen too hard."

"My public!" she said mockingly. "I'll be back."

He sat down and watched her thread her way between the tables toward the small stage. He looked at her strong flanks, the good shoulders, the long straight line of her back, the grace and balance of the way she moved, and he wondered why there were so few of them left nowadays, so few honest-to-God women on the earth, all strength and pride and warmth. It was a new breed nowadays—the whimpering ones, the squeaky little neurotic ones, all petulance and boredom. This one was so like Angela, long ago, before a sickness of the blood brought her down. It took thirteen years to kill her, but it never once made her whine. It seemed such a damnable waste to him, both Angela and this Betty Dawson. Betty was letting too many years go by. She'd lost seven good years of childbearing, of belonging to a good man and working with him, and that was what God had intended for her—not this singing dirty songs to drunks.

He remembered the odd way he had met her. A year ago March. Thirteen months ago. After losing all that money he'd been up at five the next morning, annoyed with himself, anxious to get hold of his pilot a little later on and be off the ground by eight at least. The gambling had been

84

evidence of a kind of boredom that had been growing within him for several years. He had so consolidated his power position that it had become, he realized, a little too easy to achieve his goals. Yet such was his respect for the smooth functioning of the intricately structured Gallowell Company that he could not bring himself to set up the artificial challenge of making a consciously faulty decision in order to handicap himself.

On that year-ago morning, irritable with his own unarticulated discontent, he had heard a woman singing. There were a few clots of people at the gaming tables in the casino, but most of the tables were idle. A few slot machines made isolated sounds, as opposed to the continuous roaring of the earlier hours of the night. He walked slowly across the casino floor and into the Afrique Bar.

The woman sang to eight customers in the big shadowy glossy room. Half of them were listening. One bartender wiped the bar top. The other one polished glassware.

The woman at the piano wore dark red, indecently tight, and she sat at a small white piano. A baby spot shown down on her. The husky timbre of her voice had stirred an ancient painful memory, but as he stood just inside the doorway, listening, he heard the words of a ballad overly clever, cutely dirty, and he turned to leave. But just as he turned, she ad libbed a line right along with the song, saying to him, "It isn't polite to walk out on me, sir. It hurts my morale no end."

He hesitated, shrugged, sat alone at a table for four nearest the doorway. He had a waiter bring him a pot of coffee. He learned that it was possible to listen to the cadence of her voice without following the words.

When she finished, and was applauded heartily by one drunk, she gave an ironic bow, switched off her own spot, and came directly to Homer Gallowell's table.

"I hear you used to have half the money in the world," she said. "I hear they taught you a little humility out there, sir."

He stood up. "That's your right name on that little sign yonder?"

"Betty Dawson, yes."

"Homer Gallowell, Miz Dawson. Would you . . . set for a spell?"

"Thank you kindly," she said. And sat with him.

He wondered why he had asked her. He was wary of all impulsive acts. And he had good cause to be particularly wary of all attractive young women. Angela had been the only love in his life. As his personal power increased, women had pursued him with a fervor and shamelessness and relentlessness that bemused and alarmed him. But he had evaded all the degrees of relationship they wanted to achieve. Angela had died when he was thirty-five, half his life ago. He had felt a strong and purely physical need for a woman, but Angela had left no room in his heart for any emotional relationship, and he had been far too busy building an empire to devote any time to social involvements. And so, with a cruel logic that suited him, with a characteristic, ruthless efficiency, he had solved his own problem in his own way.

One of his agents in Mexico selected the girls from small villages, picking them for health, cleanliness, poverty, good manners, industry and their sturdy, dusky comeliness. The girls were in no way deceived. Each one, in her turn, was told that she would be taken legally to the States on a work permit. She would work in the hacienda of a rich and powerful Norte Americano, and she would be expected to share his bed for a period of a year or two. She would be instructed in ways to prevent issue from this relationship. She would receive generous pay for her services, and when it was over she would be returned to her home village with a gift so generous that it would be easy for her to marry well in the village. Refusals were rare. And all those who had accepted over the years seemed well-content with the bargain they had made.

He could not sort out their names and faces, or remember how many there had been over the years. Maria, Antonia, Amparo, Rosalinda, Maria Elena, Augustina, Chucha, Dorotea. . . . There had been a comfortable sameness about them, an undemanding docility, a tremulous apprehension in the beginning that soon softened into cheerful affection, because it was easy for him to be kind to them. Almost without exception, months after they had returned to Mexico, he would receive one of the traditional wedding pictures, the bride and groom impaled on the thorn of time, staring rigidly into the unkind lens of the village photographer.

They had come to him on all those nights across the long busy years, with a reassuring sameness of firm young haunch and identical murmurs of love and healthy and strenuous participation, demanding nothing of him beyond this prearranged area of housework and bed—appreciative of his kindnesses, and devoted to giving him pleasure.

He had known it was wrong in the ethical sense. It was a voluntary slavery, but slavery nonetheless, enforced by money. He could not see how anyone was hurt by such an arrangement, yet the nag of conscience was enough to make his parting gift, each time, handsomer than he had planned.

The last one, who was sent to him six years ago, was Gigliermina, from a village in Tlaxcala. His demands upon her were much less frequent than in the days of his full manhood. She was nineteen when she came into his home. During her first two years she had taken over more and more responsibility in the running of the household. She had an unexpectedly powerful personality and a talent for administration. No matter how many weeks he might be gone on business trips, he came to know that when he returned to the old ranch it would be spotlessly clean. There would be a fire, in season, ready to light. Gigi, with a smile at once shy and proud, would be the one to unpack his things, lay out fresh clothing, make his drink, plan his meals around the foods he most relished.

After two years he spoke, without conviction, of sending her back, as had been promised to her. She told him she could stay a little longer, if her presence did not offend him. He spoke of it again at the end of the third year, and the fourth, and then knew he would not bring it up again.

She had changed in physical ways. She had grown heavier. The broad Indio structuring of her face was more apparent. She dominated the household staff, demanding and receiving obedience. And she had become much more familiar with Homer Gallowell, but in ways that did not displease him. She guarded his health like a mother with a sickly child, railing at him when he let himself become overtired. Without his desiring it or asking for it, she had made him the focus of her existence, and it would have been unthinkable to send her away. Her English had become very good, and at her gentle insistence he helped her to acquire citizenship.

When he lived at the old ranch, she made a practise of coming to his bed when he retired, massaging his back and shoulders and the nape of his neck with strong brown fingers, rubbing away the tensions of the day while she prattled about ranch affairs in a way that rested him. She would stay with him and talk, and so she was there for him when he felt any stir of physical wanting. When he awakened just before dawn, she was never there, having returned —with her understanding of the proprieties of the relationship—to her room in the servants' wing. When there were guests at the ranch, she never provided them the slightest basis for speculation. When he was alone with her he would talk out business problems, and though they were beyond her comprehension, it seemed to clarify them in his own mind. Gigi was the only one he talked to without reservation.

He had satisfied his own feeling of responsibility toward her by adding a special codicil to his will. The trusted attorney who handled his most personal legal matters had been aghast at the sum involved.

"Can this . . . uh . . . person handle an amount like this?" he had asked warily. "Wouldn't a trust fund be more. . . ."

"She will be able to handle her personal financial affairs better than you are handling your own, son."

"I just. . . ."

"You just do as I tell you."

It amused him to think how, when the terms of his will were made public, the sharpshooters would descend on this ignorant woman from a primitive village. And how they would be stopped in their tracks by a shrewdness that would see through every deception.

All of the others and now, finally, Gigliermina, had formed one line of defense against the sort of woman he had impulsively asked to sit with him.

"They took a good piece of money off me last evening," he said.

"Word gets around," Betty Dawson had said. "If somebody hits the house, they plant it in the columns. If it's the other way around it's just us captive chickens who get the word."

"I guess you like to know about the people who have enough to lose so that when they lose it, it's kind of a big thing around here. I guess right now I could win a popularity contest."

The waiter brought her coffee. As soon as he was out of earshot, she stared at Homer with eyes suddenly narrow and said, "I give not a damn, old man, how much you lost or how much you have left. I spoke to you because you happened to look depressed. You win no popularity contests with me. I'm not on the make for you or your money, and if you can't accept a friendly gesture without thinking everybody has an angle, then why don't you just get up and go right through that door. I'll miss you dreadfully."

He stared at her for a moment, and then leaned toward her, his eyes as narrow as hers. "That's just what I was a-needing, a lot of smart-alec lip from a girl makes her living singing dirty. Any time anybody has to feel sorry for me, I'll wear a sign letting you know. To me what I lost is the same as you losing a ten-dollar bill."

"Mail me a copy of your bank balance, rich man!"

"If anybody leaves this table, it shouldn't be the one who was settin' here first!"

"Why don't you buy the joint and have it torn down?"

They sat motionless, their noses six inches apart, their jaws set. The corner of his mouth began to twitch. Her eyes began to dance. And suddenly they both yelped and roared with laughter until the tears ran freely. He banged the tabletop with his knotted old fist. The bartenders stared.

When all the gaspings had died away, they were friends who could talk to each other. And both of them were ripe for talking, and for listening. He wouldn't let her go off to bed. He let her go change and asked her to come back. They breakfasted together, and on that cold bright day they took a walk along the Strip, had a long lunch at the Sahara and then taxied back to the Cameroon.

At lunch he had said, "You could get out of the business you're in, couldn't you?"

He had sensed a wariness and withdrawal in her as she said indifferently, "But why should I, Homer? I like the plush life."

"It just isn't a fitten kind of work for you, Miz Betty," he had said stubbornly.

"Oh, come now! The songs are sophisticated, but there isn't one of them that's in bad taste, actually."

"Wearin' tight dresses so the boobs will stare at you. . . ."

"That's part of the game."

"Dammit, you should ought to be married, having kids—a woman like you."

"Maybe. But you don't order up a husband the way you order a drink, Homer. They have to sort of come along, don't they?"

"But you got to do some looking. You got to help it a little."

She shrugged. "Even if the boy did show, it's just a little too . . . let's drop the subject, huh?"

"Why should it be a little too late?"

"Please, Homer."

"Has somebody got some kind of bad pressure on you, Miz Betty?"

She had hesitated just long enough to give him a certainty he was right before saying, "Nonsense! I'm free as a bird."

"I can see you don't want to talk about it, whatever it is, and it's making you uneasy. But you just remember one thing. I got a lot of weight, Miz Betty. I like you. I don't like many people. They all seem kind of dim and helpless lately. But if there's anybody got you in a bind and you want loose, you get hold of me any time, any place, and tell me who and how, and I'll get you out from under. Money is the biggest damn lever in the world."

"If I ever need a white knight on a horse, Homer, I'll phone Texas."

"You do that, hear?"

After they returned to the hotel he got hold of his pilot, and then she had insisted on driving him to the airport in her little old car, and, in the moment of parting, he had put a hesitant and leathery kiss on the softness of her cheek. A month or so later he had Neiman Marcus send her a dinner ring, a dark blue three karat amethyst, oval cut, superbly mounted in platinum.

She had sent it back to him by registered mail, with a brief amusing refusal in verse form. After ironic reflection, he had given the ring to Gigliermina.

Now her first show was over and she came smiling to his table to sit with him.

"Homer, you're looking very fit."

"Sure, Miz Betty, like an ole buzzard on a high limb. I don't know if I ought to badmouth you some, sending back that ring like you did. I thought it was a purty thing."

"It was a gloriously beautiful thing, Homer, and it took a lot of character to send it back, because I loved it on sight."

"I was thinking of that same blue you got in your eyes."

"Now be good! I didn't keep it because we're friends, I think, and I had the feeling I would see you again some day. And when I did, I didn't want to have the feeling that if I was nice to you I'd get another ring. Do you see?"

"In a manner of speaking. Maybe."

"You cannot buy my favors, sir."

"Never reckoned I could, somehow."

"It would make me feel like a kept woman, taking a mighty jewel like that."

"Well, you'd be about the longest-range, least-used kept woman on record, because I can't stand this place more'n three days in a row, once a year."

Leaning close to him and lowering her voice, she said, frowning, "Why on earth have you come back to let them clip you again, Homer? I heard you were here to gamble."

"It might work out some different this time, Miz Betty."

"Homer, Homer! That's what they all say, and it never happens!"

"If I was you, I wouldn't waste time worrying about ole Homer none. I've been studying on this thing a little since I was here last time. If a man keeps at it, those house percentages are going to sooner or later walk him down. So I don't bet often, but I bet on the heavy side." He hooked two fingers into his vest pocket and pulled out the ten chips. "Ever see any like these?"

She picked the top one off the stack. "It's just a hundred-dollar chip, is all, but it's got tape on it." She turned it toward the light. "Signed by Max Hanes! Why?"

"That raises them some. It raises them up to twenty-five thousand apiece. It's a deal I worked out with him."

She put the chip back hastily. "My God! Ten of them! Put them away. They make me nervous. When do you start to use them?"

"I started already, Miz Betty. I started with eight and now I got ten. If it goes along like I hope, I'll have me another three or four extry tomorrow, and another three or four or maybe even five on Monday, and then I'll head on back home. What's the matter? Why'd you look so funny there for a minute?"

"Nothing's the matter, Homer."

"What's the trouble?"

"I just . . . have the horrible feeling that you know exactly how to beat the casino, if anybody in the world ever can. I have the horrid feeling you're going to win."

"It's a bad thing to win?"

"I'm just kidding."

"But you looked scared like, Betty."

"Sometimes it isn't a good thing to win too much."

He studied her for a few moments. "Don't get all nerved up. I can see as how they don't like to let loose of it without struggling some. But I've been in the world for some time, Miz Betty. In nineteen eleven, when I was twenty-two years old, a man took some money off me that was mine. Three hundred in gold that I had collected from him on a note. He lathered his horse making a big half circle to come up on me, and he gut-shot me off my horse, took the gold, drove my horse away and left me for dead. I was to be married in three months, and it was no time for dying. I walked four miles, crawled three, and squirmed along for two more, rested some, then stopped a train going to San Antone by building a brush fire on the tracks. In three weeks I was mended, and I got some friends and went along to see that fella. We hung him a little bit, kept letting him down so he could talk, and when he allowed he had done it and told us where the gold was hid, we hung him for sure and certain. Since then nobody has taken anything off me I wasn't willing for them to have. So don't you worry none."

She smiled and touched his hand. "Okay, you fearless old man."

"Something's going good for you, I'd say."

"What do you mean?"

"It's writ all over you, Betty. You look like something that's come into blossom. I'd say you found you a man."

"I found him, Homer. Yes indeed, I found him!"

"Going to get married up?"

She shook her head slowly. "No."

"You're not such a fool as to get tangled with a man who's married already."

"No. He isn't married."

"Then what's holding you back, woman?"

"I guess maybe I love him too much, Homer."

"Damn if I ever met anybody of the female persuasion made any damn sense at all, half the time."

"Don't get all stirred up now, Homer. I'm happy. Can't you let that be enough for right now?"

"Sure can. You look happy, girl. You look fit to bust with it."

"He's strong, Homer. Where it counts. Integrity. Is that word out of style? That's the kind of man I need. God knows I can find enough of them who want to collapse in my lap and live off my strength. This is one I can lean on. But I won't. I know I could if I had to, but I won't. That's what makes it so good."

"Who the hell you in love with? Marshal Dillon?"

"Homer, I swear, you almost sound jealous. Thank you, dear. It's a guy named Hugh Darren. He's the new manager of this hotel . . . since last August."

"The place is better run than I remembered from last time."

"He's tops in his job, Homer."

"That's something to go by, girl. It don't much matter a damn who you hook up with, but get yourself a man who cares enough to do his job better than the next feller. It don't matter if he lays brick or runs a bank. The top men in any line have pride and guts. And that's all that counts. I'm glad you're happy, Miz Betty, and if you'll be excusing me, I'll be going along upstairs now. It's hard work standing at that table keeping track of the game ever' minute."

"Goodnight, Homer. And it's good to see you again, dear."

Hugh was in his office when one of the desk clerks phoned him and said in a somewhat nervous voice that Mr. Homer Gallowell had asked to speak to him. Hugh glanced at his watch and hurried out. It was a little after one A.M.

"Good evening, Mr. Gallowell. My name is Darren. Is there anything I can help you with?"

Gallowell's slow appraisal took so long the silence began to be uncomfortable. "Just wanted a look at you, son. It's said you do a good job."

"Thank you. Are you satisfied with the suite?"

"It shore is big, Darren."

"Any time you want anything at all. . . ."

"Whenever I want anything at all, I generally make myself heard loud and clear, son. Don't never fret about Homer Gallowell suffering in silence. One thing you could do is move that slot machine out of there. It isn't in my way at all, but I'm not about to play with it, and so it isn't earning its keep up there. And I don't like to see nothing idle, even a sucker machine like that one."

Hugh gave the desk clerk a quiet order and said, "It will be out of there before you can get to your suite, Mr. Gallowell."

"That's good service. Darren. I had made up my mind . . . from the time I was here before . . . there wasn't anybody in this place worth the trouble of digging a grave for them, with one exception—the Dawson girl, who shouldn't be anywhere near this place anyhow. Maybe you're an exception too, son."

"I like to think I am, Mr. Gallowell."

"It won't hurt you a bit to keep right on thinking that way, Darren. 'Night."

"Goodnight, sir."

As the old man entered the elevator, Hugh turned to the clerk and said, "Now just what was that all about?"

"It beats hell out of me. Maybe you're about to get a job in Texas, Hugh."

"Thanks, but no."

Before he went up to bed, Hugh had a chance to go into the Afrique Bar and catch Betty between shows. She saw him at the bar and left a table of friends to come over to him and glower and say, "Aren't you sacked out yet, lover? What good can you be to me if you don't get *any* sleep?"

"I had to take one minute before heading for the sack to look in on the only person in the hotel worth a Texas damn."

"What? Oh, my goodness, did Homer. . . ."

"He inspected the troops. I damn near saluted him. How did you worm your way into his favor, woman?"

"He's a sweet old thing and we're good friends. This is only the second time we've ever seen each other, and we're good friends in that funny way it happens sometimes."

"If Homer Gallowell is a sweet old thing, Stalin was an absolute lamb."

"You don't even know him, Hugh. He does have a very tough, hard mind. But I would trust him. And I know he would trust me. And I guess he came to look you over because I gave you the big build. The man who has put this hotel on its feet; yes sir."

"Thank you kindly. This hotel has knocked me off my feet."

"Go to bed, for gosh sakes!"

"Your wish is my command."

"Dream of me," she whispered.

"I can't. I need my rest. Go back and guffaw with your jovial friends, kid. Live it up."

"Behind this painted smile is a heart full of. . . ."

"Lust."

"You took that word right out of my mouth."

They were at a shadowy corner of the bar, so that it was safe for him to indulge himself in a parting caress, an open-handed smack where her skirt was tightest, with both the sound of the blow and her inadvertent yelp lost in the brass of the quartet on the small stage. She sank a strong elbow so far into his middle that he was unable to catch a full breath until she had walked all the way back to the table she had left, had seated herself, and turned to give him a brilliant and mocking smile. She threw him a kiss and he went trudging dutifully and contentedly to bed.

. . . six

At four o'clock on Sunday afternoon Ben Brown, Max Hanes' first lieutenant on the casino floor, came plodding sullenly into Max's office, threw himself into a chair beside the desk and said, "The son of a bitching system is still working for him, Max. Right now he's three big ones up on us for the day."

"How many bets has he made?"

"With the big ones? Five all day. He hit the first one, lost the second one, and hit the next three in a row. Honest to

God, the nerves of the boys working the shifts on that table are going bad, Maxie. He can go two hours fooling with those dollar bets and all of a sudden—Bam!"

"They know the system, don't they?"

"Sure. After any eight or more passes, he bets against the second roll of the next shooter—if the next shooter *gets* a second roll. But even knowing when he'll do it, it's still a shock, Max. He's a hundred and twenty-five into us right now, and I keep telling myself that if he bets enough the odds will swing our way."

"But he doesn't bet often enough, Benny."

"Is he going to take us?"

"It depends on how much he wants. If he settles short, he can walk away with it, Ben. He could walk away this minute. You know that. But if he wants a lot . . . if he wants a hell of a lot, we'll get back what's ours and we'll get his too."

"But, Max, he doesn't react like a gambler."

"He isn't a gambler. That leathery old bastard maneuvered me as pretty as you please, and it's something I'm not used to. He's got no gambling itch. He's fish cold. He's trying something cute and I've got a hunch it'll work, and he won't be too greedy, and he'll try to walk away fat."

"Try to walk away, Max?"

Hanes tugged at a flap of skin that sagged below the jawline of his simian face, and the deep-set eyes were venomously bright. "A manner of speaking. But I wouldn't hire a limousine so he can get away faster."

Ben Brown was a monochromatic youngish man, with tan skin, tan hair, tan eyes, thin lips without color. He had the knack of being able to roam the casino tirelessly without being seen by anybody, while he saw everything. If any slightest thing stirred his ready suspicions he would go on up to the catwalk behind the false west wall of the casino, focus a powerful 'scope down through one of the concealed observation ports and watch the questionable play with the awesome feral patience of one of the great questing cats. In addition, he had a rare talent for detecting people who had trouble on their mind long before they made their first move. When asked about them later all he could say was, "They just didn't seem to fit."

Once he became suspicious, he would alert the casino security staff and bird dog the person he was worried about. On the casino security staff of the Cameroon were several large men who had been ousted from law-enforcement agencies on charges of excessive brutality. Ignorant men often get the idea that because the crowds are heavy and money is very much in evidence, a big gambling casino is a sitting duck. Such a casino is just about as much a sitting duck as the main building of the Morgan Guarantee Trust Company.

Abortive attempts are nipped in the bud as quickly as possible, and handled with an absolute minimum of fuss so as to avoid unfavorable publicity. Often all that is necessary is for some of the security staff to take the potential offenders into a private soundproofed office, or to a remote dark corner of the vast parking lot, and, with no more emotional involvement than a crew of plumbers installing a pump, add ten dreadful years to the life of each amateur robber in six skillful minutes.

A talented and experienced crew could, of course, knock off any casino, after a professional casing job. But the skills demanded by such a project are under the control of that national hoodlum empire which has no interest in harming itself by pitting one portion of itself against another. It has been emphatically agreed that Las Vegas will be exempt from any internecine violence. So unyielding is this resolve that, even in cases where the elimination of any specific underling has been discussed in council and passed by voice vote, it has been considered advisable to lure him well away from Las Vegas before blowing his legs off with buckshot.

Ben Brown said, with a certain amount of hesitation, "Don't get sore if I say something . . . you know . . . just an idea."

"What's the idea?"

"If it was the Havana operation, there'd be no problem. I mean it would be automatic like. I got some shapes hid away. They're good ones, Max, the ones we took off those characters from Honolulu that time. So we move fat Pogo over onto that table on the stick and Willy on the bank, and that pair can switch so smooth nobody can tell. Each time after the long roll he waits for, we feed the new shooter the sure-pass dice and let him work with them through the second roll before we put him back on the level dice."

Max studied him. "And you think that's a good idea?"

"Well . . . you know . . . the old guy is taking us pretty good so far."

Deceptive as a drowsy bear, Max Hanes reached over and, with uncanny quickness, slammed the meat of his hand across Ben Brown's face. The chair went over and Ben rolled across the rug and scrambled up, his face vivid with shock and pain, the corner of his mouth bloodied.

"Goddammit Max! God!"

"Pull your goddam self together and listen to me. I can remember two other times you hinted about some kind of cute trick, Brown. This time you came right out with it. We're living in heaven, right here. We're turning the crank on a money machine. Out of every hundred thousand bucks that goes across the tables, we hold onto an average of eight, after paying the legal grease. So you're so stupid you want to diddle the machine.

"I'll draw you a picture, Brown. We'd get away with it. Let's just say, for the hell of it, we could take a million bucks off that old man. You and I would know about it. Pogo and Willy would know about it. And as sure as you're still breathing, the word would get around. I'm not talking about the state inspectors and license people, stupid. I'm talking about the important people who can't afford anybody jiggling this big apple cart.

"Stack it up against the total take in this town, and that million is cigarette money. They'd make a move, buddy boy. They'd send in the specialists. Then you and me and Pogo and Willy would get taken out into that desert out there, and when they got tired of seeing who could scream the loudest, they'd finish the job and pile rocks on the graves and go back East. It would be like an advertisement for other people who might get cute ideas."

"Jesus Christ, Max!"

"That's why your idea is stupid. Keep cute ideas out of your head. Don't ever try anything cute. I love you like you were my own son, Brownie, but if I found out you got cute with one of the marks out there, I'd help kill you, and I'd make it last. Pick up the chair and sit down."

Ben Brown sat down. He sighed. He patted his mouth with a handkerchief and then spat something into his palm and examined it.

"You busted a tooth, Max."

"Let me see. Scrooch down a little so the light is better. Yeah, I see it. It doesn't look too bad, Ben. It's like a corner came off. Does it hurt?"

"No, I don't feel anything."

"So it didn't bust as far down as the nerve. That can hurt like hell. You got a dentist here?"

"I got one I like pretty good."

"How's Sally? I haven't seen her in a long time."

"Well, this time, Max, she's sick in the mornings. I mean she had so easy a time with the first kid we thought it would be the same this time. She's still got two months to go, and that poor little chick is miserable. And you take Kevan, that little guy is walking now and he gets into everything, and she's got to watch him every minute."

Max pulled out the middle drawer of his desk, opened a Manila envelope, slid three hundred-dollar bills out and placed them in front of Ben Brown. He winked and said, "Right off the top, Brownie."

"Thanks, Max. Thanks a lot."

"We all squared away on everything?"

"Sure, Max. I got the message. But I hate to see that old bastard walk out heavy. If he does, it'll give us a bad week on the books."

"That's my worry, not yours. If he keeps playing, the house percentage will be working for us. He sandbagged me into that big limit, and Al is going to be asking too many questions if Gallowell makes out good. So I've got a special interest in making sure he keeps right on playing, and I've got some ideas about that. You run along, and just keep me up to date on how he's making out."

Ben Brown came back to the office a half hour later to tell Max Hanes the old man had dropped one.

After Ben left, Max sat at his desk, broad and heavy in the chair, his eyes almost closed, thinking about the old man who now had a total of a hundred thousand dollars of casino money, a full half of what he had dropped on the last visit.

Hugh Darren was in the swimming pool at four o'clock on that Sunday afternoon when word came to him that Al Marta wanted to see him in the Little Room. He said a hasty good-bye to Betty, changed quickly, and found Al seated in one of the big leather booths with two strangers. Al was drinking a highball. The two strangers were working on rare steaks with hungry, stolid efficiency. They were both sizable men in their late thirties, wearing conservative suits, junior executive pallor and glasses with ponderous black frames.

"Sit down, Hugh. Sit right down, boy. Boys, this is the hotel manager I was telling you about, the one that's a friend of Shannard."

As Hugh nodded and sat beside Al, Al said, "These are the boys who flew in to listen to the deal." It was the closest Al came to an introduction. The two men looked at first glance as if they could be on the intermediate executive level anywhere—in the automotive industry or a bank, or an insurance company. But there was a calculated incivility about their attitude, a grossness of table habits, and a cold appraisal behind those corrective lenses that set them apart from the unending personal popularity contest the average businessman feels obligated to enter.

"You've talked to Temp?" Hugh asked.

"Yes, and there's a problem and Shannard isn't too happy. Maybe you can help out a little, Hugh. Maybe you better explain it, Dan."

The slightly older-looking one spoke. As he spoke he had the disconcerting habit of staring fixedly at Hugh's necktie rather than at his face. "The properties look like the sort of thing we can be interested in. In one week we could make certain they have not been misrepresented in any way, and we could put the deal through on a cash basis. But your friend wants something we'd never give, because it's against policy. We have no need for or use for partners in any investment enterprise. If the properties check out, we'll pay him two hundred and twenty thousand dollars for his equity. This represents a slight overevaluation, and we're making the offer merely because we'd like to expand the resort-investment program in that area.

"Shannard is in a bind. He says that the money would not quite cover his outstanding obligations. He wants to retain partial ownership so he can share in the profits from development, or sell his share out after development. We couldn't be less interested in his personal financial problems, or what he wants or doesn't want. He seems to have the idea we're trying to bargain with him. He has something to sell. We'll buy it. We've named the price. Somebody has to convince him that we never bargain with anybody. We don't have to. If you can convince him that all he can do, dealing with us, is sell, we'll pay you a ten-thousand-dollar finder's fee."

"I told Al I didn't get mixed up in this to make money off a friend."

"Then take your fee and turn it over to him, and it will give him two thirty instead of two twenty—if you're so hot on the friendship bit. But the point is, will you talk to him?"

"I don't know if this is the right thing for him to do."

"I'd guess that so far as doing anything else is concerned, his time has run out. He's done a lot of stalling. For your private information, Darren, I phoned a contact in Nassau. He phoned me back fifteen minutes ago. They're waiting to serve Shannard with a lot of unpleasant papers the minute he steps off the plane."

Al said, "But these boys aren't putting the squeeze on him, Hugh. It's a good price. It's a cash deal. It's quick. Where can he go and get it the same way?"

"I'll talk to him," Hugh said. "I'll find out how he feels about it. It was his idea, coming out here. I didn't suggest it."

"He made that clear," the spokesman said. "We've always got the same kind of problem the depletion-allowance boys have—putting money to work and getting the diversification that makes sense, protectionwise. I admit we're moving fast enough so we're always running short on management talent, but we're not so short yet we've got to cut up the pie to attract it. This place, for instance. We got you here, Darren, without giving you a piece of it. And if you're smart you'll know it isn't a dead end. We've got resort areas we're developing. When the time is right, we can move you into something bigger."

"Thanks," Hugh said, "but . . . I've got the idea of owning my own show."

The spokesman shrugged. "Like they say, the dream of every man, huh? But it can end up like Shannard, right? Then where are you?"

"Would you hire Temp to operate those properties?"

"Offhand I'd say it wouldn't work out. He's been his own man too long." He looked at his watch. "We got a flight to catch. Shannard can tell Al what he decides."

It was dismissal with no attempt at cordiality, no slightest concession to the social amenities.

Hugh, wondering why the attitude should make him feel indignant, went off to find Temp and Vicky Shannard. Their suite did not answer. He had Temp paged, but he was apparently not in the hotel. Hugh put a note in their box.

He had been at his desk about five minutes when John Trabe, his manager of liquor sales, came in to see him. John had the pouched mournful face of an aging spaniel, the wary watchful eyes of a bank guard, and an astonishingly sweet, transforming smile.

"That bartender I mentioned, Hugh, that Chester Engler, I got him outside, and I swear I don't know whether it would be smart to get rid of him right now."

"He's worth a special effort?"

"He's a damn good man. He *was* a damn good man. I haven't talked to him about this last deal. I thought maybe if you could sit in on it. . . ."

"Bring him in, John."

Chester Engler was in his early thirties, overweight, with a round pink face, receding blond hair, blue eyes. He was obviously nervous, with a dew of perspiration on his upper lip in spite of the air conditioning.

"Sit right there, Chet," John Trabe said. "I want Mr. Darren to get the background on this. How long have you been tending bar in this state?"

Engler looked down at his hands. "Four years in Reno before I came here. Nine years altogether."

"You're married, own your own home, have a car. . . ."

"The car is gone."

"You've got two kids, two girls in grade school. It's a pretty good life. Or it seemed to be a pretty good life, up until four or five months ago. Chet, you're smart enough to take a long look at yourself. You know damn well that the people who live and work in this town don't gamble. And you also know that every once in a while somebody will start. You've known guys who have. And you know how they drop right out of sight, after everything is gone. It's . . . one of the hazards of working in Nevada. And you've said—I've heard you—that it's a foolish crazy thing for a man to do. But now you're gambling. And you're in trouble. You promised me you'd quit. I happen to know that you spent sixteen hours playing blackjack before you came on duty yesterday. How did you make out?"

Engler sighed and shrugged. "Not so good."

"Where do you stand right now?"

"Not so good."

"How much have you dropped?"

"About. . .twelve grand, John."

"Where did you get the money?"

"The savings went, and then I cashed in the insurance, and then the car went and I remortgaged the house and got some that way. And. . .I've sold some stuff. Lila took off with the kids. She said she couldn't take it. She went to her folks in Amarillo. She said she's going to get a job and her mother can watch the kids." His voice had been dead, but suddenly it strengthened and he looked at John Trabe. "But I nearly got out of the whole jam, John. Honest to God. Last week. It was what I'd been waiting for. It had to turn. I was eleven grand in the bag until then, and I built it back, almost all of it, I swear. I was damn near ten grand ahead, and I swore I'd quit forever the minute I got even. I meant it, John. I hung on, staying right about the same place for an hour. And then it went bad again."

"And you gave it all back."

"I shouldn't have started betting bigger. That's where I made the mistake."

"You made the mistake when you started gambling. You

101

know better, Chet. What happened to you? We used to shake our heads at the guys who got hooked. For nine years you've been learning you can't beat the house."

"Some do."

"Don't talk nonsense. Don't insult my intelligence and yours, Chet. You know it's asking for trouble to keep a gambler on the payroll. You'll be looking for some cute way to pick up extra money to feed across the table."

"I'm no thief!" Engler said hotly.

"That's the next step. Why should you be any different?"

"I tell you I'm no thief!"

Hugh interrupted, his tone quiet and reasonable. "What are your plans, Engler?"

The man nibbled the corner of his thumbnail. "I don't know. I mean . . . hell, I'm so far behind now. . . ."

"You think gambling is the only way you can catch up?"

"What have I got to lose? Right now I got no equity left in the house. I'm as far down as I can get. So how can I get hurt?"

"By continuing?"

"The way I see it, I can save up a couple hundred bucks at a time and keep trying. If I drop it, nobody is hurt. Sooner or later I'll make out, and then I can get well. That's all I want. I don't want to make a fortune. I just want to get well again. There's no law against that, Mr. Darren."

Hugh glanced at John Trabe. John shrugged almost imperceptibly. Hugh said, "I think we'd better let you go, Engler. You've done good work here. We'll see you get a good letter of recommendation. But, on the basis of past experience in similar situations, you're a risk we can't afford."

Engler said bitterly, "Thanks a lot. You're a couple of real nice guys to work for. Thanks for everything. Should I finish the shift?"

"You better just go clean out your locker, Chet," John Trabe said, "and turn the hotel equipment in, and wait for me out in the staff lounge. I'll bring you your check to date, with three weeks in advance."

Engler got up and walked out without a word.

"What happens to them, Hugh?" John Trabe asked sadly. "They get hooked. They throw everything away. They drop out of sight as if they'd never existed. They forget you can't beat the casinos. They live for the time they can buy at the tables. Whenever they're away from the tables they act semiconscious. They do bad work. And sooner or later they dream up some crazy scheme to tap the till so they can play oftener and heavier. People who stay immune can make a good living here and have a damn fine life."

"How did he start? Do you know?"

"He was what we call a dollar player, Hugh. A dollar player is a guy who will take his wife out for the evening, and when she goes to the women's room, he'll change a five or a ten into silver dollars and drift over to a crap table or a blackjack dealer and make a few bets. If he doubles his money he'll quit and tell his wife she was a cheap date. If he loses, he'll mentally chalk it up as part of the cost of the evening out. A dollar player isn't hooked, but with some people it can all of a sudden turn into a snake.

"The way I got the story, Chet and Lila went out one evening and they had a hell of a fight over something or other, one of those marriage battles, and she went home in a cab. He knew the fight was his fault, but he was too stubborn to follow her home right away. He played dollars at blackjack and made out well, and then started playing two hands and switched to five dollars a hand, playing with house money he had won. He kept winning, and switched to ten bucks a hand, and finally cashed in eleven hundred bucks. He used it to buy Lila a mink stole as a peace offering. About two weeks later he decided he'd try to win himself a new car. A month or so after that fiasco, he sneaked out of the house with the mink and sold it for four hundred bucks so he'd have money to play with. Now he's played himself right through everything he owned, and right through his marriage. He knows he's being criminally stupid, but he can't quit. He doesn't even *want* to quit."

"Some psychiatrists say, John, that a man like Engler wants to lose. He has a compulsion to lose and punish himself by losing. It's a sort of symbolic suicide."

John Trabe stood up. "I don't know how the shrinkers have it figured. All I know is we're doing the right thing in letting him go, but I've lost one of my best men. Joan and I have had dinner in their house, Hugh. The four of us have had a lot of laughs. She cried on Joan's shoulder before she took off. It's like somebody had died."

"Or caught an incurable disease."

"Yes. A disease. That fits better. I'll have this check sent in for signature, Hugh. By the way, I've been thinking we ought to stock a wider range of wines in all price levels. It's moving better lately, and if I can grab more storage space, we can make a hell of a saving on big purchases."

"And print new wine lists?"

"We're going to have to print up more pretty soon anyway."

"Are you thinking of any offbeat brands?"

"Hell, no! I want things we can be sure of reordering with no problems. I'll have a written recommendation ready by next week some time."

"So far it sounds good. Thanks, John."

"And thanks to you for listening to Chet. Because he's been a friend, I couldn't. . . ."

"I know."

At nine-twenty P.M. on that Sunday, the seventeenth day of April, Hugh Darren was making ready for bed. It was a rare luxury to fold so early. The hotel was full. For once every department for which he was responsible was running smoothly. He had made a final tour of inspection before deciding to turn in early. For once there were no special instructions to relay to Bunny Rice.

He soaked away his tensions in a long hot shower and slid gratefully into bed. Just as he was reaching to turn out the bedside lamp, his phone rang and he changed the direction of his reach and picked it up.

"Hugh?" the familiar voice said. "Vicky here."

"Well, hello, stranger. I left a note for you gadabouts, but. . . ."

"Perhaps Temp picked it up, because I don't know anything about it. Hugh, I'm so upset. A dreadful thing is happening, and I can't stop it. I really don't know what to do."

"What's the matter?"

"I'm on one of the house phones right now, in the lobby. It's Temp, Hugh. He's gambling."

"For heaven's sake, Vicky, he's not a child. He can gamble without upsetting you, can't he?"

"You don't understand. He's been drinking ever since he had that conference today with those horrid men. They upset him dreadfully, you know. And I can't seem to communicate with him at all. He's gambling heavily and he's losing heavily, and I don't think he really knows what he's doing. They're honoring his checks on the account he established in New York, and I have no idea what he's lost, but I really think it might be a great deal. I can't make him stop. I can't even make him listen to me. I'm hoping you can do something with him. It's really very frightening."

"You stay near the house phones, Vicky. I'll be down in about three minutes."

104

He dressed hastily. When Vicky saw him walking toward her she advanced to meet him. She took his hand in both of hers and he noticed her fingers were moist and cold. She looked trim in a severe black suit that had a slimming effect, but small flaws in her grooming testified to her agitation. The lipstick had been chewed from her underlip and some golden strands of hair were awry.

"I'll take you to where he is," she said.

Casino play was exceptionally heavy. All tables were in operation, and the customers stood two and three deep around the craps and roulette. The murmuring crowd noises blended with the chantings of the casino staff, the continuous roar of the slots, the music from the Afrique Bar and the Little Room, and the muffled bursts of applause from the big Safari Room where the dinner show was coming to an end. As he worked his way through the throng, Hugh was once again aware of how truly joyless these casino crowds were. When play was this heavy there was a special electric tension in the air, but there was something dingy about it. There was laughter, but no mirth. This was the raw and sweaty edge where luck and money meet in organized torment. Money is equal to survival. So it is as mirthless as some barbaric arena where slaves are matched against beasts. People in casinos ignore each other. It is a place where each man is intensely and desperately alone.

"Right there," she said, tugging at his sleeve. "Do you see him?"

Temple Shannard stood at a curved corner of a crap table. When Hugh worked his way closer he could see the chips stacked vertically in the half-circle groove of the rail in front of Shannard. He had a ten-inch length of hundred-dollar chips and half that amount of fifty-dollar chips. He stood with brown hands braced on the rail, watching the teasing dance of the dice. His collar was open, his face flushed, his eyes slitted and intent, his mouth entirely slack. He took some hundred-dollar chips and, with no attempt to count them, placed them behind his come-line bet, increasing his bet with the shooter.

"The point is eight," the stick man chanted. "And the shooter rolls an eleven. No bets in the field."

"Hard eight," Shannard said and tossed the hundred-dollar chip. The stick man moved it onto the double-four box.

"And a three, another number in the field, and a seven."

When the come bets were raked in and the other bets adjusted, the stick man hooked the five dice over in front of the next shooter for him to make his choice of the two dice he would use.

Hugh had managed to edge in behind Temp. "Having fun, Temp?" he asked.

Temp looked back over his shoulder. "That's what I'm here for, isn't it? A lot of big fat fun." His voice was blurred and thickened.

"How are you doing?"

"Check with me later, old boy. Check with me later. Right now I'm busy."

Hugh moved away from the table, gestured to Vicky to wait where she was, and went to the big casino cashiers' cage. The men who worked behind the windows knew him even though they did not come under the hotel operation.

"Are you cashing checks for Temple Shannard?"

The man hesitated. "Uh . . . yes, we are, Mr. Darren."

"What's the total so far?"

"Would you hold on just a moment, please?"

Hugh waited thirty seconds and suddenly Max Hanes appeared beside him. "What's on your mind, Hugh?"

"I want to know how deep Temp Shannard is getting."

"They brought the first check to me, Hugh. I checked with Al on it. We agreed we'd cash checks right up to one hundred grand. So far we've cashed one for three thousand, four for five thousand apiece, and one for ten, and it's that ten he's working with right now. Thirty-three thousand bucks, pal."

"I've got to get him away from that table, Max."

"Now that's an interesting-type idea, but do you mind telling me why you think you got to get him away from the table before the poor guy has a chance to run hot and get well?"

"He's my friend. He's had bad luck. And he's drunk. He shouldn't be losing that much money."

Max Hanes gave him a friendly thump on the biceps that momentarily numbed his arm. "Darren, I'm surprised at you. You've been here eight months now, and that's long enough so you should get the picture. The lieutenant-governor of this great state of Nevada, Mr. Rex Bell, goes around making luncheon speeches about how the whole idea of the State of Nevada is that people shouldn't be treated like children. They are grown up and they ought to be treated like adults. In Las Vegas a man gets treated like an adult. If he wants to drink, he can drink. If he wants to gamble, he can gamble. Nobody twists his arm. And if he wants to drink

106

and gamble, that's his privilege. Now you wouldn't want to go against the whole idea of this place all of a sudden."

Hugh turned to face Max Hanes squarely. "He's my friend. He's doing something he's going to regret. I'm going to have to stop him."

"Okay, so we give you a big score for friendship, buddy, but let's change that brave talk just a little bit. You can *try* to stop him. You can go right over there and talk to him. That's your privilege. Anybody who comes into my casino has that same privilege." He tapped Hugh on the chest with a thick finger. "But all you do is talk. And you do it quietly. And if he doesn't listen, that's too damn bad. Because if you try anything else, Darren, if you try pulling him away from the table, or grabbing his chips to go cash them in, you're no different from any bum who wanders into my casino making a disturbance. If you do anything except talk, I got boys who will walk you out of here so quiet nobody will know anything is wrong, but you'll maybe have lame arms for a week."

"You people wave a big flag for friendship, don't you? You leave a drunken bum in as manager because he's an old pal. But when it comes to one of my friends, he's just another pigeon to pluck. Is that it, Max?"

"You're an employee and your old buddy is a mark. You got to belong to the club."

"What do you show the membership committee? A photostat of your prison record?"

"See how I'm getting all red and confused and guilty-looking? You're hurting my feelings, Hugh." He laughed as Hugh turned angrily away from him.

Once again Hugh shouldered his way close to Temp Shannard. The dice had come to Temp. He bet heavily on himself and crapped out, then bet twice as much as before and rolled a ten. He rolled for a long time, struggling for the ten, until a five deuce showed. He was down to so few chips he took them off the rail and held them in his hand.

Hugh talked to him, his lips close to Temp's ear. He begged him, he implored him, he pleaded and wheedled.

"For me, Temp," he said finally. "Not for Vicky, not for yourself. For me."

Temp swung around, his eyes big with an animal wildness, and yelled, "Get the hell away from me, Darren!"

Ben Brown, Max Hanes' first assistant, and a big casino guard had moved in close. "I guess you're bothering the player, Mr. Darren," Brown said mildly.

107

Hugh walked over to Vicky and took her out of the crowd, over to the far wall beyond the last aisle of slots.

"He won't listen."

"Can't you ask them to stop taking the money?"

"The casino is separate, Vicky. It doesn't come under me. It's just as if he was playing at the Sands or the Tropicana. The best thing is to wait and catch him on the way to cash another check."

"How much has he gone through?"

"Quite a lot."

"How much, Hugh?"

"Over thirty thousand."

She closed her eyes. She kept them closed for several seconds, and her plump oval face looked naked and young and helpless.

"Oh, the ass!" she said, her voice barely audible in the din. "The bloody, stupid, drunken ass! It's the end of it, you know."

"How do you mean?"

"It isn't his to lose. He owes every dime of it."

"Come on! He's leaving the table."

Shannard was plodding toward the cashiers' cage, planting his feet very firmly and carefully, as though the floor were tilted.

They caught him twenty feet from his destination. "Dearest, do come up to bed now," Vicky said, standing directly in his way.

"Ganging up on me," Shannard said.

"It's a mug's game, darling. They're licensed to steal from you."

"You aren't in good shape, Temp," Hugh said. "Try tomorrow when you're rested up."

Shannard turned his head slowly to stare at Hugh with a puzzling look of mockery. "Sobered up, you mean, old pal."

"That's an idea too."

He glowered at the two of them. "You kids don't get the picture. Been a gambler all my life. Gambled on everything I ever did. So when it goes sour you got to fight it, see? You got to get in there and slug. You got to turn it back your way . . . or you're lost. That's what I'm doing. I'm standing toe to toe with it, kids. I'm fighting it."

"Temp, please. Actually, you're too stinking drunk even to know what you're saying," Vicky said.

He pushed her out of the way with one wide sweep of his arm. Had Hugh not caught her, she would have fallen.

"You don't get anywhere talking, I guess," Max Hanes said, smiling at them.

"You're a completely poisonous type," Vicky said coldly.

Max merely widened his grin. "You do the duchess bit pretty good, chick. Where'd you learn it?"

"Good night, Hugh," Vicky said. "Thanks for trying to help. Sorry I disturbed you for nothing."

She disappeared swiftly into the crowd, heading in the direction of the lobby. "That's a type broad I can appreciate," Max said with surprising warmth. "Just as mean as a damn snake. You can't cross up a broad like that. She'll beat you to it every time."

"Max, as a favor to an acquaintance . . . I won't pose as a friend . . . will you cut him off at fifty thousand?"

"It would make me unpopular with Al, Hugh. Al says he's good for a hundred."

"What about being unpopular with me, Max?"

"What the hell can you do?"

"Just stand still and think for a minute. Think of all the things I can do that'll make your operation a little bit tougher to handle, and won't be so obvious they'll get rid of me. And after you've listed all the things you can think of, multiply by three, because I sure as hell can think of three times as many as you can, if you give me this kind of a reason."

Max met his level stare for several seconds. "And I could frame you right out of the best job you've ever had, kid."

"And give yourself a chance to work with another bum like Jerry."

"You and me, we can get along. But don't push me."

"Then don't bitch up my friends."

"So maybe he takes his business somewhere else."

"It's the play right here I'm concerned about, Max."

Max knuckled him painfully in the ribs. "You know, Hughie, I think you got more working for you than I figured. If he keeps on losing, I'll cut him off at seventy-five."

"Sixty, Max."

"So let's settle for sixty-five, and I don't think he'll last to go that deep anyhow. The new limit is good only for tonight. That's the best deal you get, and I could have swore you weren't going to get yourself any kind of deal at all."

As Hugh was leaving the casino, Ben Brown moved over to stand beside Max Hanes. "That's one boy scout gives me a quick sharp pain," Brown said.

"Don't fault that boy. How much did Shannard take?"

"Another ten."

"Tell Ritchie to cut him off at sixty-five."

"But I thought you said Al said it was okay to go to. . . ."

"If I want a conversation I'll go on television."

"Okay, Max. Jeez, you're touchy lately."

"How does that goddam Gallowell stand now?"

"Just the same as he did at eight o'clock. He's still into us for one twenty-five. The dice have been too cold to give him another chance. Dom says a couple of shooters have made seven passes, but that old bastard is like a machine. You'd think he'd get impatient, wouldn't you?"

Max looked at him with contempt. "That old bastard started out at fourteen with a bedroll and a twenty-dollar horse. And I should have remembered that. He didn't pile it up as high as he did by getting impatient."

One of the floor men drifted up, whispered something to Ben Brown and moved on.

"Now it's one fifty, Max," Ben said. "The shooter rolled boxcars, so it was a standoff, and then he came back with a six he couldn't make."

"Oh, fine!"

"That old bastard is making a good bruise."

"Why do you talk so goddam much lately? Get away from me! Wait a minute! Get me that Dawson broad. I want to see her in my office right now."

Brown looked blankly astonished. "You mean you think that old. . . . Okay, okay, Max. I didn't say a word."

• • • seven

AT A LITTLE AFTER TEN O'CLOCK ON THAT SAME SUNDAY night, Betty Dawson had finished her dinner and was dawdling over her coffee, alone at a table for two in the coffee shop. She took out the letter that had come on Saturday from her father, Dr. Randolph Dawson of San Francisco, to read it again. Slowly, tentatively, in their own careful ways they had been mending the rift caused by the years with Jackie Luster.

Since she had had her own single he had come down to Las Vegas three times to visit her. He had given advance warning each time, and Max had been very decent about approving less revealing costumes and somewhat milder songs. And the staff in the Afrique Bar, alerted to the situation and understanding it, had been quick to intercept the infrequent drunk, and to explain to her special fans why she couldn't sit with them and why some of their requests had been ignored.

He was a widower, a G.P. with a large tiring practice. He still lived and had his office in the old house on the quiet street where she had grown up, and he was still cared for by Charlie and Lottie Mead, who had come to work for him when Betty was an infant. Nurses and receptionists came and went, but the Meads stayed on forever.

She had long since given up the barren exercise of wondering how it had been possible for her to hurt him so cruelly. But she had done it, and it was something she would have to live with, and the only sensible objective now was to do everything possible to heal that ancient wound and cause no fresh ones. She wrote regularly and phoned him at least once a week, and flew up to stay a day or so with him whenever it was possible.

His script had a legibility foreign to most doctors. She turned to the last page of his letter, to that part which made her uncomfortable. There was never a letter that did not contain the old question she could not answer.

"Tonight, my dear, I have once again found myself wondering why you give every evidence of remaining in that, to me, alarming community forever. As you know, I have made my reluctant adjustment to the curious fact that my only child is irrevocably established as a public entertainer. But when I peruse the newspapers here, I see that there are many places in this much more satisfactory city where you could exercise your talent. And certainly, if you lived here as I hope you would, you could make enough money to satisfy your strong desire for independence. I cannot help but feel that you are surrounded by altogether too many cheap and superficial people. I guess you would run into the same types in the night life of this community, but they certainly would not form as large a percentage of the total population. I am exempting from this indictment your Mr. Darren, who seems to have insinuated himself into both your correspondence and your telephone conversations of late. I look forward to meeting this young man.

"At the risk of imposing my talent for sentimentality upon you, I must tell you that I keep remembering you are in your twenty-seventh year. Your mother and I were married thirteen

111

years before you were born. I am now sixty-two, and reasonably sound of wind and limb, but I have a senile anxiety to become acquainted with my unborn grandchildren. If I have not misjudged the importance of this young man to you, could you not, in the immemorial way of woman, bring him rapidly to a point of decision which might gratify my wishes?

"Enough of complaint. I should be so grateful that we are once again close, after those bad years, that I would have the sense to leave well enough alone, I suppose. Things move along here with relatively little change. Charlie insists he will paint the house himself when the weather improves. We are now bickering about color. Have you any ideas I can use to silence his yearning for a rather virulent yellow? Dr. Wellborn continues to work out quite well, but somehow the arrangement does not give me the fragments of leisure I had anticipated. I suspect him of feeling some juvenile obligation to humor me. Take good care of yourself, my dear. Your hours of work and your environment could easily break the constitution of an ox. But you keep telling me you are accustomed to it. Under separate cover I am mailing you a new vitamin complex which has shown good results among my more debilitated patients. In all fairness I must credit David Wellborn for bringing these pills to my attention.

"Sometimes when I awaken toward dawn and the entire world seems hushed, I suddenly realize where you are and what you are doing. I realize that the unending noise of that place is affronting your ears, and it seems difficult to believe."

She folded the letter and put it back in her purse. There was no way, of course, to answer that last page, because the only answer was the truth, and the truth was nicely calculated to kill him. So I take refuge in pretending a fondness for this life that I have never felt.

I would like to go home, but I can't. I put myself in eternal hock to a horror named Max Hanes, father dear, and he won't let me go because I seem to be useful from time to time. But, because of Hugh, it is not as bad as it used to be. You wouldn't approve of the relationship, but it is all I am permitted to have, so I have taken it in such a way that the only person who will be hurt is me. And that is careful justice indeed.

"Max wants to see you in his office right away."

She started violently and looked up into the monochromatic face of Ben Brown.

"What's a matter with you, Dawson? Were you asleep?"

"Run along, little man. Consider your message delivered."

"He said right away."

"If he raises the question, I'll quote you word for word."

"He's ugly all day, like a goddam bear. I'm warning you."

She finished her coffee without haste, signed her dinner tab and went to Max's office.

"Siddown, cutie. Buy you a drink?"

"No thanks, Max. You're being very gracious and charming in the inimitable Max Hanes manner. Ben said you had the gritty uglies."

"For him I got them. Not for you. Never for you, sugar."

"Let me just say I'm underwhelmed, Max."

"The reason I wanted to see you, I got to toss you to a mark again, and this one can be tough."

"Max, for God's sake, think of some other way. Think of somebody else this time. Please."

"Now excuse me for saying I know the reason why you're dragging your feet. I know the whole deal with you and Darren. It's very sweet and very touching, but it isn't something that's going to get in my way, and I'm not going to let it get in your way either."

"Why don't you sell that spy system to the Russians?"

"There's no reason in the world why he should have to know a thing about it. What he doesn't know won't hurt him."

"Max, I won't do it. I just won't do it."

He leaned back and laced his thick fingers across his broad stomach and shook his head in a sorrowful way. "How many times has it been? Only twice, not counting the first time. You didn't put up this fuss the first time, cutie."

"That's when I should have. I was sick and broke and desperate, and you knew just how to put the squeeze on me, didn't you?"

"You were glad to help out, sweetie. You scratched my back so I'd scratch yours. And I did, didn't I? You've been living fat, dumb and happy ever since."

"Oh, yes, I've been deliriously happy, Max. Unspeakably content."

"So the other two times I get this same jazz—No, Max, I won't do it. And then I have to get rough with you, and it's such a damn waste of time. Okay, I'll go through the routine, if that's what you want. I've got over twenty minutes of sixteen millimeter black and white, in perfect focus. The first time you raised a fuss I tried to run the film for you to prove I had it, and you only took three minutes of it before you threw up. So, like I told you with that kraut from St. Louis and that spic from Venezuela, I own you, pretty Betty. The day after you cross me in any way by either taking off without warning or refusing to do any little favor, a special messenger delivers ten juicy minutes of that film strip to your old man and tells him to rent a projector and watch the fun."

"I guess I like to hear myself say I won't do it," she said wearily. "Lesson one—how to tame a whore."

"That's your word, cutie, not mine. I don't tell you the approach, do I? I don't care if you spend your time singing hymns to him. All I care about is he gets to like the town so well he can't leave. So he stays and gambles some more and gives us our money back, and he does his gambling right here."

"It just seems to come out the other way, Max. In some mysterious fashion."

Max put his heavy arms on the desk and glowered at her. "Honest to God, it's easy to get annoyed at you, Betty. You'd think I was using you in some stupid way. I don't ask a hell of a lot of you. If I was real dumb I could be asking you to take care of my friends when they come to town. And I could use you on those guys who have a run of small-time luck and try to walk away with twenty or thirty grand. But for jobs like that, I can hire any number of hundred-dollar broads. If I put you to work too often, it would show on you, kid."

"Gee! Thanks a lot."

"That spic got into us a year ago and. . ."

"Ten months."

"Okay, so it was almost a year. You're special, kid, so the way I see it, the smartest thing I can do is save you for special deals, the big ones. It puts them off guard, you being an entertainer. They don't figure it's a setup. And best of all, you don't look and act like you'd shill for the house."

"Thanks again. All these compliments are going to my head."

"I've used you just three times, cutie, and you've brought better than three hundred grand back into the vault. And in the process you've made yourself twelve thousand in bonuses, right?"

"Oh, I'm a very well-paid whore, Max. I can't object to the rates. But if you won't let me retire, what's the good of having a bank account?"

"Can't you relax?" he pleaded. "Can't you stop being snotty one time?"

"Do you want me to pretend I'm enjoying this? I despise you, Max, and I despise myself. And this time it's going to. . . spoil something very precious to me."

"How can it, if he doesn't find out?"

"It would be impossible to explain that to you, I am sure."

"What the hell is the use of arguing with a broad? The way it looks, it ought to take shape by tomorrow, kid. So take tonight off. I've got a fill-in for your shows. Move some of your stuff over to Playhouse 190 tonight."

"Does it have to be. . . ."

"Shut up and listen once. I'm *telling* you what you're going to do. Then you come back and stay in your room where I can get hold of you fast. And you're a very smart girl, so you can spend your time dreaming up an approach that'll work."

"And just who is the lucky, lucky fellow?"

"Homer G. Gallowell. A buddy of yours, I believe."

She stared at him. "Max, you are out of your mind! Believe me, you are completely out of your mind!"

"How do you mean?"

"It's just. . .too grotesque to think there is any way in the world I could influence that old man. The others were fools. That old man is tough-minded, Max. He's shrewd."

"When they get real old, they get real young ideas."

"Not Homer. Believe me, not Homer. I think he likes me because I don't bow and scrape. But at the first hint, the very first hint that he was being jobbed in any way. . .he'll be gone like the wind."

"Then it's up to you to make it look good, isn't it?"

"I'm not that clever, Max."

"Me, I say you can be awful goddam clever when you've got enough motive. You don't want a piece of that movie delivered to your daddy, do you? And you don't want me asking Darren back here for a private showing either, do you?"

"You enjoy every minute of this, don't you?"

"Listen, I don't understand why the fuss. All I'm telling you to do is try. I don't care what you try or how you try it. That's your business. I just want you to work that old guy into a mood where he wants to hang around and keep trying his luck. Why this big fuss all the time? You'd think I was asking you to kill somebody. What does it cost you, anyway? Just a little time. You put on an act. That's all. When it's over—win or lose—forget it."

"How nice! How easy! Just forget it. My God!"

"The way you're sitting, you ought to be the world's happiest broad."

"That's why I keep laughing all the time, Max."

"The playhouse is empty, baby. Take along enough stuff to give it that homey look."

115

"I'll take my needlework."

"You know, an old guy like that might dig the sewing bit pretty good."

"Skip it, Max."

"Don't get shy, baby. Those guys have seen so much there's nothing you could do they won't yawn at, believe me. It's like they were doctors. Take your stuff over there, then stay in your room until I clue you in. Okay?"

"Whatever I try isn't going to work."

"With this kind of money, anything is worth trying, Betty baby." And, winking at her, he handed her the key to Unit 190 in the Playland Motel.

She packed a suitcase, drove three miles back toward town, and out to the Playland. She felt a gray and hopeless lassitude, a familiar sickness of the soul. It was one of the glossiest motels in Las Vegas. The night lighting was expensive and dramatic. There were wide stretches of asphalt, lush planting areas, small fountains and rock gardens. Privacy was achieved by the placement of the luxury units, by the opaque ceiling-to-floor draperies across the window walls, by plantings and soundproofings—and also by that special and insidious anonymity of all wide-open cities everywhere. Playland even had its own small cocktail lounge and casino, and a full supply of foul-mouthed comedians.

She parked by the door of 190 and carried her suitcase in, found the familiar light switches, and unpacked with a numbed efficiency, settling herself in. She looked around, trying to be objective about the place. It was a most pleasant room, actually, and very large. Large enough for the big bed and the divans and the upholstered chairs and the small bar and the baby grand and all the draperied windows without looking cramped, without losing that upholstered spaciousness that coarse pieces of money can buy.

She checked the liquor supply, the towels and linens, the ice supply in the kitchen alcove, and the piano to see if it was in tune, knowing it would be.

She lit a cigarette and stood, her shoulders hunched, elbow in her palm, her face dulled and unhappy, looking at nothing, thinking, this is where they installed the button. They operate without anaesthesia. And once you're wired, girl, everything is easy. All they have to do is press the button, and you jump up and salute. And all you have to do is save your money and invest it wisely, because when you are at last too old and too broken down for their fun and games, they'll cut you loose, and the old lady will need a retirement income.

116

But I was so acutely, astonishingly innocent. I can think of that girl and cry.

Over two and a half years ago, after Jackie Luster had made his deathless statement, "Who needs you?" she had worked up her single, and, with the tireless and loyal and intelligent help of little Andy Gideon, the nervous agent, she had polished it and rehearsed it until they were both satisfied it was time to try to book it. Andy had set up the audition with Max Hanes. Max knew, of course, that she had been with Jackie Luster and he had cut her loose. She remembered Max's completely impassive way of listening to her routines, and she remembered she had thought him an almost comically sinister type. Bald shining head, clumsy powerful torso, squatty little legs, face half ape and half Mongol, diamonds agleam amid the flashiness of his kollege-kut klothing—he seemed more a triumph of type casting than an actual casino manager. His air of complete indifference had nearly broken Andy Gideon's heart.

But two days later Max had had her called to the phone at Mabel's Comfort Motel. "I wanna talk to you, Dawson, and I'm sending a guy to bring you over here. He'll be there in ten minutes, so be ready."

"But if you want to talk about a booking, Mr. Hanes, my agent should be there too, don't you think?"

"Have I said anything about signing anything? It hasn't got to that stage yet, honey. I just want to talk to you."

She dressed in her hasty best and was taken to Max's office. "Siddown, Dawson. Since I caught your act I've been thinking maybe it would be a good thing for us to take on something like what you've got for a fill-in on a long-term sort of deal. I mean you've got a lot of material right now, and so it wouldn't be like people getting tired because they heard the same old stuff before."

"I can keep changing it, too."

"You're built good and showing that off as much as we can won't hurt anybody, and you got a good-looking face, and I don't figure you'd be against circulating around, sitting with the marks and talking up a storm."

"Thank you, kind sir."

"It would be a hell of a lot less pay than you're going to ask for, but we'd throw in the room and meals right here in the hotel. But we can talk about that when you got your agent with you, if it gets to that point. Right now I want to arrange some good way for you to audition for some of the owners. If it was just a case of booking you in for six weeks or eight weeks, I could go right ahead with it, but I got to check my idea out with them. I'd want to put you on late in the Afrique Bar, with the idea of getting the locals in the habit so they say before they go home, 'Let's go over to the Cameroon and catch Betty Dawson.' You see what I mean? We'd promote you that way."

"It sounds good."

"I want Al Marta to hear you someplace where he can sit down and really listen, without interruptions. He's got a sort of interest in the Playland Motel, and there's a good room there empty now with a piano in it. So what I want you should do is move in out there for a few days and that'll give me a good place to bring people around to hear you and check me on my thinking."

She remembered that she had felt wary and had said, "Why don't you just phone me where I am and I can go over there any time?"

"I maybe won't get enough warning when these people can take a little time off, and we can't do it here because there's something going on here all the time. So would it hurt you to cooperate a little? I can tell you're thinking there's some kind of an angle on this, and maybe I'm setting you up for a playmate. You see this phone right here? I can pick it up and I can order me an absolute dead ringer for Liz Taylor or Marilyn Monroe any time I feel like it, at no direct expense to me whatever, and neither of them can play the piano. And so who cares?"

"All right, Mr. Hanes. When do I move in?"

"As soon as you can, kid. Here's the key. Number 190. It's way in the back of the place. You drive right through to the back and you'll see the number."

And so, vibrant with new hope after the dirty months of insecurity and panic, she had moved into 190, in a dancing way, laughing at herself in the mirrors, pleasured by the return of confidence, running sparkles of music off the keys of the piano. And for forty hours there was no contact. She was having her meals sent in. Some arrangement must have been established, because they would not take her money for the meals. The few motel-staff people she saw seemed very remote and unfriendly, and had she tried to classify their attitude toward her, she would have seen it was one of ironic, understanding contempt. She phoned Max Hanes and he told her with annoyance and impatience to sit tight.

Max phoned her back the next evening at seven and said he and Al Marta would be over later on. She spent two hours on her appearance, getting more and more nervous, before they arrived. There were three of them. Max Hanes, Al Marta, and a man named Riggs Telfert. She knew Al Marta by sight, but she had never before been introduced. He had been pointed out to her one night at the Mozambique. Riggs Telfert was a great, raw-boned, laughing man of about forty in expensive and beautifully tailored clothing which he wore with considerable assurance in spite of his piney-woods cracker twang, his big red wedge of ugly face, and his joyous, boisterous, and completely innocent air of a man having the most wonderful time of his life.

Riggs Telfert, when they were introduced, held her hand in his far too long, oblivious of her futile attempts to get it back, beaming at her with great approval as he said, "It's the Telferts from the Florida cattle country, ma'am. God knows there's enough of us now, the way we been breedin' ever since great-grandpappy moved on down from Bell County, Georgia, and grabbed hold of the biggest piece of nothin'-type swampy old land you could lay an eye on, and raised scrub cattle onto it, doin' no good at all 'til they got those tics licked by dippin' and fencin' some thirty year back. Since then, believe me truly, ma'am, all us Telferts have been livin' as high off the hog as we could reach to bite."

She backed away from him and said, "My goodness!"

Al hastily explained that if they were going to audition new talent for the Cameroon, it was only fair to bring along one of the favorite guests of the hotel, and Riggs Telfert was certainly one of his favorite people.

"I'm lovable clear through," Riggs bawled at her. "I hope you dance some, because I love to watch a beautiful woman dancin', Miss Dawson."

She had the curious feeling that if he insisted she dance, she would have to change her act. There was an uncanny force about the man, a purpose and power that was simultaneously fascinating and repelling. She recognized it as the rare impact of undiluted masculinity. He had made an erotic and a frightening appeal, which made her feel like a Sabine woman who suddenly knew she wasn't going to be able to run fast enough. And, in some strange way, the trio made her think of an animal act she had seen long ago, where two visibly apprehensive men guided, in a gingerly way, a huge, amiable, cream-colored bear into a carnival ring and made him dance. To the small girl she had been at the time, the bear seemed to be enjoying it hugely, and she could not understand why his two trainers were not having a good time too, instead of sweating and skulking around.

She tried to help Max put the three chairs in the place that seemed best, but Riggs Telfert would not let her try to move a chair by herself. She fixed the lighting the way she had planned it, sat at the piano, smiled at them broadly, winked, and chorded her way into her first number.

Riggs Telfert made her continue long after it became difficult for Max Hanes and Al Marta to conceal their growing boredom. After each number he banged his big palms together with the sound of pistols. He chuckled and roared at the lines, and kept time by thumping his heel and slapping his thigh.

"And that," she finally said, firmly, "is the end of the show, gentlemen."

Telfert stood up and said, "Al, by God, iff'n you don't hire this little gal to sing in your hotel, I swear you'll never get me or anybody I know back into your place ever again. And I mean that sure as I can see that bottle of bourbon settin' right over there, which I'm about to pour me some more of. And you pay her good, too, hear?"

"I'm sold, Max," Al Marta said. "We can use you, Betty."

"Thanks, Mr. Marta."

Al beamed at her and said, "Step on out to the car with Max a minute, honey. There's an option out there we want your signature on."

"But. . . ."

She had no chance to say more as Max took her by the arm and walked her out into the night. He walked her ten feet, whirled her around and pushed her back against the wall of the building.

"What the hell are you trying to . . ."

"Shut up and listen. We haven't got much time, kid. Get the picture first. This is about his fourth trip here. He and a bunch of his cracker pals come over in a chartered plane. They usually contribute. They get the red carpet. He's been here a week. They leave tomorrow morning. He's had one hell of a run of luck. That jackass has over a hundred and sixty thousand of casino money."

"What has that got to do with me?"

"You want the job, don't you?"

"Yes, but. . . ."

"He took a shine to you, kid. Now it's your move. I want you to change his mind about leaving so fast. You can do it."

"Now *wait* a minute!"

"There's no time for pretty talk, baby. Make the move
120

after we go back in so that he stays and we go. And you walk back in there smiling."

"I'm not going to. . . ."

"If you do it right, if you get him back to the hotel after his pals are gone, he'll feed the money right back, and you'll get a nice cash bonus, and you'll get the job you need so damn bad you can taste it. Shut up and listen. If you don't want to do this little favor, honey, I can guarantee that in one day I can fix it so you'll *never* get a job in Vegas, and in four days there won't be a joint in the country that'll book you. And to make it a little more convincing, I can have a couple of boys pick you up off the street and take you out in the desert and give you a face you can't tell from a runover jackrabbit. You're in the big bind, kid, and you're going to have to play it our way. What the hell is it to you, anyway? He isn't a bad guy, for that kind of a guy. What's it costing you? Have fun."

She stood there with her back against the wall. It was still faintly warm from the heat of the day. She could feel the heat against her bare shoulders. Max Hanes was in silhouette against floodlighted shrubbery fifty feet away.

What the hell is it to me, anyway? she asked herself. What's left of me that's so terribly terribly special—after Jackie and his fat friend? Who needs me? What am I saving, and who am I saving it for?

"How much bonus?" she asked in a dead voice.

He squeezed her arm and said, "Now you're using your head, girl. Two per cent of what he gives back."

"Suppose . . . no matter what I do . . . he leaves with his friends."

"Then we can't blame you, can we? It's a business proposition. You do your best . . . you get the job, whatever."

"But if this sort of thing is going to be part of the job, maybe it's a job I don't want, Mr. Hanes."

"Call me Max, cutie. Who said it would be part of the job? This is like an emergency. He just didn't like any of the gals who usually help me out. It would probably never happen again."

"So now I'll walk back in. Smiling," she said.

She went back in. They all had another drink. She said she had a few more songs she hadn't done. Al looked at his watch and said he had to get back. Max said, "I got to go along too, but that's no reason you got to shove off, Riggs. Look, you listen to the songs and before you leave in the morning, write a note and leave it for me, telling me which ones you like best. It'll be a help. I'll appreciate it. I think you've got a good eye for talent, Riggs."

So then she was alone with him. The bargain had been made. He began the traditional pursuit. She saw that this was a man who would place a low value on anything that came too easily to him, and so she smiled and laughed and evaded him, coldly pacing the tempo of this obligatory affair. When she saw that she might not be able to handle him, she insisted that they go out, and they went by taxi to small places she knew, with that ageless combat between them becoming ever more intense as they sat close together in quiet places—he telling her all the reasons why she should, and she giving him all the reasons why she could not. He talked with great sentiment of his ranch lands, his kids, and with weariness of his socialite wife and her continual disapproval of his habits and his friends, but who dearly enjoyed spending his money.

She sensed the times when he was thinking of abandoning the whole thing, and chose those times to nourish his faltering hopes. When it was the edge of dawn, she made the sounds of sweet and unmistakable surrender, attributing it, of course, to his charm. She sat in another taxi outside the Cameroon while he went in and left a note at the desk for his friends, telling them to take off without him. They went back to Unit 190, the Playland Motel.

They were together five days and five nights before he flew back to Florida. His winnings, by the time he left, had dwindled to a little less than twenty thousand dollars. The loss annoyed him, but he had explained with his unshakable exuberance that he had turned so lucky in love all of a sudden the other kind of luck naturally had to go a little bad for him.

For Betty Dawson it was like taking the lead in a long and rather monotonous play where all her lines had to be ad libbed. She had soon learned everything was a lot more endurable if she stayed a little bit drunk. There was no emotional involvement with him. Yet she had to pretend an emotional involvement, and she learned the cynic's truth, that it was easier to keep him contented through pretense than it would have been had she been sincere. So she faked her way through the hundred and twenty hazy hours of Riggs Telfert, bemused by her own ability to delight him with lines she took out of the grab bag of her mind, lines from old songs, old movies, old plays. She stood flankwarm against him by the rail of the gaming table, telling him his luck was good while she watched it go bad.

Had she been able to fake her way through every aspect of it, drinking herself close to the edge of control, mouthing tritenesses spiced with fond smiles that made her lips feel stiff and forced, perhaps she would have been able to convince herself that she had gone through all of it without being touched or reached in any significant way.

But his virility was a dark persuasion she could not resist. She tried but could not hold herself apart from that, succumbing each time more readily to a tumultuous reality that crumbled the walls of her pretending. It was a loss of self, like a drug that she took in a mood of defiance, using it in massive doses to get even with a world that could contain Jackie, the fat man and Max Hanes. The drug took her far back into the wastelands of sensation where she became a mindless wanderer, blinded, used, only vaguely aware of her own acts and devices.

Telfert, who treated her with a grave, sweet, measured courtesy in all small things, the light poised for her cigarette, the chair held, the door opened, the wrap gentled onto her shoulders, making her feel treasured and precious, came to her in their pentathlons and decathlons of the flesh with a compulsive, aching, greedy violence which always alarmed and astonished her before, as a result, perhaps, of that violence, she was swept into her own fierce, unwilled responses. He lamed her grievously, collapsed her into athletic exhaustion, and would then return immediately, incongruously, to that attitude of hovering, earnest courtesy which implied she was a precious and delicate vessel, fragile and tender, requiring a manly protection.

And there was, to her, a strange schism in his attitude toward her. No matter how abandoned their love-making had been . . . and he was compulsively addicted to experiment . . . he did not care to make the slightest retrospective allusion to their sport, apparently considering any such reference an indecency in which a gentleman of his stature could not indulge.

On the last evening, she learned—and it made her heartsick—that she could marry him if she wished. He had gone out for a little while in the afternoon alone, creating mystery by being overly casual, and in the evening he gave her what he had bought for her, a pair of antique gold earrings in perfect taste, delicate, set with tiny cabochon emeralds.

He cracked the knuckles of his big hands and looked at

her pleadingly and said, "I don't want it should be like a good-bye forever kind of present to you, Betty. This is something I don't want to give up, honest to God. I want you should give me some little time to kind of switch my life around so you can fit in, and I can come for you or send for you. I mean legal. I guess this is a proposal, kind of, if a man who hasn't cut hisself loose yet has got any right to ask, even."

After she had convinced him, with difficulty, that she preferred her "career" to marriage, he told her about some good ocean land he owned north of Fort Lauderdale, and the good friends he had and the good mortgages he held in Lauderdale. He could build her a good little house on the ocean and make sure she had a good job in one of the clubs in Lauderdale for as long as she wanted it, and that would be a second-best thing, but better than nothing.

After she made him understand that she would not feel right in such an arrangement, he asked her if it was all right if he came back to see her now and then, whenever he could get away, and she had no plausible objection to that.

He never came back, because he went down into the 'Glades after turkey, and in the autumn dusk he was squatting in the brush using a turkey call, and a young attorney in the party thought he was the right size in that half light to be a big wild turkey, and tore his throat away with the first snap shot. Max Hanes showed her the clipping from the Los Angeles paper, a two-inch wire service pickup, and when she was in her bed she cried a little for Betty Dawson and for Riggs Telfert and for everyone's world of what-might-have-been.

After she watched his morning flight take off, she taxied back to Playland, packed her things, left them off at Mabel's Comfort Motel, and took the key to 190 back to Max Hanes.

"Siddown and rest yourself, cutie. Now that wasn't so bad, was it?"

"It was just as easy as cutting your own throat, Max," she said, pleased that she had selected the attitude which gave her the greatest feeling of protection. Bitter, brittle, ironic. The hardcase broad. Jackie Luster had been the rest of her college education. His fat buddy had been graduate school. Riggs Telfert had been her first formal employment based on her educational record.

"You and me, we can get along, Dawson. You got to understand I could give you a very short end, but that would be stupid and I didn't get where I am being stupid."

"Your record of success should be an inspiration to every American boy."

"People you are going to work with, there has got to be fair play. You take fair play and a few laughs and the money coming in, and what more is there in life? This here is for you."

She opened the envelope and looked at the packet of bills and saw they were hundreds, and put the envelope in her purse. "Thank you, kind sir."

"Don't you want to count them?"

"I'll get around to it later in the day."

"There's thirty-five of them in there. Thirty-five bills, kid. It's more than I agreed and more than I had to give you. Right?"

"Right!"

"Would it for chrissake hurt you to smile once? Maybe I don't have to tell you this, but don't go depositing that money in an account. It's off the top, so it isn't reported from this end. Maybe you'd get away with it, but if you run into a spot-check audit, then there's a fraud rap for failure to report income, because they check out bank deposits. What you do, you put it in a lock box, and then if you want to take a risk of feeding it into a checking account a little at a time so you can live better, that's your risk. But the safest deal is spend it for fun things, in cash. They can't trace that."

"Tax evasion, hey? My next step in a life of crime."

"I'm telling you, don't declare it, baby. If you do, I don't know where the hell you got it. It didn't come from me. I can prove that by the auditors."

"The job, Max. The job. When do I go to work?"

"Soon, cutie. I got to do some shifting around. I'll get hold of you."

"This wouldn't be a brush off, Max? It better not be."

"You're too suspicious, kid. You're going to work here. You can bank on that."

She paid Mabel Huss her back rent. She bought some pretty new clothes. She bought the little Morris Minor off a used-car lot, for cash. She told herself quite firmly that it had turned out to be a different world than she had been led to believe it was, and so she had made a logical and rational adjustment to the state of things-as-they-are, and given up any juvenile wistfulness about the-way-things-should-be. She had been running full tilt into a wall and knocking herself down. So they had noticed her and opened a doorway in the wall and she had walked through and gravely accepted their brass ring, good for another ride, her order of merit.

She had to adjust to the stranger she had suddenly become. She decided that if you have built a structure in your mind and it comes tumbling down, you are under no obligation to rebuild it. You can merely cart the debris away, smooth off the area and keep it carefully swept. In that way you avoid the danger of having something else collapse on you. And it is quite neat.

She had to overcome the nagging suspicion that she had changed in some visible way. Men seemed to regard her with a more knowing interest. Did her hips swing with a new provocative arrogance when she walked down a street? Was there a sluttish contour to her lips? Had the line of her breasts become coarsely obtrusive? There was a B.T. world, (before Telfert) and an A.T. world, and she watched her friends narrowly, almost hoping to detect any slightest flavor of knowing contempt.

But she finally, in her honesty, found her friends unchanged. She caught unexpected glimpses of herself in mirrors and store windows, and was reassured. She knew that the changes in her, and they were unavoidable, were subjective changes. She was drinking a little bit more than was her habit. She, who had always appreciated the restorative effects of being alone, went to rather absurd lengths to avoid being alone. At night she slept long and heavy and awakened unrefreshed.

Max called her in at the end of a week. "You'll start two weeks from tomorrow, cutie, on the midnight to six. Four shows a night. They'll have a room in the house you can move into next week. The room will be free, and you'll sign for all meals and drinks, and we'll stake you to the kind of outfits I want you wearing for the act, and pay you a hundred fifty a week."

"I don't know if Andy will let me take that kind of money."

"Add the value of the room and food and it's far enough over minimum scale so there's no union squawk, and there'll be no squawk from you, kid."

"How can you tell that?"

"I can tell because I got a pretty good idea of the kind of gal you are, Dawson, and because you had a tour of duty in Playhouse 190."

She stared at him, wondering at the subconscious warning

126

that had suddenly turned her mouth dry. "What . . . what does that mean?"

"It means that Al Marta, through X-Sell Associates, has got his thumb in a hell of a lot of pies. There's some little unions, laundry workers and so on over into Arizona, and there's some trade associations that're into this and that, and in lots of cases Al's people can make things run a lot smoother if there's ways to put on pressure. Not the old-fashioned kind, like you bust a few arms, even though that can still be arranged, but the modern kind. Social pressure, Al calls it. One of the corporations operating out of the X-Sell offices downtown owns that Playland Motel, so when it was expanded a while back, they brought in the experts. You want to use modern methods, you get the experts. That whole unit in the back was designed for that special purpose, kid. You know, it really knocks me out the things they can do. Two-way mirrors, special lighting, concealed camera ports, superfast film. You know, they've got that playhouse bugged with induction mikes that can pick up a whisper from twenty feet, and they can amplify it loud enough to blow your head off. Al uses it twenty-thirty times a year, but even if it was only three times it would have paid itself out. There's a hundred-thousand nut just in the electronics in that place, kid."

She tried to moisten her lips. She had that feeling of remoteness which precedes fainting. "I don't . . . understand."

"Why we should have used it this time? Not because of you, baby. You're like incidental. The way Al explained, there's land operations in Florida, and that Telfert has pretty good holdings. Maybe some day there's some deal that he might want to block, and then they got a print of the film and they got a copy of the tape in the vault in Miami, and he all of a sudden gets cooperative. It's like insurance."

"The film?" she said in a fainting voice.

He stood up. "Come on back here, kid. I had Brownie set it up on the projector for me. I figured you'd want a quick look. It's all sixteen-millimeter black and white, and this is edited down to take out all the dull stuff."

She followed him into a small room behind his office, shut the door behind her at his suggestion. A projector squatted on a low table, aiming at a wall a little over six feet away.

He checked the projector, clicked it on. "There's no sound on this print. Sometimes they dub it on from the tape, but it's expensive. Click off that light behind you, kid, and I'll get this thing adjusted down sharp."

She turned off the light. The bright square on the wall came into focus. She looked through a window at the grotesqueness of her shame, stood with ice forming around her heart and looked down from a high place upon the ultimate catalogue of dishonor. Max's casual voice came from far away, barely audible over a roaring in her ears and the dutiful whirr of the projector.

"The air conditioning in that place is just a little bit noisy on purpose to cover up any camera shutter sound, kid. That guy on the camera is a real artist, you got to admit. That's a zoom lens he uses to come in for the close-ups and then back away again. You need a lot of close-ups to make sure of identification, so you can tell it wasn't faked in any way. He worked in Hollywood and got canned on a narcotics thing. By God, that Telfert is all man, isn't he? Baby, one thing you don't have to ever worry about is anybody peddling these for the smoker trade. I'm not saying they wouldn't go over pretty good, but this is a confidential deal, and no prints ever get out of our hands unless the parties involved cross us up, and then who would blame us for making the extra buck? Now on this next part the camera is shooting from a different location and the lighting isn't quite so good, but it's. . . ."

Without warning the heavy saliva ran into her mouth. Her throat filled and she bent over and, clinging to a chair with one hand for support, she vomited endlessly, agonizingly, onto the unseen rug. Max cut the projector, turned on the light and showed her to his private lavatory.

When she was alone, trying to clean herself up, the reel began to run against a wall in the back of her mind and she was sick again. It was a long time before she felt strong enough to come out. She gave herself a last look in the mirror. Her face looked gaunted and yellow-gray, and she could not bring herself to look into her own eyes.

"You look pretty raunchy, honey. You better sit down."

"No thanks," she said in a toneless voice.

"I didn't know it would get you that bad, kid."

"Who . . . who else has seen it?"

"Just me and Al and the guys in the lab. And the two guys on duty while you were at 190. That's all. I'm leveling with you, Dawson. It wouldn't do us any good to show it around. I'd figure that would be a dirty trick."

"A dirty trick," she echoed, unable to comprehend this code of behavior.

"But just keep one thing clear. I own you, Dawson. You

take the job I offer at the price I offer. And if I tell you to jump over the hotel, I want to see you out there trying as hard as you can until I decide to tell you to stop."

He came around his desk and moved close to her. "I'll be easy to get along with, but the first time you ever cross me up, I'll clip the best ten minutes out of that film strip and see they're delivered to that doctor daddy of yours in San Francisco. Have you got the whole picture now?"

She made a strangled sound of assent, turned and fumbled the door open and fled through the casino, aware that people were looking at her in a startled way. Once she was out in the incomprehensible sunshine she discovered that tears were running down her face, and she had bitten her underlip until it was bleeding.

Back in her dingy room in Mabel's Comfort Motel, motionless on the sagging bed, she accepted the fact she would have to kill herself. No matter how she tried to solve the equation, it always came out the same way. She spent two days in bed, unable to eat, unable to go out into the world, unable to answer Mabel's cautious worried questions.

And then Mabel Huss, ignoring her protests, took her out into the desert to the absolute solitude of the stone house.

"I'm leaving you here with this grub," Mabel said. "I'll be after you in a few days. Don't know what's chewing you to pieces. But if there's anyplace you can settle it, it's right here. Soon as I go you'll be finding out there's nobody here but you and God. So get squared off with Him and yourself."

She rattled away in her old car, neither looking back nor waving.

Betty Dawson mended herself in four days—or, more accurately, she adjusted herself to a future of living with what could never be mended. Mabel picked her up after the fifth day. After the first long anxious look, Mabel smiled with relief and approval.

On the way back to town Mabel said, with startling perception, "I guess you found out it's hard to think of anything you can't get along without somehow, except life itself, Elizabeth. If you have to, you can make do without legs, eyesight, freedom or love. People always have, always will."

"You just sort of . . . add up what's left, I guess."

"And keep telling yourself it's important."

"One thing, Mabel, I've got time before I have to go to work to fly home and spend a couple of days with my father. It's overdue."

"It makes a good place to start, Elizabeth."

So you build a new life within the limitations of the irreparable mistake, and do as much with it as you can. You bemuse yourself with the symbols of your own gallantry. You work hard and well at your profession, and you cherish your friends and amuse your acquaintances, and try hard to forget that you are, in the dirtiest sense of the word, on call. Just when you are beginning to wonder if that special mortgage on your soul requires no payments, Max assigns you the problem of the lucky man from St. Louis, a fat foolish man with a streak of slyness in him.

You fight that unsavory assignment, knowing it is a battle you must lose, and this time you have a stony, bitter awareness of the camera eye, and you ease your shame and your dreadful hate by enticing the fat man into those postures of intimacy which will guarantee the most ludicrous and shameful performance on his part. You feel absolutely nothing—no stage fright, no shame, no sensation. Your body is a nerveless dutiful thing you have learned how to despise. It is a gross, flexing thing, suitable only to pleasure fat fools. It takes him but two nights to prove his valor by losing back all his winnings, and a third night to lose an additional forty thousand. When he tried to find reassurance in you, he learns the heavy losses have induced impotence, and so he weeps, helpless, half drunk, rolling his head from side to side, and saying, "Mama, Mama, Mama."

After a year of waiting, and trying not to remember you are waiting, you try to bluff Max out of turning over to you the problem of the lucky Venezuelan. But Max, of course, cannot be bluffed when he knows his hand contains the case ace. At least, this time, they see no reason to record the interlude. But after the Venezuelan has prided himself upon the success of a seduction, he reveals himself in his true sadistic arrogance.

He is a small wiry man, vain, fit and rich, much given to a careful combing of his glossy hair. Once he has convinced himself that you find him irrresistible, he becomes much too free with his small, swift, hard fists, his slaps, his gutter words, his glares of contempt. He has won heavily and now that he is losing with the same rapidity, he becomes frantic, and more cruel—more like a small vicious rooster. You reach the end of endurance a little before all the winnings are gone, and when an offhand blow lands squarely upon a recent bruise, you interrupt his naked, muscle-flexing parade with a full swinging kick that makes him scream like a woman.

When he crawls toward you with simple murder on his face, you flex that solid thigh and you feel the cartilaginous tissues of his nose flatten under the blocky impact of your knee, sickening you. But he still comes on, the eyes staring murder over the ruin of his face, whimpering in his eagerness to be at you, and he is stopped only when you smash the narrow vase against his head and dress in frantic haste, trying not to look toward him, and leave his hotel suite and go directly to Max, because the special problems of a special business are taken directly to the specialist involved.

It turns out that he is not dead. He is painfully, but not even seriously, injured. Max handles everything, quiets everything down with swift efficiency.

Afterward he will not explain how it was so readily handled, but he says, "Anybody knocks you around, you let me know fast. You don't have to take that from any of these clowns, sugar. You're too valuable I should let some mark mess you up. Here's your cut, with a bonus. Take a couple nights off. Go visit your old man or something. Get yourself settled down. We're taking the very best care of you around here, kid."

And so, except for the "assignments," you live in complete celibacy. If the body is to be used in the sly ways of an expensive shill, any dual usage is not to be contemplated. It is an age, indeed, of specialization. It is odd to think that any body, used by so few, could have become so brutally desensitized. Because, after all, there have been only five of them. Jackie was shocked, incredulous and almost frightened to learn you were virgin. And after him you can count only the friend he loaned you to, and Riggs Telfert, and the fat man and the vicious little Venezuelan. The five men in your life. Who else—at twenty-six—had ever accommodated such widely disparate types in a group so small?

And then along came Hugh Darren. Along came love. But when you have gone beyond a certain point, love becomes a luxury you cannot afford. So you fight like a cornered bandit. But what's the harm in being friends? It can't hurt anything, just being friends. Can it? And in a truly inevitable way, friends become lovers. You can only pray he will not notice how soiled is the body you place on this special altar. You pretend you are the clean thing he should have. And you cannot let him know about the love. That has to be hidden. Because, inevitably, it will end, and you elect yourself as the one most deserving hurt.

Keep it a fun thing, a light and gay thing, an extension

131

of friendship, not of the heart. No implications or obligations. Just love him, and keep it to yourself, and relish the wondrous things that happen between the two of you. Pile up the memories in a trunk in the closet of your mind, because after it ends it is going to rain every day for the rest of your life, and it will be nice to have something to look at. You have known, through every moment of love, that it would end when Max Hanes made his next demand. Because, in spite of your greed for Hugh, you cannot sneak Max's dirty task into your emotional schedule, shrug it off and return to Hugh's bed, to his special deftness with you, to that something so far beyond joy it has no word. . . .

She looked, dull-eyed, at the hushed, familiar luxury of Unit 190. This is where love gets killed, she thought. This is where we knock it on the head and kick it under the rug and forget it ever was. And why, with all that I know I'm going to lose, should I still have room to be sorry about losing the good will of that old man from Texas? The others were fools. He is not. There is no possible approach, but Max won't believe me. This would be a very good night to be dead in. Just pull this night up like a blanket and be dead and safe forever.

• • • eight

TEMPLE SHANNARD WAS BROUGHT AWAKE TOO EARLY ON MONday morning, his third morning in the big bed beside Vicky's bed in the glamorous Suite 803 in the Cameroon on the Strip in Las Vegas. He was pulled up out of heavy slumber that was doing him no good, brought rudely into a painful consciousness by the brutal pains in the abused cerebral cortex—pains such as might be caused by a brace and bit being turned slowly into his skull, with exquisitely thin ribbons of bone being pared away by the cutting edge of the drill. He had a thirst so massive he knew he would be unable to satisfy it. He lay for a time with his eyes squeezed shut against the faint morning light in the room, listening to the alarming sound of his heart, and wondering if he was going to throw up. His heart felt like a bowling ball rolling very slowly down a flight of wooden stairs.

He knew he had been drunk, but he did not care to look beyond the requirements of his immediate agony. He had the wary feeling that any sort of retrospection would make him feel considerably more miserable. He clenched his teeth against the agony of sitting up, waited a few minutes, and at last felt able to stand up and pad quietly into the bathroom and close the door.

You are damn near fifty-one years old, Shannard, he told himself, and this is one hell of a stupid thing to do to yourself.

His body felt drab, sour and sticky. He leaned his thighs against the chill of the tiled counter and drank four glasses of water, paused as though listening for something, sidestepped to the toilet, lowered himself to his knees and was extremely ill. Quite a long time later, after trying another glass of water and retaining it, he felt up to taking a shower. As he stood in the harsh roaring of the shower, his eyes closed, larger events tried to work their way into his mind, but he pushed them back, knowing he was not yet ready. He sensed that there would be very little armor he could wear, but he wanted to put on all that was available to him.

On most of the mornings of his life, Temple Shannard had awakened with the conviction that life was an important and wonderful phenomenon. He sensed that it might be a difficult proposition to support on this particular morning.

After more water, he set about shaving with more care than usual. For the sake of his morale, he wanted to give himself a particularly good shave. And, in spite of the tremor of his hands, he was determined not to cut himself.

Just as he finished one long stroke, the outside thought seemed to gather itself and plunge through the wall of his brain and squat triumphantly behind his eyes. THEY WANT TO BUY YOU OUT.

He held the razor quite motionless and stared at his reflection.

YOU'RE TRAPPED, SHANNARD. YOU HAVE TO MOVE FAST. YOU'LL HAVE TO UNLOAD YOUR EQUITY. ONCE YOU'RE SQUARED AWAY, YOU'LL HAVE DAMN LITTLE CASH LEFT.

So, he thought, beginning another measured stroke of the razor, I've had little cash before, and I've made out. I'll take their offer. I'm being squeezed out of a potential fortune, so I'll just have to work twice as hard to worm my way into some more deals. I'll have a little left to start with.

OH, BUT YOU WON'T! YOU LOST IT LAST NIGHT.

133

The shock and the fear struck him with an impact that actually made him lose his physical balance, sent him tottering sideways.

How much?

Maybe I didn't lose at all!

How much did I lose?

He nicked his chin deeply, stanched it with a pasted-on scrap of toilet tissue. He opened the bedroom door cautiously. Vicky still slept. His suit was a heap on the chair. With hands made unsure by his fright and suspense, he went through the pockets and found his small notebook. He had a muddy memory of writing down the amounts of the checks they had cashed so obligingly. He turned slowly to the proper page and saw his own drunken writing, a clumsy, obstinate scrawl, but entirely legible. He added the short column, moving his lips. He added it again and got the same total. Sixty-three thousand dollars.

He looked into his wallet and found a little over a hundred dollars in cash. He went to the bureau and found three fifty-dollar chips among his keys and his pocket change. He walked naked to a deep chair by the draperies that muted the morning light, and sat down, feeling weak and confused and dizzy. He ran totals and balances in his mind. And finally he realized he had inadvertently made himself the victim of an ultimate irony—if he sold to the people Marta had contacted, and if he returned at once to Nassau and sold every other asset he had, including the house and the boat and the car, and applied every dime against his liabilities, he would very probably come out exactly even, exactly broke.

He told himself there was probably some mistake. He couldn't have lost that much. But he knew he had. And every time the figure floated into his mind, bloated and obscene, the sweat broke out on his body.

Vicky turned and sighed in her sleep and nestled down again. He felt a need to be closer to her. He went over to her bed and lowered himself very slowly and cautiously onto the edge of her bed, so as not to awaken her. She slept nude, and in her last stirring she had turned herself half onto her back, one arm curled above her head. The edge of the sheet cut diagonally across her chest, leaving one plump firm breast exposed. At thirty, it had a sag so slight that only the most absurd of perfectionists could have faulted it. The nipple was a dusky orange-pink, unwithered. The creamy globe, laced with the faintest blue tracery of veins, had a warm sweet texture well and deeply remembered in the neural patterns of his hands and his lips. Her face had that pleasant sulkiness of a sleeping child, and her body was tenderly described by the soft blue clasp of the blanket molded to it.

He felt the rising, tautening thrust of desire for her and remembered it was a phenomenon quite typical of his infrequent hangovers, as though liquor stirred up the guilts and insecurities that could best be combatted by this sweet and ready conquest.

Her eyes opened just then, and they were blind for a little while before she brought them to a focus on him. He hitched closer to her, smiled, gently cupped his brown hand on the naked impudence of the exposed breast, and whispered, "Good morning, darling."

"Take your stupid hand off me!"

There was a long moment of shock before he could obey her. He could not have been more astonished had a kitten gamboled up to him and disemboweled him. Never, except in illness, had she refused him. Never had she spoken to him in such a tone. It was not merely annoyance or irritation. It was anger and contempt, plus a much more frightening thing —indifference.

She got up slowly with one cool and casual glance toward him, went into the bathroom and closed the door quietly behind her. It seemed a long time before she came out. He sat in robe and slippers. She came out of the bathroom naked, as was her habit, and without a glance toward his chair began to busy herself with the mechanics of dressing. He had thought it a simple and endearing habit, not quite innocently provocative, a gesture of trust and closeness. Yet now, somehow, through her very nakedness and the way she handled her body, she managed to express a cool contempt.

"I guess I had a very stupid time for myself," he said.

"Quite."

"I dropped a bundle. I guess that's the right wording."

"I know. You told me how much, when you came in at three-thirty. You woke me up to tell me. Sixty-three thousand dollars. And after that exhibition, you wanted to be cuddled and comforted. You wanted me to dry your eyes and kiss your wounds and tell you how wonderful you are. You couldn't have been more revolting, dearie."

She hammocked her breasts into her bra, snapped it, hitched at it, and gave herself a profile glance in the mirror.

"I guess it was because I was disappointed, Vicky. That

135

conference came out so badly. I guess I . . . got some reckless ideas."

She came back from the closet, laid a gray suit on her bed and said casually, "I couldn't possibly be less interested in probing your motives, dearie. In the vernacular, I couldn't care less."

"It seems to me," he said with a trace of surly anger, "that if you saw I was being a damn fool, you might have stopped me."

She whirled and looked at him. "Stopped you? *Stopped* you! Hugh tried. I tried. You have no idea how ugly you were. Nobody could have stopped you, you silly old son of a bitch!"

"You've never spoken to me like that before!"

She shrugged and turned away, saying, "Haven't I, dearie?"

He watched her for a few minutes and said, "Well, worse things have happened, I suppose, but I can't seem to think of one offhand. I'll tell Al Marta I'll go along with that offer. We'll lie low here until I get the cash in hand—it should take a week or a little more, they say—then I'll go back into the den of the lions. I can unload everything and get squared away, darling. Johnny Sheldon will lend us that beach cottage of his to live in, I'm sure. And with the contacts I have, it shouldn't take long to line up something to do. We'll have the sun and the beach and each other, and that's more than a lot of people ever get. I can't run from it any longer. I just happened to get wiped out. And last night just topped it off."

"What a sweet plan!" she said.

He looked at her, puzzled. "What in the hell are you doing?"

"Why, I'm packing, dearie. I'm putting things in suitcases. That's known as packing."

"We still have a week here."

She went to her dressing table and got a cigarette, shook the match out. She studied him, her head slightly tilted. "*You* have a week here. *I* leave immediately."

"Why go back before I do?" he asked blankly.

"I am not going back there. I am leaving you, Temple. Today."

He stared at her. "I've got the crazy damn feeling I don't even know you."

"Maybe you don't. I'm luxury merchandise, dearie. So long as you were able to pick up the tab, I was perfectly willing to be your lovely-dovey sexy little honeysuckle wife. And *I* am not to blame for your not being able to afford me any longer. And if you think I am the type to grub about in a sordid little cottage and slum about in a kitchen and mend

136

our clothing, then you are right, dearie—you don't even know me. I'm something a well-to-do man can keep on display. I can entertain beautifully and run a household and decorate a dinner party. But, even if I loved you—don't feel bad, because I've actually never loved anyone—I couldn't afford to turn myself into a peasant at my age. I shall have to find someone to pick up where you left off, dearie. It shan't be too terribly difficult, wouldn't you say?"

With each phrase and intonation she had diminished him in his own eyes. She had exposed their marriage as the calculated farce it was. The older man, jolly in his conceits, and the younger wife playing the money game. He felt as though she had stripped the skin off him with the swift and indifferent efficiency of a trapper shucking a muskrat. He bled shame from every pore.

"Whore!" he whispered.

She pulled her tummy in, the better to adjust the cinnamon silk blouse under the waistband of her skirt. The posture exaggerated the soft weight of her breasts and, as she looked down, emphasized the future of the soft double chin.

"Oh, don't be tiresome and dramatic," she said. "If the word is right, you got full value, Temp. I never cheated on you, you know. And I could have, very readily. I always made you believe I was having a most glorious time, whether I was or not. Had your luck not gone bad, you would never have had to know all this. There's a certain kind of morality in deceit. You could have lived it out, all the way, and I would have buried you with all the standard symbols of grief, and cherished your memory in my own fashion, darling. But suddenly you present me with the problem of survival, long after I thought I had it solved. And survive I shall, in my own style. I shan't be alone long, I would say."

She turned to frown over her shoulder at her reflection in the full-length mirror.

"You don't leave me a damn thing, do you?"

She smoothed her skirt. "I must definitely peel some suet off these hips, you know. What did you say, dear?"

"I said you do all this so delicately, with such mercy and understanding. It touches my heart."

She put her jacket on and looked at him with a half smile. "Once upon a time a very tender-hearted man had a dear little spaniel and he learned its tail had to be docked. He could not bear to hurt it by having its sweet tail nipped off all at once, so he took it off himself, a very little bit at a time, a little bit every day." She glanced at her jeweled watch. "I

137

shall have breakfast in the coffee shop. If you care to be civilized about this, you can join me, dearie. Then I must make some toll calls. With luck, I should be able to give you an address before I leave."

She checked herself out in the mirror, straightened a seam, patted her deliberately casual curls, gave a characteristic tug at her girdle and walked blandly out through the sitting room, closing the corridor door softly behind her.

Temple Shannard stood up. He felt a curious disassociation from all the norms and logic of behavior, as though he had suddenly lost his place in the rule book.

"The head rolled into the basket and the crowd said '*Aaah*.'" His voice sounded too loud, and not quite like his own. He scratched his belly, walked to the mirror, stared into a face that was not quite his own, and spread his lips to inspect his strong, ridged, slightly yellowed teeth.

"Very few men who are close to fifty-one have all of their own teeth but one." The voice was too faint this time.

He walked with a swiftness of purpose to the desk in the sitting room, took a piece of hotel stationery and wrote, "If there is anyone who should have the least concern or pity. . . ."

He tore away the strip on which he had written, wadded it, popped it into his mouth, chewed it and swallowed it.

"In his lifetime a man shall eat a peck of dirt, but they do not mention paper."

He stood up and walked to the sliding door that formed a part of the window wall. It made a gentle rumbling sound as he slid it open and stepped from the chill hush of air conditioning to the bright heat of morning. He looked aslant at the pastel traffic on the Strip, at the tall creamy confection that was the Riviera, at the daytime silence of neon, at the oasis green of the watered places in contrast to the nubbly dun rug of the desert floor stretching to the rounded fangs of the empty hills beyond.

Temple Shannard looked up and down and to both sides and congratulated that architectural ingenuity which protected the balconies of the better suites from the surly envy of the gaze of those in cheaper quarters.

A trailered sailboat caught his eye as it was being towed along the Strip, and he felt pierced by a shaft of fierce hot joy.

We anchored, he remembered, off an island no one had ever seen, and the *Party Girl* moved lightfooted in the breeze at the end of the anchor line under a hot cardboard sun pasted to the middle of a child's blue sky. We swam to the beach and back, naked and playful as savages. Later we were forward and she sat with her back braced against the trunk cabin and I lay with the nape of my neck fitted to her thigh in a way of excruciating perfection. She fed me peanuts one by one, pretending I was a dangerous animal to be soothed and placated. I looked up, squinting against brightness, and saw the twinned fruit of breasts curving across a third of the blue sky. A gull slanted down the breeze at that moment, and the *Party Girl* swung on her line, and she laid her hand in gentleness along my lips and said in that small, clear, precise voice 'You are truly a lovely husband, husband,' and I could have died right then of joy, because we were three weeks married and I knew the twenty years did not matter to her at all.

He watched the sailboat out of sight and wished her fair winds and gentle care, then took off his slippers and spread his toes against the sun heat of the concrete.

The rail was waist-high, and about eight inches wide, with decorative tile set into the top of it. He stretched cautiously out on his back on the rail. He felt a shallowness of breath that was like a sexual excitement. He shut his eyes tightly against the sky glare. A big red sign was hung against the utter blackness in the back of his mind, flashing off and on in the same rhythm as the beat of his heart, reading GOD GOD GOD GOD GOD

There was a worm of nasty excitement burrowing in his loins, and he slipped his hand inside the robe to clasp the inert genital sac for a moment.

"I never knew what They wanted," he said in a patient voice of explanation.

And then he lifted his knees, crossed his arms hard across his chest and rolled off the railing. He opened his eyes and, with remote wonder, watched the wide blue bowl of the sky whirl around and around him.

Hugh Darren sat at his desk at noon and surreptitiously studied the face of Vicky Shannard, who sat very erect on the chair beside his desk, her hands folded placidly in her lap. Somehow she had found the time to change to black unrelieved by any ornament. Her lips were sparingly made up. Aside from the suggestion of pallor, and the rather exaggerated care with which she made each move, he could see very little change in her.

"You are being enormously kind, Hugh. I am very grateful."

"I hope this doesn't sound callous in any way, but actually a large part of it is . . . standard routine in large hotels."

"Especially here, I would imagine. Where people's reasons become . . . more immediate. I cannot get over how smoothly and quickly it was handled, the way the police officials functioned, and how few people actually ever even learned about it, Hugh."

"They avoid all bad publicity for the industry," he said bitterly.

"He was just starting to dress when I left the suite, and he said he would join me for breakfast. I hadn't the slightest clue until I looked up and saw you coming toward me with that very odd look on your face. Then suddenly I knew, before you told me, what must have happened."

"Haven't you told me that too many times?"

She looked at him solemnly. "I don't know what you mean. If I'm being a bore, it might be because I'm rather upset, you know."

"He was broke when he died, Vicky."

"Which is a rather poor reason for killing oneself."

"I can't imagine Temp killing himself for that reason. He had too much confidence."

"Then, of course, I hurled him off the balcony and scuttled down and ordered my breakfast."

"Don't be silly, Vicky. I just thought that maybe he had gotten the idea somewhere, somehow, that in losing all his money he'd lost you too."

She widened her eyes slightly as she looked at him. "I must admit, dear Hugh, that I *am* rather a luxury item, and so he could have made the perfectly absurd assumption he had lost me, but I feel rather insulted that he would. I am very tough, you know. I have survived . . . a great many curious situations. Surely I could be expected to survive a temporary setback."

"You said nothing that could have made him believe, wrongly, of course, that you might walk out on him?"

"I find that impertinent and hateful, Hugh. Had I the slightest idea it was in any way my fault, I'd be unable to live with myself, really. He seemed quite depressed about losing so much money so foolishly, but I remember telling him that pieces of monstrous foolishness are the tokens of being human. I don't know why you feel you have to be ugly to me. It's unfair, you know."

He sighed. "I'm sorry, Vicky. I just feel so damn bad about it. I'll have to stay far away from Max Hanes and that miserable Ben Brown for days. Right now I think I'd try to kill them."

"But you can get over that, of course."

"What do you mean?"

140

"You couldn't hold this job long if you went about trying to kill people, could you? And it's a very nice job."

"Okay. You're even. Let's call a truce."

"I would be delighted. I want to keep on being your friend, Hugh."

"Okay. As a friend, what are you going to do?"

"The forms and papers will be pure horror. It's terribly awkward to die so far from home. I shall phone Dicky Armbruster. You remember him, of course—our long-suffering barrister in Nassau—and unload most of this problem on him. Like a perfect coward, I wired Temp's children rather than ringing them up. But I think I should phone them, a little later. It may be possible to arrange to bury him in a family plot in the States. His first wife is buried there, but I shan't mind that. That would be a macabre jealousy indeed."

"But how will you manage, Vicky? How will you be fixed?"

"Perhaps that was what Temp had on his mind, Hugh. I believe I shall be quite well-situated after the dust settles. We have a very small estate tax in the Bahamas, you know. And poor Temp carried a large amount of life assurance. I never urged him to do so. In fact I rather resented the size of the payments we had to make. But he felt, being older than I, that it was only right to give me as much protection as he could afford. I do not believe that some of his creditors will be able to come back on me for payment. And I believe the others will be inclined to be patient. It would be dreadfully bad form to press me, wouldn't it? So I should be able to retain his land holdings and then, because I have no head for business, put it all in the hands of some terribly earnest bank officer and let him manage it for me. I will have the house, of course, and I can sell it and buy or build something smaller and easier to manage."

"I didn't know you had it all thought out."

"Oh, but I didn't! I've been thinking aloud. I know he has borrowed against his policies, but that should only be a small dent in their face value."

"I feel sick about this, Vicky. Depressed and sick."

She reached out and touched his hand with a quick and almost deliberate shyness. "Of course, you poor dear. I'd forgotten how much you were planning on poor Temp to finance your little hotel."

He felt his face turn hot. "I didn't mean that, damn it!"

She looked at him with gentle mockery, her China-blue eyes bright. "Is there any good reason, my darling Hugh, why old friends should try to play noble games with each other? Would you care to try to tell me that the money has *not* entered your mind?"

"Well . . . I think it's a perfectly natural thing that I should . . . relate it to my plans . . . when you've dreamed of something for so long. . ."

She leaned toward him in a way that created a special intimacy. "We are much more alike than you would ever admit. I know that. I've always felt that, Hugh."

"How can I possibly answer a statement like that?"

"Just don't try," she said, and stood up. "Old friends should not forsake each other, my dear. When you have reached your . . . monetary goal, please do come to Nassau and talk to me about it. You can visit me at my small house, and we shall plot and scheme to see if we cannot find a way to give you your heart's desire. You will be a great comfort to a lonely widow, my dear. I do not believe I will marry again. I shall concentrate on becoming a dowager, with many cats and jasmine tea, absolutely clanking with tiresome bracelets and brooches. As for now, I shall find you and say good-bye to you before I leave."

She turned, frowning, her hand on the door latch, and said, "Will it be necessary to tender me a bill for our charges here?"

"No. Don't even think about it."

"You're very sweet. I'll go up now and pack poor Temp's things and make those disheartening telephone calls. Oh, would you like to look over Temp's things and select something . . . as a keepsake?"

"I . . . I really don't . . ."

"I shall send you down his lighter, Hugh. You must have noticed it. It's solid gold and quite pretty. I think he would want you to have it, you know."

The door swung shut behind her. He sat very still and closed his eyes and searched his heart for the tears he had been saving to shed for Temp, but he found that she had managed to dry them up. In some way beyond his understanding she had achieved a subtle distortion in his image of Temple Shannard.

In death the man was without dignity. He was a fool who had burst his explosive blood onto the whitewalls of a parked Cadillac. He was a "fell or jumped" in the police records. He was a sealed box that would travel eastward. He had not even left a mark at the edge of the parking lot. After the sawdust had been spread and shoveled, the area had been hosed down, and the sun had dried it in minutes. The ambulance had picked up a broken something from under a tarp, and there had been no siren, and there would be no reference in any public records as to the actual name of the hotel, or to the fact that he had lost as much as one dollar in any casino.

And she had extended that distortion from Temp to him, had reduced his own stature in the same proportion. He felt smaller and meaner and more selfish than he had believed himself to be. Not only had she made him conscious of his financial interest in Temp's death, but she had sown a sickly seed of intrigue, using that talk of "great comfort to a lonely widow" to bring his inadvertent conjecture into focus upon the richness of her breasts and hips and the mature and milky textures of her. It all had the effect of burying Temp too quickly.

It seemed to Hugh as he sat there that this was a very bad place on the face of the earth, that it was unwise to bring to this place any decent impulse or emotion, because there was a curiously corrosive agent adrift in this bright desert air. Here, attuned to the constant clinking of the silver dollars in forty thousand pockets, honesty became watchful opportunism, friendship became a pry bar, love turned to license, and legitimate sentiment drowned in a pink sea of sentimentality. It would not be a good thing to stay in such a place too long, because you might lose the ability to react to any other human being save on the level of estimating how best to use them, or how they were trying to use you. The impossibility of any more savory relationship was perfectly symbolized by the pink-and-white-and-blue neon crosses shining above the quaint gabled roofs of the twenty-four-hour-a-day marriage chapels.

At two o'clock on Monday afternoon, Homer Gallowell put a $25,000 clip on the Won't Pass line, watched the shooter roll an eleven, and saw his chip slide into the banker's stack.

He had counted the exact number of bets he had made. He had reached the limit set by the young mathematician, the limit where with continued play the odds against him became too great to buck. He turned away from the table and walked to the casino cashiers' cage. A pale young man came to the window to attend to his needs.

"I got me this little stack of eight that I started with, and I got this here second stack of eight I won, and this one little chip left over, son."

"Yes sir. That'll be seventeen hundred dollars, sir. How would. . . ."

"These are worth a hair more than that, son."

"What? Oh! Oh, excuse me, Mr. Gallowell. If you'll wait just a moment, I'll get Mr. Hanes, our manager."

It was a full minute before the floridly dressed bulk of Max Hanes filled the space on the other side of the wicket.

"You're not quitting when you're into us this deep, are you, Mr. Gallowell?"

"Well, it's fun and all, and you've got a nice place here, but it's work too, all that time standing up. My legs are about to drop right off, so I guess it's time to cash in. Anyhow, Hanes, I'm not so deep into you. I got back what I give you before, and twenty-five thousand interest on it. Comes to just about twelve per cent, and I've seen fools pay more. You could rightly say we've arrived at a standoff, Hanes. So if you've still got my check, you can give me that back, plus two hundred twenty-five thousand cash money."

"That check was part of our bank deposit this morning, Mr. Gallowell."

"Then it'll have to be four hundred twenty-five thousand. I brought me a little old satchel along empty just in case, so you be getting it together while I go on up to that ballroom they give me and pack up."

"It will take time to get that much together, Mr. Gallowell."

"It shouldn't take much time. Got it, haven't you?"

"We only keep a three-hundred float on hand, and I couldn't cut it down to nothing. You can understand that."

"Then you better get on the run, boy, and start picking it up here and there, because I want to get in the air soon as I can."

"Isn't it . . . a large sum to carry around in cash?"

Gallowell looked at him with dry and ancient amusement. "Might be, if the news got around. But there's only you gambling people know about it, and I guess you don't go around stealing back the money you lose, do you?"

"No. No, I didn't mean that. I just meant . . . you know, that much dough can make a guy nervous."

"I haven't been rightly nervous since the time I was taking a bath in a crick and a bear took a dislike to me. Now you round up that money fast, Hanes. I pay some boys to keep my name out of the papers, and it would be a refreshin' project to them to spend some time getting your name in."

He turned on his heel and walked away. Max Hanes cursed under his breath. He got hold of Ben Brown. "That old hick thinks he's quitting. Get up four and a quarter. You know where to go and who to take with you."

Hanes, moving with exceptional speed, went to the elevator. Five minutes later he came out of an elevator into the lobby and hurried to Hugh Darren's office. Darren looked up with surprise and displeasure.

"You did a hell of a nice job on Shannard, Max."

"Okay, so I held his hand and told him to jump. I'm sorry. I haven't got time for that now. I need one of those special favors we were talking about."

"Take your troubles to Jerry Buckler."

"He's dead drunk. Out cold on his bathroom floor. I shook hell out of him. I threw water on him. All he does is mumble. You got to help me, and for God's sake let's argue about it later. I'll give you a thousand bucks to paste on your conscience, Darren."

"Who do I kill?"

"With lines like that, I'll book you into the Safari Room. Now shut up. Maybe I'm too damn late already. We've got to give special orders to the girl on the switchboard. She'll listen to you. I'll grease her with a hundred to keep her happy. Here's all she has to do, if she isn't too late. She's got to bitch up the phone call Gallowell is going to make to his private pilot. The old bastard won't fly at night, and I want to keep him from getting in touch until too late."

"Why?"

Max hit the desk with his fist. "I want the old guy to have a chance to keep playing. Maybe he won't, no matter what I do. But I've got to give it the best chance. Replace that girl on the board a minute and let me fill her in. Bring her in here and let me give her some orders. I wouldn't have to do it through you, Hugh buddy, except she's one of the ones I don't have on my team."

Hugh thought it over. What did it matter if one old man didn't get a call through? It was an old man he didn't know against a thousand dollars that had become a lot more essential since Shannard had flown eight stories onto asphalt. He went out, arranged for the relief operator to take over, and brought Miss Gates back to his office. She was a soured fifty, with hair died an improbable shade of cranberry red.

"This is Mr. Hanes, Miss Gates."

"Yeah, I know."

"He's got a special request to make to you, Miss Gates. It has my approval."

"Like what?"

Hanes took a piece of paper out of his pocket and handed it to her. "Eight-fifteen is going to ask for that number. If he's done it already, I'm licked. Can you remember, honey?"

"Not if I wasn't looking for it."

"So look for it. When he phones it, make like you're dialing out. You might just as well dial it, let it have a piece of the first ring, then cut the connection and change your voice and tell eight-fifteen you're the Sage Motel. He'll ask for a man named Scott. Let him hang on for a while, then tell him Mr. Scott's room doesn't answer. If he tries again, give him the same business. If he leaves a message, make like you're taking it. And you don't talk to anybody about this."

"I'm doing it just for kicks?"

"You're doing it for these here two souvenir pictures of U. S. Grant, sweetheart. And you ring my office and tell me whether you get a chance to block the call as soon as it happens. Maybe some day we want another little favor, hey?"

"I'm ready any time," she said, tucking the folded bills into her bra.

"Now get out there."

"I go off at six," she said as she moved toward the door.

"After six it doesn't matter, sweetheart."

After she was gone Hugh said, "Where did you get that number?"

"I fixed it up Saturday to get a look at whatever went into his box. I checked that name out at the airport. They got him down as the pilot of Gallowell's airplane."

Up in Suite 815, Homer Gallowell readied himself for his departure. He always carried more than his immediate needs in his big old suitcase, because his business trips often lasted longer than he anticipated. Even when he planned to stay only one night in any hotel, he always unpacked completely and repacked when it was time to leave. He traveled with one extra suit of the same cheap dark fabric and cut as the one he wore, one extra pair of black work shoes, a good supply of cheap white cotton dress shirts from J. C. Penney's low-priced racks, a few bright and knot-worn dollar ties, an abundance of socks and underwear he was accustomed to purchase at Army and Navy stores.

In the last few years he had indulged himself in an extravagance that always made him feel a guilty twinge when he exercised it. Rather than cart laundry back to the old ranch, he discarded it whenever it became soiled. This had the effect of making him more conscious of price when he replenished his supply. He had computed that this extravagance, figuring two days per white shirt, and a daily change of socks and underwear, cost him an additional $1.25 a day while away from home. Try as he might to put this figure in proper proportion to his personal income—from all sources and before taxes—of close to three hundred thousand a month, he could never drop the laundry into a hotel waste-basket without feeling reckless and slightly foolish.

It was at this point in his preparations that he interrupted his routine to call Pilot Scott. He hung up with a glare and a mutter of annoyance. Told the damn fool to stay by the phone. Maybe he just stepped out for cigarettes, or a magazine. Something like that. Try again in ten minutes. . . .

The tin voice of the telephone said into Max's hirsute ear, "This is Mabel Gates, Mr. Hanes. That call you were asking about. I just took care of it the way you said."

"Thank you so much, sweetheart. Keep up the good work."

He hung up and slowly moved a thumbnail back and forth across the shadow of bristle on his chin, making a small whispering sound. Twenty after three. There were toll phones off the lobby. Or the old boy might be sore enough to take a cab over to that Sage Motel with the idea of waiting there for his pilot. There was one idea he had previously examined and discarded, but as he appraised it again, it seemed worth the small risk involved. He picked up his phone and dialed the zero that took him off the automatic staff circuit and connected him with the central switchboard.

"Mabel, Max Hanes again. Put me through to that Sage Motel, sweetheart."

The motel operator rang Scott's room. He answered on the first ring.

"Yes sir?"

"Mr. Scott? Are you Mr. Gallowell's pilot?"

"Yes. Who is this?"

"This is the desk at the Cameroon, sir. Mr. Gallowell asked me to inform you that he won't be leaving today."

"It will be tomorrow, then?"

"He didn't say. I wouldn't know about that. I guess he thought there was no need of you hanging around the phone in a place like Las Vegas."

"I didn't know he cared."

"I beg your pardon?"

"Never mind. Thanks for calling. I'm glad to get out of here."

Max hung up. It seemed safe enough. Gallowell would probably figure it as an imaginative lie cooked up by a goof-off flyboy. But sir! They called me and told me you wouldn't need me!

The thing you had to do, every time, was maroon the winners who wanted to walk off with your money. Tie them down, no matter what you used. If they hung around, they'd

147

sooner or later put your money right back into the money machine. And you were breaking no law. The tables were honest. You were just giving the house percentage a chance to work.

And the better it worked, the more came off the top for Max Hanes.

Garages could be talked into delaying simple repair jobs. Airline reservations could be mysteriously fouled up. (But, sir, you phoned me yourself and canceled!) Sometimes it was a simple matter of sending a couple of big iced bottles of congratulatory champagne up to the winner's room. Or arranging for a hundred-dollar broad to tap on the wrong door. You had to send them all back where they came from saying bitterly, I didn't have the sense to quit at the right time. I was going to quit, but somehow I got started again. If the car had been ready . . . if I hadn't met that out-going gal . . . if I hadn't gotten loaded . . . if I hadn't been fouled up on my flight . . . if I hadn't gotten those complimentary tickets to that late show . . . if leaving when I planned to hadn't conflicted with the chance to go to Al Marta's cocktail party and meet Jackie Luster . . .

He phoned Betty Dawson's room.

"What's the matter with you, baby? You sound dreary."

"I was asleep, Max."

"I wanted to fill you in and make sure you're standing by. Our pigeon has cashed in, but somehow he isn't going to be able to get airborne until tomorrow. I don't think he knows it yet, but that's the way it stands. You got an approach worked out?"

"An approach, yes. I think. But that's as far as it will go."

"You think so?"

"I know so. He's not a compulsive gambler, Max. He's not a compulsive anything."

"He's a man, kid. I want him in the state of mind he'll lay down a couple of those special chips to show you what a big shot he is. You're the gal to do it, Dawson."

"I'm the specialist. The aging ingenue of Playhouse 190. Max, there'll be nothing to film. For God's sake, I could be his granddaughter! It makes me feel slimy for you even to think there could be . . . anything at all."

"Don't knock those old goats until you've been the route, cutie. Maybe you're his chance to regain his lost youth, like. I told you before. You make the try. For one-third of what he's carting away, it's worth the try. And we put the show on in 190, cutie, mostly because I want to be sure you go at it big. If you drag your feet just because you like the old guy, I can find that out from the tape, and you could be the unhappiest broad in Nevada."

"So that's the *real* reason why it has to be 190. You're never entirely sure you've beaten me right down into the ground, are you, Max?"

"Nobody has ever laid a hand on you, baby. Maybe it was an oversight. You keep fighting after you're licked. But there's more reasons than that. You get him talking to you, maybe there's some little thing or two he says that can be used someday for some other angle. You never can tell. Fifty million bucks, it's a good thing to listen to every word."

She sighed impatiently. "All right, all *right*! What comes next?"

"Fix yourself up pretty, sweetie, and then stand by. The way it looks, I think you can make your move about five o'clock. I'll let you know."

As soon as she had banged the phone back onto the cradle, it rang. She snatched it up and said, "What now, Max?"

"Not Max. Ol' Hugh. And what are you so steamed up about?"

"Nothing."

"Are you sore at me, too?"

"No. I'm not angry at you, Hugh."

"What's wrong with you, honey? Your voice sounds . . . dead."

"I guess I don't feel well. I'm not going on tonight, either. That's what I was arguing with Max about."

"You should see a doctor, honey."

"It's just a virus. I'll be all right."

"By the way, Betty, thanks for the note you sent me about Temp."

"I kept trying to phone you but you were busy. He was a nice man, Hugh. It was a horrible thing. Vicky told me how you both tried to stop him when he was losing all that money."

"Then you talked to her?"

"Earlier this afternoon. She seems to be taking it . . . pretty well."

"Maybe too damned well."

"I . . . sensed that. I could never feel close to her, Hugh. She looks like such a little doll, but. . . . Anyhow, I guess you found out you can't soften up the casino mentality."

"They were feeding him weak drinks to keep him on his feet. They were keeping play at the table slowed down to his reaction time. It had all the style and dignity of plucking a drugged chicken. God damn it, Betty, let's get out of here. For keeps. Maybe we shouldn't wait much longer, because it might turn out to be too late."

"That sounds almost like a proposal," she said in what was an obviously strained attempt at lightness.

"I don't know what it is. But we should both get out."

"I can't abandon my career, sir."

"You sound damn strange. I'm going to come up there and sit with the sick, girl."

"No. Please, Hugh. I don't want to see you. I might even . . . go out."

"Go out! Where?"

"Do I have to ask for your permission in writing?"

"That's sort of an ugly response, isn't it?"

"Maybe. I don't know. I don't care, Hugh. I think this whole thing, you and me, has gotten a little too involved. Maybe I don't have room for it in my life. I'll let you know."

"That's nice. Thanks. Thanks a hell of a lot, Betty."

"It isn't as if it has been a love affair, Hugh. All it has been is a . . . convenience."

"Have fun tonight," he said, and hung up on her.

After she had gently replaced the phone she sat on the edge of her bed. She combed her thick black hair back with her fingers. With a special grayness of soul, she let herself think of what her life was going to be like if Max had read Homer Gallowell more correctly than she had. She wished Homer had not sent that ring. It seemed innocent at the time, but now it made her less positive. Old as he was, if Max was right, he would be easier to endure than the fat man had been. Or the roostery Venezuelan.

But nobody in all the world could be anything more to her than a feat of dreary endurance, since Hugh. This body was his, in the ultimate sense of possession. Any act would be the theft of what was his, and such a degradation of what was his that she could never, in her guilt, return it to him.

And so, if Max was right, after tonight she would have to invent a new girl who was not in love with Hugh Darren. She would quarrel with him, and then she would become remote and cold to him. Friendship would be too much an involvement in temptation. Love would not die. She would see him here and there in the hotel, and her heart would twist and break each time.

He would not leave a job so good. Max would not let her leave.

But if, through some miracle, she could be suddenly permitted to leave, that would be the thing to do, because it would be best for Hugh. His memories of her would be good ones, warm and pleasing to him.

She was not aware she was weeping until a tear fell onto the roundness of her thigh, startling her.

People in traps, she thought, should remember they are in traps, and not get those big fancy ideas about happiness and so on. Now pretty yourself up for half the money in Texas. Silks and bows, lace and perfume, new lips and new eyes. Big seduction scene from the Book of Methuselah.

At a few minutes past four, Max Hanes led Homer Gallowell back to his private office, and there supervised the packing of $425,000 into the limp and ancient black leather satchel provided by Gallowell. Homer checked the totals as written on the paper ribbons encircling each packet of currency.

He locked the satchel, put the tarnished brass key in his vest pocket and said, "I suspicioned you were going to tell me you needed more time to get my money."

"How come, Mr. Gallowell?"

"People do hate to let loose of money."

Max Hanes slapped the satchel. "Well, here it is. You bruised us good, Mr. Gallowell. If you're heading for the airport right now, I can send you in my own car with a couple of my security guards."

"I'm not leaving right this minute."

"Then I wouldn't advise carrying this around with you. No sense in taking chances you don't have to. You can leave it right here, if you want, and get it in ten seconds at any time. I'll give you a receipt that shows what you've got in the satchel, if that would make you feel easier about it."

"You're worrying about this a lot more than I am, Hanes. They got a safe at the front desk, haven't they? I'll check it right there. Thank you kindly." He picked the satchel off the desk, turning in the same motion to march out of the office, a spare, erect old man, baked and withered by the years, with the suggestion of the ranch hand in his gait.

"We're not completely licked, Brownie," Max said after the door swung shut.

"How do you mean?"

"He could have decided to go right to the airport and buy himself a pilot."

"Oh. I didn't think of that. It gets me, the way he handles that money, like he was carrying his lunch."

151

"You're a stupid creep, Ben Brown. That money doesn't mean much of anything to that old bastard. The only thing means anything, we took him last year. If he went to a junk carnival and lost ten bucks on rollaball, he'd spend a year practising and go get his ten back and a little more if he could, and he'd feel the same way about it he feels about that sack of money. He conned me, the old fox. He conned Max Hanes. I was stupid. I figured him to play progressive, doubling the bets on his losses, and that's the same as giving me the money. So I fell for his limit, and he plays it just as smart as I've ever seen. He bet nineteen times. He hit it fourteen times and he lost five times. Two hundred and twenty-five thousand he tries to walk away with."

"Will the Dawson broad be able to work him over?"

"How the hell should I know!"

"So okay. I'm leaving. Take it easy, Maxie."

• • • nine

TWENTY AFTER FIVE ON MONDAY AT THE CAMEROON. THE sun groups around the pool and up in the rooftop solariums are thinning out. The pool attendants and solarium attendants and patio waitresses are furtively checking the day's tips. Throughout their shift they have diligently hustled the customers with a determined solicitousness about towels, lotions, drinks, and special attention to the placement of the sun cots.

There are, at this time of day, more people in their rooms and suites than perhaps at any other time. Showers create a peak water demand. Bellhops are hustling ice and setups to the rooms. Liquor waiters are making frequent trips upstairs. The doorman is busy. In addition to the late registrations, he has to cope with those beginning to arrive by private car and cab for the dinner show along the Strip, nail the cabs for those leaving for other places along the Strip, see that private cars are parked in the big lot and retrieved from the big lot with the celerity which feeds silver dollars into the depth of the special pocket in his uniform.

The Afrique Bar and the Little Room are beginning to fill up. A few people are beginning to move into the vast, plush, terraced silence of the Safari Room, preferring to get their table assignments early and do their drinking there and have ample time for their dinner before the big show begins. Bartenders at all public and service bars in the hotel are beginning to move into highest gear, making use of all the time-saving steps they have performed earlier during their shift.

The kitchens are in a clattering, frenzied crescendo of preparation, with all ranges and steam tables in operation, all chefs vigilant in their familiar jungles of stainless steel and fluorescence.

In the casino only three 21 tables, one crap table and one wheel are not yet in operation, but they are manned and ready to go. Back in the staff lounge the off-duty casino personnel, working the long shift (thirty minutes on, thirty minutes off) take their paper cups to the big coffee urn, and talk idly about their kids, their lawns, the next fishing trip on Lake Mead.

In the Little Room the piano player is working her way through all the Gershwin she knows, while the unused part of her mind prays steadily for Skippy, who is very very sick indeed, so sick he didn't even make his usual fuss about being taken to the vet's.

At the busy front desk a clerk is explaining for the third time, with a visible show of patience, that the Cameroon can take no responsibility for a camera left out by the pool.

In the Lady Eloise Beauty Salon in the arcade of concession shops between the hotel and its convention hall, an operator is working with end-of-the-day haste upon the hair of a stout saddened woman who has been saying all afternoon, "He just went right ahead and lost everything we got and now I'll have to go back to work and I haven't had to work in seventeen years. I couldn't stop him. He was like a crazy man, honest." The operator makes a comforting murmur. It is a rare week when she does not hear this story three or four times. They come to Vegas on vacation and they have no one else to talk to.

In the Afrique Bar an instrumental and vocal sextet is knocking itself out with its special slapstick version of "Chloe". A rather nice-looking woman who has been drinking with ladylike restraint for over twenty hours suddenly topples off her bar stool, and the incident is handled so deftly only a dozen people realize what happened.

The star of the big show in the Safari Room is being diligently sobered by his manager and his mistress so that he will be able to do the dinner show.

Downtown, in one of the back rooms never seen by mourners, in the establishment of Leffingson and Flass, an assistant does a brisk neat job of tacking the destination address on the special coffin approved for transportation of bodies by common carriers. It will be delivered to a funeral establishment in the East.

"Give me a hand," he says to his helper.

The coffin is on a utility cart. Together they roll it into the coldroom where it will remain until time to transport it to the railroad station tomorrow.

"Now scrub that slab down, Albert," he orders.

The assistant leans against a wall, smoking a cigarette.

"Seems funny," Albert says, "the way you gotta buy two tickets for a . . . for the remains."

"You're improving. Your language is getting much more professional, Albert."

"Why two tickets?"

"It's just a rule, that's all. But if, for example, the widow wished to go along on one of them, that would be permitted."

"Will she?"

"She isn't that hard up, Albert. It depresses them, to accompany a body."

"*You* said it then."

"I can, because I know better. Use the hose again, Albert, and we're through here."

"Since you been here, Mr. Looden, about how many would you say jumped out of hotels tall enough to jump out of?"

"Albert! You astonish me. You should know better than that. The happy vacationers in Las Vegas *never* jump from a tall building. Some of them have dizzy spells now and then. It's due to the high oxygen content of our crisp desert air, Albert. They become too invigorated."

"Sure. Just like that fella last month that wrote all the bad checks and lost the money. He went off that slanty side of Hoover Dam and rolled and bounced all the way down and ended up on top of the power plant without no skin left on him. He got himself invigorated all to hell."

"Albert, if you want to be a success in the trade, you must stop thinking the worst of people. It's a good thing you aren't the one compiling our local mortality statistics. The desert is the healthiest place in the world. Now coil your hose and hang it up and let's get out of here."

Hugh Darren and George Ladori stand in the largest walk-in cooler in the hotel. George is showing Hugh the sides of beef that have been delivered this day. With a keen and slender knife he makes a shallow slice into a flank and holds the layer of fat back. There is a quality in the hard artificial light which makes the meat look slightly blue.

"It's got the Prime stamp, Hugh, but it's on the low side of Prime. You can see. It isn't marbled the way it should be. It's more like the very best level of Choice. But we're paying Prime. What the hell do you think I should do?"

"Are all sixteen sides that came in like this?"

"Well . . . there's not a one of them *real* good looking."

"How many of them disturb you?"

"I'd say six."

"I'd say get Krauss over here in person and tell him the facts of life. Get a concession on replacement or price on those six sides. If it's price, or if you get nowhere, use these six on your convention specials, and don't menu them out to the regular trade."

"That's what I thought you'd say."

Hugh gives him a half smile and says, "So next time you don't have to ask, do you?"

Out back in one of the small rooms off the shower room used by the lifeguards, Beaver Brownell and Bobby Waldo are playing three-handed gin with Harry Charm, another one of those specialists whose names, like Waldo and Brownell, appear on the payroll of one of the corporations administered out of the X-Sell offices downtown. Their started pay is fattened by cash from Al Marta at irregular, unpredictable interviews.

"Gin!" Beaver says.

"How you making out with that showgirl, that Gretchen?" Bobby asks slyly.

"I don't know why she's so sore. I can't get near that stupid broad."

"So give up," Bobby suggests.

Brownell exposes all of his outthrust teeth in a long yellow grin. "The Beaver never gives up, men."

Harry Charm finishes checking the score. Beaver is dealing to him. "What's this about some girl?" Harry asks heavily. He is a puffy, scarred, asthmatic old hoodlum who frets endlessly about minor matters. He looks at his hand. "All my life, I never held cards. All my life, losing."

Charm has been both cop and convict. He is trusted. In the customary channel of command, when some punitive action seems necessary, Al Marta speaks to Gidge Allen, who speaks to Harry Charm, who gives the orders to Brownell or Waldo or whoever he thinks can best handle the particular operation.

"There's this Gretchen, madly in love with Beaver, only she don't realize it yet," Bobby explains.

Beaver wins the hand and the game. Bobby Waldo gets up restlessly. "Enough for me. Goddam, I get restless lately. We haven't had anything to do in a long time, you realize that?"

Beaver grins. "You bucking for sergeant, Bobby?" He turns to Harry. "Bobby wants we should get sent back to Phoenix and smack some more of those laundry workers back into line. That's the line of work he likes."

Bobby flushes and stands over Beaver, who looks up at him calmly. "The kind of work I would like, Beaver, is they decide you got too much mouth and I get to take you out on the desert and close it for good."

"Shut up, both of you," Harry says irritably. "Deal the cards, Beaver."

Jerry Buckler, the manager of the Cameroon, sleeps, bare to the waist, on the tile floor of his bathroom. The tile is cool against chest and cheek. There is a purple knot on his forehead where he struck the edge of the toilet in falling. He is still damp with the water Max Hanes sprayed upon him by holding one thick thumb against the lavatory stream, deflecting it. Jerry Buckler glides swiftly down a long snowy hill of sleep. He is on a red sled in a long-ago time, and his father is on the sled behind him, steering it, holding him safe and close, and laughing into the wind in his giant voice. The wind whips cold against their faces. But suddenly his father is gone. He cannot turn the sled. The hill steepens and the wind howls in his ears, and the hill tilts downward into some great blackness of a night that cannot end. It is late, and it is past time to go home, but all he can do is cling to the red sled, and cry unheard.

Gidge Allen is holed up back in his own room in Al Marta's penthouse apartment, and he is once again pleasuring Miss Gretchen Lane, and finding her needs to be as strenuous as before. He had found himself liking the look of her when, because of Al's lies, she had become furious with Beaver. So he had quietly sought her out, and found her quite ready to be persuaded. In just a little while now, they will rest and dress, and pick up drinks turned tepid, and wander, with some attempt at casualness, out to the random party going on in the big living room.

Gidge knows that Al will kid him again about never seeing a man work so hard to win a hundred-dollar bet, and just as the flesh beneath him begins the hungry tumult of its throes of completion, he wonders dolefully if all this is not merely an act of bravado. He wonders if he has not, at last, grown too old for all these prime young wenches who all seem to say and do exactly the same things, as though they were all graduates of the same huge underground school, veterans of endless drill teams, letter perfect in all their obligatory lines.

Vicky Shannard lies naked and alone, brushed, curled, perfumed, annointed, alone on the big bed, the draperies closed against what is left of the day, alone in the still hum of the air conditioning, her eyes closed, arms at her sides, her eyelids expertly touched with blue shadow. She has made her phone calls. Tomorrow she will fly to New York. Dicky will meet her there, bringing from Nassau the first of the many papers to study and sign.

Hugh has suggested he move her into other quarters in the hotel, but she has thanked him and told him it is really not necessary. He has thanked her for the gold lighter she sent down to his office.

She has had a long hot tub. She has scrubbed and brushed and curled and creamed and enameled herself.

She is alone. The lids hide the bland childish innocence of the slightly protruding blue eyes. She wets her lips with the sharp pink tip of her tongue. She sighs. It is a long sound in the stillness. She raises one leg and braces it there, the knee sharply bent.

She brings her hands up and presses them with a painful strength against her firm, heavy, white breasts. Something begins to well up inside her, creating a noticeable pressure. It is a feeling very like that final inevitability of sexual completion once the point of sensory endurance has been passed, but it is without any of those delicious overtones. She cannot imagine what is happening to her until the feeling wells up to its crisis. And suddenly she gives a long thin quavering cry of utter desolation and the tears burst from her eyes.

It is the first time in her life she has wept for any reason other than a reaction to physical pain. Her astonishment does not still her torment. She rocks her curly head from side to side and the tears run tickling down her cheeks to the percale pillow, and her body spasms under the continuous blows of the hard sobbing. She weeps for what she is and what she has been, and for all the empty time ahead of her, and for her sudden recognition of her beloved, too late, too long after it tumbled down through the bright morning toward the soft, horrid sound of impact.

Max Hanes led Al Marta out to the relative quiet of the foyer of Al's apartment and stood with him near the door of the private elevator.

Al said, "You see the way that boy moves? You see those goddam shoulders? He's a welter from the waist down and a light-heavy from the waist up. You want to come in on him, Max, I'll sell you a piece of my piece. Thirty-four bouts, twenty-one knockouts. I tell you, this boy is going to go all the way. I got a hunch."

"Thanks, but you know about me and the fighters, Al."

Al laughed and thumped him on the arm. "So you dropped a little on a couple of canvasbacks. Okay, you stick to the singers and the platter outfits, but don't ever forget, baby, I either get a piece of every new deal you like, or you don't get the jukebox pressure nationwide."

"I'm not that stupid, Al. What I wanted to tell you, I got Dawson set to work on Gallowell."

Al frowned, lost in thought for a few moments. "Okay. She's a good smart kid. But if she doesn't swing it, I don't want you should push too hard. Here we're not messing with some car dealer or real-estate-promotion guy. I mean if it gets obvious, here we got a guy with a lot of weight, one way and another. You've got to keep in mind that a quarter million—a little less—is going to make just one thin-type week on the books, and it isn't worth a guy with so much weight maybe getting sore and moving against us some other way."

"Like what?"

"How the hell should I know? He's maybe a little on the senile side, so he gets childish about you trying to push him around. Maybe he uses some of those millions he's got to put pressure on the Feds to give us the kind of undercover audit and investigation we could do without. He employs a hell of a lot of smart tough people, Maxie. He could just give out orders to bitch up the Cameroon any way they can think of, and some of those people could come up with something we haven't even figured on. I'm just saying you've pushed it about as far as you should, and if he don't get the hots for the Dawson broad, just let it go. Just let it go."

"Okay, Al."

"How is it with Darren?"

"He's joining the team, a little bit at a time. A little off the top looks just as good to him as it does to anybody. I overpaid him just to bring him along a little. Was that okay?"

"You know damn well it was, Max. He's worth sewing so tight he'll never leave the organization."

"What was the reaction in L.A. to Shannard taking that dive?"

"They were disappointed. It would have been good property to pick up."

"The little blonde won't sell?"

"She doesn't have to and she doesn't want to. I talked to her before I made the call. The insurance takes her off the hook."

"Maybe there's some way to change her mind, Al."

"You're a little late, Maxie."

"What do you mean?"

"I'd make book she's going to meet a very interesting guy in the next few weeks. And I bet he knows just how to make a pretty little widow forget her terrible sorrow. And I'll bet he has some plans for her."

"He better be good."

"So why shouldn't he be good?"

"That one is rough, Al. She knows every score they ever added up."

"If it's out of my territory, baby, I sure as hell know it's out of yours. So get your mind back on what the hell you're being paid for. Okay?"

"Okay."

"Tomorrow or the next day, Gidge is going to take Jerry over to Riverside and stick him back in that funny farm for a while. He's in bad shape, the worst I've ever seen him, so it may take a long time to dry him out good. Can you operate okay through Darren?"

"In another month he'll shill for me if I ask him."

"How about what I hear about him and Dawson?"

"When we own them both, Al, it's just that much easier, isn't it?"

"Sometimes you kill me, baby. Honest to God."

"I just like things to run smooth."

Hugh Darren stood behind the registration desk. He hefted the solid-gold lighter in his hand, conscious of its unusual weight. It was engraved with block initials spelling

159

T.A.S. They could be ground off and replaced. He wondered if he should do that. Would it be a morbid affectation to leave them?

"Was that all right?" the desk clerk asked.

"Was what all right?"

"What I just said, Mr. D. Mr. Hanes asked me to check Eight-fifteen to see if Mr. Gallowell was staying over. I saw no reason not to, so I did, and he is. Was that all right?"

"Yes. Yes, that was all right. But you must remember, Jimmy, that Mr. Hanes has nothing to do with the operation of the hotel as such."

"Yes sir," the man said, with a slightly skeptical expression.

"You can give him information."

"Yes sir."

"But if there is any request for any sort of . . . action on your part that you do not understand, or possibly think is not right. . . ."

"Such as?"

"Do I have to draw you a picture? Such as letting one of Mr. Hanes' people read a message that might be in the box for any hotel guest."

"Oh, I wouldn't do that!" the man said, with telltale forcefulness.

"No. You wouldn't do that. Of course you wouldn't. You check with me on the innocent acts, but not the other kind."

"I beg your pardon, sir?"

"You can create the impression of loyalty without cutting off the supply of little gifts of money."

"I'm afraid I don't understand," the man said, red and uncomfortable.

Darren slipped the lighter into his pocket. "Skip it," he said wearily. "Working here hasn't changed you at all. You just help out a little during the Saturday-night rush."

"What?"

"In the larger sense, Jimmy, this is a house of ill fame. We all make our own adjustments."

The man, looking baffled, tried to laugh at what he suspected was a joke he should have understood. As Hugh walked back toward his office he sensed that the man was still standing there, staring at him.

I am adjusting, Hugh told himself. That's all. When your stance is too rigid, they knock you down. So you stand loose, ready to bob, weave and sidestep. Flexibility is the clue to local survival. So I shall stand under the money tree and hold my pockets wide open, and if some falls in, it isn't my doing.

It's just gravity. This doesn't have to touch me in any basic way. I'll make what I have to make, and then I shall pack up and leave, and run my own show in my own way.

There are good people here. Most of the entertainers are warm, sturdy, wonderful folk, like my Betty. And the little people on the hotel and casino staffs, most of them are solid and good. In a smaller job I could afford their integrity. But I am on the level where I have to deal with people like Hanes. And so I have to adjust to his methods, or get out. Adjustment does not have to imply approval. It is only the realistic approach. Bend or break. That's the choice they give you. Only a fool would refuse to bend a little.

But I know damn well that Max Hanes could have worked his telephone deception without my ever knowing about it. That switchboard operator could not have been more obviously for sale. But he went through me, and now there are ten one-hundred-dollar bills in the locked drawer of my desk, and that is an absurd price to pay for the cooperation I gave him, particularly knowing it was not needed.

I am being purchased? No. I can let him think I am being purchased. One thousand dollars will build a good and solid piece of the dock where the sports cruisers will stop, long after I have forgotten the name Max Hanes. He thinks he is deviously entangling me in his web of deceit, but in truth it is the other way around. I am using him. I have become a realist. I stand, smiling, under the money tree.

Homer G. Gallowell sat in his big suite in his vest and shirtsleeves, his feet propped up, sipping good bourbon and watching with a patronizing contempt the details of a half-hour western on the television screen. He made no attempt to follow the story or listen to the lines written for the actors. It was a hobby he indulged himself in from time to time, relishing his own professional indignation. He would see them dally a line in a way that would pinch the fingers off a legitimate cowhand. He'd snort at a Miles City rigging or a center-fire rigging on a cow pony carrying a man who was supposed to be from Montana, or a split-ear headstall on a horse supposedly from south of the border, or a remuda containing mares that was supposed to be in Wyoming.

He got up and, carrying his glass, went to the door to answer a knock.

"Well now, Miz Betty!" he said with sudden pleasure. "Just you come on in and set."

She came in wide-eyed, hesitant, nervous, closing the door behind her in a rather furtive manner. She had a skittish look, like a mare in rattler country.

"I don't want to stay here more than one minute, Homer."

"You look like a drink would help some," he said, walking over and turning off the western.

"No. No thanks, really. Do you remember when we first met and after we'd decided to be friends, you got the idea I was under some kind of pressure or compulsion? You said you'd be willing to help if I ever asked for your help."

"I can remember that. I remember it well, because it isn't a thing I've said often in my life to many people. You said something about phoning Texas if you ever had the need of a white knight on a horse. And there's no need to ask me if it still holds good, because once I say a thing like that, I don't take it back. Now if you're ready to tell me who's got you messed up, and how, I'll get you loose of it one way or another."

"I can't talk here, Homer. I can't risk talking to you here. I've lined up a place where we can meet, where I can talk to you privately." She glanced at her watch. "Would you meet me there at about seven-thirty?"

"Anything that's got you this unsettled is worth listening to, Betty."

"It's the Playland Motel, Number 190. I'll be there first. You can come right on back to the room. It's in the rear. You won't have to stop at the office."

"I'll be proud to help any way I can, and you know it."

She left with a haste that was like flight. Homer frowned at the closed door after she left. The flavor of secret assignation set off alarm warnings in the back of his mind. Over the years many clever and unscrupulous women had attempted the entrapment of so much raw power and money. But he was not vulnerable to the scandal lies could create, and his lawyers moved with a gifted ruthlessness in such matters, shredding and flattening all guileful hopes.

This Betty Dawson was not of that breed. He knew he had nothing to fear from her. She had not simulated her own distress.

After she was back in her room, Betty felt emotionally drained. It had worked, just as she had known it would. The old man would come to the Playland Motel, and she would open the door and let him in, and the unseen reels of tape would begin to turn. But she had no idea of what she

162

would do next, what she could say to him. She would lie, and sooner or later he would sense what she was up to, and, depending on his whim, he would either make use of her or walk out. In either case it would be the death of a friendship and a respect she valued highly. But this was a loss you took to avoid taking a much greater one. You cast off the small loves to protect the big ones.

In a few minutes it would be time to drive over there and wait for him. She touched her hair and fixed her lips, and looked, with neither contempt nor curiosity, into her own dead eyes.

When the phone rang she picked it up and said, "Yes?"

"I have a long-distance call for you, Miss Dawson."

Another operator said, "Is this Miss Elizabeth Dawson?"

"Yes, it is."

"Go ahead, please. Your party is on the line."

"Betty? Betty, darling, is that you?" It was a husky voice, familiar from all the childhood years, but now broken with anguish.

"Lottie! What's wrong? What's the matter?"

"It's him. Oh, God, darlin', it's him. Gone in the twinkling of an eye. After the last patient, he went out to look at the roses in the back the way he does always. My Charlie was at the far side of the yard, and saw the doctor fall and went running to him. The doctor was trying to get up again and got up only as far as one knee, his face like paper, holding his fist against his heart, and he fell again just as Charlie reached him. Dr. Wellborn was here in two minutes, I swear, ready with his needles and all, and your father lived to be loaded on the ambulance, but him unconscious entirely. They went screaming off through the traffic, Charlie and me following in the car, not even locking the house, but he passed away before they got there. Doctor Wellborn was telling us there was no saving him in any case, child. We have just come back here, and I haven't even had the chance to cry yet, the way I will for the dear man, gone so sudden from us. . . . Betty? Betty, darling?"

"I'm here, Lottie."

"It's the blessing of the Lord you two made up so nice these last couple of years. I keep thinking of that and you keep thinking of it too, darling. He was happy, and it's a blessing these days to die fast and easy when it's your time, because we see enough of the other kind around here, dragging on in the agonies. He was struck down in the midst of life, child, and he was in happiness when it came."

"I . . . I'll fly home tomorrow, Lottie."

"It's a bitter sad thing, child. You should be able to stay here for a time and not go back into that singing and funning."

"I may be able to stay . . . quite a long time, Lottie."

She sat by the phone after she had hung up. She was stricken by such an incomparable feeling of aloneness it seemed to her she could not breathe. The wheel of the world had stopped, and there were no sounds in the dust.

Not *that* way, she thought. I wanted to be free. Not *this* way. I didn't ask for it, thinking it could happen this way.

She felt that she was straining for comprehension, but that it could not all come to her at once, that this was only a partial knowing, and all the rest of it would come, and soon.

She tried to get back into the world, and after a long time she looked at her watch and made slow sense of the position of the hands. She had a nagging sense of obligation, of a routine to be followed, and suddenly remembered Homer and the Playland Motel.

She even stood up in preparation to go, moving in a way like that of a semi-blind person in an unfamiliar environment, picking up her purse and her wrap, actually reaching her door before she remembered that the obligation no longer existed. Her father had passed beyond their ability to reach out and sicken him. The leverage was gone.

• • • ten

IT WAS A MINUTE OR TWO BEFORE SEVEN WHEN HOMER GALlowell answered the knock at the door of his suite.

"Well now, hello, Miz Betty!" he said, surprised.

"Homer," she said, and walked slowly in.

He closed the door and waited for some word of explanation, studying her, intrigued by the change in her. All tensions and anxieties seemed gone. She seemed placid. But it was a placidity that disturbed him in some way he could not define. She turned and looked calmly at him.

"I was getting about ready to go keep that date."

"What?"

"That Playland Motel place, Room 190, like you told me," he said irritably. "You want we should go there together?"

164

She frowned. "Oh, no. We don't have to do that now."

"You wanted me to help you, dammit."

"It wasn't that."

"You know, you don't make much sense along about here," Homer said.

She smiled in a tentative, almost apologetic, way, and said, "We don't have to go there now because he died. Lottie phoned me, you see, and she told me he's dead."

And, at last, Homer Gallowell knew what he was dealing with. He had seen it several times in his life. Of the memories of those times, the most vivid was of the young wife who, twenty years and more ago, had driven out to a drilling rig in East Texas in an old pickup truck to wait for her husband and drive him back home. Homer had happened to be there, checking on the progress of the drilling of this wildcat venture. The woman's husband was local labor, a farmer interested in picking up extra cash.

She had arrived before quitting time and parked next to Homer's dusty Packard, and so she had a ringside view when the hoist cable snapped and the length of casing took one awkward, diabolical bounce before sledging the life out of the young farmer. She had come running to stare, whimper once, then walk slowly and woodenly away, heading with the stubborn blindness of a wind-up toy toward the meaningless horizon line. They had caught her and turned her and led her back, and he remembered how her eyes had been, and how she had worn this same timid, apologetic smile.

He moved Betty Dawson back toward a chair. She sat, obedient as a child. He poured two ounces of straight bourbon and took it to her. She drank it down, shuddered, and gave him the empty glass.

Homer pulled another chair close and took her hand in both of his. They liked their hands held. They liked the touch of the living.

"Who died?" he asked in a gentle voice.

"My father." Her hand lay placid in his.

"So now we don't have to go to that there motel?"

"Oh, no. I had to do whatever Max told me to do, or they'd send the pictures to my father."

"That's Max Hanes?"

"Yes."

"What kind of pictures you talking about?"

He felt her hand tighten in his and then relax. "Horrid pictures, Homer. Of me and . . . a man. I didn't know

165

they were taking them. Max tried to show them to me. I threw up. I couldn't let my father ever see them. You can understand that? I would do anything to keep him from seeing them."

"Sure you would, honey. So now we don't have to go to that motel?"

She frowned. "It was stupid anyway. I kept telling Max it was a stupid idea, that it wouldn't work with you, but he kept saying you've got so much of their money it's worth trying anything. So you see, I had to do like he said. Because of the pictures."

"It wouldn't work with me?"

"No. You wouldn't go to bed with me."

He released her hand. "That's right smutty talk, girl."

"He thought it might happen. That's where they take the pictures. Movies. And they record everything you say. Al Marta owns it, somehow, I think. It's all fixed up so they can put everything on film and tape, and Max told me they use it for a lot of different reasons."

"So what was he trying to gain, girl?"

She looked at him with blank surprise. "To get the money back, Homer. So you'd gamble it all back. They fixed it so you couldn't get hold of your pilot, faking the phone calls or something, and then if you were . . . attracted to me, you'd stay in town longer and I'd have to sort of tease you into gambling some more. I told Max it wouldn't work with you, but you see he knows we're friends, and because you're . . . rich and important he didn't dare try anything that might make you so mad you'd try to get back at the hotel somehow."

"Has this Max made you do this kind of thing often, child?"

"Just three times, Homer. This would have been the fourth. But is three any different than three hundred?" She reached toward him and he took her hand again. "You see, I had no way to fight. You couldn't have helped me. Nobody could have helped me."

He looked at her with mingled compassion and anger. "I have done a lot of things in my life," he said. "I have grabbed them where I knew it was tender and I have made them do things my way. They have come at me from all the directions there are, and I have broken the ones that would break, and I have tooken the weapons off the ones with guts, but I have never done and I would never do to any human thing what has been done to you. There is maybe five thousand people cuss my name while going off to sleep and the first thing waking up, but I have never put myself in the way of cussing my own soul. When I was a boy child there was Indians still remembered ways a man like Hanes could be given ten days' dying, but that knowledge has gone out of the world. I could have a grandbaby your age, girl. If I had to think up how she would be, I'd settle for you."

"But I got myself into this . . . that first time."

"You remember why?"

"Broke, proud, scared. And I thought I didn't care what happened to me. I thought I didn't give a damn. And I kept myself just drunk enough so I could . . . go through with it."

"Show me one human thing hasn't been a damn fool at one time or another. But most don't get caught up on it. About your father, have you done your crying yet?"

"I can't. Not yet."

"It's something you should get over and done with."

"I know."

"This little airplane takes four and you could come back. . . . No, you'd have to go to the services. Didn't you tell me once you came from San Francisco?"

"That's right. I'll fly home tomorrow."

"When that's over and done, you come out. You let me know, I'll send an airplane after you."

"Thanks, Homer. I don't know. I don't know what I'll do. But thanks."

She looked a little better. He studied her for a few moments and suddenly thought of something else. "That glorified desk clerk you got your eye on, that Darren feller, he know about your . . . movie career?"

She gave him a shocked stare. "Oh, no!"

"Seems funny this happens all of a sudden and you come to me, not him."

"That's over, Homer."

"Is it?"

"He's fine and clean and good. I knew it could last only until Max . . . needed me again. Hugh deserves more than a whore."

"Maybe he ought to have the say on what he deserves."

"No. Can't you see it, Homer? If I let it . . . be as important to me as I want it to be . . . it would just give Max another hold over me. It's ended. I'll never come back here, Homer. I'll never see him again."

"He might come looking."

"It won't do him any good. Homer, please get your money

167

and your pilot and fly away from here and don't come back. These people are wicked animals. Go away and don't come back."

"We both go away in opposite directions, and nothing at all ever happens to that monkey-looking Max Hanes? Don't you think you and me, we ought to get together and bust him right down into the ground some way? Simplest thing would be to pay some fellers to come here and kill him off, but that isn't right satisfying, somehow."

"If it hadn't been Max, it would have been somebody else."

"Don't you hate him, girl?"

"I don't know. I don't know about hate, I guess. Fear, yes. Love, yes. I love Hugh. I love him so much, I can . . . give him up." She stood up.

He came to his feet, looked at her narrowly, and said, "You all right now, girl?"

"I'm . . . better, I think."

"Anything I can do for you? Anything in the world?"

"I don't think so, Homer. Thank you."

"Get your crying done," he said. He walked her to the door. In a clumsy yet courtly way, he planted a leathery kiss on the softness of her cheek. "You're too much woman to let yourself get wasted," he said gently. He watched her walk down the corridor toward the elevators, tall, staunch, graceful, her black hair glinting with health in the soft corridor lights. He sighed and closed the door and made himself a drink. So damn old, he thought. There was no fairness in it. When you got all your juice and bounce, you range the world and you can't tell brass for gold and so you grab it all and spend it all in wild ways. Then by the time when you know, when you truly know what is worth all that scrambling, there is the grave yawning, two strides ahead of you, and no time left to use what you learned in hard ways.

He paused with the drink in his hand, and he felt as if a sudden cold wind had blown across him. He wondered if this time he was, at last, going home to die.

Max Hanes took the phone call from the technician.

"Listen," he said, "I'm telling you again I don't know why nobody showed up, and I'm telling you again you stay right the hell there until somebody comes to tell you to knock off. You're getting paid, aren't you? All I can say is it was all set up and I don't know what happened."

He hung up. By his silver desk clock it was quarter after

eight. He sat in brooding silence for one long minute, then phoned Betty Dawson's room. There was no answer. He hesitated and then phoned Homer Gallowell's suite.

"Yup?" Homer said.

"Uh . . . this is Max Hanes, Mr. Gallowell."

"Something on your mind?"

"Well . . . I just thought I'd tell you the dice are running hot against the house tonight. Thought maybe you might want to get in on it and make that satchel of yours a little heavier than it is already." He forced a laugh.

"That's what was on your mind, friend?"

"Why . . . yes!"

"Want to know what was on my mind when this here phone rang?"

"Yes. Of course."

"Funny thing, I was thinking about you."

"You were?"

"I was thinking about something happening to you, and you know, I could see it and smell it, just as plain as the monkey nose on your face."

"What?"

Max Hanes listened to the leathery, sardonic old voice with growing incredulity. It went on and on. It was graphic, specific, and horrible. Max Hanes had been in many places and had seen many things. And it had been a long time since anything had made his hands sweat and had turned his belly to ice.

"What's the gag?" he yelled into the phone. "What're you trying to do, you old bastard?"

"Now you're all excited," Homer said chidingly.

"I don't get the point!"

"I was just telling you what you got coming, what you can look forward to, after I get it all planned out proper, Mr. Hanes. It's a little return for bitching up Miz Betty's life for her, then tryin' to force her to see-duce an old man and take movies of it so as you could get the old man to give back the money he tooken away from your casino. So you should know, like the feller says, what the future holds in store, so you can think on it some."

Max Hanes held the dead phone for incredulous moments, then slammed it down, scrambled out of his chair and scuttled out of his office.

Ten minutes later, in Al Marta's small office up in the penthouse apartment, Al Marta sat staring at Max Hanes with a mixture of irritation, contempt and astonishment.

Gidge Allen sat on a low table gazing quizzically, speculatively at Max Hanes. The ivory door was closed.

"You cracking up, for chrissake?" Al asked harshly.

"Listen. *You* didn't hear that old guy. *I* heard that old guy. If he wants me over in Texas, he's got the money to. . . ."

"Settle down, Max," Gidge said in his pitchman's voice. "This don't sound like you, baby."

"Let's think this thing out," Al said. "Maybe we got us a little problem here. Now from what you say the old man said to you, the only way to figure it is to agree the Dawson broad cued him to the whole bit. Right? And that Dawson broad comes in your department, Max. Right? So how did you lose control?"

"I don't understand it, Al," Max said. "I just don't understand it. I got her locked up tight."

"Your big problem, Max," Al said, "is you like to lean too hard. You put on too much pressure, so sometimes people crack open from that pressure. And when they know as much as the Dawson broad knows, you've got problems. Right?"

"You're exactly right, Al," Gidge said.

"But this Betty has a level head," Max complained. "We get along fine. She can read the score card. She's known all along that the minute she gets hairy, we could give her old man the kind of jolt he wouldn't like, seeing his only kid. . . ."

Al Marta smacked his own high forehead with the heel of his hand. "Why do *I* have to figure these things out?" He picked up the phone, asked the switchboard operator some questions, listened, hung up. "She got the call from San Francisco a while back. Half the hotel knows it, but you don't, Max. Her old man is dead. So where's your lock?"

"I didn't count on anything like. . . ."

"Shut up. I'm still thinking. She tells the old guy from Texas. She's been banging Darren, and maybe now she tells him and we can lose him. Maybe she wants to open that big mouth and tell some reform type of a newspaper. Maybe with the pressure suddenly off, she wants to talk to everybody that listens. And I won't have that, goddammit! Publicity like that stinks. The industry don't like it. I want that mouth closed up fast, Max. Has this broad ever been jolted around some? Has she ever been sharpened up on exactly where she stands, Maxie?"

"Uh . . . no, we've never had to do that, Al, but. . . ."

"What's your problem?"

"Well, she isn't just any broad, Al. This one is gutsy."

"So then it just takes a little longer, doesn't it? You seen one yet that couldn't be brought into line? Now we know where we're going, so let's move fast on this. Fast but careful."

"She'll be going to San Francisco for the funeral, Al," Gidge said. "Should we wait until after?"

"There's too many chances in that I don't want to take. Anybody out at my ranch right now?"

"Those Miami guys left two days ago. It's been cleaned up. No."

"Where is she right now?" Max said he didn't know. Al cursed him heartily, made two quiet phone calls, hung up, grinned broadly and said, "So right now she's in her room, packing maybe. What time is it? Twenty to nine. Gidge, you move fast on this. Get with Harry Charm and pick one other guy. You go along too, because I don't want this getting out of hand, and I don't want her marked up. Three guys should be able to get one broad out of the hotel in a quiet way. You got all night with her and as much of tomorrow as you want to use, and I want you should turn her into one polite, obedient, humble little doll. I want her in a condition where if she ever even thinks of opening her mouth, she gets the cold nightmare sweats. I want her tamed so good she'll be okay to go to the funeral and come running right back here all ready to stand at attention and salute any time Max here gives her any extra duties in the future. I don't care what you boys do to her, but I *don't* want you turning her into a crazy, like happened to that singer that time. Just teach her who owns her, Gidge, in all the ways that'll make it stick. Now move."

"What about that . . . Gallowell?" Max asked.

"You get this stupid one more time, Maxie, and maybe we wrap you up and ship you to Texas."

"Come on, Al. Honest to God."

"In all these years I never seen you like this before. That old boy will take his money and run, I figure. You going to dream up a new way to stop him?"

Max Hanes' smile looked wooden. "I will carry him and his pilot piggyback to the airplane, with the suitcases in my teeth. I will pack that satchel all the way full for free. I wisht I didn't know all of a sudden how you can skin and salt a man down without killing him too quick."

Gidge Allen, with a casual authority that belied a crawling tension in his belly and a sweatiness of his palms, set it up so that Betty could be taken from the hotel with no fuss whatsoever. He had agreed with Harry Charm's suggestion that the three of them, Gidge, Harry and Beaver, could handle it properly. He had Harry bring the Lincoln around and park it in the shadows behind the convention hall. They went up in the service elevator from the basement, riding up to the second floor of the old wing, the three of them sharing the service elevator with one of the larger laundry hampers on rubbertired wheels.

He left Beaver to hold the elevator door open and also act as a lookout. Harry wheeled the hamper to the Dawson woman's door, and parked it where it would be handiest the moment they would need it. Gidge knocked. She opened the door. The moment it opened they went in quickly. As Harry moved toward her, arms outspread, Gidge closed the door and took the braided leather sap from the side pocket of his jacket. He was an expert with the sap, knowing where to strike and just how heavily. It was Harry's mission to grab her and hold her just long enough for him to stun her. She would awaken in the swift black car on the way to Al's ranch house.

Her dark hair hung to her shoulders. She wore a shiny green robe. Her eyes were reddened and puffy. She backed away, startled and frightened, and in that moment when she was immobilized, Harry should have grabbed her. But he was old and tired and heavy, and she was a strong, agile woman. His reflexes were slow. As Gidge moved in quickly, she sidestepped Harry's lunge, and she began to scream. Gidge saw that she was going to try to run by him to reach the door, and he planned to spin with her and tap her solidly behind the ear as she went by, and try to ease her fall.

But as she started by, Harry Charm, half panicked by the loudness of the screams, regained his balance and turned and lunged again. She was almost out of his reach but he half fell, caught her agile thighs in a clumsy tackle and brought her down. Her head smacked with a sickening solidity against the edge of the night table and she lay silent, looking suddenly much smaller. Harry pushed himself back up onto his knees. She was face down. Gidge squatted and turned her over gently. The orange light spilled across her face.

Harry Charm, with a rusty reflex unused for many years, perhaps partially triggered by the fact that he was on his knees, crossed himself. There was not much blood. The sight of blood would not have awed Harry Charm. It was the deep groove in the right side of her forehead that startled him into the reflex of a forgotten piety of his youth. The groove was horizontal, midway between black brow and hairline, and over a half inch deep. Her eyes were one third open, showing only the whites.

"Honest to God, Gidge, I didn't mean to. . . ." Harry whispered.

"Shut up. I'm trying to think."

Gidge Allen stood up. He felt very tired. He went to the door, opened it cautiously, looked up and down the corridor, pulled the wheeled hamper in, and closed the door again. He went over to the small desk. The light was on. It shone down on a plain sealed envelope. He ripped it open and read the short letter it contained. He gave a small grunt of satisfaction and put the letter in his pocket. He looked around the room. She had packed in haste. Discarded clothing was heaped on the closet floor. Her two suitcases were packed but still open, as was her overnight case.

"Stay right here until I come back," Gidge ordered. "I'll send Beaver in to keep you company."

"Where are you going?" Harry asked in a small voice.

Gidge did not answer. Five minutes later he was in Al Marta's small office with the door shut.

"It was one of those things," he said.

Al slapped his palm on the desk and said, "All I get lately are foulups. Honest to God, I can't ask anybody to go bring a glass of water that something doesn't. . . ."

"It happened too fast, Al."

"Did it finish her?"

"What difference does it make? I know she's bad off. But the way it stands, we can't afford to have her get well, can we? And talk to the law?"

"So how does it look if she just disappears? How about that Darren? How about her missing the funeral?"

"She's all packed, Al. Getting rid of the luggage is a small problem. I know what flight she's taking. The ticket is on her desk. So let's have Muriel use the ticket, then take a bus to L.A. and fly back here."

"Hmmm. Not too bad, kid. Who can tell two pretty, good-sized brunettes apart?"

"And this will fit just right," Gidge said, handing Al the letter. "This was on her desk too."

Al read it aloud. "Hugh, my darling. Suddenly I have my chance to shuck this dream village forever, and I am taking it. We've had so darn much fun, you and I, that I don't want

173

to botch the ending with a lot of sticky nonsense in the farewell department. So take this good-bye forever bit in the warm way that I am writing it. It would depress me if you should try to get in touch with me, really, darling. I hope you do indeed fare well. You deserve the best there is, and I know you will make it your way, and reign over that little hotel on Peppercorn Cay. When you get sentimental on those balmy Bahama evenings, drink a tall one for me. And please, dearest, get out of this wretched place just as soon as ever you can. It is more foul than you yet realize, and it can do bad things to you if you let it. Of course you know that had we not been nonconformists, we would have fallen hopelessly in love. But this was our way, and, for us, the better way. So remember me in kindly ways, and stay fond of the memories . . . as I will, I promise. Good-bye, sweetie. Betty."

"It's spelled c-a-y but it's pronounced 'key'," Gidge said.

"Thank you so much. Okay. It all fits better than you deserve, boy. So take it the rest of the way. Use Beaver and Harry, and you go along so they won't pick a spot that'll get washed out, and they won't quit too shallow."

"How about where we put the Hooker twins?"

"Okay. It's your baby, so get moving on it."

Gidge went back to the woman's room. She was still breathing. He sealed the note into a fresh envelope. Beaver tied a towel around the bleeding wound. They bundled her into the laundry hamper, stripped the bed and piled the sheets onto her. Beaver brought the elevator back to two. They wheeled her in, and brought her luggage along. They went down to the cellar, wheeled the hamper back to a rear-entrance ramp, out and down the service alley to the waiting car. They put her on the floorboards in back and covered her with a dark robe. Beaver took the hamper back and, on the same trip, slipped her letter under Darren's door.

They rode, three in the front, with two folded entrenching tools tucked under the front seat. Their tension did not ease until Gidge, at the wheel, forty minutes later, made the turn into the two miles of private sand road that wound across rocky and uneven country to Al's hideaway ranch.

It was a chill bright night with the overabundance of stars that hang over dry desert lands. Gidge found the remembered place about halfway along the road, and he backed and filled until the headlights were bright on the area where they would dig. It was sand, loose and dry, and, except for being unable to lift very much at a time on the blades of the shovels, easy digging. In a short time the diggers shed their jackets. They had dragged the woman over near where they were digging. She was in the shadows of the night.

When Beaver had complained long enough, Gidge spelled him. After five minutes he shed his coat. As he moved to lay it aside, he heard a quiet sound in the shadows. He stepped toward it, straining his eyes, and then with a yell of pure fury and outrage, he took two steps and swung his leg. Beaver rolled across the sand, screaming with pain.

When he became coherent he moaned, "You hurt me bad, Gidge. You hurt me real bad, you mean son of a bitch."

"Who gave you the word you could mess with her, you goddam spook? She's dead."

"She isn't dead, honest. I wouldn't even touch her if she was dead. Whataya think I am, anyhow? She's breathing and her heart is beating. I listened."

Gidge Allen felt a disgust that was close to madness, a disgust for Beaver Brownell, and for himself, and for what life had done to both of them. He looked down at the woman, at the darkness of her hair against the starlit sand. He raised the short-handled shovel in both hands and with all his strength he brought the flat of it down on that sleeping skull. It was a monstrous sound in the night silence.

He took a deep breath and let it out. "She's dead now, Beaver. Here's your shovel. Get back to work."

"I can't dig. You busted me all up inside."

"You dig, boy. You dig right now and you dig hard and fast, or by God, you'll go right into the hole with her."

Beaver hobbled humbly over and took the shovel. Gidge put his coat back on. He stood, smoking, watching them. When it was deep enough he had them put the luggage in, and drop the woman in on top of it. They covered her up, spread the excess sand, rolled two heavy stones onto the grave in a random pattern and then returned to the car. Beaver got into the back. It was obvious he would sulk all the way back to the city, and for days to come.

Halfway back Harry Charm broke the long silence by saying, "I don't know. A young woman, it seems like a waste, you know? It's a dirty way to die."

"Any way is a dirty way," Gidge said.

"Some more than most. Tonight I get drunk, Gidge. Stinking drunk."

"I got to see a doc," Beaver said, a whine in his voice. No one answered him.

It was almost midnight when Hugh Darren returned to his room. He walked across the note and did not see it until he had turned his lights on and noticed the whiteness of it out of the corner of his eye. He thumbed it open as he walked over to the light.

At first he could not make anything of it, believing, or trying to believe, it was some complicated joke. But suddenly loss was in him like a knife slammed home, then slowly turned. He went down the hall to her room, striding long, and thumped her door, waited, thumped again, and opened it with the extra key he kept on his key ring. The lights were out, and even in the dark as he groped for the switch he felt the emptiness. The lights confirmed it.

He looked stupidly at the clutter of her hasty packing, at intimacies discarded. A wastebasket was piled high with the discards from dressing table and bathroom cabinet. He stooped and picked up from the floor a small topless vial that had held perfume. He held it to his nostril, and it was a sweet lost scent of her, faded, hurtfully nostalgic.

"But *why*?" he said aloud.

Atop discarded clothing, on a pile half in and half out of the closet, was a pair of worn whipcord slacks, stretched and faded, yet holding in slackness the faint warm hints of the long shape of her. A bra with a broken strap lay across the thigh of the whipcords, and it seemed to him a great sadness, forlorn and infinitely touching, so that in an instant the outline of it blurred and the corners of his eyes stung.

He whirled and snapped the lights, slammed the door, and returned to his own room. As he entered he realized he still held the empty vial. He set it carefully on his desk as though it were of great value.

He hesitated for one moment, then placed a call to Max Hanes' office extension. When there was no answer, he called the casino cashiers' cage. A bored voice said Mr. Hanes was still out on the floor, and he would be given a message to call back.

Hugh sat by his phone, elbows on his knees, the heels of his hands against his eyes. He snatched up the phone at the first sound of the ring.

"What's on your mind, baby?"

"Max, I got a crazy note from Betty Dawson. I don't understand it. She says she's left for good."

"You got the right message, boy. That's just the way it is."

"But *why*?"

"You tell me. She left me hung up on the late shift, buddy. That's one of the bad things about depending on the show-biz types. You'd think she was settled in here for good, happy as a clam, but they get that restlessness and what can you do? I tried to talk her out of it, Hugh. She draws, not in any big way, but nice and steady."

"Did you have any warning at all, Max?"

"None. She gave me the word . . . let me see . . . around five o'clock this afternoon. She's walking out on a contract with no notice, but what the hell. There's no point in trying to bitch her up."

"Where did she go?"

"To San Francisco, I think. That's where her old man. . . ."

"I know. She's told me about him. Damn it, it doesn't seem like her to just take off and leave me this lousy note."

"Don't get yourself in a sweat, Hugh, buddy. The wide world is full of playmates, and the ones you wish would stay take off on you, and it's hell to shake the ones you get tired of, and that's the way the ball bounces. Look, I got some potential trouble on the floor and I should be. . . ."

"Okay, Max. Thanks anyway."

"Her mind was made up. There was no keeping her here."

He undressed slowly. He searched back through memory until he found her father's name—Dr. Randolph Dawson. He wrote it down.

"It would depress me if you should try to get in touch with me, really."

One thing about that girl—when she knocked it off, she struck a very clean blow.

At seven o'clock on Tuesday morning, Scotty got clearance from the tower, pulled the Apache up off the assigned runway, tucked up the gear and headed toward the sun.

The old man sat beside him, blinking slowly in the glare, the cheap dusty old hat tilted low over his eyes.

One additional piece of luggage had come aboard, a plump old-fashioned satchel, so typical of the rest of the old man's possessions that Scotty suspected it had made the westbound trip collapsed limply inside the big old suitcase. It was a small torment to add to a mild hangover to keep wondering what was in the satchel and to be unable to ask. If you asked the old lizard he'd turn his head toward you slowly and blink his eyes a couple of times and turn his head back, and after you set the ship down, you'd be looking for work. That was for sure.

Now wouldn't it be a hell of a thing if the satchel was full of money? Wouldn't it be one son of a bitch of a thing if this dried-up old crock had clipped those slick bastards for a big piece of money? But that was a dream. Old Homer wasn't human enough to gamble. He had some private deal working, and so he met somebody secretively at Las Vegas, and skinned them clean so the Gallowell Company would be able to pick up another couple million. Maybe in the satchel he had the hearts and livers of the people he'd met with.

"How long did you stay by the phone at that motel yesterday, son?"

"All day until I got your message you wouldn't need me, at about three-thirty, sir. Then I went out."

"Had yourself some fun?"

"Huh? Yes, sir. I guess I did."

Answer the questions. Don't volunteer anything. Don't, for God's sake, chatter. Not if you want to keep the job.

It was almost a thousand air miles, right on the button. He topped the tanks at Albuquerque and they ate lunch there. After Albu-Q the old man dozed while Scotty wondered why he had taken the satchel into the lunchroom and ate with it right under his foot. Scotty wished he could stop thinking about the damned satchel. He was glad when he could begin to let the plane down onto the rough strip at the old ranch. Most of the way from the old ranch down to the company field, he sang at the top of his lungs, wonderfully alone in the aircraft.

Muriel Bentann caught the two o'clock flight out of Vegas. She checked no luggage aboard. She carried a small overnight case. The stewardess on the gate check ripped away part of her ticket and called her Miss Dawson.

She found the kind of seat she liked, just behind the wing. She kept her eyes tightly shut throughout takeoff. When she knew they were safely up in the air, she lit a cigarette, opened her magazine, and began to study the fashion ads.

Honest to God, the crazy things they tell you to do. That crazy Gidge, with all the orders. Don't talk to anybody. Don't pick anybody up. Take a cab into town. Tell the driver your father, Dr. Dawson, died yesterday and ask him if he knew him. Cry a little, if you can make it look good. Go to the bus station after you get rid of the cab. Get the first damn bus to L.A. Then get back here any way you want. They always had something crazy working for them. So the pay was real good, and they knew you did exactly like you were told and never asked any questions and never told anybody about what they had you doing. One beating had been plenty. More than enough for a lifetime. Anything the cops could do to you was nothing compared to the going over they could give you. . . .

It was good pay, and by God, this time you are going to beat that wheel, Muriel, and you're going to get it all back, kid, every dime, because you're not going to get off the system. You're going to ride that system and you're going to get it all back, starting with that lousy divorce settlement and continuing right up through every dime you've earned and lost in Vegas. Then you get back the mink and the Cad, and you go the hell back East where you belong, away from this lousy hot sunshine and being broke half the time so you have to hustle the drunks for food and rent and write those lousy lying letters back to Mother about what a ball you're having every minute of the day.

I'm still pretty, she thought. I'm still real damn pretty, so I can keep staking myself until sooner or later I hit, because, O Lord, I've been so close so many times, and it has to come true.

. . . eleven

HUGH DARREN LASTED THROUGH TUESDAY AND MOST OF Wednesday, conducting an unending argument with himself, doing his job poorly, and on Wednesday in the late afternoon he placed a person-to-person call to Miss Elizabeth Dawson at the phone listed for Dr. Randolph Dawson in San Francisco.

She was not there. He heard a fragment of the other end of the conversation before the operator closed him off—enough to know it was not her voice, but the voice of an older woman who sounded breathless and excited.

"Do they expect her there, Operator?"

"That's the way it sounded, sir. It sounded as if they have been expecting her since yesterday. I left a message for her to call you as soon as she arrives."

"Thank you, Operator."

On Thursday he placed a call to her shy and ineffectual

agent, Andy Gideon. Gideon rented desk space downtown. When he returned the call he sounded depressed and hurt. No, she'd left without any word to him at all. No note. Nothing. As soon as he heard about it, he had wired her home address, but there'd been no answer. He had no suggestion about how to contact her. Maybe if Mr. Darren would put a personal in *Variety*. . . . He knew he could get her a booking with no trouble at all, but it wasn't smart to stay away too long.

Hugh phoned San Francisco on Friday, on Saturday and on Sunday, leaving a message each time. On Monday he placed a person-to-person call to her father.

The operator, with an odd note in her voice, said, "Sir, that person is no longer living."

"What?"

"They say he died last week, quite suddenly. Is there anyone else you would care to speak to?"

He asked for Betty once more, but she was not there, and once again he left the message.

In a sense he gave up. Giving up was not the same as forcing her out of his mind. She was there for keeps, in a vividness that would not diminish. The world had moved into May, and the sun came down like molten copper. Vegas had moved into the long hot season of cut-rate conventions, with strange banners hung across main entrances up and down the Strip, and there were little clots of people in comic hats, with big badges and fines for any failure to use first names, and big luncheon meetings in the Safari Room, and political wranglings in the convention hall.

The Sales Promotion Manager for the Cameroon had done a splendid job. There were very short gaps between conventions, and thus the slack of the hot months was taken up. Some conventioneers won a very little, and lied about it grandly, and some few won respectable amounts and kept it to themselves, and a great many lost hurtful amounts and lied about that and fretted in secret, and some few lost so much it was beyond lying. The money machine chomped the conventioneers, and smashed the ones who caught the bug, and continued to enrich the owners.

They were dull days for Hugh Darren. He had gotten back into the swing of the work, but there was no satisfaction in it. Somebody had pared the bright edges off the world, and he was filled with discontent. He drank a little more than was his custom, and seldom swam, and was conscious of a new flabbiness of waist and belly, but felt no urge to

180

correct it. Max required little favors from time to time. He would stuff a bill or two into Hugh's breast pocket, pat the pocket and smile his Mongol grin and say, "A little off the top, sweetheart." It seemed to Hugh that the favors were growing more risky and cynical, but he could not bring himself to care. The extra money piled up in a private place, but there was no pleasure in it.

One afternoon in late May he went out to the pool, and he saw her there stretched sweetly in the sun, her forearm across her eyes, miraculously returned. His heart paused and gave a staggering leap of joy, and his belly was hollow and his knees weak. He went to her in a gladness almost unbearable, but as he started to speak the woman took her arm away, and he saw the hard skeptical face of a stranger.

"I . . . thought you were someone else. I'm sorry."

"My husbun' just happens to be at a meeting, wise guy."

As he walked slowly away from her, toward the pool, the final knowledge of just what it was that he had experienced with Betty came into his mind with such clarity that he was astounded it had taken him so long to find out. It was more than the bland and pretty word of the tunesmiths—love. It was that and more. It was a harsh necessity. Life was not worth a damn without her. She had been, all along, his inevitability. And so it was time to stop pretending, and get back to the basic fact of his need. The only act that made any sense in his world was the act of finding her, no matter how long it took. Everything could be dropped for that purpose. And once he found her, he knew he could make her understand. No two people had ever been as good together in so many ways, all important. Once he knew what he had to do, it was like a weight lifting off his heart.

On the following day, before he had told anyone his plans, a man came to see him, a young man with a rather pale and earnest face, sedate in dress and manner, scrupulously polite and obviously without a shred of humor.

He shook hands and presented his card and repeated the information on the card, saying, "I am James Wray of the San Francisco legal firm of Balch, Costin and Sommers." He seated himself, crossed his legs with neatness and precision and said, "The executor of the estate of Dr. Randolph Dawson authorized this trip in the hope that it might shed some light on the disappearance of Miss Elizabeth Dawson, daughter and principal heir of the late Dr. Dawson."

"Disappearance?" Hugh asked blankly.

"Since arriving in Las Vegas this morning, I have talked

to Mr. Gideon, a theatrical agent, who has had no word from her, and I have talked to your Mr. Hanes, who seems unable to shed any light upon this troubling mystery. The police have ascertained that Miss Dawson left by air on the Tuesday afternoon following the day of her father's death, en route to San Francisco. They located and interviewed a taxi driver who took her from the airport to the middle of the city, actually to the corner of Market and Van Ness. He reported her as being very upset about the death of her father."

"She knew about it?"

"Of course she knew about it. A Mrs. Mead, housekeeper for the late Dr. Dawson, phoned her right at this hotel within an hour after the doctor's sudden death, talked to her at length and described the circumstances surrounding the tragedy. Miss Dawson said she would return home at once, but we have been unable to trace her movements after she asked the cab driver to leave her on that corner. I have come on the remote chance that one of her friends here might give us some clue as to what could have become of her."

"I . . . I tried to get in touch with her."

"I know that, sir. Mr. Hanes informed me that she left a note for you when she departed. Do you still have that note?"

"I. . . . Yes, I saved it, Mr. Wray, but it's personal."

"I can assure you that my interest is professional, Mr. Darren. The deceased has left a sizable estate to Miss Dawson. We would feel remiss in our duties if we did not attempt to check every piece of information, regardless of its pertinence, or, I should say, apparent lack of pertinence."

"You wait here and I'll go get it."

He brought it down from his room. It had the frayed and worn look of a document much handled. Wray could guess at the numberless times he had read it.

James Wray took it and scanned it quickly, then read it slowly. There was a slight frown on the pale brow as he handed it back. "When did you receive this?"

"I found it under my door at about midnight the same night she left. I went to her room immediately. She had packed up and gone."

"We can safely assume," Wray said slowly, "that this message was written after her telephone conversation with Mrs. Lottie Mead. Forgive me if I observe that from the tenor of this note, you and Miss Dawson were . . . quite close. Yet the note has a certain gaiety. There is none of the flavor you would expect from a woman who had just learned of the death of a father whom she loved dearly."

182

"I guess there's only one way to explain that, and you would have to know her to see it, Mr. Wray. She is . . . a spirited woman. She doesn't have to lean on anybody or anything. She decided that it was a good time to . . . end our relationship. I don't know why she made that decision. But she wanted to keep the . . . termination on the same level as all the rest of it. So she took pains that she wouldn't get from me the . . . help and sympathy I would have tried to give her if I knew why she was leaving so suddenly. This is much woman, Mr. Wray. Proud and strong."

James Wray pursed his lips and studied his perfect but unobtrusive manicure. "Many young women disappear without a trace in this country, Mr. Darren. Most of them, at the time of their disappearance, are emotionally disturbed. You may have thought Miss Dawson a strong person, but a few facts should be considered. She is an only child. She ran away from college in the company of . . . a most unsavory sort of human being. She was estranged from her father for a prolonged period that ended only after the relationship between her and Mr. Luster ended. One can but imagine the burden of guilt she felt.

"Perhaps the sudden death of her father occured before she had what she felt was a decent chance to make it all up to him. The report given by the cab driver indicates a semihysterical condition. And why didn't she have him drive her to her home? I will ask you one last question and then I will take up no more of your time. During the time you knew her—some eight months, more or less, I believe—did she express a desire to live in any specific area? Can you think of any place she would have gone in an attempt to . . . conceal herself from her own guilt feelings?"

"I . . . I can't think of anything like that. She'd get very nostalgic about San Francisco, about the kind of foggy misty days we don't have here."

"It's always possible she may be in that city, I suppose," Wray said with a touch of wistfulness. "I could not imagine living anywhere else." He smiled and shrugged and started to stand up.

"Wait just a moment," Hugh said. "You told me she left here on a Tuesday-afternoon flight. But I know she left the hotel Monday evening."

"She did?"

"So she had to stay somewhere in Las Vegas on that Monday night." He checked his desk calendar. "That was April

183

eighteenth. Today is Monday, May 30th, exactly six weeks ago, then."

"I see what you mean, Mr. Darren. Whoever she stayed with might know her plans. Have you any idea where she could have stayed?"

"I can think of only two possibilities."

James Wray looked thoughtful. He nodded as though he had arrived at some decision. "Mr. Darren, I'm not authorized to spend as much time here as I would like. My expenses come out of the estate of Dr. Dawson. The executor has to be very careful, because the courts are reluctant to approve this sort of expenditure. You seem to me to have . . . a strong personal interest in Miss Dawson. I wonder if you could find the time to . . . investigate those two possibilities and send me a report?"

"Of course."

"Personally, Mr. Darren, I suspect . . . foul play. I don't know how else to say it. That's a terribly trite and dramatic way to put it, I know."

"What do you mean?"

"Would you say she was a hysterical person?"

"No!"

"Did she love her father?"

"Yes. They were estranged for years, and she was pleased they had gotten back on a good basis."

"In that note to you she indicates she will never come back here. But her small car, Mr. Darren, is still in the airport parking lot. A Morris Minor."

"I'm familiar with it."

"It would be worth, on a cash sale, not three hundred dollars, I would imagine. But it doesn't seem in character for her to abandon it. I had not intended to tell you all this, but since I am asking your help it is only fair. Before coming to you I visited the Nevada Security Bank. I had no proper writs, of course, but I located a cooperative vice-president, and after I identified myself and stated the problem, he was able to tell me that she maintains a checking account and a lock box there. There have been no checks written against the account in the past six weeks. The last check that cleared was her check for a one-way, first-class airline ticket to San Francisco. She made no withdrawals at the time she left. She has not visited the safety deposit vault in almost a year."

"But . . . it doesn't make sense," Hugh said.

"That's my impression too, Mr. Darren. If she was leaving, never to return, one can assume she would have used her time on Tuesday morning to close out those accounts, sell the car and so on. Perhaps something came up which kept her from doing that. But if so, why hasn't she returned here, stealthily if that is the way she wants it, and closed out her affairs?"

"Maybe . . . maybe she will."

"Possibly. But what is she living on? I find it all . . . very baffling and distressing, Mr. Darren. I suppose I am, at heart, an orderly man. I get a feeling of frustration when I deal with acts that seem utterly without logic. You have my card. I will appreciate hearing about anything you find out."

"What will happen to the estate?"

"After taxes and minor bequests, there will be, I would guess, about a hundred and fifty thousand dollars remaining. Fortunately there is a contingent beneficiary, a second cousin, a man in his early forties with a wife and two children. He is an associate professor of economics at Northwestern University. At the end of the period of years specified by law, if all reasonable efforts have failed to locate Miss Dawson, the executor will apply to the court to have her declared legally dead. My report of investigation will be submitted along with that application. If the court does so declare, the estate will be turned over to the second cousin and the executor will get a final discharge of his responsibilities."

"But if. . . ."

"If she returns at any time, she can claim it, of course."

James Wray glanced at his watch again, stood up, departed after a precise handshake and words of thanks.

After Wray had left, Hugh Darren knew that his romantic plan of quitting his job and going in search of Betty had collapsed miserably. Officialdom was looking and had been looking for six weeks. Suddenly there was no place to start. It was, though in a minor key, as though Ulysses, after planning some epic journey, went down to the sea only to find the ship had left without him.

He handled a few routine matters in an absentminded way, and he knew something was bothering him, some small thing. Suddenly he realized what it was. Betty had known of her father's death. She had received the long-distance call from that Mrs. Mead right here at the hotel. Any large hotel has a functioning information network that would awe the Central Intelligence Agency. Yet he had heard nothing about it. And he could not conceive of that sort of information being relayed without his learning about it, because his relationship with Betty was doubtless common knowledge.

After a few minutes of thought, he phoned Max Hanes and was told he could reach him at Al Marta's penthouse apartment. He phoned there and got Max on the line. He could hear background music and laughter. It was five o'clock. The unending party in Al's place was moving toward its daily peak in the cycle.

"Max, I want to ask you something about Betty Dawson."

"Who?"

"Betty Dawson, dammit! You know who I mean."

"Sure, sweetheart. For a minute there I didn't get wired up. If the question is will I take her back on, the answer is no. I got to have more notice even from entertainers hotter by a thousand per cent than she is. You seen her?"

"No, I haven't seen her. Remember on that Monday night, the night she left, I talked to you and you had no idea why she'd left so abruptly. Did you ever find out why?"

"Yes. Her old man died. But she didn't tell *me* that. If she had I wouldn't have been so sore."

"How did you find out?"

"Hell, I don't know. Somebody told me, maybe the next day. I don't remember who."

"So why didn't you tell me? You knew we were good friends."

"Kid, that broad took off and you were gloomy about it, and why should I start talking about something that makes you gloomy? Anyhow, you never brought her up in the conversation. If you had, maybe I would have said her old man died, but hell, I thought you knew it, the way I knew it. Did you just find out?"

"Yes. That young lawyer told me."

"Now there's a square type. Apparently she turned up missing or something. I told him there's no cause to sweat. She's just shacked up someplace. Maybe had a couple drinks and didn't make the old man's funeral, so she's having a ball someplace until she has to go back to work. Forget her, sweetheart. Why don't you come up here? We hardly ever see you up here. At this very moment, boy, the males are outnumbered and there is a couple of French broads from the show at the Mozambique who are getting upset because of not enough guys. So come on the run before the word gets around."

"Some other time, Max. Thanks anyway."

A few moments after he had hung up, his secretary, Jane

Sanderson, entered the big office and gave him a fragment of smile as she strode briskly to her corner desk, a sheaf of papers in her hand—departmental reports to be consolidated and summarized.

She put the reports in her working file, hooded her typewriter, took her purse from her desk drawer.

"Jane?" he said.

She turned toward him with a look of mild surprise. "Signed all that glop already?"

"I haven't even looked at it. Have you got something planned, or can you spare a few minutes?"

She came to his desk, her head tilted to one side, quizzical, moving more slowly than usual. She sat in the chair beside his desk and lit a cigarette with his desk lighter. "I have a horribly important engagement with a swim suit, a tall drink, a long novel, and the folding chair I lug out to my favorite spot beside the apartment-house pool. But I'd rather talk. It's nice to know you. What did you say your name is?"

"Darren. It's painted on that door over there."

"Oh."

"Maybe I've been away."

"That's one way to put it, Hugh."

"How do you like it here, Jane?"

She pursed her lips. "I don't suppose you want the snow treatment."

"Of course not."

She frowned. "Not as much as I did. You transplanted me from the City of the Angels to the City of the Angles— there, I've been waiting ever since I made that up for a chance to say it. Anyhow, as you know, I didn't like it at all the first couple of months. Then I adjusted, and liked it a lot better. Now it's getting a little tiresome again. I've even been feeling wistful about smog. I don't know. I'm good, Hugh. You know that. Why shouldn't I be? What the hell else have I got but the work I do? So I can write my own ticket. It's getting to the point where I have a pretty fair income from my own investments, so money isn't going to hustle me into any job not attractive to me."

"Isn't this job attractive?"

"I liked it better when we were starting from scratch, junking the old systems and putting in the new ones, fighting with everybody. Golly, I was working sixty and seventy hours a week and loving every minute of it. The pay is good, and I guess it's an interesting sort of place to work if a person likes abnormal psychology, but . . . it's pretty much a routine lately."

"The point was to get it running smoothly."

"I know that, Hugh. But there's something else that. . . . Oh, the hell with it."

"I want to know what you think, Jane."

"It may turn out to be a little more frankness than you want to take, boss."

"Don't worry about that."

"The most critical part of any job, Hugh, is who you work for. You were the tops."

"Past tense?"

"Definitely. After I came here I heard how this town can change people. I was sure it wouldn't change you. But it has—in the past month or so. It's as if you've lost interest. You're drinking too much. You're getting that puffy look. You're beginning to do things the easiest way instead of the right way. And I don't know where or how, but I do know you have a few of those little angles working for you. You're on the make, Hugh. You're . . . beginning to look and act and think just like all the rest of the fat cats around here. It isn't a change I particularly wanted to see, and maybe I don't want to hang around and watch it continue. Maybe I'm one of those dull folk who must be able to give total respect to whoever I work for. You had that respect, Hugh. And now—forgive me—I feel a little patronizing about you. A little sad, too."

He wondered if his face looked as flushed as it felt. "You come on pretty strong when you get an opening, Jane."

"We haven't talked about anything for weeks and weeks. Given the opening, I would have said it before now."

"Maybe I stopped giving a damn when Betty Dawson left."

"I could have said that too. For a week you were like a sleepwalker—a sleepwalker with one ugly disposition."

"She was important to me."

Her voice was suddenly softer. "I know that. I liked her, Hugh. Just about everybody liked her around here. A fine, warm, generous girl—who never belonged in this kind of place."

"Did you know her father died the day she left here?"

"I heard about that later."

"How much later?"

"Three days. Four, maybe."

"Did she spread that word originally?"

"I don't know. She could have. Then again, it came as a

188

long-distance call. The girls on the board are always curious about the entertainers. The operator could have listened in. Why, Hugh?"

"I didn't hear anything about it until that lawyer told me today. She's missing. She never showed up at the funeral. Nobody seems able to find her."

Jane's eyes went round. "No! Isn't that strange! I wondered what that neat little man wanted."

"I keep wondering why I didn't hear anything about her father dying that same day."

She lit a fresh cigarette. "I think I can tell you why, Hugh. Everybody in the hotel knew you and Betty were having an affair. Don't look indignant. You know you had no hope of keeping it a secret. Everybody knows she left you a note and took off, without seeing you to say good-bye."

"How the hell would they know that?"

"Don't shout at me."

"I'm sorry. Go ahead."

"You wouldn't be told because, in the first place, people would tend to assume you knew it. In the second place, you are the boss man, and the help doesn't come running to you with gossip. In the third place, you haven't been what anybody in his right mind would call approachable lately. Frankly, you've been an almost unbearable grouch, and when you have a few drinks, your disposition doesn't improve a bit. And there is a sort of fourth reason. You've been a little closer to Hanes and Marta and those people than you used to be, which sort of puts you in a different camp. Do you understand that?"

"Yes. So what else have you heard about Betty?"

"Nothing. Absolutely nothing. But, actually, I wouldn't hear very much. You brought me in here. I share a minor version of your . . . executive isolation."

"Can you do some digging?"

"What do you want to know?"

"Anything at all concerned with the way she left here. She left Monday evening and took a Tuesday-afternoon flight. Maybe you can dig up some rumors about where she spent the night, that sort of thing."

She frowned. "I can try, Hugh, and I will, of course, but —I don't know—I lack the conspiratorial touch. I get lead-footed about this sort of thing. And people tend to snap shut like an alarmed clam when I bear down on them."

"Jane . . . uh . . . stick around a while, will you?"

She smiled. "Somehow, for no reason at all, I feel better

189

about this job already. Maybe because we seem to be on speaking terms again. If you *should* get around to taking a personal interest in managing this hotel again, take my word that our system of setting up for these conventions stinks. Attendance keeps running as much as fifteen per cent above and below estimates, and both ways it's costing money. And when you get that little dandy solved, I have some more for you, boss."

One hour later Hugh Darren parked his blue second-hand Buick by the office of Mabel's Comfort Motel and went inside. It was a tiny room with a plywood counter, frayed straw furniture, a window air conditioner that sounded like a small truck on a long hill. He tapped the bell beside the dime-store registration book.

A bloated woman with colorless hair, without a trace of expression on her dough-gray face, wearing a faded cotton housecoat, opened the door behind the counter and said, "I don't take no overnights. Just by the week or longer."

"Are you Mrs. Huss?"

"Everything in the world I need I get mail order."

"I want to talk to you about Betty Dawson."

There was still no flicker of expression of any kind. "Your name Hugh something . . . begins with a D?"

"Darren. Yes."

"She described you pretty good one time. Come on in."

He went in. She closed the door. He followed her as she waddled back into the gloom, toward the sound of shots and yelpings and horses galloping hard across the picture tube. All the blinds were closed, and one lamp with a weak bulb and a fringed shade was lit. She twisted the sound off and left the picture on.

"Set anywhere," she said, lowering herself into a chair. "She write you to come and call on me? Not one word have I heard from her."

"I haven't heard from her either. She talked about you. I'd hoped maybe you'd heard from her, Mrs. Huss. I know she thinks a lot of you."

"Not enough to write, seems like. I think a lot of that girl. It was like seeing myself all over again, all them goddam dirty lost years."

"I don't exactly know what. . . ."

"One day every six months I feel like saying more than two words in a row, so you just have to set and take it, mister. 'Course she came from more than I did. I come from nothing, but the family was close, and that's what counts

190

with a family, especially once you start out breaking their hearts. Don't make no polite sounds when I tell you you couldn't hardly guess it, but I was a hell of a good-looking piece a long time ago. If I hadn't thrown all that stuff out, there's pictures I could show. I was stage struck, all right. Sixteen I was when I took off, and I thought it was a romantic world, just like Betty did.

"I got to be twenty-three—along about there—before I finally took a real good look at myself. I'd had seven years of show business by then, mister, and at twenty-three I was a wore-out bag. I'd been used too hard by cruel men, and the glamor was gone out of it, and nothing was worth what I'd gone through. So I had seven more years of it because I didn't know what else to do with myself. When I was thirty and looking forty, I had the blessing of God and found a sweet, dear man who loved me so much he didn't care what I'd done, and it didn't matter to him that I was beyond having any kids ever. I had sixteen years of heaven on earth until he died in my arms, so I'm way ahead of most folks, no matter how bad it all started for me. So when I see her, and she in the middle of her black years, it was seeing myself again."

"She told me how much it helped her—when you took her out to that little house in the desert and left her there."

"I know you were out there, mister. She asked me if it was okay before she asked you. I figured from her voice you must be somebody it would be right to take out there. I thought in my fool way she was going to have the luck I had, and find her man. Neither of us could guess you'd turn out gutless."

"What is that supposed to mean?"

"Listen how full of insult the man gets! What the hell do you think it means? If you weren't a ninny, you would have married her. In this town you make up your mind and fifteen minutes later you're married, day or night."

"If never . . . got around to marriage."

"If she loves you, what's wrong with marriage?"

"But it wasn't love! I mean, not then."

She shook her head. The harsh brilliance of the silent picture tube was reflected on her moon face. Her tone was heavy with contempt. "Sleeping with her, weren't you?"

"Yes, but. . . ."

"No buts, mister. You think she slept with you on account you used the right shaving lotion? Or ran a hotel? That's an honest to God woman, mister. Love is the only

191

thing in the world that would have her crawling into the sack with you of her own free mind and will. I can tell you just why you didn't marry her. You thought you were too damn good for her, whereas it was the other way around. You knew she had peddled her tail when Max Hanes told her to, and so that dirty word 'whore' had snuck into your mind and you were too goddam pure and clean to stop for one minute and try to figure out some good reasons *why* she had to do what Max told her to. Oh, you were willing to eat all the fruit off the tree, but you didn't want to own the orchard. All guys like you want is nice safe. . . ."

"Shut up! You've got something all wrong. You've got something terribly wrong here, Mrs. Huss. I don't know what the hell you're talking about. What's this talk about her . . . doing what Max Hanes told her to?"

"You can act real innocent, can't you?"

"Mrs. Huss, believe me. I actually, truthfully don't know what you're talking about. Did she actually. . . ."

"Let me think! Hush up a minute."

A heavy truck rumbled through the silence and he could hear faint music coming through one of the walls.

Mrs. Huss sighed audibly. "I'm sorry. I guess it could have been that way. I guess she wouldn't have wanted you to know a thing like that about her."

"She's gone now. Can you tell me?"

"I will because she should have. She phoned me that night she left. Crying. She was all packed. She told me about her father dying so sudden, and she told me she was free and she wouldn't ever have to come back. I asked if you were going with her and she said she was breaking it off with you. She cried a little harder then so I missed some of it, but it was about loving you and being too cheap to get your life all messed up. So that would sound like she hadn't told you, I guess."

"Told me *what?*"

"I don't know nothing specific, but it's an old pattern. That Max Hanes, he got something on her, some kind of proof of something she did. I'd figure he trapped her, the way men like that trap women, and after he had it to hold over her, then he could make her do things that would help him in a business way. I guess the son of a bitch is smart enough so he saw she was too valuable a piece to use real often, but when he had some big money reason why she should hop into bed with somebody important enough, he had her set up so all he had to do was say Hop!

"When they trapped her, that's what got her so low down I took her out to the desert place, having to take the chance she'd kill herself out there, but knowing her only chance in God's world was finding the strength inside herself to endure. She didn't tell me right out, but from the way she said she was free now her father was dead, it would have been something Hanes could send or show to her father. That's something a loving daughter can't let happen. After she'd done Max's little favor for him, she'd come here to me. She would hardly talk about it, but I could guess all of it. Once she was pretty bad beat by some foreigner he gave her to."

"But why would he do that?"

"Come now! You've been in Vegas the best part of a year. You blind and deaf too? Business reasons, boy. Big gambling reasons."

"Would you know . . . when the last time was that Max . . . used her?"

"Oh, that was a long time back. I told you it wasn't often. Before you came to town, even. Way last summer sometime. I don't hardly think she could get up out of your bed and git into another one and come right on back to you, smiling and happy. She's a decent woman, and that kind of trick would just be plain beyond her."

"That vile son of a bitch!"

Mrs. Huss chuckled. "Why sure he is! And he's proud of it. It helps in the kind of job he's got. Pretty women and big money—the world has a habit of working one against the other, and it's the woman seems to take the loss. So I guess if you had known all this, you wouldn't even have took the trouble coming here asking an old woman about her, would you?"

"I can't live in a world as empty as the world has been for the last six weeks. That's all I know."

"You mean that?"

"With all my heart."

She gave a snort of derision. "Mister, if what you're saying wasn't just a mess of empty words, you wouldn't even be here. You'd be with her, wherever she is. Being with her would mean more to you than the fancy job you've got."

"I'd made my decision to chuck the job and go after her, Mrs. Huss. But I found out that isn't so easy."

"Why not?"

He told her all he had learned from the lawyer, James Wray. Mabel Huss listened carefully, interrupting him with questions from time to time.

"Lord, I don't like the sound of it. I don't like the sound of it at *all*, mister. What's your name? Hugh? I'm calling you Hugh and you're calling me Mabel on account of we're the only two friends she's got in this town. Oh, there were hundreds liked her to pieces, but friends is a different word."

"So she didn't stay here with you that last night."

"I got her call saying good-bye and that was the last I heard."

"Do you think she stayed at your place in the desert?"

"I think she would have said she was going to if. . . . Say! I remember now she did say she was mailing the keys back to me. And I never got them and never thought about it until this very minute. She said she hoped I'd forgive her for not bringing them by, but she had so much to do in the morning cleaning up all her affairs, she felt she wouldn't have much time to spare."

"The bank, getting rid of the car, those are the things she was going to do. But something stopped her, Mabel."

"So why didn't she get to the funeral, and even if she didn't, why hasn't she come back and taken care of those things she left undone?"

"I don't know. I wish I knew."

"And if she'd gone out to the place, she'd have gone in that little car, and that lawyer from San Francisco said it's sitting at the airport right where she left it?"

"That's right. But I think I'll go out there and take a look around tomorrow, if you don't mind, and if you've got a key I could take."

"I'll give you one when you go, Hugh. This thing is going to worry me right out of my mind, wondering about her. I know in my bones that little lawyer man is right. If nothing bad had happened to her, she would have wrote me at least a postcard, because she's thoughtful that way. She's . . . me all over again, the way I was shaming myself and no way out of it at all, being bounced on those old iron beds in every crummy hotel from Akron to Atlantic City, just for the chance to walk on stage in sequins and hand some half-drunk magician his goddam top hat and trick cane for money they either didn't pay or borrowed back. It's a life to turn your heart to stone. But at the end I found me a man and, slow and easy, he brought me back to life again, so everything that came ahead of him was just a bad dream that almost hadn't happened at all."

He took the key with him when he left, and early the next afternoon he drove out to the little stone lodge in the desert. The silence and the emptiness of the place depressed him. He could see Betty all too clearly, every move and pose and expression, and far beyond the silences he could hear the cadence of her voice. Here love had reached its first inevitable completion, and it had been so much more than either of them had expected.

There was too much of her here, too personal, too specific, too memorable. He saw no sign that she had stopped there the last night, but if she had she would have left it as she found it.

He drove too fast when he left, punishing his car on the rough road. He left the key with Mabel and told her he had found nothing.

When he was back in his office he knew what he would have to do. He could not know whether it would work. But he knew he had to do it.

... twelve

A LARGE HOTEL IS, IN ITS MOST SIGNIFICANT SENSE, AN INTRI-cate functioning relationship of hundreds of human beings. The staff world is entirely apart from the world inhabited by the guests. Hotel workers are a special breed. They soon learn devious arts. If the most cretinous transient operator of one of the dishwashing machines cashes out a two-dollar bet on a long shot, the spinster housekeeper in charge of the fourth floor will know it ten minutes later. The day following the rabbit test, the most elderly gardener will know that the young wife of the second pastry chef is pregnant.

Hugh Darren was the son of hotel workers. He had been raised in that special atmosphere. And he knew that the competent hotel manager ignores such trivial things except when they threaten to affect the operation of the hotel. He felt a contempt for those managers who developed and carefully maintained an espionage network, using whatever unsavory bits they picked up as blackmail weapons not only to control the staff but, in many instances, to set up kickback procedures on both wages and purchases. In such hotels the guest sees the effect of bad management without knowing the cause—surly personnel, dirt, indifference.

But now he knew his personal reasons were strong enough

so that he would take the risk of destroying, without giving it a second thought, the smooth operation he had built up.

He knew that, fragmented among the memories of the hundreds of employees, was, if it could be assembled, all parts of the story of what happened on the night of April twenty-eighth, as well as all parts of the two-year story of how Hanes had blackmailed Betty Dawson. Only through force, fear and coercion could he assemble that random factual material into one complete picture.

He began on Tuesday afternoon, the last day of May.

He called George Ladori into his office, and spoke to him privately. "George, I'm making a few policy changes. From now on your recommendation for hiring and firing of your personnel will not be automatic. I'll review every case personally."

"What if you keep somebody on I don't want in my department?"

"Then you'll have to make up your own mind whether to quit or stay on, won't you?"

Ladori stared out from under heavy brows. "Who's giving you orders to do this? You know better. The hotel runs smooth, now you bitch it up."

"In addition, George, I'll reserve the right to raise the pay of any person in your department without reference to you."

"So what happens to the fancy budget system we got, huh?"

"You'll keep it in line."

"Cut quality?"

"That's your problem."

Ladori stood up. "It was nice while it lasted, Darren. Now it's the same old crap like other places. Who scared you?"

"That's all for now, George. When I want to see you again, I'll let you know."

"Make it a long time."

He gave the same orders to John Trabe, in charge of liquor, to Walter Welch, in charge of maintenance, to Byron "Bunny" Rice, his night man, and to his office manager. It created a new wariness in every one of them, and he sensed that the good relationships had been destroyed, perhaps beyond rebuilding.

And then it was necessary merely to sit back and wait.

The first customer was one of the maids. She had been employed for just four mouths. The housekeeper on her floor suspected the woman of petty theft. Guests had complained about small mysterious disappearances. The problem was brought to Hugh. With the cooperation of a guest, they set a trap for her, a stack of seven fifty-dollar chips on a dressing table. After the woman cleaned the room there were six. One of the two security officers who worked under Darren brought the woman to his office. After vehement denials that grew constantly weaker, she produced the pre-marked chip from her brassiere, flung it onto Hugh's desk and collapsed into angry tears.

Hugh typed out a confession. The maid signed it. Hugh and the security officer witnessed it. Just as he dismissed the security officer, Jane Sanderson came in and went to her desk, frankly curious. Hugh took the maid to the small conference room off the office and closed the door. The woman's name was Mary Michin. She had a weak, dull face.

When she was under control he said, "It isn't just petty theft, Mary. It's fifty dollars. You know that. I can push it, and the least you'll get is six months. I could promise you that. Six months."

After he waited out the new storm of weeping, he said, "But I might not do it if I get a few solemn promises from you, with the understanding that the first time you fail to keep them, I throw you to the cops." She bobbed her head eagerly. "Without telling a soul about this, Mary, you will dig up every scrap of information you can about Betty Dawson, who left here six weeks ago. You will report everything to me you can learn. I want every scrap of gossip about her and what could have happened to her. Do you understand? Good. Also, I want gossip about staff people who may be in some kind of trouble—money trouble, marriage trouble. Don't try to get in touch with me with any of this. Every once in a while, when I make my rounds, I'll find you and you'll have a chance to tell me these things. Keep your ears open. Ask questions. And if you can't get any information for me, Mary, I'll take this confession out of my personal private file and make sure you go to jail. Is that clear?"

After he had dismissed the browbeaten woman, he felt soiled and brutal. But he knew he was proceeding in the only possible way. In similar ways, with equivalent threats, he acquired the ears and memory of an electrician on the maintenance staff, a waitress in the coffee shop, a fat and greedy bellhop. Through their whispered disclosures of intrigue between other members of the staff he was able to acquire a bartender, a solarium attendant, a young gardener, a swimming-pool guard. He brought a cold and relentless

197

pressure down upon them, using their own fear and greed and insecurity to whip them into a great diligence of espionage.

As, piece by piece, a horrid picture began to form, he could not permit himself to realize that he was getting this information about the woman he loved. He had to steel himself to a special objectivity. The full emotional significance was there, like a presence a half step behind him, but he could not let himself turn and look into its face, because he sensed that it would break him.

He noted down each significant fragment, and as the picture began to form it provided clues to the areas where he should intensify the pressure.

At five o'clock on the fifteenth day of June, a Wednesday, Jane Sanderson marched to his desk, sat in the chair, looked at him with anger and curiosity and said, "Don't you think it's about time you told me what the hell you're doing?"

"What do you mean?"

"Oh, so bland and so innocent! For God's sake, Hugh, in two lousy weeks you've turned this whole place into a ferment of fear and confusion. Ladori is quietly job-hunting. People were in danger of liking you so much they tried to do their best for you. But all of a sudden you don't give a damn about performance. People are scared of you. You have pets. So we're getting guest complaints by the bale."

"Jane, honestly, I can't tell you what I'm doing or why I'm doing it. There's only one thing I can tell you. It won't last much longer."

"Do you realize how long it will take to undo what you're doing?"

"A long time."

"In another month we'll be right back where we started."

"I know that too."

"But why are you doing this?"

"The reason is important."

She sighed. "I give up. Some day, let me in on these things, huh?"

That same evening he sat at the small desk in his room on the second floor and carefully wrote out, in no special order, a series of statements. Though he had no proof of any of them, he believed them to be true.

1. There exists somewhere, away from the hotel, a special place to which big winners are enticed for purposes of blackmail.

2. Betty assisted Hanes in such projects.

3. Hanes, with Marta's knowledge and approval, had and

perhaps still has unsavory still pictures or tapes or movies proving Betty's complicity in this blackmail operation.

4. Gallowell won a large sum of money. On the night she was last seen, she entered Gallowell's suite in the early evening. Prior to that time she had left the hotel with a small suitcase and had returned without it.

5. Though a sealed note of farewell was presumably slipped under my door by Betty, and I mentioned it to no one, Hanes and others know of that note.

6. The airline ticket was delivered to Betty's room at 8:30. She was packing at that time.

7. Gidge Allen was seen turning out of the parking lot at one o'clock on Tuesday morning, alone in Betty's car. He returned to the hotel by cab a half hour later.

8. Brownell was seen holding a service elevator at the second floor shortly after nine o'clock that evening. He was seen again, maybe a half hour later, wheeling an empty hamper down the rear service ramp into the basement.

9. At some undetermined time that evening, Harry Charm parked Al Marta's Lincoln at the end of the service alley in the shadows beyond the convention hall.

10. (Possibly no connection) On Tuesday morning Allen was up much earlier than usual, enlisting the help of Marta's people in an effort to locate a woman named Murial Bentann.

11. Marta's Lincoln, though clean Monday, was so dusty on Tuesday it was sent down the street for wash and service.

12. Brownell, on Tuesday, required medical attention for some undisclosed injury.

13. This is indefinite, but perhaps most significant of all. There is a definite flavor of secrecy involved here. Informants have all been given the strong impression that it is "unhealthy" to be too curious about Betty. There seems to be desire she be forgotten as quickly as possible. This emanates from Marta, Charm, Allen, Hanes and their people, infiltrating my staff.

So, if I must summarize this whole thing, much as it hurts to do so, I can speculate that Betty, for some reason I do not know, was taken out of the hotel by Brownell and Charm and, perhaps, Allen, and taken away in Marta's Lincoln. I am certain that Allen drove out in her car. I have double-checked that. It is the most alarming thing I have learned. It indicates an effort to make it look as though Betty caught that flight. If she did not, someone did, posing as her. That would be the reason why the trail disappears in San Francisco. I am beginning to believe she may be. . . .

He could not write the word. He could not put that starkness, that end of hope, down on paper. He tried to tell himself they had frightened her so badly she did not dare come back.

He knew that he would probably sieve more scraps of information out of the network he had set up, but he suspected it would be repetitive, that little more of any significance would be learned.

He checked his list, and from that list he knew what he would do next. Points four and ten cried out for further investigation, and they were things he would have to undertake personally.

Muriel Bentann awoke at two o'clock on Sunday afternoon, the nineteenth day of June. It had been more than six weeks since she moved to this smaller, cheaper room on Perry Street. The two narrow windows faced west, and the sun, glaring through yellow draperies that hung lifeless in the heat, had brought the room up to an almost unbearable temperature. She lay nude and gleaming with sweat on the narrow studio bed until she was convinced she could not get back to sleep.

Though she had had nothing to drink for the past forty hours, and very little to eat, she had the dull, nagging headache of a hangover. She guessed it was the result of all the smoke and tension of the hours at the wheel.

All those lousy hours, she thought, sitting at that table, and how the hell did I go wrong *this* time. Went into Dusty's with a hundred and fifty cash dollars, and God knows how many times I got it up over two hundred, and three or four times over three hundred, and one time within spitting distance of five hundred, but every time the luck would sag off and scare me to death, and the last time it just kept right on dribbling away and by three o'clock it was gone.

She sat on the edge of the bed, gathering her strength, then got up and slipped her robe on and went down the hall to the bathroom carrying soap, towel, toilet articles and makeup kit. After her shower she avoided looking at herself too directly and too inclusively until she had fixed her hair and made herself a new mouth. She then risked an impartial examination. Her eyes were sunken and shadowed with fatigue, but she would keep her sunglasses on.

She smiled in a friendly open way at herself and thought, you'll still do, gal. And it's like a miracle, considering this life you're leading—you should look like Sinatra in a brunette wig.

200

Back in her room, she dressed hastily before the heat could spoil the effect of her shower. She put on trim blue-gray short shorts because her legs were very good, their value negotiable, and a white sleeveless blouse with a red question mark embroidered over a silly pocket, because a mild touch of insanity made conversations easier to start. With sunglasses, sandals and straw purse, she was armored for the world. She grimaced as she quickly checked her total reserves and confirmed her own knowledge that she was down to three ones and some small change.

After a drugstore breakfast, she walked another block and a half to Casa Cupid, which she had come to call her "afternoon place". It was a small cocktail lounge owned and operated by Jimmy Cupid, a husky, friendly, displaced carney who had parlayed his portable shooting gallery into a more sedentary occupation.

Jimmy was behind the bar and the place was empty when she walked into the chilly gloom, half blinded after the glare of sun outside, her sandals clacking across the floor toward one of the upholstered bar stools.

"Now isn't *this* a madly gay place," she said, sliding onto the stool, fumbling for her cigarettes.

"A Sunday afternoon in June, Muriel? If I give away the drinks I couldn't fill it."

He fixed her the customary spritzer, Rhine wine and soda, on the house. There would be as many of them on the house as she cared to drink, which would not be many, as she made each one last a long time. It was an arrangement they had drifted into without having to draw up a contract, or even talk about it. Should any customer become interested in her to the extent of buying drinks for her, she would switch, but her drink then, rum and coke, would contain but a breath of rum. On her next visit, Jimmy would have a small gift of cash. If she brought a date or a group in, the arrangement was the same. There was no set rate. A rate would have stigmatized her as a B girl.

"How did you make out?" Jimmy asked.

She made a face. "They busted me, Jimmy."

Jimmy shook his head. "I could have told you, Muriel. How long is it going to take you to get smart?"

"What the hell do you mean?"

Jimmy Cupid shifted uncomfortably. "Look what you do and how many times you've done it. You live in a crummy room and starve yourself so you can build up a stake outa what you can hustle here and there."

201

"Are you trying to call me a. . . ."

"Don't get sore. I'm not calling you anything. You don't set a cash price and you don't take all comers, so you're not a real hustler, okay? What I mean is you're not taking care of yourself. How long you going to keep your looks? Forever, maybe? Thirty already, aren't you? And where are you going from here?"

"I'll hit, Jimmy. I've got it coming, sooner or later. Honest to God, I'll hit and get my money back. Who am I hurting? I work up a stake and I play. Sooner or later, I'll hit."

"But if you hit pretty good, you won't stop."

"I'll stop. Believe me. When I got the divorce settlement, I had a Cad, a mink, diamonds and over eight thousand bucks cash, Jimmy. I'll get it all back and go home."

"Maybe it has got so the only time you feel like you're really living is when you're bucking that wheel, Muriel."

"What do you mean?"

"There are old dolls in this town who go through trash barrels to find junk to sell to get sixty cents in dimes so they can go back to the slots and pull the handle."

"Slots are for suckers."

"And wheels are for smart people?"

"Now goddam it, Jimmy, I don't like. . . ." She stopped talking as the door swung open and the street sounds came into the icy hush of the small lounge. A tall man came in, placid and unhurried, took a stool eight feet away and ordered a bottle of imported ale. Muriel gave him a careful yet unobtrusive inspection. The town was so full of phonies you had to be very careful. Usually the shoes were a giveaway. But these were black, moccasin type with a dull gleam of polish. Dark socks. (Be wary of the ones wearing bright cheap socks, or, even more emphatically unprofitable, the ones with no socks at all.) Gray slacks with a press, a dark blue sports shirt in a weave that looked like linen, a wristwatch with that flat, expensive look. Clean hands, the nails well-kept.

She sipped her drink as she looked at his reflection in the backbar mirror. Really quite an attractive guy, with that slanty bony face, that had a sort of crooked look, as if the two halves of it didn't match. A nice expression, and those big bushy coppery eyebrows, lighter than the brown short hair. But she had the strong impression she had seen him around Vegas, had glimpsed him from time to time, and that was bad. You couldn't hustle the locals. They'd seen everything and heard everything twice.

"Hot out there," the man said, and she liked his slow heavy voice.

"Shock hell out of everybody if it wasn't," Jimmy said.

The stranger turned and looked directly at Muriel for the first time, frowned in a puzzled way and said, "I've seen you before, haven't I?" He grinned. "It sounds like a dull approach. I mean really."

"I had that same feeling," Muriel said. "Do you live here?"

"I work at the Cameroon."

"Oh, hell yes! I think I've seen you behind the front desk."

"Very probably."

"Funny how you see somebody in a new place and you can't hook it up. I know a lot of people in that operation. Gidge Allen, Max, Bobby Waldo. I've been to parties up in Al Marta's penthouse. You see Gidge Allen next time, you tell him Muriel Bentann wonders what the hell happened to him."

"My name is Hugh Darren. I'll tell him, Muriel. Drink?"

She looked startled for a moment, then said, "Sure. Thanks. Make this one a rum coke, Jimmy."

Hugh Darren picked up his bottle and glass and moved over to the stool beside hers. Jimmy put the drink in front of her and then found something to do at the far end of the bar.

"Whenever I have a Sunday off," he said, "this town defeats me, Muriel. I don't know what the hell to do with myself."

"I should think you'd find enough action at the Cameroon."

"There's action, but I get sick of that place. How do you kill Sunday?"

"I just ride with it, Hugh, and see where it takes me."

"Where do you work?"

"I don't. You see, I've got this little income and I don't have to. So why should I?"

"Why should you, indeed?"

"Only I'm like broke until I get the next check. What I should do is help you kill Sunday, at an hourly rate. I'll make with conversation and ideas of things to do."

He shook hands with her. "Very creative idea." He looked around at the room. "I hope one of your very first ideas gets us out of here."

"Got a car?"

"Right around the corner."

In another few minutes they went out together. They stopped in two other places she knew and had drinks. They drove twenty miles into the empty baking landscape and twenty miles back, telling bad jokes, and laughing too hard. At six o'clock she knew that in spite of his working in Vegas, she had him properly set up for a fifty-dollar "loan" to tide her over until her fictitious check arrived. So, equipped with bottles and mix, they holed up in the air-conditioned unit of a motel where she knew, from past experience, she could get a small kickback on the rate he paid.

Hugh observed her with great care. He loaded her drinks and kept his light. He tried to avoid the necessity of making love to her because, in spite of the fact that she was passably attractive, he could feel no desire for her. But after a time he realized that his hesitancy was puzzling her, and so he began those mechanical caressings which, after a time, created enough meaningless excitement to render him potent.

It was all over quickly, and he did not know or care whether she had achieved completion or had merely pretended to. It was a trite and ordinary coupling, with mechanical love words said, stereotyped caressings, and that final hasty gallop shared, this time, by strangers enacting that final inevitable culmination of the cheap pickup. After it was over he saw that she was reassured by now being able to classify him properly—by motivation.

By about nine in the evening, when he knew the drinks had gotten solidly to her, and she had begun to make loose-mouthed hints about maybe they should have some food sent in before everybody starved to death, he deliberately encouraged a mood of confession by inventing some of his own and pretending to be very stirred by them.

And so Muriel Bentann, undone by this mood, lay in his arms and blubbered her way into full confession, telling all, calling herself a tramp, a bum, a hustler, hooked by the wheel, lying to everybody, hoping only to hit the table big and leave town forever.

He told her how much he respected her for telling him the truth, and then he gently and cautiously opened up an area she had not touched on by saying, "The trouble is, honey, when you're so down and out, it leaves you vulnerable to the sharpshooters. Then those guys can get you to do things that are a little bit outside the law, just because it's good money and you need it."

She sighed and turned to kiss the corner of his mouth and said, "You're not just whistling Dixie, lover. Honest to God, it can scare you. But the thing you do, see, is you don't think about what *could* happen. You just go ahead and do it and keep your mind on the money, see?"

"But you don't do anything worth getting scared about."

"The *hell* you say, lover!"

"Oh, sure, sure, sure. Big deal." He forced a yawn.

She rolled up onto an elbow to stare down at him, her barbarian hair hanging black and wild. She hiccupped—an echo of her recent tears. "Listen. One time I got expense money and instructions all written out to remember by heart and then burn. I flew down to Monterey and I was there two days until the box of cosmetics showed up in my hotel room, and I flew back and left it where I was supposed to. Two days after that a thousand bucks cash came in the mail."

"Which you fed to the tables."

"Sure, but what do you suppose I brought back here?"

"Drugs?"

"I don't know what the hell it was, but if I'd been picked up I wouldn't be here now."

"So you do things for the boys when you don't even know what you're doing?"

"Maybe it's better that way, lover. Like a couple of months back, I had to take a plane to San Francisco, put on an act, then take a bus down the coast and a flight back here from L.A. Five hundred bucks, and do as I'm told and ask no questions, see? You and me, lover, we're just little people. Somebody else knows all the reasons."

"Who asked you to fly to San Francisco?"

"Well, I was out digging for gold and this flying saucer landed and these little guys with the blue stalks on their heads got out and started giving me the word." She plunged against him and nuzzled his throat, saying, "Mmmm, you are such a sweetie, cutie guy, and this is enough talk about my troubles, huh? Lover, you've *got* to phone for some food, or I'm going to be too weak to do any of us any good."

There was a light on in the room when he left, quietly, at one in the morning. She was snoring as sturdily as any stevedore when he scribbled his note to her, composing it with care so as to forestall any suspicion that might attend her morning sobriety. "Honey, here is the fifty-dollar loan to tide you over, plus a little more for breakfast and a taxi. I've got to go back to work now. You told me to give your regards to Gidge Allen, but I think I'll skip that, because then you might be tied up the next time I get a day off, and I do want to see you again soon; we had so much fun. Hugh."

He got into his car and sat there behind the wheel for a few moments, feeling used and sad and dreary. Then he drove through silent streets and turned back onto the

Strip, into a sudden press of traffic and yelping of neon, back past all the boiler-room roarings of the casinos. The big machine never faltered, chomping and grinding that innocent flesh, spewing out disillusion—and keeping the money.

Hugh Darren saw Al Marta privately at five o'clock that afternoon in Al's bedroom. Al sat by the window draped in a sheet while a barber who looked enough like him to be his brother trimmed his hair.

"It's okay with me if you take some time off, kid," Al said. "You been working without a break, that I know. And if you say it's set so it runs okay without you for a week, okay. I guess you need a rest."

"Does it show?"

"Not on you. Maybe on the operation down there it shows. Things don't go as smooth as they did a while back. I hear the food is off a little. I hear we had some guests get sore and check out. I hear one of the conventions really got bitched up on arrangements. So maybe you're stale, kid. It can happen. You want a real change, you should fly to Hawaii, and Gidge has got connections there to line you up a broad and a pad, both spectacular, that won't cost you a dime. You give him the word. We like you, boy, and we want you should keep on doing the job you've been doing for us. *Cut the hair, not the ear, stupid!*"

"I'll just go find some quiet place and hole up, thanks."

He was in Dallas on Tuesday. For the rest of Tuesday and Wednesday and most of Thursday he made an unsuccessful series of attempts to get in direct touch with Homer Gallowell. Money can build a high wall. His plea that it was urgent and personal bounced off the undented formal facade of underlings who had rebuffed approaches considerably more imaginative. Late on Thursday afternoon he got in touch again with the highest echelon he had been able to reach. He said to the man at the other end of the line, "If you have any chance to get in direct touch with him yourself, please say this name to him. Betty Dawson."

Ten minutes later his phone rang in his room at the Baker Hotel and he was given an address to go to at nine that evening, and an apartment number. It was a new building, and the ground-floor apartment, listed in the name of G. L. Wells, was spacious, austere, impersonal. A robotic man who neither introduced himself nor used Hugh's name, admitted him, led him back to a small sitting room, and said that Mr. Gallowell had been unavoidably detained and would be a little late. He brought Hugh the drink of his choice and a new magazine, and then disappeared.

Homer Gallowell walked quietly into the room at ten minutes of ten, in his dark, unpressed suit, carpenter shoes, cheap bright tie, dusty black ranch hat, looking like just another one of those mild, leathery old men who sit in the heat of the sun on the park benches in Fort Worth and San Antone. But the eyes behind the slight distortion of the lenses were prehistoric, cold as geometry, merciless as a drill bit.

He settled himself into a dark-blue couch, placed the black hat beside him, and said, "You're the one she's got eyes for. I seen you behind that desk that time. You put five years onto your face since then. She send you?"

"No."

"Then, son, you better have a damn good reason for hauling me way the hell up from Corpus."

"If you give any kind of a damn about her or what happened to her, the reason is good enough. I got the impression, from her, you two were friends. But maybe a man like you hasn't got time for friendships. Maybe you can't afford it, Mr. Gallowell."

"There's no reason I should tell you this, or anything else, son. I can afford friends that don't figure on using me somehow. I got five I can count. Two are women. She's one of the two. One time I had a friend got hisself killed getting into the way of something meant for me. I would do the same for any one of those five, if that's the way it had to be. So speak your piece, hotel man."

"I'm after information, Mr. Gallowell. Not help. If that's the way you felt about her, I'll tell you the whole thing, just as it has developed. Then you'll know why I want to know exactly what happened that last evening you spent in the hotel. Have you got time now to listen to the whole thing?"

"If'n I couldn't do what I want to do with my time, I wouldn't be gettin' the full suption out of my money, son. It sounds long, so let's get some talkin' whisky in here first, if I can find that idiot I keep around here."

Darren told the old man the full story, everything he had learned. And when he was through, he said, "I think they . . . killed her. But there's a big part missing. Why would they? The death of her father meant they'd lost control over her, but why would they have to kill her?"

He had been looking down at his clenched fist. He looked over at Gallowell and saw how shrunken the spare old man looked, saw the astonishing glints of the tear tracks on the hard and ancient face. Gallowell reached to a hip pocket and pulled out a blue bandanna. He took off his glasses, wiped his face, blew his nose strenuously into the handkerchief and put his glasses back on.

"I feel like half the light went out of the world," he said, almost inaudibly.

"What happened that night?"

"You haven't come right out with it, son, but you hinted on it pretty strong. Surely, they sicked her onto me on account of I took my own money back from them they'd held so long they got to thinking it was theirs. For me it was just a game, kinda. I get so goddam bored on this end of my life. Now let me say that if it had gone like that Max Hanes wanted it to go, and she'd tried to hustle an old man like me into bed, it would have been so far out of line with the kind of girl I knew her to be I would have been too suspicious to even try to go along with it, though you can keep on finding live coals in a fire you think is dead. You set out a plate of steak for a fox, and he might circle it forty times, keeping his distance, but he won't touch it. She come to that free suite of mine twice that evenin', and it was like being visited by two different people, and here is just how it was."

After Gallowell had finished the story, Hugh said, "Just three times, then, and you were to be the fourth. The Playland Motel. Movies and tapes. So that's the mechanics of it. And the lever they used. Damn them—God damn them all."

"She loved you, son."

"That's fine. That's just jimdandy. Life is the process of finding out, too late, everything that should have been obvious to you at the time."

"I haven't told you all of it," the old man said slowly, "and maybe this is the part that's hard to tell. It riled me some, those fellers thinking they could get me to make a fool of myself over a woman. That Hanes phoned me, and I swear to God, son, I didn't even stop to think of the spot I might be putting her in, so I let him know that I knew what they had all rigged for me. And the onliest way I could have found out was from her, of course.

"I guess I figured she was out of it, and safe. So I peeled him down some. I drew him a pitcher of just what was going to happen to him, and it was so far from anything he'd ever heard of, it shoved his voice right up to a squeak, and he maybe isn't getting a good night's rest even yet. But it was a damn fool way to enjoy myself, and maybe that's what killed her, them knowing she'd crossed them before she had a chance to get out of town. If she talked to me, then maybe she'd talk to other people too."

"But wouldn't they have learned that anyway? She would have had to give some kind of report, some reason why she didn't go to the Playland Motel."

Homer Gallowell looked slightly relieved. "Hadn't thought of that. Hell, all I've done for you, son, is make it look more and more like Miz Betty is dead. But now I'm in this all the way, son. You got a partner."

"I . . . I just don't know what to do next, Mr. Gallowell."

The old man stared at him with open astonishment. "It looks like they killed your woman, didn't they? You only got one direction you can go. You didn't have to tell me it's no good going to the police. It's all covered up too good for that. You only got one direction left, haven't you, son?"

"What I'd like to do, and what I can do, are two different things. This isn't the Old West, Mr. Gallowell. I could get close enough to them so that if I didn't drop the gun, I could hit at least one, and maybe two. And I might have two whole seconds of satisfaction before somebody else would blow the top of my head off. All very gallant and bold, I guess." He leaned forward slightly. "I want all of them, Homer. Hanes, Marta, Allen, Brownell and Charm. And, like the old Spanish toast, time to enjoy them. And there might be more people involved, and I'd like to get them too. But I'm not going to kid myself. I'm not the same kind of a man you are. If I held a gun against Max Hanes' head, I don't know—I couldn't be sure I could pull the trigger. I don't feel any less of a man because of that. But before I do anything, I had damn well better be aware of my own limitations, so I won't get into something I haven't got the instinct to finish."

Gallowell blinked slowly. "First things first. Got to make sure of exactly who all was in on whatever it was, and at the same time break our own hearts by provin' we're guessin' right. Of the five you named, son, which one do you guess would bust open easiest with a little pressure on him?"

Darren thought for a moment. "Brownell. Beaver Brownell. Do you really understand what I mean about . . . not knowing if I could pull a trigger even if. . . ."

"Had me a hand one time, way back, couldn't gun a rabbit or spur a horse. Couldn't bring himself to draw on a man, no matter what he got called. One night over Kerrville way

209

a bunch of the boys were funnin' him and made like to take his britches down to get a close check on whether he was a man. Before they busted his left wrist he fixed three of them up for the hospital, and after the wrist was broke, he took care of the other two. He still couldn't gun a jack rabbit or stomp a toad, but the word got around he was a man in his own way. If you wasn't a man, Darren, she wouldn't have give you a minute of her time, so don't apologize to me about not being able to handle it in an old times' way. Like they say, your ul-tim-ate ob-jec-tive is jes' fine. Now the thing to do is to leave this Brownell up to some of my people and we'll find out just what happened and who all was in on it."

"And where do we go from there?"

Gallowell's smile was slow and thin. "What is the one thing in the world most important to those fellers? What do they love the best?"

"Money."

"And what's the greatest weapon in the world?"

"Money."

"Now you tell me every damn thing in the world you happen to know about this Beaver Brownell."

• • • thirteen

BEAVER BROWNELL DISAPPEARED ON THE LAST DAY OF JUNE. IT wouldn't have been noticed so soon had he not been told to report to Harry Charm for orders at eight that evening. That was the one obligation he would never forget—those infrequent assignments that made possible the lush life. Someone, probably Al Marta, ordered an immediate and thorough but unobtrusive investigation. When Max Hanes questioned Hugh Darren, Hugh was able to say, truthfully, that he had no helpful information whatever.

As near as it could be pinned down, Brownell was in the Afrique Bar at one in the afternoon and had struck up a quick and apparently warm association with some unknown woman, a handsome and mature blonde, richly and smartly dressed. After much murmured conversation and some laughter, they had walked out to the big parking lot and had driven off together, heading west, in a large, shiny car, make and plate unknown, with the woman at the wheel.

By Monday, the fourth of July, if the search was continuing Hugh could see no evidence of it. He did hear one rumor, which seemed a little too pat, that Brownell had been sent East on business and would be gone a long, long time.

At six o'clock that evening Hugh found a sealed note on his desk. On the envelope it said, in Jane Sanderson's hand, "Delivered 5:22 by special messenger." The note inside consisted of a local phone number and a request to call a Mr. Wells. He was reaching for his phone when he remembered the name plate on the Dallas apartment. He drove down into town and phoned from a drugstore booth. "Sandspun Motel," a woman said. He asked for Mr. Wells. An unfamiliar male voice answered. He gave his name and was answered almost immediately by Homer Gallowell, who sounded very wary until Hugh said he was phoning from a booth in a drugstore.

"Good boy! Get on out here. You can't tell what nervous people will do, so make sure nobody is following you around. If you don't know where this place is, look it up. I'm in Twenty. Last one on the right-hand side as you face it."

"I know about where it is. It should take me ten minutes."

It was a new motel, on the main highway east. He drove by at a good speed and on into the empty land. Then he pulled off and stopped, watched traffic while he lit a cigarette, and drove back to the Sandspun.

Homer admitted him to Number 20 when he knocked. The old man was alone.

"Fix yourself a drink afore you set, son."

"It's bad?"

"I'll wait until you get yourself ready to set and listen."

Gallowell started with Brownell. "A good gal I known most all her life noosed him easy and led him away like a little child, and it don't matter to you where she took him to. But when he walked in there with his chest stuck out, all smiles and set for one hell of an afternoon, he got hisself greeted by a couple of good boys I sent over to work with the gal. They're wild boys that have worked for me on Ayrab matters. I won't exactly say they're purposeful, but if you closed a door on either one of them they'd walk through it, and they got a natural dislike for people like that Brownell.

"Anyhow, Brownell, he didn't crack for ten whole minutes. About the end of that time he come to realize this was a brand of man he hadn't never run into before. He even figured it for some kind of a bluff, when they were getting him ready to geld him like you would a stallion that's turned

211

too mean to handle. But when it come to him these boys were in dead earnest, it about turned him into an idiot right then and there, because he figured it for that fate worse than death they keep talking about."

"Is she dead?" Hugh asked.

The old man's face changed, the narrative light fading out of his eyes, leaving them as lifeless as pebbles.

"She's dead," the old man said, gently. "I'm sorry, son."

Hugh carefully set his drink aside and lowered his face to his cupped hands. There was a long silence in the room. He lifted his head and picked up his drink. "Go on with it."

"I'll get rid of that Beaver first, son. After my boys milked him empty without quite knocking his brain off center, they drove way out to check on where she's buried. We want to steer the police to the exact place, when this is all over, without the police knowing who told it. There was a question about what to do with Beaver and how to handle it quiet, but he fixed all that for himself. He'd had all he could take and a little more, so all of a sudden he yanks himself loose and starts running across that empty land, giving a couple of yelps at first but then saving everything for running.

"One of my boys took off after him, sprinting to catch up at first, and then just loping along right behind him, nice and easy, grinning like a young wolf lapping vinegar. Ever' time Beaver would begin to lose his top speed, my boy would make some appropriate speech about just what Beaver was going to lose when he caught him. The information kinda spurred that man on. All of a sudden Beaver stopped running at top speed and pitched onto his face and slid a little ways, probably dead before he hit the ground.

"My boys aren't doctors, but they guess his heart blew up.

"He was carrying a good piece of money on him, and I let the boys keep it as extra pay for having to work out there in that hot sun with sticks and stones, scraping a groove deep enough to bury him in. He made it maybe a whole half mile into that desert, up and down little rises in the ground, before he come abrupt to the end of himself. We had no more need of him anyhow, having the whole story by then."

"Don't edit it for me, Homer."

"I wasn't fixing to. Hanes, Marta and Allen had a little conference after I talked so damn fool free to that Hanes, and they had found out, somehow, her daddy was dead, and so they had to find some other way of controlling her. So it was agreed that Allen, Charm and Brownell would take her to Al Marta's ranch, about thirty-five miles out, and break her down to the point where from then on she'd do like she was told.

"But when they went up to the room to take her out, there was a scuffle and she tried to break loose and got knocked down and hit her head bad, so bad you don't have to ever think about her knowing a thing from then on. They wheeled her out in a laundry cart, along with her luggage. Allen talked to Al Marta about what happened, and they plain couldn't risk putting her in a hospital where they couldn't get to her, even if she could have recovered, which didn't seem promising. And if she died in the hospital it was going to make a lot of awkward questions being asked by police and such. So they took her out to that private road leading to Al Marta's ranch and . . . she was dead by the time they got her there and so they buried her and her stuff, come back and parked her little car at the airport, and sent that Bentann woman to San Francisco on her ticket."

"Have you left anything out, Homer?"

"Only if that Beaver happened to leave anything out, and from what my boys said, there wasn't anything in the whole world he wasn't right anxious to tell them all about. We know the five that were in it, and now there's four. Having that Beaver run hisself to death sorta cancels off any idea of bringing in the police, even if we'd ever had that in mind. So we got to go at it in our own way, son. You give any thought to how we can use the weapon I spoke of?"

"I have a few ideas, but. . . ."

"Slide that there satchel out from under the bed and open it up, son."

Hugh opened the small suitcase on the bed. It contained packets of currency, neatly banded and labeled.

Gallowell walked to stand beside Darren. He took one packet out of the suitcase, bounced it in the palm of his old misshapen hand, and flipped it back with contempt. "Pretties," he said. "Toy things. The whole sad batch of human kind sweatin', strainin', cheatin', bustin' their sorry guts trying to pile this here stuff up so high they can't see over it. But it was this stuff killed Miz Betty. And it killed that Beaver. And . . . it's got some more killing to do."

"It looks like . . . quite a lot."

"I got me a deal coming up later on this year that'll take cash money, so to save trouble I forsook the interest money on what I flew away from here with, and this is part of it. It's still banded up like they done it in that money room

213

over at your hotel. I separated out the packages of hundreds they wrapped up personal, no new bills and no serial order. There's twenty-two of them, fifty in each package, which makes a hundred ten thousand. It should be enough to make all the trouble we got to have. Now look here, at this one. It's just like all the others. This is the type band they get from the bank, saying five thousand, right here. Now here's two sets of initials, so you can figure one man counted it and wrapped it and initialed it and another man checked up on him and initialed it. This here is the date, writ in pencil, so it's no trouble for you to change the date some. Anybody like Hanes or Marta looking at one of these would know right off it come out of the money room. So you can see how all the rest of it is up to you, once you get this cash money smuggled into that hotel and hid."

"All hundreds?"

"It's the logical kind of cash money to stick to a man's fingers. Smaller bills are too bulky. Bigger ones get checked too close and they don't spend so easy." Gallowell walked back to his chair and sat down. Hugh closed the suitcase lid over the money. He turned and looked at Gallowell.

"I want to know what you think of the risk of turning it over to me."

Gallowell chuckled. "You mean like you taking off with it? I thought of that, sure enough. You fixin' to?"

"God no!"

"So let's stop talking kid stuff and get down to a little planning, son. You know what's possible and what's impossible, so you try the ideas you've had on me and I'll see what holes I can pick in them."

When Hugh Darren returned to the Cameroon at ten o'clock that evening, he was carrying the money in a large brown paper bag, with the top securely crimped. He shrugged off the offer of one of the bellhops to carry it for him. He had the feeling that anyone who glanced at the bag would know at once what it contained. He felt sweaty and short of breath by the time he reached his second-floor room. After he had locked and bolted the door and adjusted the blinds, he dumped the money out onto the bed and lit a cigarette with trembling hands. When he discovered he could not think clearly with the money in plain view, he covered it with his robe.

After he had sat for a time in the big chair by the window, he was able to control his random thought patterns and force himself into a logical evaluation of those factors necessary to the plan. There was no need for all the money to be hidden in one place. The hiding places had to be safe, yet so readily available to him that he could quickly take advantage of unanticipated opportunities. It might be wise to carry a couple of packets on his person, he thought.

In Gallowell's room they had carefully erased the penciled 2's, 3's and 4's that indicated the month in the written dates, substituting 6's and 7's according to the indicated day, so as to label the packets as having been bundled in the money room during the latter part of June and the early part of July. The dates had to be very recent, because it was logical to assume that a thief would place such a packet in a temporary hiding place with the idea of moving it to a better place, such as a lock box, as soon as was convenient. And during that second transfer remove the band.

After a careful evaluation of all possible hiding places in his room, he settled on the trite device of concealing a dozen packets, $60,000, in the bottom of an ancient musette bag that hung on a hook in the back of his closet. He stuffed an old shirt in on top of the money. After a few rehearsals he found that it took a very few seconds to enter the closet, slide his hand down past the shirt and select, by touch, one to four packets to transfer to his pockets. At eleven o'clock he went down to his office, with the rest of the money packed in the briefcase.

The office hiding place was logical and obvious. He maintained one drawer in a safe file for personal matters, letters, credentials, tax forms, confidential reports. He had the only key. That particular file stood in the corner behind his desk, and his was the bottom drawer. He packed the money into the front of the file and relocked it.

He sat at his desk and realized his jaw was clamped so tightly the muscles ached. Now all doubt was gone. And because doubt was gone, so was hope. Death is a wind slamming a door that can never be opened again.

Hanes and Allen. Marta and Charm. Max, Gidge, Al and Harry.

Here I come. Ready or not.

There is no living space in any hotel which is off limits to the hotel manager. Improvements, repairs and redecoration can always be arranged by order of the manager. And there is no reason why he should not, during his inspection tours of the hotel, look at the work he has ordered done.

During the balance of the week of July 4th, three projects were begun. Al Marta's penthouse apartment was scheduled for redecoration. Al's current showgirl helped him make the color selections. Work was begun in Gidge Allen's room.

On the second day, Hugh Darren went to see how the work was coming. He said to the boss painter, "How about the interior of the closet over there?"

"Well, it looked okay to me. I checked it."

Darren stepped into the large closet. He found Gidge Allen's topcoat hanging near the back of the closet. He took the six packets of bills from his pockets and slipped them quickly into the deep pockets of the topcoat.

He stepped out and closed the door and said, "It's good enough, Hank. We'll catch it the next time around."

It was summer, and the desert city lay dazzled under the white torch of the sun. It would be months before Gidge Allen would touch that coat.

In the room occupied by Harry Charm, and in the three adjoining rooms, the scuffed and battered floor of asphalt tile was torn up and replaced. When Hugh Darren left Harry's room, after a perfectly normal inspection visit, he left two packets of bills in the flap pocket of a heavy red-and-black mackinaw.

When one wall was torn open in Max Hanes' suite, Darren found the quiet and swift opportunity to leave eight of the packets divided between the two pockets of a black overcoat with a fur collar.

When he had disposed of the sixteen bundles of currency, he had six left. Five of them were locked in his file.

It seemed to Hugh to be a satisfying irony that he was able to set up his crucial appointment with Al Marta on a Monday. It was the twelfth Monday since Betty had been killed.

It was six o'clock. Al had had a couple of drinks. Al locked the door of his small personal office and said, "So you want it private, you got it private, kid. The place isn't bugged. Now what the hell is on your mind you got to put on an act like this?"

"You've been very fair to me, Al."

"You trying to quit or something?"

"I . . . I think I might be in serious trouble, Al."

"So tell me what it is and we'll get it fixed up."

"I can't even convince myself I'm doing the smart thing in telling you."

Al looked at him with impatience and annoyance. "I was having fun, kid. You're taking up time. So get off the dime."

"You see, I want to handle this in such a way, Al, that I won't get what Beaver got."

It seemed to Hugh that Al Marta stopped breathing for a moment. The shape of his mouth changed and flattened.

"What do you know about Beaver?"

"I know a little and I've guessed a little."

"Do I get somebody to come and slap it out of you?"

Hugh reached into his side pocket. He took out the packet of bills and tossed them onto the table. "This should tell you something about the reason."

Al Marta picked up the bills and suddenly slammed them down. "Oh, dammit, no! Oh, goddammit, no! It would have to be some way through Max. You better do some talking, Darren."

"I'm no part of whatever has been going on, Al. I'm coming to you with it. I've been sitting on the information for some time. I want to make a deal."

"Keep talking."

"I want protection. I don't want to be put in the middle on this. I'll tell you everything I know, and based on that, you can probably make better guesses than I can. I want to keep on running this hotel, and I want the pay and title of manager. In return for that, I'll never tell another soul what I'm about to tell you."

"If what you tell me is worth it, it's a deal, Darren."

"I think it's worth it. You'll have to be the judge. Three days before he disappeared, Beaver Brownell came to my room at four in the morning. He acted furtive and peculiar, but he wasn't drunk. He said he had something important on his mind, but he couldn't seem to get to the point. He acted nervous but confident. He kept telling me he had decided he could trust me. He said he had a big deal working for him. He said it was a money-room deal. I said I wasn't involved in that part of the operation. He said that was why he had come to me.

"Now I'll try to say it in his words. 'Harry and me found out about it, like by accident, way back, and so the two guys working this deal, they had to cut us in, and they cut me in small, less than Harry. So now I'm putting the squeeze on. Harry says I'm wrong. But I'm telling them I get cut in equal, or I go to Al. So what I want from you is, you take this here envelope and don't open it and put it in a safe place. It's my protection. If something happens to me

—and I think it won't on account of I got those guys bluffed good—you take this to Al because it's the proof, and you tell Al that Max and Gidge are taking him. You tell him to move in on them real slow and he'll find they hide the take in their clothes in their closets until they get the chance to move it out to a safer place. Tell him Harry is in on it too. Tell him they've took a fortune off that money room.' "

"And he disappeared . . . eleven days ago? Where have you been?"

"Thinking. I opened the envelope and the money was in it. That's the proof he was talking about, I would say."

"It sure as hell is!"

"I didn't want to get mixed up in a thing like this. And I couldn't understand why Beaver didn't let the others know that he'd arranged for somebody to tell you all this as soon as anybody started to get tough with him."

"So why didn't he?"

"I think he started to tell it, Al, but he didn't finish his story."

"Why not?"

"Maybe they roughed him up a lot before he was given a chance to say anything. And you remember his bad heart."

"Bad heart?"

"I know he was ordered to go on the wagon and leave women alone. I forget who told me."

"I just can't believe Gidge would. . . ."

"There's more."

"You're giving me the worst night in ten years already, kid."

"I don't know what he said or how he said it, but I think somebody has the idea I know something about all this." He glanced toward the door. "Could anybody hear what. . . ."

"This room is soundproofed, kid. For business reasons."

"Good. Somebody got into my room this morning, probably with a passkey. They pried open the locked drawer of the small desk in my room, and broke the lock. Everything is mussed up in all the other drawers. Maybe they were looking for that money, or a letter written by Beaver. I wouldn't know. But I don't like it. I want protection, Al."

"And if you hadn't started to get nervous, you would just have held onto this five grand. That's right, isn't it? Isn't that why you waited so long, figuring you could keep the money?"

"I could have kept it anyway."

"How?"

"I could have given you a different package, even. Mainte-

218

nance is laying a new floor in Harry Charm's room. I had a chance to check his closet. It was locked, but I have a key that opens that type lock in all the rooms. He's got ten thousand dollars, I think, in two packages like this one, in an old red-and-black jacket."

"Harry Charm has ten thousand dollars!"

"I didn't want to risk checking either Gidge's closet or Max's. I'm no hero, Al. I'm in over my head. I'm sorry I ever came out here. And I wish to God Beaver hadn't picked me to trust."

"He picked pretty good," Al said softly. "He picked pretty good."

"Does my deal stand, Al?"

"What? Oh, hell, yes. Now stay right there a minute."

Al went out and closed the door. Hugh sat and stared at the pursed and pulpy mouths of the actresses in the fondly inscribed photographs on Al Marta's office wall. When Al returned, a full ten minutes later, he slammed the door, emptied his pockets and tumbled six packets of bills onto the table.

"I sent him into town on an errand. And I was thinking what a damn fool thing to do. I knew Gidge couldn't be on the clip. Maybe Max, even. But not Gidge. Jeez! All the laughs we've had. All the years of kicks. All the broads and all the bottles."

He spun around, hands spread in a gesture of appeal, his face contorted like a child fighting tears. "But I had to look, didn't I? I didn't have any choice about that. I had to know Gidge was okay, didn't I?"

Hugh sat silently, knowing Al did not want an answer.

Al picked up a bundle of money and dropped it. "All these were taken in the last ten days," he said wonderingly. "I loved that guy. I trusted that guy. Why should he do this to *me*?"

"Maybe he . . . was just bored," Hugh said cautiously.

"I got this soft heart. I treat everybody too good. So that makes me good old Al. Some kind of dummy, maybe. I think they're laughing with me and all the time they're laughing at me. For chrissake, they figure me for such a meathead, they even do a sloppy job! He's so confident he doesn't even take the wrappers off and hide it better! And they just don't give a damn how bad I look if it ever comes out."

"I guess they didn't expect you to find out, Al."

Al seemed lost in brooding thought for a long minute. He

219

sighed. "I got to stop kidding myself about there being any other way of handling a thing like this."

"How will you handle it?"

Al grinned without mirth. "You got yourself into this sideways, kid. This has tired us both out." He looked at his watch. "We need a rest. Use all the pressure you got to get us a couple of airplane tickets for tonight, to two different places. Set me up for El Paso, and get me out of here before midnight, and make it a round-trip first class. Get a reservation to come back, say, next Sunday. Better make it for two people. I'll take a broad along. I got friends there, and they're going to see a lot of me. You take your choice where you go, kid, but stay at least until Sunday, and if you got friends you can move in with, it's good policy. Phone me the word soon as you line up the tickets."

"Okay."

"I like the way you don't start asking questions. This is like an impulse, kid. I don't even get time to say good-bye to anybody, not to any of my old buddies."

"You haven't proved that Max. . . ."

"He'd *have* to be in it. It'll be checked out. Everybody gets every break, Darren. I'm a very fair guy. I'm very warm hearted. For old friends I'll do one big favor. I'll put in the request it don't hurt."

Al Marta picked up the money and dropped it into a desk drawer. He hesitated, then flipped one bundle into Hugh's lap. "Wherever you go, buy yourself a big week, kid."

"Thanks. Is there anything else I can. . . ."

Al sat down. "Now you can just get out. Thanks for everything. I am a guy who always likes the action, and I like a lot of people around, having fun, laughing it up. But right now for one time I am going to sit right here all by myself for a little while."

Just as Hugh pulled the door shut as he left the small study, he caught an incredulous glimpse of tears shining and quivering on thick black lashes.

The newspapers, television and radio and, a little later, the news magazines hit the incident heavily—as though the men who edited the news realized that it would never be a continuing story, that nothing else would ever be discovered to keep it alive. An itinerant laborer spotted the gray sedan at dawn next to the main highway, just twelve miles west of Phoenix, Arizona, on a Friday morning, the fifteenth day of July. The car had California plates and was later identified as having been stolen in Los Angeles the previous Wednesday noon. It had been driven off the shoulder and parked behind a fringe of small trees.

The three men sat in the back seat, wedged upright by their own bulk, with wrists, ankles and mouths bound with wide surgical tape. Their three heads were bowed. In each forehead, almost perfectly on center in each case, was a single dark hole, ringed by powder burns. There was no identification on the bodies, and all surfaces on the sedan that could have taken fingerprints had been wiped clean.

The autopsies disclosed a misshapen .32-caliber pellet deep in the torn brain tissue of each body. Aside from the fatal wounds, there were no marks of violence on the bodies. The autopsies disclosed the presence of alcohol and barbiturates in sufficient quantity to have rendered the three men helpless, if not unconscious, at the time of death.

The routine check on the fingerprints taken from the bodies and relayed to the Central Files of the FBI identified the three men as Maxwell Hanes, Harold Charm and Dillard "Gidge" Allen.

All three men had criminal records, and it was soon learned that all of them had been connected in one way or another with the Cameroon Hotel in Las Vegas. When Al Marta was located and questioned about these men, he said that to the best of his knowledge the three of them had left Las Vegas together on Tuesday night en route to Los Angeles to investigate personally some sort of investment proposition in which they all seemed to be interested. Marta told the reporters that it had evidently turned out to be a bad investment. The reporters laughed. Al Marta was a very funny man.

. . . fourteen

THE BLUE SHADOWS OF THE LATE SEPTEMBER DUSK HAD begun to stretch across the flatlands of Texas.

There was a wind-beaten porch along the west side of the old ranch house, and Homer Gallowell sat there with the black hat tilted to shade his eyes, wearing a wool shirt and stained work pants, the heels of his riding boots hooked onto the railing, his chair tilted back precariously.

"So what did you do about your own job?" Homer asked.

Hugh Darren sat lean on the railing, his back braced against a pillar. He sipped his drink slowly. "I don't know why I had to give a damn about the hotel. But I'd put a lot of thought and time into it. I'd put a good staff together. And so—when it was all finished—that thing we had to do—I knew I had to stay around for at least a month and work along with the new people who came in. But I thought I'd just put in time."

"But you couldn't do that?"

"No. Hell, I had to get things back on the track. My gestapo technique did a lot of damage, Homer. I weeded out all those bad apples. I had no more use for them. I made my peace with the top people on my staff, who just couldn't figure out what had happened to me. Ladori, Trabe, Welch, Sanderson, Rice. Decent, capable folk. Maybe I owed them that final effort. It took more than a month. When I left, three days ago, it was a good, tight operation, just about ready to show the first operating profit on the hotel, food and liquor end since the place was built."

"Where do you go from here, son?"

"I couldn't say, Homer. Everything I own in the world is in two suitcases, if you don't count that car out there. I've got more money in hand than I've ever had before, and I was piling it up to use for a special purpose, but that little dream has gone sort of dead on me."

"What's the dream you were saving for?"

Hugh explained it all, and then said, "Nothing is going to be any good without her, I guess. Maybe for a long time. Maybe forever. Right now I'm sick of people. I'm sick of hotels. I'd go crazy trying to loaf, and I have the feeling I ought to work with my hands. Can your empire offer me some brute labor, Homer?"

"Get you something real different if you want a big change in your life. Put you on an oil rig out in the Gulf, boy. It's good money and it'll either toughen you complete, or kill you dead."

Hugh thought it over. "Sounds about right, if you mean it."

"Gave up saying things I don't mean long ago. I got to talk to Gulfport in the morning. I'll fix it then."

"Thanks."

"When you got enough of it, you come on back here and we'll talk about that Peppercorn Cay of yours. It might look better to you, say, by next year this time."

"It might. Right now I couldn't say."

The two men sat in a long silence watching the slow violent explosion of the sunset.

"We did it," Homer said. "Just the right combination, you and me, each needing just what the other feller could provide to get the job done. Maybe it don't make her rest any easier way off there in San Francisco next to her maw and her daddy, but it sure makes me grin like a snake."

"Your idea of how to work Beaver's death into the story I told Al was what made it work."

"All my life I been good at thinking up the stories men are likely to listen careful to. But it was you had to make it sound just right, or you'd be long dead by now. You know, there's just one thing wrong with the whole business, son. It's like missing the best part of it I don't so much mind those other fellers not knowing why their life was over, or knowing it was you and me cooked them on account of what they done to Miz Betty. But I sure wish that top man, that Al Marta, could have knowed."

"I think he did know, Homer."

"Now how the hell could he know?"

"Because he had time to realize that what was happening to him was just another variation on what had happened to the others. And he got it in the spine, so he was a long time dying—maybe longer than what they planned for him. It would have given him time to tie me into it. He would remember letting me know the name of the man he reported to, the man responsible for all operations on the West Coast."

"What did you say in the note you sent that man, son?"

"I wrote it over and over until it sounded right, and then I printed it, using a ruler. I said something like 'Al had my man Beaver and those others killed to shut them up, because he was in it too. Before they killed him, Beaver told me Al keeps getaway money in a coin locker at the airport. The key is taped to the underside of the middle drawer of his desk. He is a dirty thief and murderer and he had my man killed.' And so on. A woman after revenge."

"It worked just fine, son."

"I was very unsure about it. I was afraid Al would talk too fast and make too much sense, and be too well trusted. But now I think I know a couple of reasons why it worked. When they checked it out and found that cash in the locker, there was enough of it to numb their minds. Thirty thousand, Homer. Because I donated the five he'd given me in return for exposing the others.

"But suppose it didn't daze them enough so they swallowed

223

the story whole? Suppose they figured it as a plant, a frame-up?" Hugh said. "Would it have mattered too much? Al was losing control of the operation. They knew that the men closest to him had crossed him. They all give high points to this love and loyalty and old-buddy bit, but there is no such thing as firing any executive personnel. There's just one way to get rid of a top man. The decision was made and they had a job to do, so there was no reason to give Al time for any summit conference."

"I read about how they found him in that ditch," the old man said.

"He had time to think about it, Homer. They tumbled him out into a deep ditch not far from Riverside, California. When the body was found they saw how stubbornly he had clawed at the wall of that ditch, trying to pull himself up so one of the passing motorists might see him in the head-lights."

The two men sat in the silence of the evening, in the changing light as the afterglow of the sun diminished.

Hugh thought: That night while Al was dying, and tonight too, it is all just the same back there. The cabs are bringing the marks in from McCarran Field to fill up the twelve thousand bedrooms. At all the places in the gaudy roster of the Strip—El Rancho, Sahara, Mozambique, Stardust, Riviera, the D.I., Sands, Flamingo, Tropicana, Dunes, Cameroon, T'Bird, Hacienda, New Frontier—the pit bosses are watching all the money machines. Smoke, shadows, colors, sweat, music, the bare shoulders of lovely women, the posturings of the notorious—and that unending, indescribable, clattering roar of tension and money. I shall never see it again, but I will always know it is going on, without pause or mercy, all the days and nights of my life.

The old man sighed and said, "Wish that damn woman would ring for supper."

Just as he sighed again, they heard the clang of the triangle calling all hands. The sun was gone; the long land was purple dark. They stood up together and went into the old house where the smiling Mexican woman awaited them. The screen door slapped shut behind them as they walked into the orange glow of the lights.